Julie Ann Walker

COL...
COLU... P9-CCY-686
WITHDRAWN
OCT 2017

"Edgy, alpha, and downright HOT, the Black Knights Inc. will steal your breath…and your heart!"

— *USA Today* bestselling author Catherine Mann

"Exhilarating…Walker consistently delivers on alpha males and laugh-out-loud banter."

— *RT Book Reviews*

"A nonstop, action-filled thrill ride. The author has such a wicked sense of humor and an amazing talent for phrasing. Reviewer Top Pick!"

— *Night Owl Reviews*

"Julie Ann Walker is one of those authors to be put on a keeper shelf along with Nora Roberts, Suzanne Brockmann, and Allison Brennan."

— *Kirkus Reviews*

"One of the funniest military romances ever written and an instant favorite. Action-packed with hilarious dialogue."

— *Booklist*

"An intriguing mix of fast-paced action and sizzling romance! Walker delivers a story that is fraught with sexual tension."

— *Fresh Fiction*

"Winning romance…Walker takes readers on a high-speed adventure."

— *Publishers Weekly*

"Walker does a fantastic job…a perfect combination of humor, suspense, and romance."

— *Literary Escapism*

"I absolutely love Julie Ann Walker. Her stories are always addictive and packed full of heart-pounding action."

— *The Book Whisperer*

"Turn up the heat with
Julie Ann Walker's Black Knights Inc.

Also by Julie Ann Walker

Black Knights Inc.

Hell on Wheels

In Rides Trouble

Rev It Up

Thrill Ride

Born Wild

Hell for Leather

Full Throttle

Too Hard to Handle

The Deep Six

Hell or High Water

Devil and the Deep

WILD
A BLACK KNIGHTS INC. NOVEL
RIDE

JULIE ANN
WALKER

sourcebooks
casablanca

Copyright © 2017 by Julie Ann Walker
Cover and internal design © 2017 by Sourcebooks, Inc.
Cover image © Georgijevic/Getty Images

Sourcebooks and the colophon are registered trademarks of Sourcebooks, Inc.

All rights reserved. No part of this book may be reproduced in any form or by any electronic or mechanical means including information storage and retrieval systems—except in the case of brief quotations embodied in critical articles or reviews—without permission in writing from its publisher, Sourcebooks, Inc.

The characters and events portrayed in this book are fictitious or are used fictitiously. Any similarity to real persons, living or dead, is purely coincidental and not intended by the author.

All brand names and product names used in this book are trademarks, registered trademarks, or trade names of their respective holders. Sourcebooks, Inc., is not associated with any product or vendor in this book.

Published by Sourcebooks Casablanca, an imprint of Sourcebooks, Inc.
P.O. Box 4410, Naperville, Illinois 60567-4410
(630) 961-3900
Fax: (630) 961-2168
www.sourcebooks.com

Printed and bound in Canada.
MBP 10 9 8 7 6 5 4 3 2 1

To all the BKI fans out there. This one's for you.

If you are going through hell, keep going.

—Winston Churchill

Prologue

FROM THE CORNER OF HER EYE, SAMANTHA TATE SAW him make a move.

He pushed up from the booth in the back corner where his friends and coworkers sat. She tracked his progress as he sauntered across the peanut shell–strewn floor, past the pool tables, and through a sea of female admirers. Seriously, every double-X chromosome in the place turned to watch him go by.

Some XY chromosomes too.

Not that Samantha could blame anyone for eye-guzzling him. The man had one of those faces that managed to be both beautiful *and* masculine. Square jaw, defined lips, and eyes as blue as Lake Michigan on a windless summer day. Combine his mug with his boyish, flyaway blond hair, his half grin, and the kind of loose-hipped swagger that could only be pulled off by the supremely fit, and what you ended up with was the whole package. We're talking the kind of package seen on the silver screen. The kind of package that—

Oh no, he didn't.

As if he'd read her mind, he reached down and adjusted *his* package as he strolled past a table full of coeds. Samantha watched the young women zero in on the bulge behind the fly of his well-worn jeans before they dissolved into a fit of titillated giggles. When his half grin stretched into a full grin, Samantha realized he'd purposefully drawn the ladies' attention to his unit. *The lecherous cad.*

With a roll of her eyes, she turned back to her drink. For having come from a rough-and-rowdy biker bar on the edge of one of the city's sketchier blocks, her martini was surprisingly good. The redheaded bartender, the namesake of the place, had made it extra dirty. Just the way Samantha liked it.

She slid an olive off a blue cocktail sword and popped it into her mouth. While chewing, she studiously avoided eye contact with the bearded old biker at the end of the bar who kept waggling his bushy eyebrows at her, smiling to reveal tobacco-stained teeth. The crack of pool balls could be heard over the clinking of glasses and the music coming from the jukebox parked by the front door. The air was filled with an odd mix of smells... salty peanuts, motorcycle exhaust, and many decades' worth of spilled booze. There was denim and leather as far as the eye could see.

All of this Samantha noted as an aside. Because even though she was no longer looking directly at him, her focus remained on the man and the journey he made toward the bar. If she could just get a couple of minutes alone with him, she might get him to answer a few questions. Then she could write the damn article—*Correction! Damn puff piece*—her editor had assigned her.

"They've been in business for a while, and we've yet to do a write-up on them. Just give me two good paragraphs and a quote or two from one of the employees," Charlie had said. "This one's a piece of cake."

Yeah. Right. It *should* have been a piece of cake. Trouble was, nobody at the custom motorcycle shop known as Black Knights Inc. had returned her calls. So she'd been forced to do what any reporter worth her salt would do. She'd followed them to their local watering hole and covertly grabbed a barstool that afforded her an unimpeded view of the crew as they shared pitchers of beer and lively conversation.

It hadn't taken her long to select her mark. Of all the hulking, rough-looking men in the back booth, Mr. Movie Star was by far the most animated. He also appeared to have a weakness for women, grinning that grin and flashing those eyes at everything with boobs.

Good news! she thought. *I have boobs!*

They weren't anything grandiose. Certainly nothing like the bazoombas on the bartender. But they would do in a pinch. And just to make sure, she unbuttoned the top two buttons on her blouse and tried not to retch when the grizzled old biker licked his lips and leered.

"Hey, Delilah!" Mr. Movie Star hollered at the bartender over the din as he leaned one leather jacket–clad arm against the bar top. "Two more pitchers for the boys in the back booth! And I'm taking requests for the jukebox!"

The redhead slanted him a cat-eyed look, shoving a clean pitcher under the draft nozzle of Goose Island 312—a local brew. "If you have any love for me," she yelled, "you'll lay off the eighties!"

"Aw, Delilah." Movie Star shook his head sorrowfully. "You know I love you! Why else would I ask you to marry me every time I come in?"

Samantha raised a brow at this, but the look on the bartender's face convinced her the marriage proposal was nothing more than hot air. *Figures. He seems the type.*

"But right now, I cannot resist the siren's call of a good hair metal band!" Movie Star continued. "So your choices are Van Halen, Def Leppard, Quiet Riot—" He ticked off bands on his fingers.

"Which means your invitation for requests was nothing but a tease!" Delilah harrumphed, handing him two pitchers full of perfectly poured beer.

"First of all, as Twisted Sister says, 'I wanna rock!'" Movie Star winked. "And second of all, don't pretend you don't love it when I tease you!" He blew her a kiss before turning to make his way back toward the booth.

After depositing the pitchers on the table, he made a beeline for the jukebox, stopping along the way to lean down and whisper something to the coeds. Samantha watched the young women's cheeks flush in concert as their mouths slung open…also in concert. Then Movie Star continued his journey toward the front of the bar, a knowing smirk on his lips. The coeds' eyes dutifully followed his retreating back—*ass?*—and two of them vigorously fanned their faces with their hands.

Samantha gave in to another eye roll while grabbing her purse from the hook under the bar. She slung it over her shoulder and took a big gulp of martini. *Come on, gin, you beautiful elixir of life, don't fail me now.* Hopping from the stool, she made her way toward the jukebox.

"Hi!" she yelled at the movie star without preamble, placing a hand against the wall and staring at the jukebox's screen as though she had any interest in his song selection. She opened her mouth to add something witty to her utterly mundane *hi*, but the words stuck in her throat when he turned to her.

To be the object of his full, undivided attention was… *wow*. Just wow.

When he gave her a quick once-over, his eyes lingering briefly on her newly exposed cleavage, she knew she should feel insulted. But she didn't. Somehow, the way he looked at her wasn't lewd or lascivious. Instead, it was highly complimentary, like an artist eyeing a model.

As if he saw, appreciated, and enjoyed the female form in all its various shapes and sizes and was genuinely pleased just to be able to stand there and behold it. Behold *her*.

Then he smiled at her.

To her complete horror, she felt her cheeks heat. *Just like those silly coeds*. And when he leaned close so he wouldn't have to shout, saying, "Well, hello there," in a deep voice that was as smooth as silk sheets, she was hard-pressed not to fan herself. *Also like those damned coeds*. Now she got what all the fuss was about. "Do you have a request?"

"Huh?"

"For a song?" One eyebrow quirked as he straightened, his blue eyes threatening to suck her in.

Oh, for fuck's sake, Sammie. Well done. So far, you've managed "hi" and "huh." Someone's going to run in here and rip up your Mensa card.

"Uh…" She sifted through hair metal bands, realized her mental inventory was scanty at best, and settled on, "How about the one that starts out with 'Come on, feel the noise!'"

"Quiet Riot!" He nodded, eyeing her speculatively, probably trying to decide if that was her pick or if she'd overheard his conversation with the bartender.

When he turned and entered her selection into the jukebox's screen, she noted how wide his palms looked, how knobby-knuckled and callused his fingers were. A workingman's hands. Made sense, since he used those big hands to build badass bikes.

And speaking of…

She opened her mouth to segue into her reason for being there, but once again, words failed her. Because once again, he was looking at her. Like, *looking* at her.

She'd never felt so...*looked* at in her entire life. It was disconcerting.

"I'm Samantha Tate!" She extended her hand, needing to do something to distract him from all that looking.

Uh-oh. Big mistake. Because he didn't just shake her hand. He seduced it. His palm was warm and rough against hers, his fingers firm yet gentle. When he slowly pumped, the motion was strangely reminiscent of two bodies locked together in a vigorous bout of lovemaking.

"Ethan Sykes," he said, or rather purred like a cat— like a big, warm, highly dangerous cat. Once again, he leaned close to be heard over the noise. The bad-boy smell of him—all worn leather and harsh soap and sexy, *sexy* pheromones—mixed with the sweet smell of the hops on his breath. "But everybody calls me Ozzie."

Ozzie...

It fit. She wasn't sure why. Maybe because he was a little mysterious, a little dangerous, a little rock 'n' roll.

Ohhhh, Momma like!

To Samantha's chagrin, she was a total sucker for a bad boy. In theory, anyway. In reality, she knew they were far more trouble than they were worth. But all that was beside the point. Because she had no time for boys, good or bad. She had a career to advance. And that started with getting a grip on her wildly celebrating hormones and getting the scoop on Black Knights Inc.

"Are you part of—" she began but was cut off when one of Ozzie's friends sidled up beside them.

If Ozzie was the perfect mark, this new arrival was the *opposite* of the perfect mark. For one thing, he was huge. We're talking arms that could easily Hulk-smash someone. For another thing, with all the scars on his face, he looked like he'd gone ten rounds with a wood chipper and lost. Definitely not the kind of countenance to encourage questions. And last but not least, she hadn't seen him utter a single word the entire time she'd been watching the group.

She barely refrained from grumbling her displeasure at his ill-timed arrival.

"Hey, Boss Man!" Ozzie crowed, smacking a hand on the Hulk's shoulder. "I'd like you to meet Samantha Tate. She's got wicked good taste in music. Samantha, this is Frank Knight. But everyone calls him Boss."

"Hi!" She forced a friendly smile and extended her hand. Unlike Ozzie's handshake, Frank Knight's was cool and perfunctory.

"Why does your name sound familiar?" he asked over the thumping racket of Quiet Riot as they yelled for the girls to rock their boys. Before Samantha could answer him, he answered himself. "Oh, right! You're that rookie reporter from the *Trib* who wants to do a story on the shop."

She bristled at the term. She might only be twenty-four years old, but she'd been working at the paper for two years, which meant her rookie days were far behind her. *Not that you'd know it from the assignments Charlie gives me.* It took some effort, but she managed to broaden her smile. "Nice to know my reputation precedes me."

"More like your incessant phone calls precede you." Frank's tone was as firm and clipped as his handshake had been.

Her eyelid twitched, a sure sign her temper was spiking.

"You're a reporter?" Ozzie asked.

All the smooth, unstudied charm was gone from his expression. Now he looked like the guy sitting behind him was a proctologist who'd decided to give him an impromptu exam.

"That a problem?" she asked curiously. Now it wasn't her eyelid that was twitching; it was her reporter's nose. The Black Knights' blatant refusal to return her phone calls and Ozzie's obvious aversion to her profession combined to have her smelling a story. Maybe a juicy one?

Man, I hope so. I need a break, or Charlie will never take me seriously.

Before Ozzie could answer, Frank/Boss leaned over and whispered something in Ozzie's ear. After he straightened away, Ozzie said, "Well, it was great meeting you, Samantha Tate."

She blinked at him and spun around when she realized the men who'd been in the back booth were now arrayed behind her, heading toward the front door. "Wait a minute!" she yelled. "You're leaving?"

"You know what they say." A glimmer of that sexy twinkle was back in Ozzie's eye. "All work and no play!" He shrugged laconically.

The move drew her attention to two things. First thing: underneath his biker jacket, he wore a black T-shirt that sported a drawing of the Starship *Enterprise*. Printed beneath the ship were the words *Property of Starfleet Academy*. So the man wasn't just a pretty-boy biker with a sinful smile and a bad haircut. He obviously had a little sci-fi geek in him too. Beautiful and brainy. She found the combination wildly intriguing. Second thing: she was fairly certain she'd caught a glimpse of a leather strap up near his shoulder. A shoulder holster, perhaps? And that she found even *more* intriguing.

As she watched the group of men push through the swinging front door, a lone question banged around inside her head. *Who the hell are these guys?*

One way or the other, she was going to find out…

Chapter 1

Red Delilah's Biker Bar
Six years later…

"I REFUSE TO SPEND ANOTHER NIGHT IN THAT RUDDY henhouse. My plan is to find a willing woman who'll take me in like a puppy in a rainstorm."

Ozzie took a measured sip of his beer and glanced over at Christian, one eyebrow cocked. "Henhouse, huh? You saying there's too much skirt and not enough steak back at the shop?"

Christian offered him a derisive glance. The man was British. He could do derisive like nobody's business. "Speaking of steak," he said, "I think I can feel my prick getting smaller every minute I'm there. The amount of estrogen in the air is intolerable."

"You two realize bartenders hear every-freakin'-thing, right?" Delilah was polishing a pilsner glass and freezing them both with a look colder than a winter wind in Chicago. The bar was unusually quiet, the jukebox turned down to humane levels.

"Hey! Don't look at me." Ozzie hooked a thumb at the culprit. "Christian's the one complaining."

He covertly reached beneath the edge of the long mahogany bar to massage his battered thigh. He pointed his booted toe against the brass footrail and shifted his weight on the leather barstool, but nothing brought relief. He'd gone off his pain meds ten weeks ago, and his damn leg had been barking at him like a rabid junkyard dog ever since. A constant reminder of all he'd lost and all he might never regain.

But loss was life, right? He had known that since the tender age of four. Still, *this* loss promised to bring him to his knees. *This* loss was one he might never fully recover from.

Fuck, shit, damn, and dick.

"Aw, what a good boy you are, Oz." Delilah's tone was more than a touch patronizing. "Here you go." She slid a bowl of pretzels in front of him. "Here's your Scooby Snacks."

Now it was his turn to try a derisive look. Delilah seemed unimpressed. She skirted around her goofy, yellow Labrador retriever where he lay sprawled on the floor behind the bar and went back to polishing glasses.

Ozzie lifted his beer and took another sip. The movement reflected in the mirror on the back wall, snagging his attention. He studied himself for a moment, no longer recognizing the man who stared back at him. The one with the wilder-than-usual hair and the facial scruff that hadn't been trimmed in…what? A week? Two? The one with the bags under his eyes, the lines on his brow, and the sullen scowl. The one who looked…*so much like my father*.

The twin pits of self-pity and remorse he'd been carrying around in his stomach ever since that assignment in Malaysia—when he had become the only living victim of a series of terrorist bombings—pulled total Grinch moves and grew three sizes larger. The self-pity was a result of the damage to his leg, which was assuredly permanent. And the remorse was for those who had been lost and who would probably have given *both* their legs to still be drawing breath. He was a shitheel for feeling even the tiniest bit sorry for himself. He hated himself for what he was becoming, for *who* he was becoming. But he didn't know how to stop his own downward spiral.

Shaking his head, he forced his thoughts to something he *did* know how to do. Namely, help Christian locate the lucky lady who might enjoy her own private British invasion.

Not that the former SAS officer *needed* his help. With the accent and the designer clothes and the smooth way he carried himself, Christian was pretty much the walking equivalent of barfly paper. Still, Ozzie used the mirror to scan the prospects behind them.

It was half past eight on a Wednesday night, so pickings were slim. Most of the patrons were single dudes looking to tie on a buzz before heading home to fall into bed, catch a few z's, then wake up and start the daily grind all over again. A few couples were snuggled into the booths or sitting at the high-tops having a nightcap before calling it a day. And then there was the foursome of ladies playing pool. In their late twenties and dressed to the nines in business attire, they seemed the answer to Christian's prayers. Except for the fact that they were hooting and hollering, kicking off their high heels, and doing their best to get sloppy.

Girls' night out.

Ozzie knew better than to intrude on *that*.

"You might be out of luck," he lamented to Christian, eyeing one of the pool players as she stumbled toward the jukebox. "And worse still, this one looks like a Taylor Swift fan."

Christian glanced over his shoulder at the woman as she drunkenly studied the jukebox's screen. "If she plays sodding 'Shake It Off,' I grant you permission to unholster my Walther and shoot me in the face."

"Let's hope it doesn't come to that."

They waited, shoulders tense, as the jukebox loaded the woman's selection. It was "Shake it Off."

"Right-oh. Never mind the shot to the face," Christian declared. "I have a better idea. Let's get good and pissed and then ring up a cab to take us home. Delilah, luv, fetch us two vodka shots, yeah?"

"You're both pathetic," Delilah declared after plunking the vodka down in front of them. "It's not like they *wanted* to leave either of you behind."

And by *they*, she meant the Black Knights. The most select, most secretive group of covert operators ever to sign up to do Uncle Sam's dirty work. They were Ozzie's teammates. His friends. And they were all now half a world away, disrupting the Islamic State's supply lines in order to weaken the group's defensive and offensive capabilities.

Well, except for Zoelner. He was somewhere in Europe helping hunt down a mysterious underworld crime lord aptly named Spider.

But that's just splitting hairs. Because whether it was chasing ISIS or shadowy international figures, it all came down to one thing. Every Black Knight was engaged in making the world a safer place. Every Black Knight except for Ozzie and Christian. And Christian would be heading into the field again soon. His burst eardrums, courtesy of a recent mission when he'd been forced to fire a .50-cal. in an enclosed space, were mostly healed.

And there they were again, the self-pity and remorse. Ozzie tossed back the shot and welcomed the burn of the liquor, hoping it would pickle those stupid pits in his stomach.

"It's not that we feel sorry for ourselves," Christian

said after downing his shot. "It's that we're sharks. If we stop swimming, we die."

"Oh, for the love of tequila." Delilah's expression was unsympathetic. "Neither of you needs to do anything but what you're doing, which is healing up. Besides, we like having you around, Christian. You brew a freakin' mean cup of tea."

"God save the Queen." Christian winked and saluted her with his beer.

The *we* Delilah mentioned were the wives and girlfriends of the Knights—Delilah being one of the former. All the ladies had taken to gathering in the big warehouse in the evening, because at precisely seven p.m. local time, one of the guys in the field would make an encrypted satellite call back home to say a quick hello to his better half and let the other better halves know that everyone in Syria was A-okay. The tension in the shop in the minutes leading up to that phone call each day was palpable. Just one more reason he and Christian were sitting at a bar in the middle of the workweek. *Just a little nip to take the edge off.*

Ozzie lifted his beer to wash down the bite of the shot. No sooner had he set his glass on the bar than the front door burst open, and a Tasmanian devil, otherwise known as ace reporter Samantha Tate, came barreling in. Her right shoulder drooped under the weight of one of her giant oversized handbags, which was stuffed full of the myriad piles of crap she carried around.

Christian took one look at her, turned to Ozzie, and started whistling the tune to "Me and My Shadow."

Ozzie elbowed him.

"Watch yourself, wankstain." Christian pretended to reach beneath his jacket for his Walther.

"Please. You wouldn't shoot me. I'm the only one who'll go to Fadó's to eat bangers and mash with you."

"True," Christian admitted. "Still, remind me why you think it's a jolly good idea to go mucking about with a reporter? I cannot wrap my mind around you knowingly shagging someone who could blow your cover. You off your trolley, or what?"

"First of all," Ozzie assured him, "I'm not shagging her." *Although every time I see her, I'm damned tempted.*

"Well, that *is* a first," Christian said.

"And second of all," Ozzie went on as if Christian hadn't spoken, "you have nothing to worry about. I treat her like a mushroom."

"Pardon?"

"I keep her in the dark and feed her shit." *Which is really starting to bother me. I fucking* hate *lying to her.* Of course, Ozzie kept that last part to himself.

Christian narrowed his eyes. "You filched that line from a movie."

Ozzie feigned a playfulness he hadn't felt in a long time. "Movie quotes and song lyrics, home slice. They're my bread and butter. Besides, you know that old saying." Ozzie saw the moment Samantha spotted him and started heading in his direction. The woman had a way of walking that reminded him of female sailors. They had hips, so they moved like women, but their naval training taught them efficiency of motion. That was Samantha Tate in a word. Efficient. And *beautiful*. Last weekend, when they met in Lincoln Park for a picnic on the grass, the sunlight had dappled through the leaves of the trees, bringing out the auburn and gold highlights in her curly, mink-brown hair, and he had been so stunned by her simple loveliness that he hadn't been able to breathe.

"Which old saying would that be?" Christian asked.

"'Keep your friends close and your enemies closer.'"

Christian narrowed his eyes again. "You expect me to believe she's your *enemy*? That all these lunch dates and coffee dates are...what? A smoke screen?"

They had started that way. But it'd quickly become... more.

"So you got me," Ozzie admitted. "I *like* her. The woman burns words the way a magician burns flash paper—quickly and with a lot of show. It stimulates my brain."

"I'm certain it stimulates *something*," Christian scoffed, the end of his sentence a bare whisper as Samantha closed in on them.

"I see you have your boyfriend with you tonight, Ozzie." She hopped onto the barstool beside him. Her soft, powdery-smelling body lotion reached out to him, filling his nose and triggering a cascade of goose bumps. It happened every damned time she got close. He'd scoured the shelves at Walgreens, sniffing every bottle of body butter and balm they sold, trying to find out which brand she used so that he could...what? Use it to whack off with? For the love of Spock's ears. He was pathetic. "Good to see you again, Christian." She waved across him at the Brit.

"Ah, Christian's not gay," Ozzie assured her, ignoring his body's interest at her nearness and focusing on the lively banter she had come to expect from him. "He's just really pretty. But I can see how you'd make that mistake, what with the hair product and the tailored clothes."

Christian grunted.

Samantha nodded, waved her hand through the air, and was on to the next subject. "Well, gents, it's official.

The zombie apocalypse has started. On my beat today, I covered a police-on-police shooting, a ten-car pileup on the Kennedy Expressway, an outbreak of salmonella brought on by a restaurant knowingly serving tainted sushi, and a string of B and E's where the perps turned out to be two thirteen-year-olds who claimed to be in love"—she rolled her eyes at this—"and fancied themselves the modern-day Bonnie and Clyde." She signaled Delilah. "Make Momma one of your specialties, would you, please? Extra dirty with three olives." Then she turned back to Ozzie and Christian. "But you two have nothing to worry about. Zombies eat brains, so you'll both be fine."

See. Verbal flash paper. *Crackle! Poof! Ahhhhh!* Ozzie felt a smile—a *real* smile—tug at his lips.

Christian harrumphed. "I shouldn't think you know me well enough to judge my mental acuity."

"Maybe not. But you have to be a little lacking in the IQ department to willingly pal around with this one." Samantha hooked a thumb toward Ozzie. The sparkle in her dark eyes was positively mercenary.

"That's a bit like the pilot calling the hippie high, yeah?" Christian raised a brow.

"Oh, you think I *want* to spend time with Mad Scientist Hair here?" Samantha pretended incredulity. "No, no. I feel sorry for him. I mean, who wouldn't? Just look at him."

Ozzie made a face and gifted her with a terse hand gesture that used his third digit.

"Spoken like a true scholar," she said.

A crack of laughter blasted out of him. And when Samantha turned to thank Delilah for the martini, he took the opportunity to study her profile.

She *was* beautiful. Her brown eyes glowed with

intelligence, and she had one of those faces that drew you in. No one feature stood out as terribly arresting or unique, but all her features fit together to make an enchanting whole.

And then there was the gap between her two front teeth. It was small. Just a sliver of space. But it was totally, wonderfully *her*.

Samantha tipped back her martini glass and took a giant sip, eagerly sucking down the gin and olive brine like it was a gift from on high. When she lowered her glass, she wiped the back of her hand over her mouth and let loose with a dainty, feminine-sounding burp. "I am woman. Hear me drink."

Another bark of genuine laughter shot out of him, and all he could think was… *God, that feels so good*. Most of his jocularity was forced these days. But when she was around, he felt…more like his old self.

Then it occurred to him. Samantha Tate, the woman he and the rest of the Black Knights had avoided for years, the woman he should probably *still* be avoiding, had somehow wormed her way into his life, under his skin, and in so doing had become…his *friend*.

Who'd a thunk it?

How was it possible she could not only *like* but *lust after* a complete sociopath? A lying, gunrunning piece of shit?

That's taking a penchant for bad boys to a whole new level, don't you think?

Problem was, the Ozzie she'd gotten to know didn't *seem* like a bad boy. In fact, she'd come to believe that everything she suspected about BKI was dead wrong. After years of dodging her, a few months ago, the Black

Knights had finally invited her on a tour of their shop. Ozzie had been her guide, and he had managed to convince her that the brusque men of BKI weren't hiding anything nefarious and that the big compound with its various outbuildings and huge factory warehouse was exactly what it was purported to be, a top-of-the-line custom bike-building shop that catered to an elite crowd of motorcycle enthusiasts who didn't just want a form of transportation but a piece of rolling art. He'd won her over with his smile, his razor-sharp mind, and his geeky penchant for all things *Star Trek* and eighties.

Her mind flashed back to a day six weeks earlier. Winter had finally released its icy grip on the city, and the first true promise of spring had hung in the air. Ozzie had phoned her at work, telling her it was the perfect day for a motorcycle ride and begging her to come for one. As soon as she'd typed up the last of her assignments, she had run out the front door of the Tribune Tower to find him idling by the curb on his big purple-and-green custom Harley.

The bike was a wonder of chrome and steel and whimsical paint.

The man was a wonder of muscle and strength and funny quips.

They had ridden along Lake Shore Drive for hours, watching the sun turn the waves on Lake Michigan to burnished gold. And she had fallen for him then. Just a little. Fallen for how easy he was to talk to. Fallen for how fun he was to be around. Fallen for the simple *joy* he brought to her heart.

But it's all a lie!

A big, fat, stinking lie. And she didn't know whether to scream with disappointment or scratch his gorgeous, criminal eyes right out of his gorgeous, criminal head.

Keeping up pretenses, acting like nothing had happened earlier, like she didn't know the truth, was taking everything she had.

Beneath the bar, her knees shook. The gin, which usually gave her a warm, rosy glow, soured in her stomach. And emblazoned on the backs of her eyelids every time she blinked was the look of frightened sincerity in Marcel's eyes when he told her who the Black Apostles, Chicago's most notorious South Side gang, were buying their guns from.

Play it cool, Sammie, she coached herself.

Yeah, right. Easier said than done when she was sitting beside two arms dealers. But if she had any hope of blowing the lid off Black Knights Inc., of getting the evidence she needed for Legal to sign off on the investigative story she would write, she had to maintain the status quo. And lest she make Ozzie suspicious, she had to keep on keeping on as if she didn't know what he was.

"Well, hello, Ozzie," a pert blond in slacks and a formfitting maroon blouse slurred, sidling up to Ozzie like a cheerleader to a quarterback. Somehow, she managed to squeeze herself between Samantha and the lying asshole. That's how Samantha was going to refer to him from here on out. Not Ozzie, but Lying Asshole. Lying *Criminal* Asshole. "My friend over there told me I should come and introduce myself to you."

"Oh, uh…" Ozzie said haltingly, glancing into the mirror at the women by the pool table. "Hi. Which friend is—"

"The redhead. Gloria. She was a brunette when the two of you hooked up." The blond tried to bat her lashes, but the booze in her blood made the move look less sexy and more like she had glue stuck in one eye. "My name is Janie, by the way. And Gloria told me to tell you I have a really small…" She glanced around and leaned close to whisper something in Ozzie's ear.

Even though he was a lying criminal asshole, Samantha felt jealousy bubble in her guts, all green and gross and altogether obnoxious.

But it's not for this *Ozzie*, she assured herself. *It's for the Ozzie I* thought *he was*.

Fake Ozzie was wonderful. Fake Ozzie had walked around Lincoln Park Zoo with his face painted like a lion because they had passed the kiddie station and she had dared him to have it done. Fake Ozzie had hired a singing stripper telegram to stop by her apartment the morning of her birthday. When the "UPS driver" began to take off his shirt while doing his best Paul McCartney impression and serenading her with the Beatles' "Birthday" song, she had never laughed so hard in her whole life.

Fake Ozzie had brought her chicken soup, the entire DVD collection of *Orange Is the New Black*, and two bottles of NyQuil when she came down with a wretched cold. He had knocked on her door and left all the stuff outside with a card that had the Starship *Enterprise* printed on the front. Inside had been an inscription in his decisive hand that read: Get well soon so you can… *live long and prosper*.

Yes, Fake Ozzie was a gorgeous, geeky, wonderful man. Too bad Fake Ozzie was a big ol' phony.

The laugh he managed when the blond trailed a bloodred fingernail over his jaw before turning to stumble back to her friends was forced and hoarse-sounding. If Samantha wasn't mistaken, there was a slight flush on his cheeks when he pinned his eyes to his pint glass, refusing to meet her stare in the mirror.

"Sweet fuck all." Christian's face was the epitome of incredulity. "Do you have some sort of magical pecker?"

"I—" Ozzie began but was cut off by a discordant jangle coming from Samantha's purse.

Saved by the bell. She was a wreck, completely devastated, and the last thing she wanted to talk about, to *think* about, was Ozzie's penis. His lying, criminal— *likely big and lovely*—penis.

She rummaged around inside her purse, pushing past a Snickers bar, a can of Diet Coke, and all the various notebooks, pens, pencils, and whatnot. But her phone was nowhere to be found. She was left with no other recourse. She upended her purse, spilling its contents onto the bar.

She could feel the men beside her raising their eyebrows as she located her phone. Ozzie picked up a tampon from the pile, his expression bemused. *Probably fake bemused.* She slapped it out of his hand at the same time as she glanced at her phone's screen and saw she had a text from Donny Danielson, her best friend and mentor. Also the man she tried to beat when it came to getting her byline above the fold.

Holding her purse beneath the bar and opening it wide, she used her arm to sweep everything but her phone back inside.

"It's all essential to my daily life," she assured Christian, keeping up pretenses when he leaned around Ozzie's back to blink at her haul. Punching in her security code, she went to her text messages and felt her heart freeze into a solid block of ice.

Isn't he one of yours? the message read, followed by a crime-scene photo of Marcel Monroe lying in a dirty alley somewhere, his dark eyes unblinking on either side of a gruesome, wet-looking bullet hole. Her mind flashed back to the crime-scene photos of her father's murder. And the gin sloshing around in her stomach threatened to reverse directions.

Terror grabbed hold of her with sharp teeth and shook her savagely. She must have made some sort of noise, because Ozzie asked, "You okay?"

She turned to him, a million thoughts spiraling through her head. Had Marcel fallen victim to the life of an Apostle, taken out by a rival gang member? Or had someone discovered he had talked to her today and decided to end him before he could give her more? Could that someone have been one of the Black Knights? Could it have been...*Ozzie*?

She searched for the truth in Ozzie's eyes but reminded herself that he wasn't the man she had thought he was. He was a lying criminal asshole. There wasn't one *true* thing about him.

"I...uh..." She had to swallow. Her voice sounded like she'd taken sandpaper to her vocal cords, and her heart was a lead fist pounding against her ribs. "I need to hit the ladies' room."

And get the hell out of Dodge.

Because if they'd killed Marcel, they wouldn't hesitate to kill her too. Was that why Ozzie had texted her to meet him here for drinks? Because he planned to take her out back and put a bullet between *her* eyes?

A part of her, the part that had fallen for all his bullshit, didn't want to believe it. That part of her *hurt* to believe it. But the rest of her was screaming one and only one word: *Run!*

Chapter 2

FULL SITUATIONAL AWARENESS...

It was a phrase the Navy SEALs used to describe an operator's ability to focus on a million things at once and quickly come to conclusions about who or what in his environment posed a potential problem. As far as Ozzie could figure, his environment posed three potential problems.

The first was Janie. She was gearing up to make another pass at him. He could see it in her come-and-get-me-big-boy stare. And what the hell was Gloria thinking? That he was some toy to be passed around? Sure, he deserved an ass-kicking for not immediately recognizing her. But in his defense, they'd only had sex once. And besides being a brunette back then, she'd also been about twenty pounds heavier. And just to be clear, *she* was the one who never called *him* back.

Pretty much the story of my life, he thought, quickly followed by, *Damn you, self-pity!*

His second problem was Samantha. Something was off with her. He hadn't noticed it at first, but then he'd detected the edge in her voice, the slight trembling of her lips. Both subtle tells had increased exponentially after she read that text message. *Not good*. The woman was like one of those damned truffle pigs when it came to sniffing out trouble, and the thought of her pretty neck on someone's chopping block had anger burning low in his belly and fear crawling up his spine like a poisonous spider.

And then there was *problema número tres*, otherwise known as the big, burly biker who had shouldered his way into the bar. He was wearing the colors of the Basilisk MC, one of Chicago's true-blue motorcycle clubs, and the expression on his face said he hadn't come in for a drink. He was searching for someone. His eyes were barely visible between his shaggy hairline and the dark beard that grew up over his cheeks, but they zeroed in on Samantha's back as she made her way down the long hall leading to the restrooms, making it seem that he'd found his quarry.

Ozzie's heart rate spiked, the feeling as familiar as breathing. The blood rushing through the injured muscles of his thigh caused them to twitch, and the resulting pain was *also* now as familiar as breathing. He tried to take comfort in that. Pain meant life. He should be grateful to still be alive. He *was* grateful to still be alive. Even if it appeared that his life wasn't going to be anything like what he had planned or hoped.

"Heads up," he murmured casually.

"I see him." Christian took a slow sip of his beer as they watched the biker skirt around tables until he stopped at the high-top closest to the mouth of the hallway.

"Hard to tell what he's packing beneath his cut," Ozzie observed. *Cut* was the term bikers used to describe the jackets that sported their colors and patches. Those colors and patches not only told the world which MC the rider was affiliated with but also who the rider was *within* the MC and the various things the rider had done *for* the MC. According to this dude's patches, he was the sergeant at arms, the enforcer for the Basilisks, and he'd killed for his club. More than once.

Well, piss, shit, and suck a potato dick.

"Judging by the size of that bulge," Christian speculated,

his accent thickened with adrenaline as he nonchalantly unhooked his heels from the brass footrail and prepared to make a move, "I should think it's either a small side-arm or a bloody big knife."

"Trouble brewing?" Delilah asked beneath her breath, coming over to them and pretending to wipe down the bar. "First time I've ever had a Basilisk in my place."

"You still got that sawed-off back there?" Ozzie asked. One of the many things they all appreciated about Delilah was the shotgun with the aftermarket shortened barrel she was known to keep behind the bar.

A faint smile curved her lips. "Wouldn't leave home without it."

"Good," he told her. "If shit goes sideways, I want you to grab that scatter gun and duck down behind the bar."

"But—" she started, only to have Christian cut her off.

"Oy. Shut your gobs. Here comes Samantha." When Christian got really worked up, a little Cockney slipped into his highbrow London speech.

But Samantha wasn't coming. Oh no. She was *running*. Running out the door leading to the alley like the place was burning down behind her.

Ozzie's pounding heart jumped into his throat when the Basilisks' sergeant at arms slid from his chair at the high-top and bolted after her, reaching into the back of his waistband for the weapon he'd stored there. Reaction time for men in Ozzie and Christian's business was faster than the speed of thought, so a split second later, they were off their stools, weapons out, and barreling across the room.

Samantha!

Ozzie wasn't sure if he screamed her name aloud, or if that was just his soul crying out in terror.

"Stop!" he yelled, blasting through the back door

and sighting down the barrel of his Beretta 92FS at the Basilisk's beefy back. The biker had an eight-inch hunting knife fisted in his hand, and he was closing the distance to Samantha.

"I said stop!" Ozzie shouted again, plowing down the dark alley and darting around a big, blue dumpster that, from the overpowering smell of it, was in dire need of a visit from the trash man.

The pounding of his feet on the dirty asphalt sent daggers of pain slicing through his injured thigh. The agony traveled up his spine to stab into the base of his skull.

Neither the biker nor Samantha bothered to glance back, prompting him to make his intentions crystal fucking clear. "Drop that pigsticker, asshole! Or I'll put a bullet in the back of your skull and then piss on your corpse!"

That did it. The biker skidded to a stop, slowly lifting his hands in the air. Ozzie blew out a relieved breath when Samantha made it to the mouth of the alley and escaped around the corner.

What the hell have you gotten yourself involved in this time, Samantha?

"Was the pissing-on-his-corpse bit really necessary?" Christian asked as they slowed their momentum to stalk toward the Basilisk.

"I don't believe in pulling my punches." Ozzie skirted around the biker so he could get a good look at the man's face. And, conversely, let the man get a good look at the business end of his Beretta to discourage the dickwad from attempting any funny business.

The light from the street lamps in the parking lot filtered into the mouth of the alley and lit the Basilisk's hairy face. Ozzie could see the words forming in the guy's beady black eyes before he hissed them aloud.

"Who the fuck are you?" His vocal cords sounded like they'd been marinated in years of bad bourbon.

"Friends of the lady," Ozzie said. The sound of the biker's heavy breathing filled the alley. His robust middle said he wasn't a stranger to milk shakes and cheese fries, and it'd likely been years since he'd managed more than a brisk walk.

When the biker smiled, it revealed his front teeth, all of which were gold and speckled with flecks of chewing tobacco. To call the dude ugly would be an offense to the word. He was *fucking* ugly. "Aw, I wasn't gonna hurt her," Fugly said, adding a wink that set Ozzie's blood boiling.

His finger twitched against his trigger. The day they'd pinned his SEAL Budweiser to his chest was the day killing had become a part of his life. But taking out jihadists in the backwoods of Afghanistan was a far cry from punching a fat biker's ticket in a Chicago alleyway. Through gritted teeth, he managed, "Drop the knife."

"Now why would I do that?"

"Because if you don't, you won't be able to see or pee straight by the time we're finished with you."

"Big talk."

Ozzie wiggled his Beretta from side to side. "Backed up by a big gun. Now drop the blade."

"You won't shoot me," Fugly declared, his smile stretching to reveal back teeth yellowed not by gold but by poor dental hygiene. Just looking at them made Ozzie feel filthier than the floor of a taxicab.

"Look, rotten mouth." His patience was stretched tight. "I'm trying real hard to be polite, but I have to tell you, it's not something I excel at."

"Fuck you."

"Oh, now see?" Ozzie shook his head. "That just got

you removed from my Christmas list. You've got two seconds to comply before I add you to my *other* list. It's titled: Dickheads I've Shot in the Gut."

The biker eyed him for a good two seconds. Then he uncurled his fingers from the hilt of the knife. The blade caught the light and glinted as it somersaulted through the air, hitting the asphalt at his feet hilt-first.

"There," Fugly said. "Happy now?"

Getting there. "You hiding any other weapons?"

"Just my dick." The dude spat a huge glob of tobacco juice on the ground next to Ozzie's boot. It was a visual *fuck you*.

"Comedian, huh?" Ozzie asked.

Now that Samantha was safe and the adrenaline was letting down, he realized he was sweating. June in Chicago usually went one of two ways. Either spring held on with a fierce grip, keeping temps mild. Or summer came on like a she-devil, setting the city on fire. This year was the former, but since there wasn't a breath of wind in the alley, the coolness of the night barely penetrated the insulation of his biker jacket. What little air there was felt thick…*expectant*, like an electrical storm rolled in the distance.

A trickle of perspiration slid from his temple to his chin. He was using his free hand to wipe it away when a noise from the parking lot had his blood running cold and goose bumps crawling over the back of his neck. It was a squeal of alarm. And it came from Samantha.

"Watch him!" Ozzie shouted, turning and running for the mouth of the alley without a backward glance.

~~~

"Come on! *Come on!*" Samantha cried, on her knees beside her classic 1976 Ford Mustang Cobra, searching for the key ring she'd dropped from her shaking fingers in her hurry to save her own life.

The car had been her father's, one of the only things she still had of his. And usually she loved it, loved its cobalt-blue paint, white racing stripes, and manual four-gear transmission. But right now, she'd give anything for a brand-spanking-new vehicle with a keyless entry.

Her heart raced out of control. The smell of fear was ripe in the thin layer of sweat slicking her skin. And her scalp burned like a colony of fire ants had taken up residence on her head.

He's trying to kill me!

She could not *believe* he was trying to kill her. There was no mistaking his words, though. Her chest hurt. She wondered if that was the feel of her heart breaking.

As soon as she had the thought, she squashed it. Surely the ache behind her breastbone was simply heartburn brought on by the dirty martini and the fact that a man she'd thought was her friend—and had hoped might be something more—was trying to feed her to the fishes.

"Gotcha!" she crowed, snagging the keys from where they'd rolled behind the front wheel. She straightened, then spun like a top when she heard Ozzie yell her name.

The Taser she'd pulled from her purse while in the bar's bathroom was in her right hand. Her keys were in her left. And in front of her was the most gorgeous, most treacherous man she'd ever met.

"You okay?" he had the unmitigated gall to ask, jogging toward her. His gait was a little uneven due to his injured leg. He had told her he'd wrecked his motorcycle. But now she wondered if the trauma to his thigh had been caused by something far more corrupt.

She pointed her Taser at him, which caused her

purse to slip from her shoulder to dangle at her elbow.
Silently, she cursed herself for carrying around so much
shit. Aloud, she screamed, "Stop right there, Ozzie!
Don't take another step!"

He stopped dead in his tracks and cocked his head.
"Samantha? What's wrong, sweetheart? Why are you—"

"Shut up!" she yelled, her arm shaking with the effort
to keep the Taser pointed at his chest when all twenty
bazillion pounds of her purse were tugging her elbow in
the opposite direction.

Sweetheart? *Sweetheart?* He'd never used an endear-
ment on her before, but he whipped one out now? She
tried to wrap her mind around the disparity between his
mouth, which dripped honey, and his heart, which was
as black as the ace of spades. She couldn't do it.

How could you? she wanted to scream at him. The
words burned the edge of her tongue, sharp and bitter,
but she bit them back.

Looking at him standing there reminded her of the
time he had taken her to a concert in Millennium Park.
She had danced her ass off to the blues band, and he had
stood watching her, hands stuffed in the pockets of his
jacket, a bright twinkle in his blue eyes and a sexy smirk
on his mouth.

He wasn't smirking now. But his eyes were certainly
twinkling in the glow of the streetlights.

"Samantha, I—"

That's all she heard. That's all he managed to *say*.
Because he started to lift his hands, and her gaze
snagged on the matte-black metal of his handgun. These
past few months, she had convinced herself that she had
imagined the glimpse of that shoulder holster the first
night she met him. She hadn't seen a trace of it since.
Of course, now she understood that the biker jacket he

always sported helped to put the word *concealed* in the phrase *concealed carry*.

She didn't hesitate.

She squeezed the Taser's trigger, releasing the barbs attached to the wires, and let him have all fifty thousand volts.

———

During his thirty years, Ozzie had taken a baseball bat to the back of his head, been shot in the gut, and had his leg nearly blown off. But being tased was its own special brand of misery.

As he flopped on the ground, his muscles spasming and his brain frying inside his skull, he vaguely registered the sound of Samantha's muscle car rumbling to life and the feel of flying gravel pelting him as she fishtailed her way out of the parking lot.

When the spasms subsided, he found himself on his back, staring up at the few stars that managed to shine through the city's constant glow. He wasn't big on heaven or the afterlife, but for a brief moment, he wondered if his mother might be looking down on him. He hoped not. Because the sensation he was experiencing was similar to the one he felt after vomiting…shaken and weak and so glad *that* was over.

"Shit yourself?" Christian's voice sounded like it was coming from a great distance. But when Ozzie lifted his chin, he discovered his teammate standing by his feet.

"Hope not," he admitted. Then he realized Fugly wasn't with Christian, and his heart started beating faster than the Starship *Enterprise* at warp nine. He glanced around. "What the hell happened to the biker?"

"The tosser set off two seconds after you did. And I couldn't shoot an unarmed bloke in the back."

At least Samantha is hell and gone from him, Ozzie thought, relief washing through him as he let his head fall back against the gravel. "He wasn't unarmed. He had his dick, remember?"

"Delighted Samantha didn't fry your sense of humor, Ozzie ol' boy." Christian squatted near his shoulder. "And I take back what I said about the two of you not being enemies. The look on her face when she pulled that trigger was positively exuberant."

Ozzie was having trouble concentrating. His brains were scrambled. The only thought that seemed to have any consistency was *I cannot believe she tased me!* And that was quickly followed by *Why the hell did she tase me?*

Before he could begin to figure it out, Delilah came barreling through the front door of the bar, wild-eyed and blowing like a spooked horse. She had the sawed-off in one hand and Fido's collar in the other. Sensing his owner's distress, the dog had his lips pulled back in a snarl. Considering he was a soft-eyed, floppy-eared, veering-precariously-toward-chubby Labrador, the sight struck Ozzie as funny. It was like a bunny trying to look badass.

"I thought I told her to duck behind the bar and stay there until we said we needed help." He watched her and the dog make their way toward him.

"Telling one of the BKI women not to do something is as effective as telling Fido there not to lick his balls," Christian observed, the last word sounding more like *bohls*. Christian had lived and worked with the Black Knights long enough that his syntax and slang had become Americanized, but there was no getting rid of that London drawl.

"I can freakin' *hear* you," Delilah huffed, coming to

stand beside Ozzie's head. "How many times tonight am I going to have to say that?"

"Maybe just once or twice more." Ozzie grinned up at her, hoping to allay the deep scowl of concern knitting her brow.

It worked. Her expression relaxed, and the instant the tension drained from her shoulders, Fido slipped from watchdog back to his happy-go-lucky self. He plopped onto his haunches, pink tongue lolling, and grinned up at Delilah with dopey doggy adoration.

"What are you doing laid out in my parking lot?" she inquired with a raised brow.

"Samantha tased him." Christian picked up one of the wires still attached to Ozzie's T-shirt.

"You might try saying that *without* a note of glee." Ozzie scowled, ripping the probes from the fabric of his shirt and tossing them aside. *I cannot believe she tased me. Why the hell did she tase me?*

"Jesus, Mary, and Joseph. What did you do to deserve *that*?" Delilah asked suspiciously.

Ozzie pushed up to his elbows. The world did a quick spin. "Why do you automatically take *her* side and assume *I* did something wrong?"

"Puh-lease. It's one of the rules of the sisterhood. When in doubt, blame the man."

"Good to know." He nodded. "Is there a copy of this rule book somewhere? I'd love to thumb through it. I suspect so much about life would be clearer afterward."

"Undoubtedly," Delilah agreed. "Alas, the first rule of the sisterhood—"

"Is there's no talking about the sisterhood?"

"Is that all rules will remain unwritten," she continued as if he hadn't spoken.

"Figures."

"So what happened to Samantha and the Basilisk?"

"Samantha sped away in her car," Christian said, helping Ozzie struggle to stand. His bad leg hummed with pain. The electricity Samantha had shot through his body had forced injured muscles to contract.

Speaking of contracting muscles, amazingly, Ozzie's Beretta was still in his hand. He thanked his lucky stars for the training the navy had ingrained in him, especially the part about never curling his finger around the trigger until he was ready to pull it. If he hadn't been holding the trigger guard when Samantha tased him, there would have been nothing he could do to keep from firing off a wild shot. "The biker knocked off down the alley and—"

That was all Christian managed. The roar of a big bike coming to life sounded from somewhere around the block. A few seconds later, the Basilisk buzzed by the parking lot, his motorcycle eating up the asphalt like a wheeled beast.

While the Black Knights rode fantastical creations of steel and chrome, the Basilisk's bike was bare-bones. Lackluster design elements aside, it was obvious from the well-tuned growl of the engine that the motorcycle was meticulously cared for. And fast.

It was this last bit that had fear grabbing Ozzie's heart and shoving it against his rib cage. Samantha's name whispered through his brain like a call to vespers as he took two painful steps toward Violet, his custom chopper. "He's going after her."

"That would be my guess," Christian agreed. "Are you keen to ride? That jolt gave you crazy eyes."

"I'm okay," Ozzie assured him, his skin itching from latent electricity and a prickly sense of foreboding. "I'll follow you." He motioned to Christian's car. The Brit was the only one of the Black Knights who refused to saddle up on a steel horse, and his sports car looked decidedly out of place in the biker bar's parking lot.

"Brilliant." Christian nodded, pulling his key fob from his jacket pocket. "Now the only question that remains is…follow me where? Where is she likely to go?"

Even though a normal person would probably head straight for the local police station in a situation such as this, reporters, in Ozzie's experience, were far from normal. Whatever mess Samantha was involved in, it would end up on the front page long before it ended up in a CPD report.

It was obvious Delilah and Christian were thinking the same thing, because after a second, they all answered in unison, "The newspaper."

Chapter 3

"HE WON'T TELL YOU ANYTHING!" DONNY CALLED AS Samantha hopped into the elevator. "It's an ongoing investigation!"

She slapped a palm against the edge of the closing door and stuck her head back into the chaos of the *Chicago Tribune*'s bullpen. A sea of messy desks and bright computer screens met her eyes. The sound of clicking keyboards and people yelling good-natured obscenities accosted her ears.

In many places, newspapers were a dying breed, with people getting their daily dose of the world's woes through the nightly news or streamed straight from the Web onto one of their many mobile devices. But lucky for Samantha, who had never wanted to be anything other than a newspaper reporter, the *Chicago Tribune* was holding its own both digitally *and* in print. And even at this late hour, plenty of her colleagues were racing to meet their deadlines.

"He might not come right out and tell me anything!" she called back to her best friend and professional rival. "But I've got mad skills when it comes to reading between the lines!"

"Trouble with that, sweetie, is you can't print something you've scooped from between the lines!"

Before she ducked back inside the elevator car, her indolent shrug said, *We'll see about that*.

She'd gone back to the *Trib* to do two things. The first was to write down—with shaking fingers and a heavy heart—everything she knew about the Black Knights, including what Marcel had told her this morning, as well as to document all the bad business that'd gone down outside Red Delilah's biker bar. The whole sordid tale was tucked in an envelope secured beneath a paperweight on Donny's desk, only to be opened if something bad happened to her. And by *bad*, she meant kidnapping, assault, and/or death.

This wasn't the first time she or Donny had gone after a story that was just as likely to put them six feet under as it was to see them in the running for a national journalism award. They had an understanding that should one of them pay the ultimate price for shining a light in the places that dangerous and powerful people would rather keep dark, then the other would do their best to see that justice was ultimately served.

The second reason she'd gone back to the *Trib* was to suss out which Chicago police detective had caught Marcel's murder case. She couldn't go home. Ozzie's duplicity and her raw emotions would get the better of her there—plus, he knew where she lived. Which left only work. Work was good. Work kept the heartache at bay.

After a couple of calls to her sources within the CPD, she had a name in hand. She was headed to one of the South Side's homicide divisions to see if she could squeeze anything out of Detective Curtis Carver.

"Hey, Sammie?" Donny called just as the elevator doors were about to slide shut.

She stopped their progress with a quick jab of her hand through the narrow gap. The rubber bumpers squeezed her forearm in an ungentle vise before sliding open once again, this time with a high-pitched *ding-ding-ding* of irritation. "What?" She poked her head back into the bullpen.

"Be careful, okay?" Donny Danielson was ten years her senior. But his whip-thin body, kept going with a steady diet of caffeine and chasing down leads, made him look much younger. His dark hair was always impeccably stylish, and beneath his black glasses, his face usually had the craftily expressionless look of a poker player. But right now, as he stared at her over the top of his lenses, his concern was evident.

She blew him a kiss and ducked back into the elevator through the closing doors. Then, shoulders sagging, she let out a ragged breath and punched the button that would take her to the underground parking garage.

She had been deceived before. Bamboozled by sources, conned during interviews, hoodwinked by a local businessman whom she'd written a glowing article about only to find out later that he was a total cocksucker. But never before had she felt someone's betrayal all the way down to her bones.

Ozzie had cut her that deep. Deeper even. She would swear she could feel the slice of his treachery in the very fabric of her soul.

How could he? How could *he?*

How could he have sat with her all those hours in all those different coffee shops, acting like he was just a regular Joe, making her think he was a good guy, one of the *best*, when, in fact, he was a lying criminal asshole? How could he have laughed with her, joked with her, finished crossword puzzles and Sudoku with her when he was hiding *who* and *what* he really was?

And why? Why had he gone to all that trouble?

To distract me, she realized. *To get me to quit nosing around the Black Knights*.

And it had worked. She had fallen for his bait—hook, line, and sinker. A couple of weeks from now, when she wasn't nearly doubled over with hurt and shock, she was going to have to kick her own ass.

The elevator announced her arrival in the parking garage with a cheerful *ding-dong*. She gritted her teeth and determinedly fisted her keys in her hand. Despite the warmth of the air in the garage, an icy chill slipped up her spine. She'd always considered the place well lit. But now the shadows in the corners seemed inky and deep, alive with vile possibilities. And the smells of spilled oil and old exhaust were tinged with an ominous undertone. Something darkly sweet and sinister.

Like death. Like something has died in one of the drains.

Even as she convinced herself it was just a mouse or a rat or a poor pigeon that had flown in and been trapped, she reached into the side pocket of her purse where she kept her self-defense apparatus. Unlike all her other crap, she always made sure to keep her defense stuff handy. She pulled out her rape whistle and her can of pepper spray, since she'd used her last Taser cartridge on Ozzie. Looping the whistle over her head, she thumbed off the plastic safety gadget on the side of the can and scurried across the garage in the direction of her car.

The clomping sound of her bootheels against the concrete was particularly loud, echoing around the cavernous structure and between the parked vehicles. The garage's location off Michigan Avenue, one of the biggest tourist draws in the city, meant it pulled double duty. The first three floors were filled with assigned spaces for the guys and gals working in the Tower, and the remaining three floors were open to the public. Despite that, she seemed to be the only person around.

Which was why she nearly jumped out of her skin when someone called her name.

Ozzie…

She'd know that silky, sinful baritone anywhere.

She spun as a filament of fear unspooled in her chest and tangled with her lungs. There he was, big as life and leaning against the hood of Christian's parked car, booted ankles crossed, big arms stretching the leather of his biker jacket. His colorful motorcycle was angled into the spot beside him.

The audacity of him!

"There are security cameras everywhere!" she yelled, holding the can of pepper spray out in front of her while shuffling backward toward her Mustang. Her car was still a good twenty feet away, but since the elevator doors had long since closed, the small safety the Mustang could provide was her only hope. "You kill me here, and there'll be no getting away with it!"

"Kill you? What the hell are you talking about?" He uncrossed his arms and pushed away from the Porsche.

"Oh, right!" Her voice bounced shrilly against the cement walls. "Like you don't know!" Her heart had gotten tangled up in that filament of fear unspooling in her chest. It beat like the Fourth of July bands at Navy Pier, trying to fight its way free. "You must think I'm an idiot. But fuck me once, shame on you. Fuck me twice, shame on *me*!"

"Samantha, I don't know what the—"

When he started to make his way toward her, she lifted the rape whistle to her mouth. Blowing it with all her might, she felt its strident squeal nearly burst her eardrums. Turning, she bolted for her car. This time, her shaking hands didn't fail her. Her key slid into the lock as easily as a hot knife through butter.

A second later, she was behind the wheel, door closed and locked, and cranking over the big engine. With a pump of the clutch, she put the Mustang in gear and left rubber on the parking garage's pavement as she screeched up the ramp, sending silent thanks to her father for rebuilding the Mustang's engine with such love and devotion that in all the years since his death, it hadn't failed her even once.

Adrenaline burned through her blood. Fear tasted metallic on her tongue, like an invisible hand had shoved an old penny between her teeth. And in her rearview mirror, she saw Ozzie standing there, hands on hips, head cocked. He looked so normal. So...*unthreatening*.

But it was a big, fat act.

Tears she refused to shed burned the back of her eyes as she peeled out of the garage at breakneck speed. She crested the small rise that would dump her onto the street and quickly flipped on her blinker. As she waited on an opening in the traffic, she darted another glance into the rearview mirror. Nothing. And then something across the street caught her eye. There was a big, burly biker parked there. He was covered in hair and leather.

Now, *he* looked like the kind of person who would show up in a parking garage to help someone shuffle off their mortal coil. *He* looked like the kind of guy to chase a woman out of a bar and threaten her at gunpoint.

But it's never the ones you suspect, she thought.

Then she quickly reminded herself that she *had* suspected the Black Knights. Ever since they refused to do an interview. Ever since she thought she'd caught a glimpse of Ozzie's shoulder holster. Ever since Patti Currington, secretary for the shop and wife to one of the Knights, had caught a stray bullet during a drive-by shooting. Ever since any *number* of curious and deadly things had happened to or around the Black Knights.

Then there had been Ozzie. Ozzie with his smile and his charm. Ozzie making her forget herself, making her ignore years' worth of gut instincts.

What a fool she'd been!

The roar of the biker's motorcycle competed with a cannonade of thunder that boomed through the sky overhead, shaking the city below. *Great. Just what I need. A deluge that'll bring traffic on the Dan Ryan to a standstill.*

No sooner did she have the thought than a space opened up in the traffic. She gunned the Mustang between two vehicles as the clouds gave birth to fat drops of rain that splattered against her windshield. Clicking on her wipers, she tried to shake off the sensation that the almighty seesaw of life was doing its best to drop her ass in the sandbox tonight.

Dan Ryan Expressway, Southbound

"In any given situation, I'm usually the one with a clue. But I cannot imagine what that woman is thinking."

Christian glanced over at Ozzie in the passenger seat. "I shouldn't think Walt Disney could have imagined what's in her head." He snapped on his turn signal and changed lanes to take advantage of a paper-thin slice of space.

After Samantha set off with the pudgy biker hot on her heels, and after the heavens opened up, Ozzie had decided it would be best to jump in with Christian. Now they were crawling along at a snail's pace in traffic, doing their best not to lose sight of Samantha or the biker through the driving rain.

That daft Basilisk is serious about getting his hands on Samantha if he's willing to withstand this deluge.

Christian did not understand everyone's mad fascination with motorbikes. Sure, they were cool. And the ones built back at Black Knights Inc. went beyond cool to completely badass. But they were not all-weather vehicles. *So why would someone fancy tying themselves to a mode of transportation that is dependent on the weather?*

He thought to stick with his Porsche, thank you very much, and all those lovely horses she kept under her bonnet.

"But how could she think I'd want to kill her?" Ozzie demanded, drumming his fingers on the dashboard impatiently.

Christian gritted his teeth around an order for Ozzie to quit abusing the leather and narrowed his eyes at Ozzie's expression. If one were to look up the word *wounded* in the dictionary, one would find Ozzie's puckered puss pictured beside it. It was obvious that despite what Ozzie proclaimed, Samantha Tate had come to mean more to him than a mere gal pal.

"It boggles the mind," Christian mused, "given you've gone through birds the way a bloke with a cold goes through tissues, that none of them have formed a negative opinion of you. But the one Betty you haven't shagged thinks you're evil incarnate."

Not that Ozzie had been going through women of late. In fact, as far as Christian knew, Ozzie hadn't hopped aboard the shaggin' wagon since the night he nearly lost his leg. Christian wondered if perhaps it wasn't just Ozzie's *thigh* that had sustained an injury. Of course, he dared not ask. Talk of whether or not a bloke's manhood was up to snuff was best done over a pint. Or rather many, *many* pints.

"First of all," Ozzie said, sliding him a withering look, "when it comes to bagging babes, I'm not like a man with a cold. I'm like a connoisseur of fine wines. Sampling comes with the territory, and those who are sampled love the fact that they've been savored by someone who truly enjoys their unique bouquet."

Christian's snort was the audio version of an eye roll.

"And second of all, you could look a little less delighted that Samantha is operating under some misguided notion that I…that I…"

"Kill people for a living?" Christian lifted a brow while making another lane change. "If the shoe fits, mate, lace it and wear it."

Ozzie's scowl deepened. Then he sat forward, pointing. "She's exiting. Get over. Get *over*! Oh my God! Why are you driving like an elderly turtle? Let's chew up some asphalt!"

"Cool your heels," Christian muttered, downshifting and shoving his way between vehicles, ignoring the irate honks that followed his progress.

"The Basilisk is following, but he's not trying to advance on her," Ozzie observed. "He's happy just to remain on her tail. What the hell is going on?"

Uh…like Christian should know? "Sorry. I left my crystal ball back home. Shall I pull over and fetch my tarot cards from the boot?"

"You, sir, are a boorish lout." Ozzie's affected English accent was actually quite good.

"And you, sir, are a slang word for male genitals." This was a game they used to play before Ozzie's accident. They lessened the tension of any given situation by devolving into name-calling and smack talk. Immature? Sure.

But bloody good fun.

"Speaking of male genitals," Ozzie said. "I saw you staring at my rig yesterday when I was wearing those tight jeans. But just to be clear, while I love you, it's more like brotherly love than—"

"I only stared because I've never laid eyes on anything so woefully minuscule."

"Oh, you mean the minuscule bit of space left in the crotchal region of my Levis due to the enormity of my—"

"In fact," Christian went on as if Ozzie wasn't speaking. "I shouldn't begin to imagine how you managed to bag all those babes, as you so eloquently put it, given you're working with such limited equipment."

"When it comes to women, I've found it's best to lead with confidence, follow with comedy, and close with red-hot sex. I could give you some pointers."

"I'm sorry." Christian kept one hand on the wheel but used the other to cup his ear. "What language are you going on in? It sounds quite a lot like bullshit, but since I don't speak it, I can't be certain."

"I'll release the Kraken and prove it." Ozzie pretended to reach for his fly. "Prepare yourself to behold the majesty of the ol' Ozzie meatsicle. But fair warning, it's been known to make folks faint."

"From despair?"

"Nah. From its overwhelming size and majesty."

Christian lost it. As he exited the highway and laid on the gas to close the distance to Samantha's Mustang, he couldn't stop laughing. Having a war of wits with Ozzie was always fun, despite Christian usually losing the final battle. But since Ozzie's jocularity had dimmed of late, seeming pressured and somehow *less*, this bout felt particularly good. It was as though, after the bombing in Malaysia, all the Ozzie had been scooped out of him, leaving behind a dry husk.

"You keep your iPad back here, don't you?" Ozzie reached into the backseat, foraging around inside Christian's rucksack.

"Yeah, so?"

"Do you pay for Internet service for it?"

"I…" Christian frowned. "No. I connect to Wi-Fi and… What are you on about?"

"I'm going to use your iPad to hack into the police databases to bring up the CCTV and POD footage as we go. That way, if we lose Samantha, we can still track her through the city's cameras. But since you don't pay for Internet service, I'll have to use my iPhone as a hot spot."

"Oh, brilliant." Christian had stopped being amazed at Ozzie's ability to make magic with all things electronic and geeky years ago. The bloke was a mad genius. He could hack anything, program everything, and always make it look easier than tea cakes and scones on a Sunday.

"I think she's turning." Ozzie's head whipped around just as he settled the iPad in his lap. "And the Basilisk just peeled off in the opposite direction. Why did he—"

But that's all Ozzie managed when they saw Samantha's destination. It was a police station, lit up like a Roman candle against the dark, rainy night.

"This should be interesting," Christian muttered as he pulled into the station's car park and chose a space three over from the one Samantha slammed into with a squeal of brakes that sent twin fans of water kicking away from her tires.

"While I figure out what the hell is going on, you call back to the shop, or *ring* back to the shop, as you like to say, and let them know we're okay." Ozzie's hand was already on the Porsche's door handle, despite

Christian having yet to put the vehicle in park. "I'm sure Delilah called them as soon as we left the bar. No doubt they're worried."

Christian scowled as he switched off the engine. Ever since the BKI women had descended on the shop, he'd been made to feel like a teenager instead of the trained agent he was. "You realize those three sentences made my willy invert," he grumbled.

"Oh, poor you." Ozzie feigned a pout. "It's so hard having a handful of beautiful women care about you, isn't it?" He opened the door and jumped out, tossing Christian's iPad into the passenger seat. The sound of the rain crashing onto the car park's pavement was relentless before the door closed with a perfunctory *thunk*.

*And the most beautiful of them all is...*her, Christian thought grumpily.

Her was Emily Scott, Black Knights Inc.'s new secretary, den mother, and all-around girl Friday. She was a former CIA office manager, a born-and-bred Chicagoan—which meant a tough, take-no-prisoners kind of bird—and though she had only worked for BKI a little over a month, she already ran the place like she owned it. With long, brown hair that always looked a bit messy, as if she had just returned from the beach, and a beauty mark high up on her cheek, physically, she was just his type.

But for reasons unknown to him, she had decided to make him her personal punching bag. Which wouldn't be a bad thing if he could punch back. But one look from her twinkling brown eyes, one word uttered from her pursed, disapproving lips, and he found himself tongue-tied. Speechless. Mute as a turnip.

Smitten.

Such a benevolent-sounding word. Rhymed with

kitten and *mitten*, which were both fairly pleasant things. But now that he found himself suffering the affliction, Christian could say with authority that being smitten was anything but nice.

It made him forget which way was up and which way was down. Caused him to break out in hot sweats at night and slink around the shop like a shadow during the day, hoping to snatch a glimpse of her unobserved. Because when she *did* observe him, she gave him loads of tosh with that sharp tongue of hers.

And what *really* cheesed him off was he…*liked* it.

Which proves you're a sick shite.

With a groan, he pulled his mobile from his hip pocket and thumbed through his contacts until he found the one titled *Shop*. Holding the phone to his ear, he was dismayed to discover his heart thundering right along with the clouds overhead. Then, sure enough, Emily answered. And what were the first words out of her mouth? They weren't *How are you two getting on with the reporter?* Or even *Is everything okay?* Oh no.

"Hey, Fancy Pants." Her accent was pure Chicago. Her *A* sounded long and somewhat drawn out. But her voice? Oh, it reminded him of actresses in old movies. Low and smoky and full of sexual innuendo. "Are you pissing in your Post Toasties about your pretty car getting all wet? And speaking of… How are those six-hundred-dollar shoes faring in this weather?"

Chapter 4

"GOD BLESS AMERICA! HOW DO YOU MANAGE TO PUT your pants on every morning?" Samantha yelled.

"I'm sorry! What?" Ozzie tried to blink the water from his eyes. The second he had exited Christian's car, he'd been drenched to his skivvies. Samantha was doing a pretty good impersonation of a drowned cat herself, all ragged hair and bristle as she skirted around the back of her Mustang where she assumed some sort of martial-arts pose. Ozzie felt his lips twitch at the ridiculousness of the situation.

"You know, over those massive balls of yours!" she cried. "You realize we're at a police station, right?"

"So?" He was completely flabbergasted. It wasn't a sensation he enjoyed.

"So I called ahead when I saw you following me!" she yelled just as an angry bolt of lightning sizzled overhead. The zigzag of electricity was followed by the deafening boom of thunder. Ozzie winced. A storm like this forced a man to admit his weakness, his feebleness in the face of Mother Nature. And this one in particular seemed to be personally mocking his plight when it came to making heads or tails of the crazy, stubborn, *confounding* woman in front of him. "They'll be out here any second to take you into custody!"

"Take me into custody? Samantha, what the fuck are you—"

That's all he managed before the door to the police station burst open and six uniformed officers came barreling down the steps, sidearms out and unmistakably aimed in his direction.

Here we go, he thought, automatically assuming the position, hands laced behind his head. He didn't know what the hell Samantha thought he had done or was about to do, but one thing he did know. When it came to the CPD, you didn't even *hint* like you were considering resisting arrest.

"On the ground!" the beefy officer at the front of the pack bellowed.

Ozzie immediately dropped to his knees. His injured thigh called him dirty names on the descent.

"He's armed!" Samantha yelled oh-so-helpfully.

Ozzie groaned, bracing himself for what he knew came next.

Right on cue, he was hit by the crowd of policemen and shoved face-first into a shallow puddle. The water smelled like dirt and grease. It tasted worse. When his hands were whipped behind his waist and a knee shoved into the middle of his back, there was no way to stop his grimace and keep the foul sludge from slipping between his teeth and coating his tongue.

"It's a nine millimeter in a shoulder h-holster," he sputtered, trying to be helpful as rough fingers fumbled beneath his body, searching for his weapon. "I have a license to carry it."

He was rewarded for being a good Samaritan. And that reward was the knee in his back doing its damnedest to break his spine.

"Oy!" he heard Christian yell. "What the bloody hell do you coppers think you're doing to my—"

Ozzie turned his head and blinked the water from his

eyes in time to see two things. The first was Christian stepping from his Porsche. The second was four of the six policemen charging toward Christian like a hulking group of Klingons rushing into battle, all bared teeth and bristling rage.

Christian took an instinctive step back. But it was too late. One officer broke away from the pack and took a flying leap toward the Brit. Two minutes later, they were both handcuffed and being gently—*Ha-fucking-ha!* If you believed the CPD boys were gentle, Ozzie had some beachfront property in Utah he could sell you—marched up the steps and into the police station. His teeth were chattering with the cold and the wet by the time they pushed through the front doors. But everything inside him was burning hot.

He was surprised the combination didn't have steam pouring from his ears, especially when Samantha came to stand in front of him, her brown eyes searching his blues. "You have no one to blame for this but yourself," she said.

He could have asked, *Blame for what?* But she'd been unwilling to provide any goddamn answers all night, and he was sick and tired of begging her to explain herself. And beyond that, he was…*hurt.* Hurt that after all the hours they'd spent getting to know each other, all the lunches and coffees and walks through the park, she could actually accuse him of…whatever the fuck she was accusing him of.

"Maybe," was all he allowed through gritted teeth.

"And for the record," she said, sniffling, "I'm blaming you too."

Some of the fire inside him burned away. That sniffle had less to do with the cold rain dripping from her hair and more to do with the pain he saw in her eyes.

"Samantha, I—"

"Haven't you ever heard the old newspaper adage that you should never pick a fight with someone who buys ink by the barrel?" she interrupted.

He'd always had a soft spot for the fairer sex. Supposed that protecting things smaller and weaker than himself had been stamped into his DNA at conception. He could remember being barely four years old when he jumped in front of the little neighbor girl after the dog from across the street lunged at her with slavering jaws and snapping teeth.

His terrified mother had barreled out the back door of their suburban Indiana home, shooing the dog away and taking Ozzie into her arms. With one breath, she had scolded him for being so reckless. With another breath, she had praised him for being brave and selfless. He could still remember the love and the tears in her eyes when she had brushed his hair back from his face. It was one of his last memories of her, and—

He pushed the old pain away and focused on the present. "Samantha, whatever you've got going on inside that head of yours, it's just flat-out wrong. I wish you'd tell me—"

"Wrong? *Wrong?*" A hysterical edge entered her voice. "After everything that's happened tonight, you're still trying to convince me I'm wrong?"

His attention was drawn to her rapidly rising chest and the thin sweater that covered it. The weight of the sopping wool pulled the garment down until he could see the top swells of her breasts and the barest edge of hot-pink lace.

Hot pink.

Samantha was so pragmatic, so sensible in everything she wore—take tonight's black sweater, unadorned jeans, and low-heeled boots—that he'd pictured her as the typical white-cotton-underpants kind of woman. Then again, she did tend toward colorful designer handbags. So maybe that was her nod to her own femininity. Handbags and lingerie.

I can get on board with that, he thought, and felt movement behind the fly of his jeans.

After the bombing and the trauma to his thigh, not to mention all the pain meds he'd been taking, the mornings he woke to a pup tent in his sheets had been rare. He'd thought getting off the painkillers would help. And it *had*. Physically. His morning wood had been restored to its former glory.

But mentally?

Yep, that was another matter altogether. Those months when he'd been recovering, those months of *abstinence* had brought clarity. He'd realized that the way he'd been going about life, hopping from bed to bed, wasn't getting him what he really wanted.

Not that he had gone on a woman diet, per se. More like he had lost interest in the *hollowness* of it all. Then Samantha had arrived on the scene. Samantha with her eager mind and biting sense of humor. Samantha with her gap teeth and long, lush hair that tempted his fingers.

She made him want to throw his convictions right out the window. He might have done just that if not for the teensy-weensy fact that he *liked* having her around. And in his experience, ladies tended to love him and leave him. So it stood to reason that if he wanted to *keep* her, he needed to avoid the "love him" portion of that equation so the "leave him" portion never happened.

Unfortunately, his dick hadn't gotten on board with the plan. Anytime she was near, it took notice. And right now? Well, it saw that hot-pink bra and decided

to stand up and wave a happy *Hi, how are ya* to the
whole world.

"Sweetheart, if you would just explain what you think
is happening or *has* happened, then I'm sure we can—"

"Oh, you just ooze charm like an oil spill oozes..." She
blinked, seeming to search for the correct comparison.

"Oil?" he finished helpfully.

Her left eyelid twitched. A bright-red flush of anger
stained her cheeks. "But I'm not buying it."

His patience snapped. "Well, that's good, because
I'm not trying to *sell* you anything! For the love of
James T. Kirk, could you please just—"

"Ma'am," the officer who had been the first to tackle
Christian butted in. "I think Detective Carver is waiting for you." Of all the times for Barney Fife to find
his voice. Ozzie wanted to deck him. "And we'd like
to take these two into an interrogation room. Check
them out, and see if they really do have licenses for
their weapons."

"Yep." Ozzie nodded with mock enthusiasm. Since
he couldn't pop the po-po in the puss, he'd satisfy himself with sarcasm. It was *nearly* as gratifying. "As men,
we will go and discuss important things. First thing we
should talk about is the phone call you owe me. I'd like
to make it to Lawrence Washington. You've heard of
him, right? He's your police chief."

That seemed to set the officers back on their heels.
Lawrence P. Washington was a former marine who had
a tendency to bark orders at his rank and file with rapid-
fire, machine-gun precision. He also happened to be the
only civilian not affiliated with the Black Knights who
knew the true nature of their business. More than once,
the police chief had come to their rescue, helping them
keep their real identities secret when the work they did

for the government ended up intersecting with the mean streets of Chicago.

"Well?" Ozzie didn't have to feign annoyance. He had it in spades. And the fact that his thigh was screaming due to his recent brute squad manhandling wasn't helping matters. "Let's get going. The sooner I figure out what I'm being accused of and why my night has turned into such an unholy dick suck, the happier I'll be."

Samantha stood silently as the officers marched him and Christian toward the back of the building. When Ozzie glanced over his shoulder, he was taken aback by the look on her face. There was only one word to describe her expression. It was *betrayal*.

—————

Samantha drummed her fingers on the metal table and impatiently glanced at her reflection in what she knew was a two-way mirror. With a start, she realized the drowned rat with the smeared mascara and the shiny, red nose staring back at her was, in fact, *her*.

Good Lord.

Licking the tips of her fingers, she wiped the mascara from under her eyes as best she could. Then she finger-combed her quickly drying hair into some semblance of order. With curly hair, that was a challenge. As for her red nose? It'd just have to stay. She was so weighed down by disappointment and heartache that she didn't have the desire or the energy to go rummaging through her purse for her compact powder.

She didn't like that Detective Carver had insisted on answering her questions inside an interrogation room instead of at his desk. She liked it even less that she'd barely had time to ask him if he had any concrete leads in Marcel's case before his cell phone rang and he ducked into the hall to take the call—which was almost forty minutes ago. And the fact that she felt guilty for turning Ozzie in? Well, *that* she liked least of all.

He's a gunrunning piece of slime-sucking scumbag criminal crap who spent months buttering me up and then tried to kill me. He deserves anything and everything he gets, she forcefully reminded herself.

Except…

Well, except something wasn't right. Now that her adrenaline was wearing off, now that time had been allowed to euthanize the fear that had savagely ripped at her heart like a rabid animal, she was beginning to wonder if she'd been wrong about something. None of Ozzie's recent behavior made sense.

She was frowning, trying to figure it all out, when the door burst open and Detective Carver sauntered in. He was quickly followed by Chief Washington and…Ozzie and Christian. The latter two were uncuffed and carrying steaming cups of coffee.

Warning! Warning! A buzzer sounded in her head.

She gripped the edge of the table and blinked in mute disbelief.

"Seems there's been some sort of misunderstanding between you and these two gentlemen tonight," the chief said, hitching up his pant leg so he could perch on the corner of the table.

Samantha had interviewed Chief Washington on two occasions. Once during protests in the city brought on by a case of police brutality. The other for the quick write-up she'd done to commemorate his ten-year anniversary as police chief. She'd found him to be plainspoken and given to impatience with anything that whiffed of bullshit. In short, her kind of man.

But tonight, he seemed to have aligned himself

against her. She narrowed her eyes as Carver, Christian, and Ozzie each took a seat opposite her. And then Ozzie had the gall to slide her one of the two cups of coffee he carried.

"Two sugars and a crap-load of creamer. Just the way you like it," he said.

"Excuse me?" She glared at Washington. "How is it possible to misunderstand someone who threatened to shoot me in the back of the head and then piss on my corpse?"

"Saman—"

"No." She pointed a finger at Ozzie when he tried to interrupt. "You may have everyone fooled, but I'm on to you. *Big time*. You prance around all suave and charming—"

"I don't prance. I'm not a show pony."

"But you can't put flowers in an asshole and call it a vase," she went on as if he hadn't spoken. It burned her that his expression was the only friendly one in a room full of taciturn scowls.

"I wasn't talking to *you* when I said that stuff in the alley." He looked for all the world like he meant it and expected her to believe him.

Ha! She was finished falling for his horseshit.

"No?" She cocked her head, narrowing her eyes. "Well, were you talking to Christian? If so, that's no way to treat a coworker."

"He was talking to the Basilisk," Christian said.

"Huh?"

"The Basilisk who followed you out the back of the pub," Christian clarified, his English accent making him sound condescending. *Or maybe that's just my imagination?* "The one hefting this hunting knife."

He lifted a plastic bag from beneath the table,

slapping it down on the surface. She leaned forward to see that inside the bag was a blade that looked huge and razor sharp.

Her mind blanked. Just...full stop.

"Huh?" she managed again, proving her degree from Purdue was some sort of hoax.

"Maybe it's best if you start at the beginning, Miss Tate," Chief Washington said, unbuttoning his cuffs and rolling up the sleeves of his dress shirt to reveal muscular forearms and deep-mahogany skin. He'd always reminded her of a slightly leaner, determinedly tougher Idris Elba. A handsome man, to be sure, with a larger-than-life personality.

"The beginning of what?" she demanded, not liking this at all. A basilisk had followed her out of the bar. *As in the mythological Greek monster?* She must have misheard. *Perhaps it's Christian's accent.* "The beginning of my investigation into these assholes?" She flicked a finger toward Ozzie and Christian. "Or the beginning of this day? Or maybe the beginning of tonight, when I found out one of my sources had been shot and killed only hours after he gave me a vital piece of information pertaining to these assholes?" Again, she gestured toward Ozzie and Christian.

"She keeps going on about us being assholes," Christian fake-muttered to Ozzie.

"I don't know where she gets that," Ozzie fake-muttered back. "We're as sweet smelling as a summer breeze."

Washington lifted a hand for silence, and both Christian and Ozzie obeyed, albeit with smirks on their faces. Samantha was sorely tempted to reach into her handbag, pull out her pepper spray, and give them both a squirt. *That* would show them.

"How about we start with this evening," Washington

said, "and work our way backward, see where the misunderstanding happened, and take it from there."

"Fine. Good." She crossed her arms, realized the gesture looked petulant, and forced herself to simply fist her hands in her lap. Then she told Washington about the text message she had received from Donny, her suspicion that Ozzie and the Black Knights had been involved in her source's death, her fear that Ozzie had invited her to the bar to silence her, and finished by reiterating the threat Ozzie had yelled at her as she beat feet down the alleyway in back of the bar. When she was done, she lifted a brow that succinctly said, *Now are you getting the picture? How about you put these two back in cuffs?*

Instead of handcuffing Ozzie and Christian, Washington turned to Carver and said, "Go grab that POD footage from outside Red Delilah's. Bring it in here for Miss Tate to see."

POD footage? Samantha knew that stood for police observation device. The security cameras installed throughout the city, but particularly in high-crime areas, were just one more tool the CPD used to try to combat pockets of lawlessness.

Carver pushed up from the table and exited the interrogation room, and then there was silence. Deep, penetrating silence. Samantha's stomach rumbled, and she realized she'd skipped dinner. The sound of Christian nonchalantly sipping his coffee was like nails down a chalkboard. And the clock on the wall ticked away the seconds, each one straining the atmosphere inside the room just a little more.

Samantha was tempted to look at Ozzie. But she knew what she'd see. Charisma and sex appeal and a blatant expression of innocence.

No, thank you.

She wasn't sure what they hoped to show her on that footage besides Ozzie chasing her out of the alleyway, gun in hand. And truthfully, she didn't look forward to seeing the moment of his betrayal playing out in front of her. After all, she'd already *lived* it. She was *still* living it.

Her stomach grumbled again, and she reached for the coffee Ozzie had brought her. Before she closed her fingers around the Styrofoam cup, a thought occurred. *What if he poisoned it?*

Okay, so maybe she was teetering toward paranoia, but better paranoia than death. She opened her purse and pulled out the warm can of Diet Coke she kept inside. Popping the top, she enjoyed the *psssffft* that broke the silence of the room. She had just lifted the can to her mouth when Carver returned carrying a laptop.

He set the machine in front of her and said, "The footage is loaded. Just press Enter."

Her heart fluttered as she set aside the Diet Coke. She fisted her hands once—to stop any tremors that might linger—and pressed the button. The video was so grainy that she couldn't make out much on the screen. "Is this as good as it gets?" She frowned at the police chief.

Washington glanced at the screen and sighed. "I'm afraid so. Sometimes the cameras…"

"Do you mind?" Ozzie grabbed the machine from Samantha, turning it toward himself. "I can route this through my server back at the shop and use some software I created to clean up the image."

"Suit yourself." Washington shrugged.

Route it through his server? Use software he created?

She knew Ozzie was good with computers. Ten minutes in his company, and she had known he was a bit of a tech geek. And then a month ago, he had spent two full hours shopping with her for a new laptop when her old one finally gave up the ghost. He had pointed out the different bells and whistles of each machine. Once she picked one, they had gone to a coffee shop where he had patiently helped her install the software needed. So yeah. She knew the man was good with computers.

But by the sounds of things now and the sight of his fingers absolutely *flying* across the laptop's keyboard, he wasn't just *good* with computers, he was great. *We're talking the kind of guy who belongs in Silicon Valley running a multibillion-dollar tech company, not selling black-market weapons to Chicago South Side gangs.*

"Done." He turned the laptop around and slid it toward her. "Just press Enter."

She did as instructed and blinked in amazement at the new and improved images sliding across the screen. There was no sound to accompany the footage, but she had no trouble making out the parking lot at Red Delilah's biker bar. For a couple of seconds, the only things the video showed were a few cars driving by and her Mustang parked beneath the closest streetlight. Then, there she was.

She leaned forward and watched her video self dart from the mouth of the alley. Bile climbed up the back of her throat, the horror of the moment fresh once again. When she saw herself fumble the keys and drop to her knees, she nearly cried out her frustration.

Then, there was Ozzie running toward her with that awkward, limping gait. The gun in his hand was easy to see, and she was about to point at it and say, *There! See? I told you so*, when a dark shadow emerged from the alleyway. That shadow turned out to be a big, bearded biker. He seemed to hesitate when he saw Samantha pointing her Taser at Ozzie, then he darted up the street and out of the camera's range. Christian arrived in the mouth of the alley a second later, a huge knife clutched in his hand—the same knife now gleaming on the table—just as her recorded self lit Ozzie up.

She winced and closed the laptop lid, having seen all she needed to see. The uncertainty she'd been toying with earlier rolled in like an undertow, pulling her down and away from the shores of her conviction.

She glanced at Ozzie, only to discover his expression was guarded. Gone was his smirk. His mouth was now set in a hard line, and she marveled at how his lips could appear simultaneously sensual and severe.

"I, uh, I may have rushed to judgment," she admitted. The coals of embarrassment smoldering inside her were stoked into a flame when Christian snorted.

One eyebrow climbed Ozzie's forehead to disappear into a shock of sand-colored hair. "Sweetheart…" His voice was low and liquid. It flowed over and around her until she felt as though it was just the two of them alone in the room. "I think you had judgment preprogrammed on your speed dial."

Chapter 5

CAREFUL WHAT YOU WISH FOR.

It was good advice. On the one hand, Ozzie was tickled pink that Samantha no longer thought he was trying to kill her. On the other hand, he would've done just about anything to smooth away the look of mortification that contorted her pretty face.

"I never saw him," she said. The dry parts of her hair sprang out in loose coils, while the wet parts continued to lie lank against her skull. Her nose was auditioning to be the next stand-in for Rudolph—that would be the reindeer, not Valentino. And her damp sweater kept slipping off her shoulder to reveal the strap of that hot-pink bra. "No, wait. That's not true. I saw him when I exited the parking garage at the Tribune Tower, but I never saw him before that. I swear it. I… Oh jeez!" She turned to Ozzie, a flush spreading over her cheeks. "I *tased* you!"

He rubbed his chest where the barbs had stuck in his skin. "Not something I'm likely to forget anytime soon."

"I…" She blinked, then scowled. "But hang on a minute. You might not have been talking to me when you promised that bullet to the brain." He was glad she left out the pissing part this time. "But you're involved in *something* nefarious. Why else would you walk around with a piece in your pants? Come on, I watched *Sons of Anarchy*."

"Well, to be clear, I don't keep my piece in my *pants*." He couldn't help himself. "At least not the piece *you're* talking about." Her scowl deepened. So did her blush. "I keep it in a shoulder holster. My business isn't exactly located in the nicest part of town, and ever since I left the navy, I feel naked without a sidearm. You get used to having that level of protection on you. It's a psychological thing."

At least those were the reasons he'd given the cops when they asked him about his Beretta. The same reasons Washington had backed up once he arrived at the station. But now, the confession sat like an aspirin on Ozzie's tongue, chalky and sour.

One more lie in a long line of lies. One more betrayal.

Samantha searched his face for a time, and he could see her wanting to believe him. The moment she did, the moment doubt gave way to faith, ranked right up there as one of the worst of his life. And that was saying something. He wasn't quite sure what. But *something*. Maybe that he was sick and tired of lying to her? Sick and tired of *hiding* from her?

If that was the case, he was in some seriously deep shit.

"So now that we have *that* cleared up," Washington said, "how about you tell us about your meeting with Marcel Monroe this morning." Washington had been born and raised in Chi-Town, but he tended toward a Dixieland drawl. "Specifically what he said to make you believe the boys and girls at BKI would want to kill him…and *you*."

Ozzie saw the indecision in Samantha's eyes. The journalist part of her didn't want to give away anything that would jeopardize her ability to scoop the story. But the *Samantha* part of her—the part that valued justice, honesty, and integrity above all else—won out in the end. "He told me the Black Apostles are getting their weapons from a group of motorcycle mechanics who have a shop here in the city."

Christian made a rude noise. "And obviously that had to be us, yeah? Because in a city of nearly ten million people, we're the only motorbike mechanics."

"No." Samantha gifted him with a dirty look that would have put a lesser man in his place. Christian simply raised a brow. "Marcel *also* said these motorcycle mechanics used to be in the military. Which made sense to me, since the whole reason I asked him to do some digging was because the gun that was recently confiscated after a Black Apostle drive-by shooting had a serial number matching a weapon that was supposed to be in Iraq. You lot"—she waved a hand in a circular motion toward Ozzie and Christian—"have military backgrounds and likely military connections both foreign and domestic. So I figured it was a sure bet that you were the motorcycle mechanics Marcel was talking about, getting your guns from some contact you kept after leaving the armed forces. I added two and two and got four."

"More like *negative* four," Christian insisted. "The *opposite* of the correct answer."

Ozzie agreed with Christian but held his tongue because (a) he liked Samantha too much to pile on, and (b) while he was shocked that she would actually think for one minute that he was capable of running black-market guns and offing one of her sources, he could sympathize with how much those conclusions must have shocked her…*hurt* her.

The look of betrayal he had seen in her melted-chocolate eyes suddenly made sense. And that gave him hope. If she cared enough to feel betrayed, then maybe she cared enough to stick around.

Washington stood up. "Hang on." His back was ramrod straight, a testament to his military training. "How the hell do you know about that Glock, Miss Tate?"

Ozzie turned from Washington to Samantha. He could see her mentally backpedaling. "Oh, uh..." She rolled in her lips, then offered a smile that brought to mind images of a cat after it'd been caught in the cream. One look at the sliver of space between her two front teeth had his jeans feeling tighter and the torn muscles of his thigh twitching.

Great. Just great.

"Don't bother." Washington shook his head. "I should've known you had a source in the evidence department. You're too quick to get details, stuff the other newshounds have to wait to read in the press releases."

"Hey." Samantha sat up straighter. When her sweater slipped off her shoulder again, revealing that wonderfully intriguing bra strap, Ozzie had to adjust his position in his seat or risk injuring himself. It was like his damn prick was trying to make up for those days and weeks and months of zip, zilch, nada all at once. "Have I ever printed anything that sidetracked an investigation?" She hoisted up her sweater—*on the one hand, a crying shame; on the other hand, a blessed relief*—and answered before Washington could. "No. I have not."

"All the same," the chief harrumphed. "Might be time I cleaned house over there."

When Samantha started to sputter, Ozzie figured he might as well jump in and get the conversation back on track. "So let me see if I have this right. A Glock that was recently used in a drive-by shooting was found to have a serial number that matched that of a weapon supposed to be in Iraq." It was no secret that the American government had armed the Iraqi military and police to the teeth in the hope that they could impose some sort of rule of law over their own fractious population.

"Yes," Washington admitted through pursed lips. "The

number had been filed off just like all the others we've confiscated from various Apostle crimes. Usually, we can use acid to read scratched-off numbers. But these guys are no amateurs. They use a stippling machine to… Never mind. The point is that, for whatever reason, the machine wasn't used on this one weapon. We were able to read the number, and when we ran it through the databases, we got a hit. A hit that, like Samantha said, led back to a weapon that had been shipped to Iraq. As far as the Department of Defense is concerned, it should still be over there. We've been trying like hell to figure out why it isn't."

"And what does the DOD say?"

Washington sent him a look, soldier to soldier. "They don't seem all that concerned. It's just one gun. Their explanation is that a contractor or a soldier or, hell, even an Iraqi delegate could have gotten their hands on it, brought it back to the States, and either sold it or given it away. And in the usual course of events for undocumented weapons, it found its way onto the black market and into the hands of a gangbanger here in Chicago."

"But you're not buying it." Ozzie leaned back and crossed his arms over his chest, eyeing Washington. He admired the man not only for his service to his country, but for his continued service to the good people of Chicago. And for a moment, he wondered if Washington might offer him a job once the Black Knights realized he was physically as good as he was ever going to get and decided to—

He stopped the thought right there. It hurt too much to let it reach its inevitable conclusion.

"Maybe they're right," Washington said with a shrug. "Maybe they're not. I have enough firefighter friends to know that where there's smoke, there's usually fire."

"Mmm." Ozzie nodded his agreement before turning back to Samantha. "And this Monroe character—"

"Marcel," she said, something flickering in her eyes. It looked a lot like regret…or maybe recrimination. No doubt she was blaming the conversation she had with Mr. Monroe this morning for his death this evening.

"Marcel," Ozzie repeated, softening his tone and hoping she could read in his face the sympathy he felt. There was nothing worse than shouldering the blame for someone else's death. And he would know. The memory of the bombed-out hotel room, of Julia Ledbetter's charred corpse, flashed through his head. It was followed by the memory of his father wailing his mother's name over and over again as the paramedics took her draped body from their home on a gurney. The flashbacks made his stomach somersault, caused the ache in his leg to increase tenfold. Reaching down to massage his mangled flesh, he continued, "He's a Black Apostle?"

"Recently joined." Samantha's throat worked over a hard swallow. "His mother worked the streets over in Englewood. I used her as a source a couple of times before…" She trailed off and looked away, her jaw sawing back and forth.

Ozzie wanted to reach across the table and grab her hand, but something stopped him. Which was when he realized that, to his recollection, he'd never touched Samantha other than a quick handshake or friendly pat on the back. Since he was the touchy-feely sort, this was rather odd. Then again, considering how *touchable* she looked, and given that once he started touching her, he might not be able to make himself stop, perhaps it wasn't so odd after all.

"Suffice it to say," Samantha went on, "that the streets finally got the best of Sheena. Marcel had just turned eighteen when she died, and I tried to help him stay out of the life. I got him a job bagging groceries at a corner store. For a while, he seemed to be doing okay. But it's hard to work your ass off every day for minimum wage, barely making ends meet and constantly worrying if your water is about to get shut off. And it's *especially* hard to live that way when you see the kids you grew up with lazily slinging dope and then driving around in tricked-out SUVs. Four months ago, Marcel told me he'd joined the Apostles. Two weeks ago, I found out about the Glock and asked him if he knew anything about where the gang members were getting their guns."

Ozzie watched her glance into her lap. He couldn't see what was happening beneath the table, but from the way her arms moved, he figured she was absently picking at a loose thread on the hem of her sweater or the seam of her jeans. She bit her lip, and he was certain that any second now, he'd see tears fall. He clenched his hands into fists in readiness, his heart rate going into warp drive. But when she lifted her head, her eyes were clear.

Tough. It was a term he used to describe many of the women he knew, particularly those associated with the Black Knights. But this was the first time he looked at Samantha and realized she was cut from that same cloth. A pride he had no business feeling expanded his chest.

"At the time, Marcel didn't know anything," she admitted. "But he said he'd do some digging, ask some questions." Her shoulders drooped. Once again, she looked into her lap. "I should've stopped him. I should've—"

Everything inside Ozzie urged him to reach for her. He was about to throw caution to the wind and do just that, but Washington beat him to the punch. The police chief put an arm around her shoulders, giving her a fatherly pat.

"You start blaming yourself for other people's choices, and you'll quickly find you don't have time for much of anything else," Washington told her. "Marcel was a full-grown man. He knew the risks and the consequences of the life he was choosing."

Julia had been a full-grown woman and known the risks of her job, but that doesn't stop me from feeling some measure of responsibility for her death. And then there was Mom...

No doubt Samantha felt the same, and nothing anyone said would assuage her guilt. Still, she firmed her jaw and got right back to business. "So obviously Marcel wasn't talking about the Black Knights. But who *was* he talking about? Who was... Who *is* that biker?"

And that's my cue, Ozzie thought. "He's the sergeant at arms for the Basilisks. Or so say the patches on his cut."

"Basilisks?" Samantha shook her head. "Is that, like, the name of a gang?"

"A *biker* gang," Washington clarified. "And not the snuggly, teddy bear sort that do good deeds like coordinate charity rides and blood drives. We're talking old school. The one-percenters."

"One-percenters?" Samantha frowned.

Ozzie explained. "Years ago, the AMA—"

"That would be the American Motorcyclist Association," Christian clarified.

"Right." Ozzie nodded. "Anyway, they commented that ninety-nine percent of motorcyclists were law-abiding citizens. Which, of course, implied that those in the last one percent were *not*. Since then, outlaw biker clubs have glommed on to the notion and started referring to themselves as the one-percenters."

"Exactly," Washington agreed. "The Basilisks are

the same kind of bikers as those who perpetrated that bloodbath down in Waco, Texas."

"So you're telling me these guys are the real, honest-to-god Sons of Anarchy? An outlaw biker club running guns?" Samantha blinked owlishly. "Doesn't that seem a little…"

"Coincidental?" Washington asked.

"Well, *yeah*." She hitched one shoulder.

"Fiction often mirrors fact. And if the Basilisks *are* running guns out of Iraq, it'd be one more entry on a long list of criminal enterprises they've embarked on over the years."

"Such as?" Her dark eyes gleamed. She was fanatical in her desire to unearth corruption and crime. Ozzie couldn't help but think there had to be a story behind her rabid hunt for the truth, but in all their time together, he had never gotten up the guts to ask her about it. Maybe because he had sensed how personal the subject was for her, and he had known that if he asked her to open up *her* Pandora's box of deep, dark secrets, then she might want him to open up *his*.

"Such as nothing that we've been able to prove beyond a shadow of a doubt, but a whole host of stuff we suspect. Like extorting corrupt city officials, running prostitutes, maintaining protection rackets, and so on and so forth," Washington said.

"Shit," Samantha said.

"That pretty well sums it up," Washington concurred.

Carver joined the conversation for the first time. "Their sergeant at arms goes by the road name of Bulldog."

"You know him?" Ozzie raised an eyebrow.

"Liked him for the murder of a shopkeeper a couple of years back," Carver explained. "But like always with these guys, I could never get enough proof to arrest him.

They're slimy as eels. And good news, ladies! Most of them are single!"

Carver's frustration was clear, as was the fact that he'd had a chili dog for lunch. The yellow and brown stains on his shirt were impossible to miss.

In Ozzie's experience, homicide detectives always looked like a dry-cleaning nightmare. Hunting down murderers was a 24-7 job that required catching meals on the go. Carver also had the prematurely graying hair, the slight paunch, and the weathered complexion of a quintessential murder cop.

"Do these Basilisks run some sort of motorcycle mechanic shop?" Samantha asked.

"It's small. Just one of their many businesses," Carver said. "Many *fronts*," he added with disgust. "But yes. They do."

Samantha took a deep breath. "So Marcel tells me the Apostles are getting their guns from motorcycle mechanics. Eight hours later, Marcel is dead, and a motorcycle mechanic, a *Basilisk*, is chasing me down an alleyway with…*that* in hand." She flicked a finger at the knife lying in the center of the table. "I'm thinking that's no accident."

"I'm thinking you're right," Washington agreed.

"So what now?"

"So now I thank you for giving us our first real lead in figuring out how the hell that Glock got here," Washington said. "And I ask you to butt out and let us do our jobs."

Samantha frowned, glancing back and forth between Carver and Washington. A million questions burned behind her eyes. Ozzie thought if he squinted, he'd be able to see her putting on her reporter's cap and adjusting it to a jaunty angle.

Cue the music.

"What else do you know about the Basilisks?" she asked. "Do they have military connections? Have they partnered with the Apostles on anything else? Will you—"

"Miss Tate." Washington cut her off. "You've been in this business a while now, so you know how this goes."

Samantha crossed her arms and gritted her teeth so hard, Ozzie was pretty sure he heard her molars creak. "I just gave you everything, and you're going to give me nothing."

Washington shook his head. "Because you did give us our first break, and because I happen to like you—you've got gumption, remind me of my oldest daughter—I'm willing to let you be the one to break the story once we have a firm hold on it and an arrest pending. Seem fair?"

"Marginally," Samantha allowed. Then, "But you could use me as a source, couldn't you? Or better yet, as bait? The Basilisks—"

"Over my dead body," Ozzie growled before he'd made the conscious decision to speak.

There was so much fire, so much *conviction* in his voice, that everyone turned to gape at him. Well, everyone except for Christian, who just leaned back in his chair and shook his head like he wasn't at all surprised.

Well, that makes one of us.

Ozzie was as surprised as hell. Sure, he was naturally protective. Sure, Samantha was his friend and his secret midnight fantasy. But his vehemence went beyond both those things and skated along the edge of something deeper, something more substantial, something that scared the ever-loving shit out of him.

Over my dead body…

Ozzie's declaration, spoken in that low voice, rubbed over Samantha's skin like a tongue. All smooth and seductive. Then, the more she thought about it, the more his words grated.

Sure, they were friends—and she was beyond relieved to discover he wasn't a lying criminal asshole; in fact, she was so elated, she wanted to grab his ears and kiss the stuffing out of him. Then again… *How dare he think he has any right to tell me what I can and cannot do!*

She opened her mouth to tell him it was none of his damned business if she wanted to volunteer to be the carcass the police used to lure in the big, bad wolves, but she hesitated. Because the look on his face said he was the human equivalent of a cluster bomb. One wrong move from her, one wrong word, and *boom!* Detonation.

She did a double take. The Ozzie she knew had always seemed so good-natured, so charming and easy-going. Okay, sure, there were times when he got quiet, got serious, and his expression turned…*sad*. But never had she seen him looking like this. He was still Ozzie, still handsome as homemade sin. Still wearing that ridiculous T-shirt that read *Keep Calm and Klingon*. But there was something else in his face. Something *more*. Some sort of knowledge or understanding or—

And then she realized what it was. He was sitting there in his young man's body, but his eyes…

His eyes were those of an old warrior.

When Washington cleared his throat, she realized that some time had passed since Ozzie had spoken. Time when she and Ozzie simply stared at each other, neither able to look away. Her mind felt fuzzy, as though someone had installed shag carpeting along the inner curve of her skull. Which was why it took her a second to understand what Washington was getting at when he said dryly, "Thanks for the offer, Miss Tate, but we'll have to pass. There's that whole *protect* nonsense in the oath we took to protect and serve."

"And speaking of that"—Ozzie gave Samantha a quick glance—"are you going to assign her a marked unit as escort? Put a uniformed officer at her house? Bulldog doesn't strike me as the kind of dude to simply give up once he has his mind set on something. And judging by this evening, his mind is set on getting his hands on Samantha. She needs protection 24-7 until you guys resolve this thing."

Samantha knew how it was supposed to go at this point. She'd seen enough TV, read enough books. This was where she was supposed to object. Where she was supposed to say she was capable of looking out for herself and didn't need police protection. But in all those TV shows and books, the oh-so-brave heroine eventually found herself in the clutches of the big, bad men, and the audience or readers just rolled their eyes, unsurprised, since the heroine had made a decision that put her in a category labeled Too Stupid to Live.

That being the case, Samantha kept her mouth shut. Not that she looked forward to the inconvenience of having a bodyguard. But if the alternative was a body *bag*, you can bet your sweet ass she'd take the inconvenience every day of the week and twice on Sunday.

"Well…" Washington rubbed his chin, glancing back and forth between Ozzie and Samantha. "I could do that," he mused. "But if you're worried about her safety, you know there's no place in the city safer than—"

"The shop," Ozzie finished for him.

"Oh no." Christian shook his head adamantly. "That's a bleeding, buggering cock-up of an idea if ever there was one."

Samantha saw Ozzie's expression turn contemplative. That contemplativeness quickly morphed into determination. "Why?" He pinned a frown on Christian. "With all the others away at that *conference*"—he seemed to stress the word unnecessarily—"the place is empty."

"Except for the wives and the girlfriends," Christian grumbled.

"All the better. She'll have plenty of female company."

Since Samantha had been inside the Black Knights compound, she knew Washington was right. Not taking into account the massive brick wall topped by razor wire that surrounded the place, the warehouse itself was a throwback to a bygone era, with masonry walls that were three feet thick and insulated with what was probably clay and horsehair. It was a fortress. She would certainly be safe from the Basilisks in there.

And honestly? She was curious to get back inside. Maybe there she'd find the answers to why Ozzie had those old warrior's eyes.

I mean, they have to come from somewhere, right?

Somewhere other than the year he matriculated at Stanford before going to see his nearest navy recruiter. Somewhere other than the three years he spent as a rescue swimmer attached to a navy aircraft carrier, because as far as she could figure, he hadn't seen much action. Maybe he had acquired those eyes during the year following his stint with the navy. In all her research, she hadn't been able to account for those thirteen months postnavy and pre–Black Knights Inc.

"And the days?" Christian asked.

"What do you mean?" Washington frowned.

"I mean, if we muck about and do your dirty work, providing Samantha with protection at night"—she wasn't sure she cared for being labeled anyone's *dirty work*—"who will follow her around all day while she's at work or…or…" Christian shot her a dagger-eyed look. "Whatever else she gets up to, including but not limited to accusing innocent men of murder?"

"I said I was sorry about that." She frowned at him.

"Indeed?" He raised one dark eyebrow. "I must have missed it."

That took her aback. She glanced at Ozzie, then at Carver, and lastly at Chief Washington. "I apologized, didn't I?" She was sure that she had.

"Not that I recall," Washington said.

Carver's answer was a succinct "Nope."

Ozzie remained silent.

Despite her dark hair and dark eyes, her complexion was rather fair, which meant there was no way to hide the color that stole into her cheeks. *Damn.* "I'm sorry." She forced out the words.

"What's that?" Christian cupped his hand around his ear. "You were mumbling, so…"

"I'm sorry!" She glared at him, her fingers inching toward the side pocket of her purse and the pepper spray inside. They started inching faster when his face split into a smug grin.

"I forgive you," he said magnanimously.

Her hand was suddenly around the canister of pepper spray. *It would be so satisfying.*

Unaware of the violence bubbling in her heart, Washington said, "You can call me in the morning when you're ready to leave the shop, Miss Tate. I'll arrange for a police escort to follow you while you're out and about."

"No need," Ozzie said. "With everyone gone from the shop, we've pretty much stopped production on new bikes. So I'm free to do a little work as a bullet catcher."

Chapter 6

Basilisk Clubhouse

THE NAME ON HIS BIRTH CERTIFICATE READ JOHN George Peabody III. But nobody dared call him that. Sometimes he wondered if his parents had saddled him with the highfalutin-sounding name in the hopes he'd do what John George Peabody Sr. and John George Peabody Jr. had not. Namely, rise above the poverty and the violence that was life for so many on Chicago's South Side. Of course, if that was their aim, they had failed utterly.

When it comes to rising above the violence, he conceded. As for rising above poverty? Not to toot his own horn or anything, but he'd kicked that in the pants pretty early on. The platinum Rolex glinting on his tattooed wrist proved it.

He only allowed himself two overt luxuries in life, the watch and his motorcycle. Any more than that, and he might draw the attention of law-enforcement types. Now, as he glanced at the first of those luxuries and noted the time, his lips curved into a severe frown. "How fucking long does it take to bag up a hundred-and-twenty-pound woman?"

When silence stretched, he realized his question had been construed as rhetorical. He made it clear it was *not* when he lifted his eyes to Crutch, his vice president.

"It's raining cats and dogs out there," Crutch said, leaning back in his chair and crossing his arms over the patches on the front of his cut. The overhead light caught the scar running across Crutch's temple and the occasional sandy-colored strand of hair that salted his bushy brown beard. "It might've put a crimp in Bulldog's plan if she ran in somewhere to wait out the storm. But don't you worry, Venom, he'll get it done."

Venom. *That* was his name—the only one he'd gone by since way back in basic training, back around the time he met Crutch and found the man to be a kindred spirit. At first, Venom had been his nom de guerre. Now it was his road name. And it suited him just fine. Because in war and on the road, Venom was the same. Toxic to his enemies. Lethal to anyone he decided to sink his teeth into.

"I don't know." He shook his head. "It's possible that fat fuck finally stroked out."

Bulldog was the club's enforcer because he was tough as nails, enjoyed knocking heads together, and was ruthless and single-minded when you set him on a task. But if he kept ballooning in size, he would no longer be able to do his job. That would become an issue. Venom would have to delve into the ranks of the club for a replacement. Trouble was, though most of the Basilisks were tough and unafraid of getting a little bloody, none of them had Bulldog's special brand of unyielding tenacity.

Shit. I gotta get that asshole to lose some weight.

He glanced down at the big table, then let his eyes travel around the empty clubhouse and marveled at how quiet it could be. When Devon Price, the leader of the Black Apostles, told him that one of Devon's new homeboys, some skinny fuck named Marcel Monroe, seemed mighty interested in the *who* and the *what* and the *how* of the weapons the Black Apostles were using, Venom had called an emergency session of Church, and the clubhouse had been packed. In the front room, club members had lounged around with their old ladies or their current hardbelly of the month. But in the back room, Venom had gathered his executives.

"We might have ourselves a bit of a problem, boys," he'd told them as the sound of crashing pool balls and blaring classic rock slid under the locked door. Cigarette smoke hung heavy in the air, as did the smells of warm beer and pussy.

After he'd outlined the problem, it hadn't taken long for the committee to agree that Marcel Monroe needed some watching. And perhaps some *killing* if the reason the gang member was asking questions about the guns turned out to be more than just personal curiosity. The plan had been set. Bulldog had been ordered to stick like glue to the gangbanger's heels and see what was what.

For a while, Bulldog had turned up a whole lot of jack shit. Then, this morning, the Basilisk's enforcer had called to say he was sitting in a parking lot across from a coffee shop where Marcel Monroe was meeting with Samantha Tate.

Initially, Venom had drawn a blank. Then when Bulldog said, "You know, she's that hotshot reporter who blew the lid off the City Hall scandal last year," it'd all come back Venom. The story in the *Tribune*. The quarter-page photo of the pretty little journalist with that sweet gap-toothed smile.

Venom had held on to that paper for a week, jacking off to that photo as he imagined the reporter on her knees in front of him, those sexy teeth of hers raking not-so-gently against his hard cock as she hoovered him dry.

His decision had been instantaneous and his instructions to Bulldog succinct. "Kill the banger. Bring me the woman."

His first duty was always to his club. But nothing said he couldn't have a little fun along the way. And silencing a sexy bitch who dared stick her nose into his business was *beyond* fun.

"What's the plan once she's here?" Crutch asked now, reaching inside his jacket pocket and snagging a pack of Marlboro Reds. He shook out a smoke. With a *flip* and a *snick* from his Zippo lighter, the end of the cancer stick glowed bright orange.

"Find out what she knows, what that Marcel prick told her. Then…" Venom shrugged, spreading his hands wide. He could no more stop the smile that split his face than he could have stopped the tide from rolling in.

"Your old lady isn't going to like you plugging some young reporter," Crutch said conversationally. "We're not out on the road. You're breaking a cardinal rule."

In MC culture, a biker out on a ride was afforded the freedom to get himself a little strange, no questions asked once he got home. The caveat being that once he *was* home again, the only Twinkie he could cream was his old lady's. So yeah, Venom was breaking a cardinal rule by asking Bulldog to bring the pretty reporter here with the intention of screwing her brains out after he'd learned all she could tell him about her meeting with Marcel. But so what?

"Rules are made to be broken."

Black Knights Inc. Headquarters, Goose Island

"Beware. The coven has hopped aboard their broomsticks."

Ozzie closed the door to the third-floor room where Samantha was changing out of her wet clothes. They'd stopped by her apartment, Ozzie waiting out in the hall while she packed an overnight bag, before making their way to the shop. Now, the delightful thought of her behind that metal door—no more than five feet away while she stood in nothing but her hot-pink bra and panties—was replaced by the imagery Christian's words evoked.

Coven? Broomsticks? The Brit really did *not* like having the shop overrun by women. "They blame me as much as you for this brainiac scheme," Christian continued in a conspiratorial whisper. "And, mate, in the future, if you plan to shag me from behind, at least do me the courtesy of holding my hair out of the way."

"Mental image be gone!" Ozzie hissed.

Tiptoeing down the hall, they passed doors that concealed the many loft-style bedrooms that had once been the personal lairs of BKI's bachelors. Now, those rooms stood mostly empty since so many of Ozzie's teammates had wives and children who required homes that didn't pull double duty as a motorcycle shop and defense firm. Under *normal* circumstances, the rooms were empty. Right now, some of the aforementioned wives and children were in residence, and Ozzie was careful not to wake up the latter even as a deep, aching longing for things he might never have filled his chest.

"My point is, if bodyguard duty is your way of auditioning for the douchebag Olympics," Christian continued as they quietly descended the metal staircase, "then, Ozzie ol' boy, I should think you're a shoo-in."

Ozzie didn't dignify that with a response other than a clear and concise hand gesture.

His thigh ached from the night's activities, a constant reminder of the precariousness of his future. The hot, dark despair that had been threatening to consume him for months felt particularly oppressive in the moment, but he did his best to ignore it as he stepped off the last tread and was met by a sight that warmed his soul and beat back some of the blackness. Namely, two of the eight gorgeous gals who loved his brothers-in-arms with all their fierce, loyal hearts. Two gorgeous gals he'd come to adore. Two gorgeous gals who turned to him with so much fire in their eyes that he instinctively stumbled back.

Christian had used the word *coven* to describe them. Ozzie was beginning to see the accuracy of the term. He got the distinct impression he was one *bubble, bubble, toil and trouble* away from being turned into a toad.

He opened his mouth, but Becky lifted her hand. "Can't you see we're having an event here?" She was wearing a bright-green mud mask that had images of flying monkeys whirling inside his head.

"What event?" he asked.

"Your funeral."

"Hear me out." He patted the air in a conciliatory fashion, thanking his lucky stars he was *only* dealing with two of the eight women who were attached to his teammates.

"Oh, goodie." Becky rolled her eyes. "He's about to start man-splaining, using his ever-lovin' man logic to validate this idiotic idea. But don't let him sway you, Michelle. This situation he's created is a frickin' problem."

Blond, bossy, and no bigger than a minute, Becky was the original owner of the motorcycle shop that had become Black Knights Inc. She was the artist responsible for the fantastical bikes they made and the one who ultimately provided their cover. Ozzie loved her to pieces. *Usually*.

"*Problem* is just another word for *challenge*," he assured her, grabbing Christian's arm when the Brit began backpedaling. "Stay right where you are," he demanded. The air inside the shop smelled pretty much the way it always did, eau de rubbing compound, burning metal, and strong coffee. But if he wasn't mistaken, there was now a tinge of napalm wafting toward him from the direction of the women. If he was about to get his ass fried, he didn't want to be the only crispy critter in the room.

Misery loves company, right?

"Piss off, knobhead." Christian jerked his arm free.

"You." Becky pointed to Christian. "Those curse words sound kinda pretty in that accent, but they're still curse words. Don't forget there are children upstairs." Ozzie found it hysterical that the woman who could outcuss all of them turned into a profanity Nazi anytime the little ones were around. "Also," she continued, "go stand by the base of the stairs and make sure our conversation isn't being overheard by…you know who."

After watching Christian happily retreat to the stairs, Ozzie turned back in time to see Becky's eyes blasting into him like photon torpedoes.

"And you," she said. "Please explain what *she*"—she shoved a finger toward the ceiling—"is doing here and why we had to run around like frickin' chickens with our frickin' heads cut off trying to make sure this place was…" She stopped herself and seemed to search for the right words. Her voice was barely a whisper when she finished with, "…fit for company."

Ozzie knew that meant locking doors, shutting down computers, and squirreling away evidence that BKI was anything other than a motorcycle shop. Not that it would have taken much. He and the rest of the Knights kept the place in company-ready condition, since one of the little ones, Jake and Michelle's son, Franklin, was now old enough to start asking questions. Keeping BKI clandestine meant keeping it kid friendly. Which, in turn, meant it was naturally *reporter* friendly.

He could have pointed this out to Becky. He decided it was in his best interest to keep his mouth shut.

Apparently that wasn't what Becky wanted from him. She glowered so fiercely, her mud mask cracked. "Speak!" she demanded.

"There really wasn't much choice." Ozzie quickly outlined the events of the night. And just in case Becky and Michelle weren't convinced, he finished with, "From all I've heard, those Basilisk bastards are bad news. *Evil* men. And you both know as well as I do that the only thing that's necessary for evil men to triumph is for good men to stand by and do nothing. I wasn't about to stand by. Are you both saying that *you'd* just stand by?"

"Oh, for Pete's sake." Becky rolled her eyes. "I bet your ass is jealous of all the crap that just came out of your mouth."

"He's doing his best to be a tube steak tonight, isn't he?" Michelle spoke for the first time, eyeing him consideringly. Not only was Michelle Boss's sister and Snake's wife, but she was the mother of two darling little boys. She was kind and soft-spoken—*usually*—and she was *not* supposed to use terms like *tube steak*!

Ozzie felt his hackles stand stick straight. "So what's the plan then, ladies? For me to stand here and take it on the chin until you finally insult me to death?"

"We're *trying* to see this from your point of view," Becky insisted, adjusting the collar on her striped cotton pajamas. Given the lateness of the hour when he called to inform them he would be bringing company home for the night, it was no surprise he'd caught them in various states of dishabille.

"We're trying to see this from your point of view,

but we can't get our heads that far up our asses," Emily Scott, BKI's new secretary, quipped as she appeared from one of the offices. Looking at the lithe brunette, one would never know she was a tough, streetwise Chicago gal who had worked as the assistant to one of the most powerful men inside the CIA. Her girl-next-door looks were currently compounded by fuzzy slippers, silk sleep pants, and an oversized sweatshirt.

"*Ba-da-bum!*" Becky mimicked a drum solo.

Emily and Becky, whom Ozzie was pretty sure were sisters from another mister, exchanged a high five as Emily took a seat at the conference table.

And now it's three on one. Perfect. Kill me now.

He decided it was time to change the setting on his charm ray gun from stun to kill. Donning his best puppy-dog expression, he hooked his thumbs in his belt loops and allowed his shoulders to slouch. "She's in *trouble*," he insisted. "And I…I *care* about her." It was meant to garner sympathy, but the minute he said it aloud, he realized it was true. He *did* care about Samantha. A lot.

Holy shit.

Suddenly, he understood his vehemence at the police station when Samantha offered herself as bait. That something he had felt in the moment, that something that had been deep and substantial and scary as hell, was back in full force. He wasn't just fond of Samantha. He didn't just lust after her. He…*adored* her. Everything about her—from her natural nosiness to her sharp mind and her quick quips.

The epiphany must have registered on his face, because when he glanced at the group, his heart pounding in his chest, he found every eye glued to him. Like, *glued* to him. As if they had the ability to Vulcan mind meld with him and could see all his inner workings.

A bolt of lightning blazed overhead, flashing through the leaded-glass windows like a strobe light. A *crack* of thunder followed an instant later.

He braced for the fallout. Samantha was a *reporter*, after all. In the Black Knights' line of work, that word was found under the *Family Feud* category of Things You Don't Want to Find Stuck to the Bottom of Your Shoe. But to his surprise, the fallout never came. Instead, the women just got quiet.

Very quiet. *Uncomfortably* quiet.

He tugged on his collar, shuffled his feet, and felt a bout of indigestion stirring.

Finally, Becky said, "Care about her, huh?"

Before he could nod, Emily piped up with, "If by *care about* he means *tap that ass*, then sure."

A tsunami of anger crashed over him. He felt the tips of his ears ignite. "Excuse me? She's my *friend*. And I'll thank you not to reduce her to a sex object."

"She might be your friend, but that doesn't mean you don't want to eat her cake," Michelle said. "What?" She lifted one sable-colored eyebrow when she saw the incredulity on his face. "Oh, for goodness' sake, you think I don't know about cake eating?" When he just blinked, a smile that was decidedly feline appeared on her lips. "Believe me I know all about cake eating. In fact—"

"Stop right there." He lifted a hand.

"I suspect we *all* know about cake eating," she continued. "How about it, ladies? Like having your cakes eaten? Thumbs up or thumbs down?"

"Thumbs up," a duo of voices declared.

"Look at him," Becky said, unwrapping a Dum Dum lollipop and plugging it into her mouth. "You can see the wheel is still turning, but his brain hamster frickin' up and died of mortification."

"You're all going to catch pneumonia from the ice in your hearts," he gritted between his teeth.

"Maybe we should give the poor guy a break," Emily muttered. "He can't help that God saddled him with a penis *and* a brain but only enough blood to supply one at a time."

"That reminds me of a joke I recently heard," Michelle said. "Why do men name their penises?"

"Ladies—" Ozzie tried to interrupt.

Michelle just barreled ahead. "Because they don't want a stranger making ninety percent of their decisions for them!"

Cackles of laughter erupted.

"Stop! Stop!" Becky howled. "You're ruining my mud mask! It's cracking into a million pieces!"

"I'm melting! I'm melting!" Michelle did a dead-on impersonation of the Wicked Witch of the West.

"Enough!" Ozzie chopped his hand through the air. The two syllables echoed around the shop like blasts from a double-barrel shotgun. Three pairs of eyes blinked at him in surprise.

Damnit all! It was *never* his intention to raise his voice. Not with them.

"Sorry," he mumbled, blowing out a deep breath and reaching down to massage away the shooting pain in his mangled thigh. "Look, I know it's not ideal. I know you're all under a lot of pressure right now, and the last thing you need or want is this. But I *do* care about her, okay? Despite what you might think of her chosen profession, she's a good woman. And I want to help her through this. I *need* to help her through this. I'd appreciate your support."

For a long time, silence ruled the room. It was only broken when Peanut, BKI's mascot and former tomcat

turned fat tub of lard, launched himself onto the conference table with a weird, grunt-like *mrrreow*. He
slunk to the middle of the table where he collapsed as
if he'd been held up by marionette strings that had suddenly been cut. His notched ears twitched. His crooked
gray tail flicked back and forth. And he let loose with a
very unfeline fart.

It effectively broke the tension hanging in the room.

"Dear sweet baby Jesus! You *have* to change his diet,
Becky," Emily said, waving a hand in front of her face.
"At this point, he's nothing but a fart factory."

"The one who smelled it dealt it." Becky grinned
around her lollipop stick. She intentionally mispro-
nounced *smelled* as *smelt* for a poetic touch.

"Don't blame that on me!"

"The one who denied it supplied it!" Becky wheezed,
doubling over with laughter. And despite everything,
Ozzie felt his anger melt and his lips twitch.

This was what made Black Knights Inc. more than
just a job. *They* were what made it more. And the
thought that he would lose his spot in the fold because
he was no longer able to—

"Okay, Ozzie," Becky cut into his thoughts. Good
thing. He was tired of the same old refrain. "We've got
your back on this one. But if you do anything to jeopardize our men, I'll—"

"You *know* I'd never do that," he told her, a muscle
twitching in his jaw, his blood simmering anew that she
would even consider mentioning it.

"I *do* know." She nodded. "But shi…uh…*stuff* happens. And just be aware, if it does, we'll kick your butt
up between your shoulder blades and make you wear it
like a cape."

"Great. Hunky-dory. And now that we have *that* all

cleared up," Michelle announced, pushing from the table, "I'm off to bed."

Becky agreed, and the two of them stopped beside Ozzie on the way upstairs to impart private bits of advice.

"She might look like a delightful lady lollipop, wonder boy. And I'm sure you're tempted to take a lick," Michelle whispered in his ear. "But remember she's triple dipped in nosiness. She's going to snoop while she's here. Yessiree, Bob. Without a doubt."

Before he could respond, Michelle drifted off. He turned back to find Becky the Green-Faced Goblin glaring up at him. "Well?" he asked. "Let's have them."

"Have what?"

"Your two cents."

She grinned. Her mud mask was a spiderweb of cracks. "Oh. Well, that's simple. Don't make me go Gitmo on your ass," she warned, her brown eyes flashing, her blond ponytail swinging.

"Oh, talk like that really steams my trousers," he told her, forcing the kind of easy, flirtatious response she expected from him. The kind of response that would have come naturally before the bombing. "I can understand why Boss put a ring on it. With a dirty mouth like that, you're a catch. How about you ditch him and marry me instead?"

"Rrrright." Becky rolled her eyes just as he had known she would. "You couldn't handle me even if I came with a set of instructions." She trailed after Michelle.

Ozzie looked toward the table where Emily still sat, stroking Peanut. The attention had caused the feline colossus to turn over his motor, and the tomcat's loud purr rumbled through the entire room until Ozzie could feel it in his chest. "Staying down for a while?" he asked.

Emily was a new addition to the team, but she fit

in like she'd always been there. "Yepper." She nodded. "I'm too wired after all the brouhaha." Her Chicago accent made the word *the* sound more like *da*. She focused over his shoulder on the spot Christian occupied, looking like she was gearing up to do what she did best—give the poor guy shit.

And that's my signal to leave, Ozzie thought.

When he got to the base of the stairs, Christian grabbed his arm and pleaded, "Don't leave me alone with her. I'm pretty sure she bites."

Christian liked to pretend Emily Scott's arrival was the prelude to Armageddon and that the woman herself was none other than the Antichrist. But Ozzie knew better. He knew better because Christian's pupils dilated every time he looked at Emily.

"And if she *did* bite, you'd love every tooth mark she left behind," Ozzie told Christian with a confident smirk, pulling his arm free to tiptoe up the stairs.

"You, sir, are proof that shit can grow legs and walk!" Christian hissed after him.

Ozzie didn't have time to jump into the ring for another fun round of name-calling. He needed to grab a quick shower and some dry clothes and check on Samantha.

Samantha…

Her name seemed to wind itself around his brain, pulsing, sliding, rubbing…

Chapter 7

EMILY SCOTT HAD NEVER MET A MAN QUITE LIKE Christian Watson.

And that was a bold statement, given that she'd spent seven years working for the CIA and was used to that whole International Man of Mystery thing. But Christian…well, Christian took the word *mystery* and raised it to the power of ten.

He was a former SAS officer, but he was working for the U.S. government. Since coming to Black Knights Inc., he hadn't set foot in England and avoided the subject of his friends and family the way one avoided poison ivy. And he'd chosen to accentuate his ridiculous male perfection not with a biker jacket and faded jeans like the rest of the BKI crew, but with designer clothes, Italian-made shoes, and accessories that would make a fashionista weep with joy.

But it was like he was a shined-up wooden nickel. Emily was certain that underneath that thin veneer of pomp and circumstance lay a rough core. A deliciously *intriguing* core that she only caught glimpses of when she scratched his surface.

Which I do every chance I get.

"Go on, then," he said, still standing by the bottom of the steps, all long and tall and handsome. It wasn't the *pretty* kind of handsome or even the *cute* kind of handsome that had been popularized in America, but the *manly* kind of handsome. The kind of handsome that came with harsh features, strong bones, and a mop of wavy dark hair that seemed to cry out for the caressing touch of a woman's fingers. The kind of handsome she had grown up with in her working-class Bridgeport neighborhood. "Speak your piece so I may—"

"Shhh." She raised her hand from scratching Peanut's furry belly. "This is such a rare moment, you standing there looking like something I'd draw with my left hand. Mind if I take a couple of minutes to savor it?"

Mrrreow! Peanut complained, so Emily resumed her petting duties while still eyeing Christian's delightful level of dishevelment. With his hair all wild, his clothes damp and conforming to every bulging muscle, and a smudge of dirt across his brow, he looked more like what she thought he *really* was. A barbarian. A savage. An uncivilized man who had been forced to live in a civilized world.

Ohhhh, be still my heart.

"As a matter of fact," he replied darkly, his expression shuttered. "I do mind. I'm knackered. I'm wet. And a long, hot shower is calling my name."

So much sophistication. So much *control*. But there was heat in his spring-green eyes. The kind of heat that made a woman imagine he was tamping down embers in a place only he could see.

"You're no fun." She shook her head sorrowfully. "In fact, you remind me of a Cubs fan at Sox Park. A total wet blanket. Emphasis on *wet*." She laughed at her own wit.

Instead of coming back at her, he turned toward the stairs.

"Aw, come on now!" she called after him. "Don't walk away like that!"

"I'm sorry." She could tell by the flatness of his tone that he wasn't anywhere *close* to being sorry. "I'd do a funny walk, but I don't feel much like Charlie Chaplin at the moment."

Her grin stretched from ear to ear as she watched him disappear up the steps, his high, tight ass and muscled thighs a sight to behold in those clingy, wet slacks.

———~~~———

"Welcome to the jungle," Samantha breathed aloud as she sat on the bed and glanced around.

The room Ozzie had assigned her was small, with brick walls and exposed piping running across the ceiling. But the utilitarianism of the loft-style space was softened by a big four-poster bed topped by a quilt striped in various shades of blue. A triptych painting hung on the wall over the bed. The three separate canvases formed the Chicago skyline as seen from the water. And *behind* that painting, just on the other side of that wall? Well, that was Ozzie's bedroom.

She couldn't shake the feeling she'd be spending the night next to the lion's den.

Welcome to the jungle, baby!

The line from the old Guns N' Roses song whispered through her head again. Her knowledge of eighties hair bands had been increasing exponentially since she'd starting hanging out with Ozzie.

She took a deep breath, hoping the exercise would settle her nerves. Then she glanced at the mirror hanging over the dresser. She'd taken a quick shower and changed into a pair of slouchy boyfriend jeans and a centuries-old sweatshirt with *Da Bears!* printed across the front in faded letters. Her feet were bare. Her hair was drying into a mass of soft curls. And her stomach was doing its best to gnaw its way clean through her backbone.

The Snickers bar in her purse was temptation itself,

but Ozzie had offered to take her down to the kitchen to get something more substantial to eat once he finished showering.

Or did he say for me *to come get* him *when I was ready?*

Shit a brick. She couldn't remember. But the sight of her bag reminded her of the envelope on Donny's desk. Digging inside her purse, she located her phone and sent Donny a quick text. **I was way off base. Shred the envelope. P.S. Love your funny face.**

After that task was completed, she was once again forced to wait. The old-fashioned alarm clock beside the bed softly *tick-tick-ticked*. When her stomach made an impolite inquiry about whether her throat had been cut, she bolted up from the bed and padded over to the door. Leaning her ear against the metal, she held her breath and listened.

She'd met the ladies currently in residence at Black Knights Inc. before. And while they had *seemed* happy enough to see her tonight, made the right noises about her being welcome, their eyes had looked too brilliant. Too brittle. Samantha recognized forced politeness when she saw it.

Not that she could blame them. For so long, when she'd been convinced the Black Knights were involved in something depraved, she'd been a bit of a pain in the keister.

Oh, who are you kidding, Sammie? You were all over them like a cheap suit.

Girding herself, she turned the handle and peeked into the dimly lit hall. Looking right and left, she was relieved to find the place empty. And *quiet* despite the constant drumming of rain falling on the roof.

Taking a deep breath, she was hit by the subtle smells of motor oil, ground-down metal, and brake fluid.

Memories of her father's repair shop—the shop that had brought about his ultimate demise—threatened to overwhelm her, but she beat them back and set her jaw at a determined angle as she tiptoed to Ozzie's door. She scratched the metal surface, fearing a knock would be too loud in the narrow hall.

"Coming." Ozzie's deep, smooth voice sounded from inside.

When he swung the door wide, every thought fell out of her head, and her breath strangled in her lungs. He was toweling his hair dry with one hand and holding the door open with the other. His raised arms lifted the hem of his T-shirt away from the waistband of his ratty, low-hanging cargo shorts. She could see where his belly tan faded, the whorls of golden brown hair that made up his love trail, and the big veins that ran down the insides of his hip bones…the ones that fed blood to his…

Holy fucking smokes!

She gulped. *Audibly.* Were the walls sweating? No? That was just her?

She barely recognized her voice when she said, "Nice shorts." But she gave herself credit for having the wherewithal to speak at all, because, *man*, he looked good enough to eat. *Smelled* good enough too. All clean, healthy skin and masculine heat.

"Why, thank you." He winked and tossed his towel onto the chair pushed under the desk in the corner. She got a quick glimpse at his room. At the ridiculous number of laptops he owned. At the T-shirt that hadn't quite made it all the way into his wicker laundry hamper and dangled half over the side. And at the big bed dominating it all. "They're my favorite pair."

Huh? Oh, right. His shorts.

"I can see that," she said, so distracted by the nearness

of him, the sexy, *sexy* nearness of him, that the only way she could keep from standing there and stuttering like an idiot was to fall back into her usual role as bandier of witty repartee. "Because I was joking about the whole *nice shorts* things. Those, my friend, are not shorts. Those are loose molecules of fabric held together by desperation."

Any minute now, she expected the material to disintegrate—*yes, please*—and leave him standing before her in nothing but his drawers.

Then again, he might not be wearing *drawers.*

It was official. She would deposit the glorious moment when he opened his bedroom door directly into her spank bank.

"Are you really ribbing on my shorts when you're wearing a sweatshirt that looks like it was minted around the time Reagan was president?" He flashed her that incredible grin and closed the door. He bent to give his thigh a quick rub. For a moment, she thought she might catch a glimpse of his injury—she was crazy curious. But then he straightened and gestured for her to precede him down the hall.

Is he going to touch me? Her shoulder tingled as if his hand hovered there, but the feel of his fingers never came. She blew out a breath of relief.

One brush of his fingers, and her control might snap. She could very easily see herself pouncing on him like a cat on a canary. Only instead of biting his head off, she'd lick him from stem to stern. Including that terribly intriguing trail of hair arrowing from his belly button into paradise.

And then she'd lick paradise.

Whew! Is it hot in here? No? That's just me?

Her legs wobbled as she took the stairs to the second

floor. And even more annoying than the Jell-O knees was the hot ache between her thighs. It would be one thing if Ozzie had given her any indication he wanted something more than friendship. But he hadn't. Since their first meet-up for coffee, he'd been nothing but a gentleman.

A gentleman swimming in so much testosterone that he gave off the vibe that he was your guy if you liked your sex down and dirty. And guess what? That's *exactly* how she liked it.

"This way." He guided her across the conference area, then down the second set of metal steps that led to the shop floor. Most of the lights in the warehouse were shut off for the day, but the ambient glow of the city outside cut the driving rain and streamed in through the two-story leaded-glass windows along one wall. It was enough to see where she was going. Good thing, because a gray steak of fur darted in front of her. She jumped back and slammed straight into Ozzie.

Her spine pressed tight against the immovable wall of his chest, and she marveled at the heat coming off him. He was a human blast furnace. She felt singed through her jeans and sweatshirt.

But then he was gone. Just like that, he stepped back. "Damnit, Peanut!" he hissed. "Go catch a mouse or something, would you?"

Peanut, who was quite possibly the biggest, *ugliest* cat Samantha had ever seen, heaved himself onto the leather sofa shoved next to the base of the staircase. In response to Ozzie's suggestion, the mangy-looking feline lifted his leg over his head and thoroughly licked his balls.

"I don't get no respect," Ozzie chuckled, doing a spot-on Rodney Dangerfield impression as he motioned for her to follow him down a long hall leading to the back of the warehouse.

The smell of the shampoo in his damp hair wafted back to her. She could still feel the pressure of him against her back. And was it her imagination, or had his shoulders somehow grown a foot wider?

What the hell is my problem? Why is every sense, every sensation amplified?

Maybe it was the god-awful day she'd had. The last thirteen hours had been the equivalent of a double shot of espresso mixed with a can of Red Bull. The Basilisks, Marcel—all of it was surreal, terrifying, spinning through her mind in Technicolor clarity.

Then Ozzie flipped on the kitchen light and sauntered over to the refrigerator. When he opened the door, bent over, and gave her a picture-perfect, high-definition shot of his ass, any fear or guilt or uncertainty was instantly replaced by one thought.

God bless America!

"God bless America," Ozzie muttered to himself, using one of Samantha's favorite phrases and trying to cool his ardor with the icy blast of the refrigerator.

The second, the very *second* she backed into him, he'd sprung a length of lumber that would put a twinkle in the eye of a logger. Her lush ass had bumped against his crotch. Her soft hand had brushed his thigh. And her sweet-smelling hair had tangled in two weeks' worth of beard growth on his chin. Apparently that's all it took for his own personal pocket rocket to shoot for a trip to the moon.

It was a problem. One he hadn't the first clue how to solve.

Sure you do, whispered a voice of impeccable reason.

Okay, he *did* know how to solve it. The solution was

to lay her naked across the island countertop, kiss every inch of her pale skin, and then hammer away between her pretty thighs until he was sweaty and spent.

But then what?

Well, then she'd leave him. Like all the others. And he couldn't have that. Didn't *want* that. Wasn't sure he'd be able to *live* with that.

Then again, it was a moot point. While she was always up for a laugh and a joke and a rousing game of Who Can Solve the Crossword Puzzle First, Samantha had never expressed any interest in taking their relationship to the next level. She had always seemed completely content with friendship. And he had grown to appreciate and depend on that friendship, so heaven forbid he do anything to fuck it up.

Forcing himself to concentrate on the contents of the refrigerator, he swallowed the wad of cotton sitting at the back of his throat. "So your options are a turkey sandwich, a mushroom and cheese omelet, or leftover Thai food." He grabbed the box of leftovers, lifted the lid, and gave the contents the ol' sniff test. "Correction." He lobbed the container toward the trash can in the corner. "I'm pretty sure the Thai has turned."

Careful to keep his overeager johnson pointed in the direction of the milk carton, he glanced over his shoulder and lifted a questioning brow.

Samantha had hopped onto a barstool and propped her adorable bare toes with their glittery, hot-pink painted nails against the metal footrest. She was such a wonderful mix of contradictions. Plain clothes but flamboyant underwear. Designer handbags that she carelessly chocked full of crap. Unpainted fingernails, but toenails that belonged on a showgirl. He was captivated by her. Charmed. Completely fascinated.

"I'd love a turkey sandwich," she said. "Fast and easy."

Fast and easy. His mind knew she was referring to the time and effort it would take to make the sandwich. His cock? Yeah, well, it took the phrase to mean something else entirely.

For the love of Leonard McCoy, this has got to stop.

"You're sure? Because if I made an omelet, I could also whip up some sausage and bacon. What are—"

"Stop right there." She lifted a hand. "You had me at bacon."

"A woman after my own heart." He winked at her, sending a small word of thanks skyward that she'd agreed to the meal. It would give him something to do besides fantasize about pulling that wide-necked sweatshirt off her shoulder so he could kiss the soft skin over her clavicle. Give him a reason to keep pointing his undercover brother in a direction that *wasn't* straight at her.

Of course, given his current condition, the stove might prove a dangerous concept. Then again, perhaps thoughts of burning his dick off would help keep the silly sonofabitch in check.

At least it's worth a shot, he thought, pulling all the ingredients from the refrigerator.

"Anything I can help with?" she asked.

"No!" He realized he sounded a little frantic and softened his tone. "No. This is a one-man show." That's what he said aloud. Silently, he added, *So stay way the hell over there. Out of my line of sight. And definitely out of my reach.*

"A one-man show, huh? Well, consider me an eager audience of one."

Hang on a second. Is she…

He glanced over his shoulder to discover a flirty light in her eyes.

Sonofa… She is! She's coming on to me!

His heart started pounding, and a weird buzzing sounded in his ears as his vision tunneled. But then she added, "Because I can't cook for shit. The last time I tried to heat up a can of soup, I turned it into baked-on industrial waste." With that, he was left to conclude that perhaps what he'd thought was *flirting* was just her being *friendly*.

Obviously, he needed sleep. And a heating pad for his leg. And ten minutes alone with his own hand.

But not necessarily in that order.

"I don't think I ever thanked you," Samantha said, shoveling a forkful of omelet between her teeth, closing her eyes, and savoring.

True to his word, Ozzie had whipped up a meal worthy of one a.m. on a Thursday morning. And watching him work had been both heaven and hell.

Heaven because he was a sight to see. The muscles had rippled in his broad back and wide shoulders when he'd stirred the eggs. His tan calves had flexed as he'd made trips between the fridge and the stove. And his ass… Oh, his ass had been particularly special. All round and tight, and the only thing holding up that sorry excuse for a pair of shorts.

Hell because the ache between her legs hadn't been alleviated by squeezing her thighs together. Quite the contrary—that only made her predicament worse. And her nipples? They had been hard for so long, rubbing against the lace of her bra with every ragged breath, that they were starting to feel raw.

"Thank me for what?" he asked, noshing on a strip of bacon and eyeing her curiously from his barstool on the opposite side of the kitchen island.

The *opposite* side. *Because he wouldn't want to get too close and touch me now, would he?*

She sighed at her own thoughts. They seemed to be on a loop. Or maybe *she* was the loopy one. Loopy over Ozzie and his infuriating sex appeal. *I mean, seriously, are teeth really supposed to be that perfectly straight and white? Does anyone really have eyes the hue of rich sapphires? Is it really humanly possible to have a jaw that angular and defined?*

Apparently so. And though she'd been attracted to him from day one, all the night's hubbub—thinking he was a lying criminal asshole one minute and finding out the next minute that he wasn't, that he really was the man she'd come to adore—seemed to have intensified her lust for him.

"For saving me from that fat biker," she said, dragging her eyes away from his male magnificence and forcing herself to pay particular attention to the business of cutting her sausage patty into bite-size pieces. "For not being mad at me for tasing you. For bringing me here. For agreeing to be my bodyguard. For the food. For…everything. For being *you*, I guess."

When he was quiet, she glanced up, expecting to see that devilish gleam in his eye. Instead, his expression was somber, *intense*.

"What?" She blinked. "What did I say? I'm sorry, was I—"

"No," he responded, cutting her off. "Don't apologize. It's just…" He shook his head. It caused his shaggy hair to riot, and she was forced to use every ounce of self-discipline she possessed not to reach across the countertop to smooth those sandy locks with her fingers. "It feels like I've been waiting a long time to hear those words," he finally finished.

"What do you mean?"

He held her gaze forever. So long, she lost track of time. Of space. Of *self*.

How does he do that? How does he make me feel looked *at in a way I've never been looked at before?*

Then he chuckled and shook his head. "Nothing. I don't know. I guess I'm feeling a little… I don't know," he said again, seeming uncertain, embarrassed even.

It was so unlike his usual cocksure self that Samantha could only blink in confusion. Something important had been on the edge of his tongue before he bit it back. She was reminded of how little she knew about him, despite all the time they had spent together. How much she *wanted* to know about him.

Why do you get that sad, faraway look in your eyes sometimes? she wanted to ask. *What were you doing the year after you left the navy? Why don't you talk about your injury when it hurts you? Why don't you ever touch me?*

Of course, that all felt too personal, too probing. So what she said instead was, "So why *Star Trek*?"

"Huh?" He stopped chewing to cock a brow.

She pointed at his freshly laundered T-shirt. It was gray and well worn and sported the phrase: A Vulcan in the Streets, a Klingon in the Sheets.

Apparently he has an inexhaustible supply of the suckers.

"How'd you become such a huge fan? I mean, why not Star Wars or Doctor Who or any of the other fandoms? Why *Star Trek* all day, every day?"

"For the record, I think the first three Star Wars films, which were really the middle three—"

"Duh." She rolled her eyes. "I spend my days in the Tribune Tower, not under a rock."

"Touché," he allowed with a dip of his chin. "Anyway, I think those are amazing. I've seen *The Empire Strikes Back* at least fifty times. As for Doctor Who, which incarnation are you talking about? Which Doctor? There have been twelve, you realize, with some others thrown in for fun and confusion." He started talking faster. "For instance, I think David Tennant absolutely *rocked* the role. I mean, did you *see* the episode where he was inconsolable after the Master's death? Just perfection. But ultimately, I think Matt Smith played the best Doctor, because he was able to combine Who's childlike energy with his darker side, and... Oh my God. I just revealed my über-geek status, didn't I?"

Samantha realized she was grinning like a goof, and it didn't immediately occur to her that he hadn't answered her question about why *Star Trek* all day, every day. "Sorry to tell you, friend, but your über-geek status became apparent the afternoon you dragged me around Comic-Con like a kid in a candy store."

He made a face.

"Don't worry. I think it's adorable," she told him. And it was. He was such an intriguing juxtaposition of dark and light, tough and tender, alpha and beta. He was the best of both worlds. All hot testosterone-y goodness, but with the brains and the wit and the boyish enthusiasm to match.

In a word...*perfection*.

"*You're* adorable," she added before she could stop herself. "And I think the world would be a better place if all you über-nerds—"

"Geeks," he corrected. "There's a difference. Nerds are prone to obsess about stuff, but they don't usually have a social life. Geeks, on the other hand, are prone to obsess about stuff *and* have vast social lives, sharing their obsessions with the world." He pointed to his T-shirt. "See? Geek."

"So tell me, how did you manage to find the time to watch all those shows and become an über-geek, what with your…ahem…rather stacked dating calendar?"

"I don't know what you mean." He pretended ignorance, but there was a devilish glint in his blue-on-blue eyes.

They were back to their regular ol' banter, and Samantha could not have been more relieved. That he could forgive her for all she had put him through that night spoke to his innate generosity of spirit.

"Please," she scoffed, then raised her voice to a falsetto and batted her lashes. "I'm Janie with the really small…"

He winced. "That was an aberration."

"*Pfft*. I'm pretty sure it was SOP where you're concerned. Don't forget, I've seen you walk into a room and watched every estrogen receptor in the place light up."

"I haven't the first clue what you're talking about."

"Cut the bullshit. You know what you look like. You own a mirror."

He dropped the pretense, wiggling his eyebrows at her. But then he shrugged and sighed, and his grin turned from cocky to self-deprecating. "Believe me. My dating calendar wasn't always stacked."

"No?" She forked a bite of omelet between her lips, cupped her hand in her chin, and chewed. She was enjoying this conversation more than she'd enjoyed any conversation since… *Uh, probably since the last time I met him for lunch*.

"No," he assured her. "My body didn't catch up with my bones until I was way past high school. At nineteen, I was still gangly. It wasn't until I'd been in the navy a couple of years that I was able to pack on some pounds. Miraculously, around the same time, my acne cleared up. Throw in some Lasik surgery to get rid of my glasses…and *voilà!*" He held his arms wide. "That's right, take it all in."

Oh, I have been, she thought with a covert leer. *All. Night. Long.*

"Interesting." She nodded, crunching a slice of bacon. Her stomach was singing praises to the chef. "I always imagined you were the type to shoot out of the birth canal, make the delivery-room nurses gasp and titter, and then exchange a high five with the obstetrician."

He laughed. The sound was low and rolling. A good laugh. An honest laugh. The kind of laugh you could listen to for the rest of your life.

Whoa there, Sammie. That's dangerous thinking.

"I can assure you, that was *not* the case."

"So what then?" She cocked her head. "You've spent the rest of your adult years making up for the nookie you didn't get as a teenager?"

"Why do I get the impression you're calling me a manwhore?"

"Hey." She lifted her hands. "No judgment here. I fully support playing the field. What's love got to do with it? Am I right?"

"Tina Turner." He nodded with satisfaction. "Nice."

Although, in reality, the thought of all the women in his past made her want to chew nails. Or maybe *use* nails. *Her* nails. To scratch out their eyes. Starting with Janie with the really small… *Grr*.

"So what about you?" he asked.

She frowned. "What do you mean, what about me?"

"Were you always as beautiful as you are now?"

The piece of bacon in her mouth exploded in size and started choking her. She hastily grabbed the glass of orange juice by her right hand and gulped down half the contents. *He thinks I'm beautiful?* "You think I'm beautiful?" Her voice was wheezy.

"Of course."

"There's no *of course* about it."

"Sure there is. You own a mirror, right?"

She glanced around, feigning confusion. "Is there an echo in here?"

"No need to rephrase a perfectly good argument."

When she looked back at him, he was…*smoldering* at her.

And now he's whipped out his tough, alpha, testosterone-y goodness!

Then, just like that, the heat in his eyes banked, and his mouth curved into a decidedly chummy grin. "Don't worry though," he said conversationally, spearing a piece of omelet with his fork. "I won't jump your bones. I know you just want to be friends."

She was pretty sure her mouth was hanging open. She was *completely* sure she was blinking. Rapidly. The room looked like it was lit by a strobe light. "I do?"

The look he pinned on her then was penetrating. Dark. That terribly intriguing warrior's gleam was back in his eyes. "Don't you?"

"No!"

Chapter 8

OZZIE FELL OFF HIS BARSTOOL.

Or at least he *almost* fell off his barstool. He *would* have fallen off his barstool, knocked silly by Samantha's vehement proclamation, if he hadn't instinctively curled his fingers around the edge of the countertop.

For a second, he thought he might have misheard. But then he realized he hadn't misheard; he'd just misunderstood. His heart sank. Down. To. His. Knees. It took his stomach with it.

I should never have said anything. Should never have flirted. Should never have—

"I get it," he said, trying to hide the hurt in his voice. His omelet was suddenly threatening a reappearance. He had been so worried that taking Samantha to bed would lose him her friendship that he hadn't considered their friendship might be one-sided. "You've got plenty of friends already. You probably don't need one more. And it's not like we have all that much in common, so—"

"No, you idiot." She harrumphed, crossing her arms. "What I mean is I don't *just* want to be friends. Not counting today's misunderstanding, I've been waiting for you to jump my bones or even just…even just *touch* me for…well, forever!"

This time, he *did* fall off his barstool. Luckily, he caught himself, so he hoped it looked like he'd *intended* to dismount. He pushed, albeit it a little shakily, to his full height. And his heart? Well, it'd bounced from his knees up into his throat, where it proceeded to strangle him.

He assumed that was why his voice was hoarse when he said, "You have?"

"For a guy who's supposed to have a high IQ, you sure are dumb."

"I am?"

"What's the matter with you?" She frowned at him. "Did you pop an aneurysm or something?" She waved four fingers in front of his face. "How many fingers am I holding up? What day is it? Name a compound that contains both ionic and covalent bonds."

"Uh...four, Thursday morning, and sodium phosphate. Am I right?"

"I can only vouch for the first two. It's been too long since I took chemistry."

He realized he'd been stock-still and blinking for a really long time when Samantha threw her hands in the air.

"Well, don't just stand there. Say something!"

"I..." *Haven't the first clue what to say.* He was both ecstatic and scared to death. Ecstatic because...well, it was obvious why he was ecstatic. Just look at her. She was everything, and she was interested in *him*. Scared to death because...what happened *after* he jumped her bones? Would she leave after her itch was scratched? Stop calling and drift away?

She made a disgusted sound. "Great. Wonderful. I've rendered you speechless. That's just what a woman hopes for when she makes her intentions toward a man known. Look." She pushed up from the barstool and grabbed her plate. "I get it." She walked over to the trash can and used her fork to scrape off the leftovers. "You have women chasing you all the time." She deposited her plate in the sink and turned to lean a hip against the counter.

"The last thing you need is another one. You've

probably looked at me all these months and thought, 'Now here's a woman who doesn't want to rock my bod. A woman I can relax and be myself around.'"

His lips twitched at her fairly spot-on impersonation of him, then he frowned when he realized the second half of that sentence was true. He *was* himself around her. His *old* self.

"Sorry to disappoint you. But I'm no better than all the others. You're funny. You're smart. You're brave and courageous. And you're *hot*. And I *do* want to rock your bod. But—"

"Samantha…" He tried to cut in, even though he had no idea what he wanted to say. She thought he was smart and brave and courageous and hot? He wanted to howl! He wanted to jump in the air and click his heels! He wanted to…screw her brains out.

"I'd much rather lose you as a lover than a friend." She spoke over him. "So can we just forget the last five minutes? Can we go back to the way things were?"

"No," he said. Or rather croaked.

Her shoulders slumped. "Damnit." She stared dejectedly at her sparkly toes.

He'd never been a foot man, but right then he wanted nothing more than to kiss every one of those dainty digits.

"I should never have—"

"I don't want to go back," he interrupted. And like so many times that night, the minute he said the words aloud was the minute he realized they were true. But there were so many obstacles between them. There'd been so much deception. And what about afterward? What happened then?

"You don't?" Her eyes searched his face. Her breaths came short and fast.

He was sure he could see the gentle jut of her nipples

against the fabric of her sweatshirt. His dick, which had been seesawing between semihard and rock-hard all night, took one look at those sweet peaks and rose to the challenge.

"No." He shook his head. In that moment, he didn't care about the obstacles or the deception. In that moment, he couldn't think about the future. There was only now. Only her. Wonderful, adorable Samantha.

She wants me! She wants…ME!

If his heart had a voice, it would sing the refrain over and over.

The rain was still coming down by the bucketful outside, but the storm had released the last of its electrical energy. Inside, however, the atmosphere was charged. Ozzie imagined he could see bolts of sexual lightning arcing through the air, making the entire kitchen crackle and glow, making the torn flesh of his thigh tingle.

He knew that thunder followed lightning. And he waited anxiously for the explosion.

"But…you never *touch* me," she whispered, her voice sexy in its hoarseness. "You touch everyone else, but you never touch me."

"Because if I started, I'd never want to stop." And there it was. Another truth. Perhaps the most important truth of the night.

One of those gap-toothed grins took up her whole face. Then it happened. She ran across the room, launched herself into his arms, and slammed her mouth over his.

BOOM!

The minute Samantha's mouth touched Ozzie's, she was completely obliterated. His lips were hotter than dynamite, and the first slick glide of his tongue between her teeth was an atomic blast that sent wave after wave of molten fire through her body.

There was no hesitation. No tentative exploration. It was pedal to the metal from the get-go. Which might have been a turnoff, had they not been engaged in foreplay for the last few months. At least that's how it felt to her. All the talks, all the smiles, all the jokes and the gibes and days out and about had been leading up to this. This moment, right here, right now, when she *finally* got her hands on him.

Her fingers tangled in his crazy, wonderful hair. It was softer than it looked. Her aching breasts smashed against his chest. It was harder than she'd imagined. And her belly cradled the evidence of his desire. Which, *holy smokes*, was larger than she'd expected.

He was hot. A wall of heat against her front, making the air in the room feel cold against her back.

She ate at his mouth, one kind of hunger quickly replaced by another. He met her carnal demands with more of his own. It was all teeth and tongues, lips and scratchy beard and...*hands*. Hers skated over his broad shoulders, down his back. She dug her fingers into the groove of his spine. His were on her face, cupping her jaw. He curled his fingers around the back of her head to hold her in place.

She had no idea how long they stayed that way, how long they ravaged each other before he pulled back slightly. She murmured her disappointment, then hummed with delight. He was only adjusting the angle so he could kiss her more deeply.

So deep.
So good.
So sweet.

The stroke of his tongue was an experienced glide of velvet warmth. He knew just what she liked, just what she craved. In and out. Mimicking the joining of two bodies. Tasting. Savoring. *Rejoicing*.

Pleasure rippled down her spine, making the place between her legs feel even achier and hotter. She lost her breath. He fed it back to her. Her heart pounded out of control. His matched the rhythm. She lost her mind. But it didn't matter, because he was the one in control, molding her, shaping her, loving her lick by deep, penetrating lick. Suck by wet, wonderful suck.

"God, you taste good," he murmured against the corner of her mouth, leaving a trail of hot kisses along her cheek back to her ear. He gently bit the lobe, his warm breath whirling against the shell. The muscles of her vagina clenched like a fist. "Samantha, I—"

"More," she demanded, guiding his mouth back to hers. She wanted to kiss him forever. And then kiss him a day past that. "Please, Ozzie. I want more."

With a sound of need, or maybe it was impatience, he wrapped his large hands around her hips and hoisted her onto the kitchen island as if she weighed no more than a feather. Just to be clear, she weighed *a lot* more than a feather. But in his strong arms, she felt fragile, *feminine*.

Everything that was woman in her responded to the man in him.

When he stepped between her thighs, her warmth and wetness welcomed his steely hardness. His callused hands slipped beneath the hem of her sweatshirt, finding bare flesh, and goose bumps followed the path of his fingers.

"Samantha…" The way he said her name, enunciating each syllable, made it sound sexy. Or maybe that was just him. Just Ozzie. Just the sexiest man alive. "Slow down, sweetheart. Let's—"

"No!" She was quick to cut him off, feeling desperate in a way she never had before. "I can't stop. Don't make me stop." The thought of not touching him, not kissing him, not tasting him for even a second when she'd waited so long... No. Just...*no*.

A moan—*of surrender?*—rumbled from the back of his throat. And then he grabbed her long hair in his fist and wrapped a loop of it around his thick wrist, pulling her head back and exposing her neck. He bent to suck the spot where her heart beat close to the surface of her skin. Her blood bubbled up to meet the wet suction of his lips, the heated stroke of his tongue. And lower, her body began to hum in earnest.

"Ozzie..." His name was an entreaty, a plea, a prayer all rolled into one.

"Say it again," he commanded in a low growl, all that amiable charm having disappeared. This was Ozzie at his rawest. Ozzie pared down to his truest essence. And it was nothing more, nothing less than one-hundred-percent alpha male. He was all passion. All assertive control. And she was such a cliché, because that just did it for her.

It lit her up.

It burned her down.

It made her a pliant supplicant in his arms. Ready to be ravished, to be taken, to be made into whatever he wished as long as he would keep touching her, keep kissing her, keep giving her pleasure with his mouth and tongue and body.

"Ozzie," she whispered again, her nails digging into his muscled shoulders when he cupped her bottom and pulled her to the very edge of the counter so he could more fully align their bodies.

His hard shaft pressed into the seam of her jeans. Answering wetness slicked her panties. She thought maybe he felt it, felt the pulse of sultry heat against his cock, because he took her mouth in a kiss that was a little crude and totally, completely, bone-meltingly delicious.

The slow, deliberate bump and grind of his hips mimicked the thrust and parry of his tongue. Both created a friction that drove Samantha insane, pushed her up, coiled the ache inside. Ozzie even *tasted* alpha. Bold. Barbarous. Completely untamed.

"I want to touch you," he said between soul-drugging kisses. "I want to put my hands on every inch of you."

There was no asking for permission. No *waiting* for permission. The next instant, his hands were once again beneath the hem of her sweatshirt.

She moaned at the feel of his rough palms skating over her tender flesh. Without hesitation, he slid his fingers up her sides, over her rib cage, stopping when his thumbs bumped the lace covering the undersides of her breasts.

"If you want me to stop, tell me now," he rumbled against her throat, sounding like the lion she'd imagined earlier. *Welcome to the jungle, baby. Indeed.*

But stop? Was he crazy?

She could have gone with the obvious… *Don't stop; never stop.* Or the comical… *Bang me like a drum, big boy.* But all she could manage was "Please." She pulled him closer, rubbing herself against his throbbing hardness and closing her eyes as the friction jangled the bundle of nerves at the top of her sex. "Please," she begged again.

And he didn't disappoint. He cupped her breasts in his large hands, lifting them, plumping them. Her nipples had been saluting him like little soldiers all night long, and now they received their reward for good behavior when his thumbs passed over them. The resultant pleasure bordered on pain, because the tips had been so hard for so long. But she wanted more.

It was so good.

The best.

She wondered why that should be. Was he better at it than her previous lovers? Or was it something else? Was it because she'd never felt about any other man the way she felt about him? Like he was Prince Charming riding in on his white stallion. Like he was Romeo climbing onto her balcony. Like he was Superman, able to leap buildings in a single bound. Like he was…Ozzie. Just everything a man was supposed to be and then some. Was it so good with him because it wasn't just her hormones involved but also something that started with an *H* and rhymed with *dart*?

The thought terrified her. Mostly because she had no idea if Ozzie felt the same. In fact, she figured chances were good he did *not*. The man was a playboy, a lothario, a wolf in…*wolf's* clothing.

Lion or wolf, Sammie? Pick one and stick with it.

Problem was, she couldn't find one that fit perfectly. He had all the cunning and stealth of a wolf, all the majesty and big-boned grace of a lion. He was just animalistic. Just unrepentantly *carnal*. Just…Ozzie.

Pushing all thoughts but those of pleasure from her mind, she grabbed the hem of his T-shirt and yanked it over his head. His hands had to stop doing those wonderful things to her breasts. But she was rewarded for her sacrifice when he stood in front of her naked from the waist up.

Sweet, merciful fuck!

She thought she'd been drowning in desire before. But

she'd only been swimming in it. *Now* she was drowning. Unable to breathe. Unable to move. Unable to do anything but look at inch upon inch of tough, tanned flesh.

She ran her eyes over every light-brown whorl of hair that curled between his bulging pectoral muscles. Saw the clutch of violets tattooed over his heart twitch when his chest flexed. And took a cursory glance at the *Star Trek* Starfleet insignia inked on his right bicep.

On his left side was a scar. A jagged wound still angry and puckered, even though it was obvious from the faded white color that the injury was old. She wondered if it was from the same motorcycle wreck that had injured his leg. And speaking of injuries, she couldn't help but notice the two little red circles like mosquito bites on his chest, courtesy of her Taser.

She winced, prepared to apologize yet again, but every thought in her head dripped out of her ears when she saw the head of his cock protruding past the waistband of his loose shorts. It was bulbous and red, thick and shiny. *And sonofa—!* It would have taken a crowbar to pry her eyes away from the drop of pre-ejaculate that formed at his tip.

Before she made the conscious decision to move, she reached for him.

Ozzie's dick jumped when he saw Samantha go to grab him. But he knew he'd never last if she touched him. He was too hard. It'd been too long. He wanted her too much.

"Don't," he gritted between his teeth, catching her delicate wrist before her fingers could reach their intended target. The force of his grip and the vehemence of the command startled her. She searched his face with eyes that had gone dark and half-lidded. The sweetest, sexiest bedroom eyes he'd ever seen.

"Why?" she whispered.

"It's been too long," he admitted without shame. He'd never been a man to mince words, especially when it came to sex. *What would be the point? The only way you get what you want is to ask for it, straight out.* And when it came to the bedroom, he *always* got what he wanted. When it came to the bedroom, he dropped the charm, dropped the jokes, and *took*.

And he gave too. Oh, how he *loved* giving. Loved learning a woman's body. Loved hearing the noises she made when ecstasy overtook her.

And Samantha... Samantha was his greatest challenge, greatest triumph yet.

"Too long since what?" She was still watching him.

"Since I had sex. If you touch me now, I won't last. And I want it to last. I want it to go on forever."

"Wh—"

Before she could ask whatever she was poised to ask, he whipped her sweatshirt over her head and tossed the garment onto the island beside them.

"Turnabout is fair play," he told her when she blinked in surprise. Her dark hair cascaded around her slim shoulders. Her pale skin was pink with a blush of desire. But the lacy cups of her bra—this one, bright red—were what held his attention. Because the bra was peekaboo lace. And her nipples showed through the material, taunting him with their hardened peaks, beckoning him with their sweet, rosy color.

His tongue glued itself to the roof of his mouth. His balls pulled up close to his body. And his dick flexed and bowed as another drop of pre-ejaculate rolled over his heated crown to dampen the waistband of his shorts.

She was beautiful from the top of her dark head to the tips of her sparkly toes. Beautiful in the way only a woman in her prime sexual years could be. Gone was the skinny, tomboyish angularity of youth. She was all soft curves and smooth skin. Narrow waist. Flaring hips. And red lace that covered creamy mounds of flesh.

Their breaths were ragged as they stared at each other, *wanting* each other. Their eyes hot as they devoured inches of flesh and sought more. She caught her lower lip between her teeth when, with one finger, he slowly traced the edge of one cup, savoring the contrast between her silky skin and the lacy material. Savoring the moment before he pulled down the cup and revealed her, like a kid opening his last Christmas present, trying to draw the moment out for as long as possible.

"Beautiful," he whispered, trailing his finger over the strap, gently pulling it from her shoulder.

"I could say the same about you." She ran her hands over his shoulders, down his arms, across his chest. The blood beneath his skin rose to her delicate touch until every inch of him was vibrating, even the torn muscles in his leg. When she feathered her fingers over his nipples, causing the centers to contract into tight nubs of pleasure, he hissed. And when she used the edge of her thumbnail to gently abrade the skin, he begged for mercy with one breath and egged her on with the next.

He wanted to stand there, just stand there and let her touch him, but his control was dangling by a thread. And before it snapped, before reason left him, he wanted to see her. Appreciate the subtle nuances that made her *Samantha*.

The female form in all its glorious incarnations had always brought him pleasure. There was nothing in the world, to his mind, more marvelous than a woman. And a woman being ridden by lust? One who was soft and sexy in her need? Forget about it. That was the closest thing he'd ever seen to heaven.

"I want to look at you. *All* of you," he told her.

"Then look." She crossed her ankles behind his thighs and pulled him tight against her. She was so unabashedly sensual. So brazenly wanton.

His eyes crossed when the heated head of his dick kissed the warm, soft flesh of her bare belly. His own wetness slicked her skin, and the satiny feel of it must have turned her on, because she moaned, low and long, and once again wrapped her arms around his neck, pulling him down to press her mouth to his.

There was nothing gentle in her kiss, nothing hesitant. Just female need. Just a woman's demand.

He gave in to it. He couldn't *not* give in to it. As if he were a junkie taking his first hit, Samantha's initial kiss had caused an addiction in him. Now, the exotic taste of her ran hot in his blood. He craved her. He *needed* her.

He met her kisses with everything that was in him— all the fight, all the knowledge, all the passion. And still it wasn't enough. He wanted to devour her, consume her, become so much a part of her that it would be impossible to tell where she started and he ended.

Her catching breaths urged him onward. Each flick of her tongue between his teeth felt like a benediction. Samantha was a star, burning bright and hot in his arms. Shining all around him until the darkness inside him had nowhere to hide. He was washed clean by her glow. Doubts? Gone. Self-pity? Gone.

It was just her. Just glorious, wonderful Samantha clinging to him so tightly that he felt every breath she took, every beat of her wild heart.

He couldn't wait another minute.

Never breaking the suctioned wonder of their mouths, he softly pulled her remaining bra strap from her shoulder. Using his free hand, he reached behind her back to unhook her bra. But his fingers fumbled with the task, shocking him. He hadn't bumbled a bra in years, knew every kind of closure and snap there was and could undo them without thought. But now, when it mattered most, he botched the job like a horny teenager trying to cop his first feel.

He knew why. He was shaking. She made him shake. With need. With desire. It was too much...and not enough. Part of him wondered if it would ever be enough.

Get out of your own head, you idiot!

Right. Sound advice. He made a second attempt at her bra.

Success!

The closure popped open, and she shivered when he carefully pulled the scrap of lace from her body, tossing it aside. And then, with a nipping kiss to the corner of her swollen mouth, he lifted his head and did what he wanted to do. He...looked.

Fuck. Me.

The air wheezed from his lungs. The tips of his ears burned hot. His whole body thrummed with tension.

She was lovely. Her breasts weren't too large, but they weren't too small either. Like Goldilocks and the Three Bears, he had finally found a woman who was *just right*. Her flesh was dewed with the sweat of desire. Her breasts were heavier on the bottom than on the top, causing them to point slightly toward the ceiling, toward his devouring eyes. And her rosy nipples were the size of quarters, furled tight around their centers.

When she breathed, those creamy mounds rose and

fell. It occurred to him that she was exactly where he
had wanted her earlier. She was on the island. All but
naked. And if he had his way, he'd be hammering away
between her pretty thighs, emptying himself into her
very soon.

"Please, Ozzie," she rasped, reaching out to him,
taking his hand and guiding it toward her. "I want you
to touch me. I *need* you to touch me."

Her voice was a stroke against his balls. Her words a
warm, wet mouth devouring the head of his cock.

He never lost control. *Never*. Not even with the first
woman he'd ever touched. But Samantha made him
crazy. Made him lose the ability to reason. To think. To
do anything but feel…

The smooth weight of her breast in his palm.

The hot flush of her creamy skin beneath his fingers.

The hard jut of her nipples as he feathered the rough
pads of his thumbs over the tips.

She hissed and let her head fall back. His heavy erection ached at the sight. Now she was an offering. His
gift. A feminine sacrifice to his masculine desires.

Just the way I like it…

Chapter 9

WHEN OZZIE'S HOT MOUTH CLOSED AROUND HER nipple, Samantha's whole body buzzed. She could feel the suctioned pull of his lips…everywhere. The wet sweep of his tongue…everywhere.

"Ozzie!" She croaked his name.

"Shhh, sweetheart," he rumbled against her flesh. "I know it hurts so good. But it's okay. I got you."

And he did. With an arm behind her back, he held her up as he feasted at her breast. With her legs wrapped around his waist, he supported her even as he continued to grind against her, never letting the friction ease, keeping her climbing ever onward, ever upward.

"Are you wet for me?" he asked.

And even though she was sure he knew the answer, she gave him the words anyway. "Yes. Please touch me. I ache so much."

He reached for the button of her jeans, expertly flipping it open. The *scrrriiitttch* of her zipper was a whisper of sound compared to her moans and the suckling noises he made against her breast.

So close. So close. So close.

The friction of his hips combined with the pull of his lips on her nipple, coiling the spring in her center tighter and tighter and…

His hand snaked between their rubbing bodies. His fingers delved beneath the waistband of her panties. And the moment he touched the distended bud of her clitoris, her orgasm hit her full force. Her hips bucked against him as her entire body locked in exquisite ecstasy.

Wave after wave of delight crashed against her, a storm of passion finally reaching the shore and obliterating everything in its path. She was carried aloft for... she didn't know how long. It seemed like forever that Ozzie used the rough pads of his fingers, drawing out her climax, keeping it rolling through her, over her, beneath her.

"That's right," he whispered against her nipple. "Ride it out, sweetheart. Ride it all out."

And she did. Her body spasmed and contracted, flowered and spasmed and contracted again. Until, finally, she collapsed back onto the countertop, completely spent but still wanting. Wanting *him*. Wanting all of him.

He was a mind reader, apparently—or maybe she'd voiced her needs aloud and had just been too undone to realize it?—because the next words out of his mouth as he lifted his head from her breast were, "You want me to put my cock in you?"

"Yes," she admitted breathily, pushing up to her elbows. Or at least, that's what she *tried* to say. Instead, the only sound to come from her throat was a needy whimper.

He must have taken it for the affirmative it was. "God, I want that too. I want it so much, I'm weeping for it. Feel."

He pulled her back into a seated position and put her hand over the head of his dick. The searing evidence of his desire slicked his heavy crown.

"Ozzie," she whispered, reaching into his shorts so she could fist him, gasping when she realized his true girth.

He let his forehead rest against hers, his hot breath

coming in panting puffs that tickled her lips and cheeks. Before he could say anything, a strange sound invaded the sanctity of the kitchen. A weird *clickety-clickety-click* that reminded her of…

"Sonofa—" Ozzie growled, pushing out of her grasp. The tug of his wet dick through her fisted fingers was so erotic, she felt her inner walls clenching once again. He grabbed her sweatshirt and tossed it at her. She caught it against her chest, confusion and disappointment filling her just as Delilah and her dog stepped into the kitchen.

"Holy freakin' shit!" the redheaded bartender yelled, covering her eyes with her hands. "Sorry, guys. Sorry!"

Samantha felt heat wash over her. *Busted. Like horny teenagers beneath the bleachers.*

If she'd wanted to ingratiate herself with the women of Black Knights Inc., this was definitely *not* the way to do it.

"I could have gone two, maybe three lifetimes without seeing that. Thanks, you two," Delilah said.

"Sorry." Samantha hurriedly tugged her sweatshirt over her head, glancing around frantically for her bra. She spied it just as Ozzie tucked the scrap of red lace into the pocket of his shorts, then he bent down to retrieve his T-shirt from where she'd tossed it on the tile floor, wincing slightly from the pain in his injured leg.

She could still feel him in her fist. Still taste him on her tongue. Still smell him and her and them and *sex* all around her, which didn't do much to dampen her libido. What dampened her libido was the sight of Delilah still standing there covering her eyes and Fido eyeing them and grinning that goofy doggy grin. "I… We…" she stuttered.

"No explanations necessary. I suspect Delilah knows exactly what we were up to." There wasn't a hint of remorse in Ozzie's voice. Quite the contrary, he looked amused. Horny and blue-balled, certainly. But underneath that was definite amusement. "Especially considering I've caught her and Mac going at it in some pretty unique places. The coat closet comes to mind."

"But never in the kitchen!" Delilah harrumphed. "Never where we prepare our freakin' food! Yeesh!"

"Then you might be the only one." Ozzie tugged his T-shirt over his head. His hair was going every which way. "Because I know for a fact that Boss likes to have Becky up against the refrigerator whenever he gets the chance. Something about the vibrations of the motor and—"

Delilah waved her hands in the air, but her eyes were still screwed shut. "Stop it! Stop it! TMI!"

Now Ozzie had the audacity to chuckle. Samantha found nothing humorous in this situation. "You can open your eyes, my dear sweet Dee," he said. "Everyone is decent."

Samantha decided her position atop the island countertop was now wildly inappropriate and hopped down before Delilah opened one eye, then the other. Peanut, who came to investigate the ruckus, slunk by Fido, and the dog immediately gave chase. Before Samantha had time to move, both animals were doing laps around the island and her legs, Peanut hissing and Fido barking.

Christian appeared in the doorway, yawning and scratching his bare belly. Even dressed for bed in flannel PJ bottoms and nothing else, he looked like he should be walking down a runway. "What the bloody hell is happening here?" he demanded.

Ozzie shrugged, looking bemused. "Not my circus, not my monkeys."

Delilah rolled her eyes and clapped her hands. "Hey! Cut it out!"

"Is she talking to you two," Christian asked over the pandemonium, glancing between Samantha and Ozzie, no doubt noting their dishevelment, "or the dog and cat?"

"What the hell is going on in here?" BKI's newest employee, Emily…something—Samantha had forgotten her last name—appeared beside Christian.

Ozzie shook his head. "Oh good. Say, Emily, mind going up to gather the rest of the peanut gallery? I mean, everyone deserves to see this show."

"Huh?" Emily cocked her head.

"Never mind." Ozzie grabbed Samantha's hand, carefully extricating her from the path of the canine-feline footrace. "Come with me," he said in a low voice. "Let's leave the zoo to the animals."

She squeezed his fingers in agreement. But before they could go more than a few steps, Delilah stopped trying to catch Fido's collar and instead caught Samantha's arm. It effectively jerked her hand from Ozzie's grasp. He turned to lift a brow.

"Run along." Delilah shooed him. "She'll follow in a second, after I tell her something important."

Ozzie's other eyebrow climbed up his forehead.

"It's a sisterhood thing," Delilah assured him.

"Why do you insist on rubbing that in my face tonight?" he demanded, and Samantha felt like she was missing something.

"Tell him to run along," Delilah instructed. "He's in big, bad protector mode and won't go unless you say it's okay."

Samantha wasn't sure it *was* okay. "It's fine," she assured Ozzie, forcing a smile.

After searching Samantha's eyes, Ozzie nodded and turned to join Christian and Emily in the doorway.

Fido was still barking. Peanut was still yowling and

hissing. But Samantha had no trouble hearing the words Delilah whispered in her ear. "Okay, *sister*. Hear me and hear me well. If you hurt him, I'll murder you in your sleep and toss your bloody carcass into the Chicago River."

Samantha opened her mouth, but Delilah kept on. "No, I talk. You listen. Ozzie is the best of us. The absolute *best* of us."

A lump suddenly grew in Samantha's throat. To inspire such loyalty, such fierce protectiveness, Ozzie had to be everything she'd always thought he was.

"I know that," she assured Delilah, placing her hand over the tight grip on her arm and giving the woman's fingers a squeeze.

"He's suffered enough recently. I don't want him—"

"I know that too," Samantha insisted. "He told me."

"He did?" Delilah frowned.

"Yeah." She nodded. "I know the motorcycle wreck nearly killed him. I know he almost lost his leg. I *know* he's suffered. I won't make him suffer any more. I promise."

Delilah searched Samantha's eyes for a long time. The bartender must have seen what she was looking for, because she finally released Samantha's arm.

Samantha turned and scampered toward Ozzie, who was waiting for her with an extended hand. She thrilled at the memories of what those skilled fingers had accomplished such a short time ago. And she couldn't wait to get upstairs and finish what they had started.

Emily watched Ozzie and Samantha disappear down the hall into the shop and took a tiny step closer to Christian. Just to test him. Just to see if he noticed her proximity.

Yes, sir, he noticed. He immediately stepped away, taking all his delicious body heat with him. *Damn.*

The devil in Emily made her close the distance again. Since his shoulder was now pressed against the doorframe, there was nowhere left to run.

"Does the concept of personal space mean anything to you?" he asked, his voice wonderfully raspy. Barefoot and bare-chested, he was the visual equivalent of *Whoa, baby!* His skin had the healthy, golden glow of having been kissed by the sun shining over six of the seven continents. And his tattoos… Given the way he dressed, one would never know his arms were covered in deep, black tribal designs that didn't appear the least bit civilized.

She had to tuck her hands inside the sleeves of her sweatshirt to keep from touching him. "Just making room for Delilah," she lied, glancing over her shoulder.

Delilah finally caught Fido's collar and dragged him toward the door. No longer forced to escape and evade, Peanut hopped onto the lid of the trash can and eyed the dog from his superior position, taunting the poor pooch with the angry, side-to-side flick of his crooked tail.

Turning Emily's lie into a truth, Delilah joined them in the doorway. "Ugh. I'm not sure how to feel about those two hooking up." She shook her head and eyed the empty hallway.

"I do," Christian said. He smelled like expensive aftershave and designer deodorant. But underneath that was…man. "It's bad news. Ozzie leads with his heart, which is why we love him. But this time…" He shrugged. "This time, I wish he'd lead with that stonking brain of his. It won't work between them. It *can't* work."

"Well, aren't you Mr. Glass Half Full?" Emily glanced up at him. *Whoa, his eyes are pretty.* They were such a light green that they were almost yellow. "I never knew you were a pessimist. An overweening dandy, sure. But never a pessimist."

He glared down at her. His harsh features and bright eyes made him look positively terrifying. She shivered in delight and decided to press on. "Just because you're emotionally constipated and—"

"Why do you *insist* on raking me over the bloody coals every bloody minute of every bloody day?" he interrupted.

"Um, 'cause it's fun?"

He made an exasperated sound and turned to stomp down the hall.

"Oh, for crying out loud! There you go again!" she called to his back. "Walking away from me!" After he turned the corner, she saw Delilah eyeing her speculatively. "What?" she demanded, thickening her South Side accent so that it sounded more like *whut*.

"There are better ways to seduce a man than verbally ripping off his dingle every freakin' chance you get."

"Who says I'm trying to seduce him?" Emily fisted her hands on her hips, jutting out her chin like she'd been taught to do on the tough Chicago playgrounds. "Maybe I'm just trying to knock him down a peg or two. All that lofty air he breathes has to be getting thin."

Delilah snorted and shook her head. "If that's how you want to play it…"

That he was standing in front of Samantha's bedroom door, rejecting her offer to come inside, made it official. Ethan "Ozzie" Sykes was…an…*idiot*.

"You're an idiot," Samantha confirmed with a frown. "I'm not suffering from PTSD or some shit. I'm a grown-ass woman who knows what she wants, and I want *you*." His heart thrilled at the words even as she pointedly glanced down at the fly of his cargo shorts. "And you want me too. No use denying it."

Nope. None whatsoever. His johnson was making its ever-intrepid presence known far and wide.

"I *do* want you, Samantha," he admitted, reaching down to adjust himself into a more comfortable position.

She watched the maneuver with ravenous eyes, catching her bottom lip between her teeth and grinning up at him. *God help me!*

"But cooler heads have prevailed, and I realize that tonight isn't the right time. For one thing, you were nearly knifed by a fat, bearded biker. For another, you've been up for going on twenty-four hours. Not to mention the fact that you lost someone you cared about." She opened her mouth to argue, but he talked over any objection she might have made. "You *did* care about Marcel, even if you didn't know him well. And I *know* you feel responsible for what happened to him, so add a heaping helping of guilt into the mix. Do you know what that all adds up to?"

She started to answer, but he did it for her. "A woman who's vulnerable. A woman who's looking for something to help her forget what's happened. A woman who might have second thoughts in the cold light of day."

Everything he said was true. Every word of it. What he *didn't* say was that on the walk up the stairs from the first floor to the third, his conscience had started gnawing at him, taking huge bites that left gaping holes of doubt behind. There was a bigger issue working against him than the possibility of her taking off down the road after he scratched her itch.

And that was the chance that she *wouldn't*.

She was a reporter bent on uncovering the truth.

He was a covert operator whose entire existence was built on a lie. She lived in the light. The shadows were his stock in trade. She thought she knew him, thought him funny, smart, courageous, and hot—her words still echoed inside his head. But she didn't know the first thing about him, not the *real* him.

He *couldn't* follow her into that bedroom no matter how much he might want to, because there was no way to make it work with her in the long run. The long run would require him to tell her the truth about himself. The truth about Black Knights Inc. And that wasn't his secret to share. Especially not with someone who could print that secret for the world to see.

It's better to be friends, he told himself. *Staying friends keeps her in my life while allowing me to keep quiet*. Although, in truth, keeping quiet was beginning to grate on him. Every half-truth he fed her weighed heavier and heavier on his heart, his *soul*.

She eyed him for a long time, frustration obvious in the lines on her brow and the twist of her delicious lips. Then she shrugged. "I'm not going to talk you out of acting on this misplaced chivalry, am I?"

He shook his head, afraid to open his mouth. He wanted her so badly that one stroke of her hand, one lick of her tongue, and he would be dunzo. The *need* for her was an all-encompassing physical ache.

She blew out an exasperated breath. "Jeez. Have it your way. But I have two things to say on the subject."

He lifted a brow, waiting.

"Number one." She held up a finger. A finger he was fiercely tempted to suck straight into his mouth. "I have no regrets about what happened down there in the kitchen. And the cold light of day won't change that. I hope the same can be said for you."

"Regrets?" Was she insane? "Are you kidding? Having you nearly tackle me to the ground is pretty much a dear diary day for me."

She gifted him with that gap-toothed grin, and he nearly fell to his knees battling the urge to drag her into his arms and kiss her until her smile turned into a gasp of pleasure. He knew now. Knew what it took to make her shiver, make her moan.

"Good." She nodded. "So, then, number two is this. Thank you. Again."

"For what?"

She shrugged. "For being you."

And there they were again, offered so freely, so easily. The words it felt like he'd been waiting a lifetime to hear. *Damnit all to hell and back! She's trying to kill me.*

When Samantha went up on tiptoe to press a sweet, chaste kiss to his lips, he had to curl his hands into fists to keep from wrapping his arms around her.

"Good night, Ozzie," she whispered.

"Good night." His voice was hoarse with unquenched desire.

The instant she closed the bedroom door, he slammed a hand against the doorjamb, his shoulders shaking, raspy air sawing from his lungs. He gave himself a couple of seconds to breathe, to ensure his injured leg wouldn't give out on him, before he turned and headed to his own room. *Alone.*

It was a state he was used to. A state he'd been raised in since the moment his mother died and his father lost himself in the bottle and an endless string of women. Ozzie could still remember every detail of his childhood room. He had spent so much time there, avoiding his dad's drunken rages or the looks of pity or, worse, *affection* in the eyes of the ladies who had shared his life for a week or a month or a year, until they left too.

Quietly opening his bedroom door, he realized the old memories, painful as they were, had done nothing to quench his desire for Samantha. He didn't bother with the lights. Didn't bother with his clothes. He fell onto his bed, stuffed his pillow over his face, and groaned loudly, hoping *that* would alleviate some of the lust riding him hard, spurring his body to hum with hot, fruitless passion.

It didn't.

Knowing there was nothing else to be done, he shoved the pillow beneath his head and reached for the button on his shorts. Releasing his dick, he pushed the waistband of his shorts beneath his ass. But not before pulling Samantha's bra from the pocket. A naughty souvenir of their time in the kitchen. A little part of her he planned to keep for himself.

He brought the scrap of red lace to his face and inhaled that soft powdery scent that was uniquely Samantha. She was on his fingers. The sweet, musky smell of woman and sex and climax clung to his skin. It traveled up his nose and hit his brain like an H-bomb.

Closing his eyes, he rubbed her bra over his chest, letting it abrade his nipples until they pebbled and throbbed. Lower, along his belly, he trailed the delicate morsel of fabric until he finally brushed the lace over his swollen member. His toes curled as he remembered how she looked with her head thrown back and her perfect breasts bare and begging for his mouth.

He wound the shoulder strap of her bra around the base of his dick, trapping the blood there, making him harder still. So hard, he knew if he reached over and clicked on the lamp, he'd see the skin of his cock stretched tight, the whole thing shiny and red.

Then, with the picture of Samantha firmly fixed in his mind, he touched himself.

A moan escaped his throat at first contact. His shaft was burning hot against his rough palm. Without hesitation, he began to stroke. Soft at first and then harder and harder, his hips bucking in counter rhythm to his hand, the muscles in his battered thigh aching as a thousand different images of Samantha danced in his head.

The taste of her was still on his tongue. The smell of her still tickled his nose. And the sounds she made. That low, keening moan as climax overtook her. It was the sweetest damn music he'd ever heard and—

His orgasm burst from him, traveling like lightning up his shaft to explode in a torrent of need and lust. He had no idea how long he convulsed and stroked while whispering Samantha's name into the darkness. But finally, long moments later, he was spent, shaking, and weak as a newborn kitten.

Chapter 10

Hog Help Motorcycle Repair Shop, South Ashland Avenue

THREE. THERE WERE THREE STORIES IN THE DAY'S edition of the *Chicago Tribune* bearing Samantha Tate's byline. But none of them gave Venom any clue to what she was after.

With a growl of impatience, he folded the newspaper and lobbed it toward the trash can in the corner of his office. When the edition bounced off the rim and landed on the floor in a mess of scattered pages, he barely resisted the urge to smash his fist against the top of his desk.

He had been in a terrible mood ever since Bulldog returned empty-handed the night before. Apparently Bulldog's plan had been to abduct Samantha at knifepoint and force her to drive her car to the clubhouse. It was a decent enough idea. Not earth-shatteringly brilliant, but Venom didn't expect brilliance from Bulldog. Just results.

Unfortunately, Bulldog had been thwarted. First by some mysterious blond asswipe wielding what Bulldog called "a well-used Beretta." *Then* by the police when the sweet-assed journalist decided to make a stop at a cop shop on Wentworth.

What are you planning, you sly minx? Venom wondered.

Not that he was too concerned she could actually out him for his gunrunning business. Which, he had to believe, was what she was after, given that her little snitch inside the Black Apostles had been sniffing around and asking questions about that very thing. No, the guns were safe. They were buried beneath so many shell companies, the money routed through a dozen offshore accounts, that it'd take a genius, a forensic accountant, and someone with the clearance to view his military records to be able to connect all the dots. All things Samantha Tate and the CPD were *not*.

So it wasn't the possibility of having the Basilisks' most lucrative line of cash flow interrupted that made him grit his teeth so hard his molars creaked. It was the fact that having her sniff around for one thing could very well lead her to discover *other* illegal businesses the Basilisks were involved in that *weren't* so airtight.

He'd gone home to his old lady, climbed naked into bed beside her, and after pulling the crotch of her panties aside and doing her the service of a quick squirt of lube, he'd screwed her long and hard. Poured his foul temper and volatile mood into her willing body, which usually worked to satiate him.

Not last night. He'd wanted Samantha. And nothing else, *no one else*, would do.

Curiosity had him leaning forward and moving the mouse on his computer. The monitor flickered to life, and he immediately did a Google search on her. A second later, his screen was filled with links to the articles she'd written. But it was the images of her he was most interested in.

Clicking through them, he saw neither hide nor hair of the blond guy Bulldog had mentioned. Instead, there was often the same small, dark-haired man at her side.

Venom lifted a brow. The guy was obviously important to her. A boyfriend, perhaps?

"Not the kinda man I woulda thought she'd go for," he muttered to himself.

While handsome, the bespectacled man also seemed a little effeminate. But maybe that was how Samantha liked her men. Maybe she *liked* being in charge, running the show, wearing the pants in the relationship. She looked like the ball-busting sort.

Venom smiled, growing hard at the idea of giving her a taste of what it was like to be taken by a *real* man.

He clicked on one of the pictures, which took him to a newsy website that featured a blog post written by Samantha. After reading the first few paragraphs, he realized the dark-haired cat in all the pictures wasn't her boyfriend but a coworker. And, according to her blog post, her best friend, even though they often competed for line space in the paper.

Boring.

He wanted something juicy. Something *personal*. He looked for her on Facebook. But before he could click to the social media site, the bell above the repair shop's front door trilled its dainty-sounding *tinkle*.

He *hated* that noise. Thought it made it seem like a bunch of pussies ran the joint. But Crutch assured him that connecting a bullhorn to the front door would scare away business. And *that,* they couldn't have. The repair shop was the front they used to launder most of the money they made from extortion and prostitution, which meant keeping the place in well-paying customers was a must so that the books looked good.

Venom was only a little bit scared of the nosy reporter and the Chicago police. But he lived in terror of the IRS.

After switching off his computer and exiting his office, he walked to the front of the shop to see a cop waiting on the other side of the counter. *Speak of the devil*.

Venom knew the newcomer was a pig not because he sported a uniform or flashed a badge, but because he wore a rumpled, off-the-rack suit and had a terrible haircut, but despite this, carried himself with a certain arrogance.

Venom had assumed he might get a visit from the police after last night's shenanigans. Bulldog had been wearing his cut—and broadcasting his affiliation with the Basilisks—when he was confronted by the blond in the alley. But being prepared didn't make it any easier for Venom to stomach having the law inside one of his establishments. He recognized no authority above his own, but for a while, he would be forced to act like he did.

That didn't mean he couldn't get in a few digs. A man had to take his fun where he could find it.

"You smell that?" He was sniffing the air when Crutch strolled into the front of the shop through the door that led to the mechanics' bays in the back. Wearing coveralls and biker boots, Crutch wiped grease from his hand onto a blue terry-cloth rag.

"Yeah." Crutch nodded, instantly clueing in and playing along. "What is that?"

"Pork." Venom sneered. "Makes me wanna fry up some bacon for lunch. How 'bout you?"

"You know I love cooked pig."

"Ha-ha." The cop reached into his jacket pocket to pull out his credentials. "Like I've never heard that one before." He placed his badge on the countertop and adjusted his suit coat over the bulge of his shoulder holster.

Venom wondered if the doughnut eater realized both bikers standing in front of him had Glocks hidden in their boots. *Probably not*, he decided. *Or else the cop wouldn't be playing the big, bad cock of the walk.*

"My name is Detective Curtis Carver, and I need to ask you boys a few questions about a murder that happened yesterday."

Boys. Venom wanted to make the detective eat that word. Instead, he said, "And here I thought my day was gonna be boring." Grabbing the stool behind the counter, he casually took a seat. Crutch came to stand at his shoulder, ever the loyal sidekick.

"But before we get to that," the detective said, "let me be clear who I'm talking to. You are…" He looked at Venom, brow raised in bored interest as if he already knew the answer to his question but was determined to wait on the reply anyway.

"Name's Venom."

"Ah." Carver nodded and pulled a small notebook from his breast pocket. He flipped it open and licked his finger, thumbing back a few pages. "John George Peabody the Third." Venom's jaw clenched at the hated name. "Which would make you the president of the Basilisks."

Venom wasn't surprised by the detective's knowledge. The Basilisks had had enough run-ins with the CPD to warrant familiarity. Luckily, few of those run-ins had resulted in jail time.

"So then you are…" The detective let his eyes run over Crutch. "Let me guess. Denis Cook, a.k.a. Crutch."

In answer, Crutch reached into the pocket of his overalls, pulled out a pack of Marlboros, and shook out a smoke. With a leisureliness that made Venom fight a smile, Crutch lit the tobacco, inhaled deeply, and blew a smoke ring toward Carver's face.

The detective's eye twitched as the smoke wafted over his head. "In the city of Chicago, it's illegal to smoke inside buildings open to the public."

"You goin' to arrest me, Detective Carver?" Crutch asked with a lazy drawl.

Instead of answering, Carver reached into his back

pocket and pulled out a photo of a smiling kid in a striped sweater. He set the picture on the counter beside his shiny badge. "You ever seen this man before?"

Venom recognized Marcel Monroe right away. Although the photo—obviously a school picture— showed a completely different young man than the one Bulldog had tailed and finally taken out. *That* Marcel had sported the baggy jeans, cocked ball cap, and black-and-purple colors that shouted his affiliation with the Apostles.

"Nope," he said, his face carefully blank. "Can't say that I have." He turned to Crutch. "You?"

"Maybe." Crutch shrugged. "Hard to tell. He looks like all the other kids 'round here. Why? He into motorcycles or something? He doesn't look the sort."

"No, he isn't into motorcycles." Carver frowned. "He's into running drugs with the Black Apostles. You two have any knowledge of that?"

Venom laughed loud and long. Made sure it was a good belly-roller. Then, pretending to wipe a tear, he looked the detective straight in the eye and declared, "You're funny. Surely, you know gangbangers and MCs don't mix. I'm not saying it's a race thing, but…it's a race thing."

Carver held his stare, the detective's poor opinion of Venom's prejudice evidenced by the curl of his upper lip. Venom didn't blink. He couldn't be arrested for being a bigot. They both knew that.

Finally, Carver reached into his pocket again. This time, the photo he placed on the countertop made Venom's heart race. Behind the fly of his jeans, his dick flexed hungrily. He wanted to snatch that picture, shove it into his pocket, and keep it for later. Instead, he blinked and stared impassively at Carver. "Who's the hottie, and where can I find her number?"

"Her name is Samantha Tate. She's a reporter for the *Chicago Tribune*."

"Fancy."

"You ever seen her before?"

"I'd remember if I had." Oh, he remembered all right. He remembered *well* the first time he'd seen that face, that smile.

"Any idea where Bobby Garrett might be?" Carver asked, tucking both photos back into his pocket, along with his badge.

"Who?" Venom asked, just to make the man work for it.

"Bobby Garrett." Carver's expression said he wasn't fooled for a minute. "I think you guys call him Bulldog. I went by his residence, but his wife—"

"She's ain't his wife," Crutch said, laying the poor grammar on thick. It never paid to act as cunning as you really were. A lesson they'd learned during their first tour in Iraq. "She's his old lady."

"Fine." The detective couldn't have looked any more bored if he'd tried. "His *old lady* said she hadn't seen him in a few days."

"Maybe he decided to go out on a run." Venom's smile was forced. "That's the thing about us bikers. You never know when the open road is gonna call our names, and off we go."

"He was in the city as late as last night," Carver said. "We have an eyewitness putting him at Red Delilah's a little before nine p.m. As well as POD footage of him outside the establishment not too long after that."

Venom hated the police observation devices spread throughout the city. Luckily, he didn't have to worry about Big Brother looking in on *his* neighborhood. Between the Basilisks and the Black Apostles, within twenty-four hours of a camera going up, someone made sure it came down again. And then, surprise, surprise, that same someone smashed it into a million pieces. Venom hoped it wouldn't be long before budgetary restrictions and apathy made the CPD give up trying to install the damn things.

"So you're telling me those nifty cameras of yours got footage of a biker at a biker bar." He widened his eyes. "Imagine that."

"He seemed to have ill intentions toward Samantha Tate. He went after her with a knife."

"She the one who's dead?" Venom played the ignorant card. "You said you were here to ask us questions about a murder."

"No." Carver shook his head. "She's alive and well. It's the other one, Marcel Monroe, who's dead."

Venom shrugged. "Gangbanging is a dangerous job. So what's a dead dope dealer got to do with Bulldog and this reporter chick?"

"How about you let me worry about that?" Carver said smugly. *The prick.* "And since we're back on the topic of that murder, mind telling me where you two were between the hours of three p.m. and five p.m. yesterday?"

"That when the Monroe kid was killed?"

"Answer the question."

Venom's fingernails cut into the palms of his hands, his fingers curled around the urge to punch the paunchy detective right in the middle of his stupid pig face. But assaulting an officer of the law, while fun, was also a straight shot to an eight-by-ten. "We were here until seven thirty. We got the footage to prove it." He pointed to the ceiling where the bright-red eye of a surveillance camera blinked.

"Mind getting me the tapes?"

Tapes? Venom snorted. "What year do you think this is? Nineteen ninety-five? The footage is saved straight onto the hard drive of my computer." He waved a hand over his shoulder, indicating the direction of his office.

Carver pulled out a business card and slid it across the countertop toward Venom with one finger. When the detective leaned close, Venom could smell coffee and jelly-filled doughnut on his breath. "Then mind emailing me the file?" Carver asked, his tone more demand than request.

Venom glanced at the card, wanting to tell the detective to go fuck himself and come back when he had a warrant. But he figured playing nice served him better in this instance. "Sure."

"And if you see Bobby…uh…Bulldog," Carver continued, pulling back, "tell him to give me a call. I have some questions about why he was chasing Samantha Tate with a knife."

"Maybe she *wanted* him to chase her with a knife. Ever think of that? Some chicks go in for that kinda thing. Rape fantasies, I think they're called."

"She *didn't* want him to chase her with a knife," Carver gritted between his teeth. "I can assure you of that."

"Well, of course she wouldn't admit it to *you*, but—"

"I think that's all for now." The detective cut him off, his audacity making Venom's blood boil. "I look forward to reviewing that video. And don't forget to send Bulldog my way when he shows up."

Venom's jaw sawed back and forth as he watched the detective take his time sauntering toward the front door. Before he pushed outside, Carver turned back. "One more thing."

There always is. "What's that?" Venom asked, all smiles and false curiosity.

"You ever do any time in the military?"

Venom felt Crutch tense beside him, but he made sure to keep his own muscles loose, especially those in his face. "Yep. Army for eight years."

Carver nodded. "Spend some of those eight years in Iraq?"

Now Crutch was vibrating, the waves of his unease reaching out to Venom and nearly making his teeth rattle. "Two tours," he admitted, because all of that was easily accessible information, and lying would only draw future suspicion when the detective checked his story. "Why do you ask?"

"No particular reason." Carver shrugged. "You just have that military bearing about you." And with that parting shot, the detective pushed into the cool summer day. The *tinkle* of the bell above the door was a further taunt Venom could have done without.

Crutch waited until they heard the engine on the cop's car turn over before blowing out a blustery breath that was thick with cigarette smoke. "What the fuck was that last part about? Why was he asking about Iraq?"

"Dunno," Venom mused, narrowing his eyes.

There was no way to trace the guns. Raheem made sure of that, made sure all the serial numbers were eradicated with a stippling machine. So even if that douchewad Monroe was able to find out his homeboys were scoring their weapons from the Basilisks, there's no way he could have known where the Basilisks were getting the guns. *No way*. Even Devon Price, the leader of the Apostles, didn't know that the shit he fired on the Chicago streets originated in the hot Iraqi desert. Still, *somehow,* Iraq had come into the conversation, and Venom desperately needed to find out how.

"But I know one person who can probably tell us," he said between clenched teeth. "Samantha Tate."

Even her name was sexy. Like a cheerleader or an actress or the high school slut. "Call Bulldog. Tell him to up his game and grab her." He watched Crutch reach for the burner phone he kept in his pocket. "And tell him to take off his cut, and for fuck's sake, stay away from the damn PODs while he's at it."

Tribune Tower

"What are your intentions toward Samantha?"

Samantha walked into the bullpen's break room where Ozzie was in the middle of making himself a cup of coffee. And where Donny Danielson was in the middle of…what? Interrogating the poor man?

Oh, Donny…

She could have put a stop to it then and there, but she was interested in Ozzie's reply. She ducked out of the doorway, flattening herself against the wall and turning her head to listen.

"I…uh…I'm not sure what you mean." Ozzie's tone was guarded.

"I mean, are you just in for a little slam-bam, thank-you, ma'am? Because if that's the case, then let me warn you, I—"

"That's definitely *not* the case," Ozzie interrupted. "I like Samantha. And I respect her. More than that, I consider her my… She's my *friend*."

Samantha warmed at the words. Very soon, she hoped to make him *more* than a friend.

"Friend, huh?" Curiosity laced Donny's voice.

"Yep."

"Hmm. Well, in that case, feel my shirt."

What? Samantha peeked around the doorjamb to see Donny offer Ozzie a sleeve.

Ozzie raised a brow but dutifully rubbed the material of Donny's shirt between his thumb and forefinger.

"Know what that's made out of?" Donny asked.

"Cotton?"

"No." Donny waggled his dark eyebrows. "*Boyfriend* material."

If there were two things to be said about Donny, besides her loving him to pieces and respecting the hell out of his journalistic integrity, it was that he was a purveyor of terrible pickup lines, and when it came to men, especially *handsome* men, he didn't do subtle. *Ever.*

It had gotten him into trouble a time or two with some less-than-broadminded individuals. She held her breath and waited to see if it would get him into trouble now. Ozzie *was* an über-alpha male, after all. How would he handle the blatant come-on of another man?

She should have known better than to worry.

Ozzie slung a friendly arm around Donny's shoulders. "If I leaned that way, you would *so* be my type. Dark hair, dark eyes, and a killer smile. It's the kryptonite to my Superman." Samantha couldn't help but note that *she* had dark hair and dark eyes. She wasn't sure about the killer smile though. The little gap between her two front teeth probably knocked her out of the running on that one. "Unfortunately, my inclinations run strictly *not* dickly."

Samantha bit the inside of her cheek.

"Oh. I thought maybe the whole *friends with Samantha* thing meant you…" Donny shook his head and feigned a windy sigh. "But never mind."

When Ozzie slapped Donny on the back, it occurred

to Samantha that Ozzie hadn't touched *her* since last night. Not this morning when they stood side by side in line at the bagel shop. Not when they rode up together in the Tribune Tower's elevator. And not once in the hours he sat beside her reading the day's edition while she put the finishing touches on the two stories due to her editor before noon.

He hadn't shied away from touching everyone else, she recollected with a frown. He'd shaken the hand of her editor. Bro-bumped knuckles with that meathead sports reporter who couldn't stop using dangling modifiers if his life depended on it. And fiercely hugged the freelancer who'd been diagnosed with breast cancer and who was submitting weekly articles about her battle with the disease and her journey toward recovery.

But when it came to Samantha? Ozzie was back to employing his hands-off strategy. Which didn't work well with *her* strategy of getting him into bed at the earliest possible opportunity. In fact, she'd been having trouble thinking of anything else.

Take, for instance, the minor inconvenience of writing the same sentence five times because she'd been distracted by the flex of Ozzie's triceps when he turned the page of the newspaper. Or when she couldn't think of the word "accordingly"—*accordingly, for shit's sake!*—because her mind had turned to soup the minute he started chewing on his lower lip as he read something particularly interesting. And *then* there was the embarrassing occasion when she'd typed the word *cock* instead of *cook*, and she hadn't caught it until Ozzie, who'd been reading over her shoulder, pointed it out with a wry twist of his delicious, totally edible mouth.

Jeez. Either she jumped his bones, and jumped them

soon, or she'd find herself the butt of all the copy editors' jokes.

"You hetero types always get the good ones," Donny lamented in a whisper once he'd drawn even with her in the doorway.

"We do *not*," she assured him. "Remember the last disastrous blind date I went on? The high fives the asshole couldn't stop giving me? The Brut aftershave? The fact that he wore a T-shirt that read: *Save a lollipop; suck a dick*? Any of that ringing a bell?"

"Are you kidding? I tell that story at parties. It always gets a big laugh."

"Glad my trip through the seventh circle of dating hell has become fodder for your cocktail conversations." She jerked her chin toward Ozzie. "*He's* the exception, not the rule."

"Mmm," Donny hummed. "That he is. Military man, motorcycle hottie, bodyguard bent on *guarding your body*." He unnecessarily emphasized the last three words before giving her a once-over that was thick with green-eyed jealousy. "Some girls have all the luck. If I didn't love you so much, I'd hate you."

When he whisked by her, nose held firmly in the air, she smiled at his retreating back. Then she turned and made her way into the break room. Cocking a hip against the counter, she crossed her arms and eyed Ozzie as he stirred his coffee.

"What?" he demanded.

"Do you ever feel drained?"

"Drained?" He stopped stirring to frown at her. *How the hell does he make wild, every-which-way hair and untrimmed beard stubble look sexy?* "From what?"

"From the way men and women alike just drink you in."

"Ha!" he barked. "Try telling that to your editor. The guy gave me a look that was meaner than Worf on a Wednesday not ten minutes ago."

"Worf?"

"*Star Trek: Next Generation*." He waved a dismissive hand. "What'd I do to piss him off? We seemed to get along just fine when you introduced us this morning."

Charlie had barely batted a lash when she arrived at work with Ozzie in tow and announced he would be shadowing her for a few days. In fact, *she* was the one to blink in surprise when Charlie told her, "Yeah. I know. Police Chief Washington called and said you were working on something that might prove dangerous, and he'd assigned you a bodyguard." More like Ozzie had volunteered, but who was she to split hairs?

"He's mad because half my coworkers have spent the morning ambling by my desk to get a better look at you, and they're all likely to miss their deadlines as a consequence."

"Just half?" The corner of Ozzie's mouth quirked. "You wound me."

"The other half are…" She wrinkled her nose. "How did you put it? Strictly *not* dickly."

When Ozzie barked out a laugh, she wondered if there was any sweeter sound on earth. She found herself grinning up at him like a fool. "Ozzie," she began, wanting to tell him…something. She wasn't sure what, but *something*. She was thwarted, however, when the angry buzz of his cell phone sounded from his hip pocket.

"Whatever thought that was…" He reached into his jeans pocket. "Hold it for a second." He glanced at the screen. "It's Washington." Thumbing on the device, he pressed it to his ear. "Ozzie here, Chief. What do you know?"

Samantha *should* have been on tenterhooks waiting to hear what Washington had to say. Instead, she
found herself mesmerized by the golden-brown beard
that peppered Ozzie's jaw. Hypnotized by the way his
mouth formed words. Completely captivated by the
deep rumble of his voice.

Ladies and gents, there is no more use denying it.
Samantha Tate, the woman who always prided herself
on not getting caught up in all that hearts-and-flowers
nonsense, was completely, utterly, entirely infatuated
with the man standing in front of her.

Chapter 11

Downtown Dogs, North Rush Street

THE MOOD-SWING ROLLER-COASTER RIDE OZZIE HAD been on all day long took a nosedive off a steep hilltop when he and Samantha walked into his all-time favorite hot dog joint and he saw the looks on the faces of Washington and Carver.

"Wow." He glanced back and forth between them. "Are those supposed to be smiles?"

"Subtle, right?" Carver asked.

"If by subtle, you mean pissed and painful looking, then yep." Ozzie nodded. "Totally subtle. So who kicked your cats?"

"First, let's order," Washington said. "I'm starving. Spending a morning running around and getting nowhere whets my appetite."

Samantha turned and gave Ozzie *That doesn't sound promising* eyes but said nothing as she got in line to place her order.

Ten minutes later, they were seated on barstools at the counter that ran the length of the front windows— *all the better to keep an eye on the street*—with loaded Chicago-style hot dogs and fries in red plastic baskets arrayed in front of them.

After they had a chance to dig in to the food, Washington said without preamble, "It's shit. There's just no other spin to put on it."

Samantha was taking a bite of her hot dog but halted,

lips open in a round O that made Ozzie wish he'd opted for a looser pair of jeans.

"What's shit?" she asked.

"There's no evidence to prove a connection between the Apostles and the Basilisks besides the vague confession of a gangbanger to a local reporter," Carver answered from his seat at the far end of the group.

"Don't forget that after that confession, the gangbanger"—Samantha made a face as if the term tasted sour on her tongue—"took a round to the head, and the reporter was followed out of a bar by a knife-wielding member of the biker gang in question."

"Circumstantial," Carver said, taking a giant bite of hot dog. "Or coincidental," he garbled around a mouthful, "to use Judge Maple's words."

"Who's Judge Maple?" Ozzie asked, swirling two fries through ketchup and welcoming the salty zing of flavor when he popped them into his mouth.

All the better to sop up the saliva caused by Samantha's proximity.

He'd been careful not to get too close to her all day, fearing if he did, he'd touch her. And if he touched her, he'd *keep* touching her until—

"Maple is the judge we approached about getting a warrant to tap the Basilisks' phones and confiscate their PCs," Washington answered. "But like Carver said, the good justice didn't think we presented a compelling enough case."

Samantha's jaw firmed, and one eyelid started to twitch. It was one of her tells. "What about the ballistics from the round you pulled out of Marcel?"

"Nothing." Carver had already wolfed down his hot dog. His french fries were quickly heading toward a similar fate. "Doesn't match any other cases. The gun that killed Mr. Monroe hadn't been used in a previous crime."

"And Bulldog?" Ozzie asked. "Any luck locating him?"

"Nope." The detective shook his head. "He's in the wind. I went to the motorcycle repair shop run by the Basilisks this morning. Had a chat with their president and vice president."

"What are *they* like?" Samantha asked curiously. Ozzie did not notice the way her red lips wrapped around her hot dog when she took another bite. No, he did not.

"I'll say this much." Carver's expression was anything but favorable. "Jesus might love them, but *I* think they're a couple of assholes. And they claim they haven't seen Bulldog in days."

Samantha pointed a fry at the detective. "Bullshit."

Carver shrugged. "You'll get no disagreement from me. But I got no way to prove they're lying."

"And where were they when Marcel was killed?" Samantha demanded, dark eyes flashing. "Did you ask them that?"

"They were at their repair shop. And *that's* something I *can* prove. They showed me the security footage that backs up their claim." Carver noisily slurped the last drops of Sprite through his straw.

"That doesn't mean they weren't responsible," Samantha insisted. "It doesn't mean they didn't order Marcel's murder. Any member of the Basilisks could have—"

"We know." Washington cut her off. "But short of rounding them all up and waterboarding the information out of them, we're left holding the bag. And guess what's inside. A big, stinking pile of shit. Which, if you'll remember, was my original point."

"But there is one lead we still might be able to follow," Carver mused.

Samantha turned to look at him, meal forgotten. Good thing, since Ozzie didn't think he could take watching her eat one more bite of that damned hot dog. For months, he had wanted her. But now that he knew what it was to hold her, to kiss her, to watch her come apart in his arms, the word *want* didn't even live on the same continent as his feelings for her.

"The Basilisks' president admitted to being in the military," Carver said. "His vice president too, come to find out. They were both army—went through basic training together and then deployed together. Two tours in Iraq."

Samantha gaped. "And *that* wasn't enough of a connection to make this maple-syrup judge"—Ozzie chuckled at the nickname—"grant you the warrant you want?"

"Judge Maple's argument is that a lot of men did tours in Iraq. We can't start investigating all of them based on one weapon that's supposed to be half a world away and, again, the vague confession of a gangbanger to a local reporter."

The sound Samantha made then could only be described as incredulous.

"I'm assuming you pulled their military records," Ozzie said to Washington. The police chief nodded. "Find anything interesting?"

"As a matter of fact," Washington drawled, looking at him meaningfully, "it wasn't what we found but what we *didn't* find that was interesting."

Ozzie raised a brow. "Redacted?"

"Their records are blacker than I am." Washington grinned at his own joke, revealing a set of dimples that rarely made an appearance. "I tried to use my pull as police chief to get an unedited version. Told the DOD and anyone else who would listen that the ex-soldiers in question were suspected of running guns and a whole mess of other criminal activity. But I got the Do Not Pass Go, Do Not Collect Two Hundred Dollars card for my efforts."

The look in Washington's eyes was worth a thousand words. Ozzie heard every one of them. If they had any hope of forwarding the investigation, Ozzie would need to put a call in to his connections.

Unfortunately, there was a teeny, tiny, itty-bitty problem with that. Neither Samantha nor Carver knew about his connections. And Ozzie was bound by duty, honor, and his unsigned but understood contract with all the men of BKI, not to mention the freaking president of the United States, to make sure neither Samantha nor Carver ever found out about the afore-mentioned connections.

Seated between Ozzie and Washington, Samantha glanced back and forth between them. "*What?*" she finally demanded. When neither of them spoke, her impatience erupted in its usual way…with foul language. "Oh, for fuck's sake, are you two sharing the same brain right now, or what? And if you are, could you please stop? It puts the rest of us at a distinct disadvantage."

Okay. So he could do this. He could admit to being able to get the information Washington needed. He just needed to be very careful how he couched his explanation.

"What you…uh…what you might not know about me is that I have some pull with the military brass." He didn't want to flat-out *lie* to Samantha. He was tired of doing that. So he tangoed his way around a half-truth. "It's possible I could use that pull to get an unredacted version of their military records."

Samantha cocked her head. "And why do you have pull with the military brass?"

"Oh, I could tell you, but then I'd have to kill you." He waggled his eyebrows, hoping to distract her.

It worked. She rolled her eyes. "Fine. Keep your secrets if it tickles your pickle. But tell me, what—"

She was interrupted by the sound of her phone jangling inside her purse. His lips twitched—a condition he rarely suffered nowadays except when he was in Samantha's company—as he watched her dig around inside the bag.

Wait for it…

She quickly got fed up and upended the purse. The usual culprits tumbled onto the countertop. Pens, pencils, and notepads. Two Snickers bars and one dented can of Diet Coke. There was a scarf, a wallet, a rubberbanded stack of note cards. Three tampons. A book of stamps. An electric bill and a cable bill. Two tubes of ChapStick. Fingernail clippers. A rolled-up pair of dress socks. And a Kindle e-reader. Beyond that, Ozzie couldn't tell. It became a blur.

Carver pulled back as if she'd dumped a slithering pile of snakes onto the counter.

"Don't judge me." She glared at the detective as she located her phone in the mess. "It's not my fault I was raised in a society of rampant consumerism."

She's adorable, Ozzie thought, pressing a hand to the center of his chest where a strange ache had set up residence.

It's just indigestion, he assured himself.

Himself answered back with, *If that's what helps you sleep at night, brother*.

—◦◦◦—

"What do you mean, you're spiking my second piece?" Samantha growled at her editor over the phone. She pressed a finger into her opposite ear, blocking out the sounds of traffic on Rush Street and the bawdy laughter drifting through the open front door of the bar next door.

She'd been forced to take the call outside because a large group of tourists had packed into the small eatery, all talking at once. Dedicated bodyguard that he was, Ozzie had followed her out onto the sidewalk. Now, he leaned against the side of the building, hands stuffed into the pockets of his biker jacket, injured leg bent, and boot resting flat against the bricks. He looked for all the world as lazy and bored and *gorgeous* as ever.

That was, if you didn't take the time to watch his eyes. Those were intense, bright with intelligence, and cataloging every facet of the world around him. She cocked her head, wondering where he had learned to do that. Then Charlie accused her of writing her last piece with an opinionated slant, and she forgot everything except for the conversation at hand.

"I did *not* editorialize!" she yelled into her phone. "That was a direct quote from the asshole."

Charlie made some rumblings about defamation and having to print a retraction if he let the article run. Samantha wondered if Charlie was more worried that they were about to drag the guy's name through the mud or that the dick munch had close ties with the mayor.

"How about this." She hated to compromise but knew that was the only way. "You mark it up and send it to me. I'll make some changes, and we'll bump it to the next edition."

She curled her hand so tightly around her cell phone that the casing emitted a pained *crackle*. But her grip wasn't because Charlie was pissing her off. Oh no. She was used to that. Two women in power suits and sneakers—out for a walk during their lunch break, apparently—were making a beeline toward Ozzie, and *that's* why she was trying to throttle her poor iPhone. Ozzie, the cad, was grinning at them, his easy, open expression inviting conversation.

Can't take him anywhere, she thought uncharitably, remembering the time they'd gone to the movies together and the over-perfumed seventy-something lady sitting next to him had tried to hold his hand. By the end of the film, Ozzie had let her. Because he was kind and adorable and just the best thing since sliced bread.

Samantha had never been a jealous person. But the minute Ozzie reached out to shake the ladies' hands, to *touch* them when he hadn't touched her all fucking day long, she was pretty sure that if she looked in the mirror, she'd find her brown eyes had turned green.

"Hang on, Charlie," she grumbled. To Ozzie, she said, "I'm going to finish my call in the car!"

If he wanted to follow her, he was welcome to. Or he could just stand there and be admired.

Yuck. She did *not* like feeling this way.

Quickening her steps, she made her way up the block, heading to the spot where she and Ozzie had parked their vehicles. She'd driven her Mustang to the lunch meeting, and Ozzie had retrieved his motorcycle from the parking garage at Tribune Tower.

And yes. Okay. So she'd nearly wrecked twice on the short drive from Michigan Avenue to Rush Street because she'd spent most of her time gazing at Ozzie in her rearview mirror instead of watching the street in front of her.

But can you blame me? By himself, Ozzie was sexy as hell. Ozzie on a motorcycle was so hot, it should be outlawed.

Sandwiching her phone between her ear and shoulder,

she dug into the side pocket of her purse for her keys. She was curling her fingers around the key ring when Ozzie yelled from behind her, "Shit! Look out!"

"Huh?" She turned to look back at him but was distracted by the white van that squealed to a stop at the curb, tires smoking as rubber melted onto asphalt.

What happened next was a blur. She *thought* she saw a big-bellied man with a dark beard hop out of the van and rush toward her with his arm raised menacingly. She *thought* she recognized him from the video footage of the night before. And she *thought* she heard Ozzie yell her name as the sound of his big biker boots pounding on pavement struck a quick, frantic rhythm. But she couldn't be certain of anything. Because, just like in the cartoons, an anvil fell on her head, and she was suddenly seeing stars.

Ozzie had his Beretta out and aimed through the driver's side window a split second after Bulldog tossed a dazed Samantha into the back of the van. He didn't dare take a shot, however. The street was bustling with people, and he couldn't chance a ricochet that could injure or kill an innocent bystander.

Bulldog took advantage of Ozzie's momentary hesitation by putting the van in gear and peeling away from the curb with an ear-piercing squeal of tires.

Shit, fuck, damn, and dick!

"What the hell?" Washington thundered from the corner. The police chief had seen Ozzie and Samantha leave the sidewalk in front of Downtown Dogs and decided to investigate. But that was too little too late. Bulldog was barreling down the street, blowing through stop signs and traffic lights, leaving swerving cars and honking taxicabs in his wake.

Ozzie didn't hesitate. He holstered his weapon and ran to his motorcycle. "Bulldog just whacked Samantha over the head with a billy club! He's got her in that white van!" He rocked Violet off her kickstand, gritting his teeth when a lance of razor-sharp agony stabbed through his thigh. *Don't fail me now*, he silently commanded his bum leg. "I'm going after them! Follow me if you can!"

"Wait! Let me—"

Ozzie didn't stick around to hear the end of Washington's sentence. He roared down the street, dodging in and out of traffic, all while quickly working through possible scenarios of how this could play out.

He could catch up with them and shoot out the tires. But if he disabled the vehicle, Bulldog's options would be twofold. Run, or take Samantha hostage inside the van. Ozzie didn't like the sound of the latter. Not one bit.

So maybe he could ride up behind them, jump from Violet onto the van's back bumper, and hope he could wrench the cargo doors open. But if Bulldog was packing, once Ozzie was in the back of the van with Samantha, he'd be an easy target. Not to mention that Samantha could inadvertently take a round meant for him. He liked the sound of *that* less still.

Or there was a third option. He could pull even with the van and try to shoot Bulldog through the driver's side window. But without a driver, the van could spin out of control, no doubt plowing into civilians and likely injuring Samantha in the inevitable crash. That seemed to be the worst option of all.

Ozzie had been scared before. Plenty of times. There was his first year in the navy when he'd been riding copilot in a helicopter that suffered catastrophic engine failure, forcing the pilot to ditch the bird in the ocean.

There was that incident in Afghanistan when he'd been left to make like Usain Bolt and hightail it out of a Taliban leader's hideout after one of his teammates called in an impromptu air strike. And last but certainly not least, there was the hotel in Kuala Lumpur where an incendiary device had nearly blown his damn leg off. Proned out and bleeding in the hallway, he hadn't known whether he would live or die.

In fact, it was a great fallacy that spec-ops guys in general, and SEALs in particular, didn't get scared. The misconception was promoted by Hollywood, which liked to portray men in his profession as macho, grunting hulks muscling their way through every situation. But in truth, all SEALs shared one trait. Brainpower. And being smart meant knowing how easily one could bite the bullet.

So yep. Ozzie knew fear. But never had he felt it sink its teeth into him with as much vigor as it did when Samantha was in danger. And when he wasn't sure how he was going to get her out of it.

Think, man! Think!

He'd been taught how to slow his heart rate, but the usual trick didn't work. The stupid organ was doing its best to make a jail break through his rib cage. He'd been drilled on tactical breathing. But no matter what he tried, his lungs continued to work like bellows. The only part of his training that seemed to be functioning normally was his ability to ignore pain. Because even though he knew on a strictly intellectual level that his thigh was screaming with the effort he was putting it through, he didn't really feel it. All he felt was...

Desperation.

The thought of never seeing Samantha grin at him over a steaming cup of coffee, or never hearing her take him to task for not combing his hair, or never smelling that soft, powdery scent when she leaned close to elbow him after a good joke was—

He couldn't even countenance it as he shifted gears and blazed through a red light. A black Beemer laid on its horn and its brakes at the same time. Its front bumper clipped Violet's back fender with a loud *whack*. The contact was enough to send Ozzie fishtailing as prickles of dismay skittered across the back of his neck. Thankfully, the little collision wasn't enough to make him lose control of the big bike.

"Come on, come *on*," he encouraged the motorcycle, urging more speed from her, more maneuverability. In response, she roared like a caged beast. The sound echoed against the buildings lining the street, drowning out all other noise. It was enough to have most people stopping and staring.

Most people…

A woman carrying a double handful of shopping bags and wearing headphones suddenly stepped into the street in front of him. He missed her by inches, her scream of alarm piercing his eardrums like daggers as his heart kicked up another notch. He'd barely completed his livesaving swerve before a cyclist darted between a couple of parked cars, forcing him to wrench his handlebars hard right and take the motorcycle onto the sidewalk.

No longer on the road, he felt his vision tunnel, his concentration complete as two trash cans, a newspaper dispenser, and a fire hydrant rushed by in crystalline clarity. Then he hopped back onto the street, his rear tire bouncing off the curb with teeth-clacking force. Luckily, the unexpected maneuver had gained him some ground. The white van was visible four blocks ahead,

darting and weaving between slower-moving cars and
honking like it was the end of days and the devil himself
was riding shotgun.

Ozzie knew where the asshole was headed. The on-
ramp to I-90. And if the van made it to the interstate,
Ozzie would be hard-pressed not to lose it. There were
so many exits. So many cars that could cut him off.
Not to mention, Violet was made to look pretty and run
smooth at around sixty-five miles per hour, a cruising
piece of art as opposed to a racer. When Mötley Crüe
sang about *a custom-built bike doing one-oh-three*, they
hadn't been singing about Violet. He didn't know what
the van had under the hood or if it could outpace his
motorcycle, but he sure as shit didn't want to be put in a
position to find out.

"Shit!" he yelled when a woman pushing a stroller
tried to cross against the light. He slammed on Violet's
brakes, feeling the bike's fat front tire dig into the pavement at the same time as her rear tire threatened to leave
it. The smell of burning rubber and hot brake pads tunneled up his nose. "You idiot! I should report you to
child services!"

The woman turned and shot him a double bird,
screaming at him to do something with himself that was
anatomically impossible. Shaking his head, he revved
his engine and darted across the intersection at his first
opportunity. As fate would have it, the white van was
stuck in traffic, closed in on all sides by cars waiting at
a red light.

A hard *thumping* noise made Ozzie wonder if he'd
pushed Violet too hard. Then he realized it was his
own heart. The wind sent fingers of warm air tunneling
through his hair, alerting him to the fact that he hadn't
taken the time to put on his helmet. The protective

headgear was still strapped to the back of his seat, where it wasn't doing him any good.

Too late now.

He tightened his grip on the handlebars and shifted gears. His world existed in the distance between him and the van. Between him and Samantha. Closer. Closer. Closer still. Each inch coincided with a beat of his heart.

Looking at the red light, Ozzie wished with everything in him that it would *stay* that way until he got there. Knowing it wouldn't, he realized what he had to do…

Chapter 12

"LET ME OUT OF HERE, YOU BASTARD!" SAMANTHA screamed, slamming her hand against the wire mesh separating the cargo hold of the van from the two front seats. Her head ached. Her vision was a little wonky, spots occasionally blooming in front of her eyes and bursting like fireworks.

She still wasn't sure what had happened out on the sidewalk. Although she was fairly certain it wasn't an anvil that landed on her head. *I mean, that doesn't happen in real life, does it? Who uses anvils anymore?* All she knew for sure was that one second, she was talking to her boss and digging for her keys, and the next second...*Bang! Zoom!* Only she wasn't headed to the moon. By the looks of things, she was headed toward the highway.

Bulldog turned and snarled, "Sit down and shut up, bitch!" His breath was ripe with the smell of chewing tobacco and greasy chili with onions. It had the room-clearing capacity of a bad fart, and Samantha gagged, stumbling back.

Bulldog laid on the horn again and again, and the noise felt like a violation. A cleaver to her cerebral cortex. She grabbed her head and felt the lump behind her left temple. Probing it gently, she winced at the pain. A brief inspection concluded that her skull was still intact. She'd live. At least for the next couple of minutes.

And since she *would* live for the next couple of minutes, she should use them to her advantage. Her first thought was to look around for her phone and her purse. But a quick scan told her she'd dropped them on the sidewalk. Her next thought was to try to escape the van. But the rear doors revealed no interior handles. There was no way to open them from the inside.

Honk! Honk, honk, honk!

Bulldog would *not* lay off the horn. Samantha couldn't imagine what the stupid dill weed was thinking. He was stuck at a light, bumper to bumper with the cars around him. Even if the drivers had been inclined to listen to his insistent honking and *wanted* to open up an avenue of escape—and, come on, Chicago motorists were not known for being the obliging sort—there was no way they could have moved. Not even an inch.

So stop fucking honking! she wanted to scream. Instead, she forced herself to concentrate on what to do next. Escape was impossible. Phoning Ozzie or the police was impossible. But so was sitting back like a good girl and accepting her fate.

"Did you kill Marcel Monroe?" she demanded, lacing her fingers through the wire mesh, daring to get close enough to take a hit of Bulldog's foul breath.

The biker didn't say anything, just continued to pound on the horn.

"Why have you taken me?" she screamed. "Is it because I know you and your douchewagon band of biker brothers are selling weapons to the Black Apostles? How are you guys getting the guns from Iraq? Who is your source over there?"

"I said sit down and shut up!" Bulldog shouted. He didn't turn to her, but she was still overwhelmed by a wave of hellacious halitosis.

She beat back the urge to retch and shook the metal wiring like a lunatic. It rattled Bulldog enough to make

him turn away from the light that suddenly flicked from
red to green.

"Stop it!" he bellowed, foul spittle flying from his
mouth to stick in his beard. Samantha wouldn't have
been surprised if the stuff grew legs and walked right
back into his mouth. "I told you I—"

HONNNNNKKKK!

Now it wasn't Bulldog causing the head-splitting
ruckus. It was the cars piled up behind them.

"Hey!" Samantha yelled, trying to keep Bulldog's
eyes on her. But it was no use. He turned back, saw the
light was green, and put his foot on the gas.

The van lurched forward, forcing her to cling to
the metal mesh to keep her balance. But before the
vehicle could go more than a couple of yards, she
heard it. A noise like rolling thunder. The sound of a
two-wheeled beast with a badass set of pipes eating up
the asphalt.

Ozzie!

"Shit!" Bulldog cursed before the impossible
happened.

Ozzie darted in front of them on his big motorcycle,
cutting them off. Like a hero from a comic book, he
leapt from the bike onto the van's front bumper.

Crash!

The van hit the abandoned bike, knocking it to the
road and forcing Bulldog to slam on the brakes. But it
was too late. The van rolled over the bike and got high-
centered on its metal and chrome chassis. The resulting
screeeeech of steel against blacktop reminded Samantha
of metal fingernails down a chalkboard.

Her first thought wasn't *Thank goodness! I'm saved!*
Oh no. Her first thought was *Noooo! Not his motorcycle!*
He loves that thing!

But he'd sacrificed it. For her.

Ozzie rolled onto the hood of the van in a move that would have done a stunt man proud, stopping with one knee planted above the engine and one big biker boot slammed against the windshield as the van rocked to a stop. His handgun was out and aimed straight at Bulldog's head. The look in his eye was one Samantha recognized.

The warrior is back…

All the noise of the past few seconds was replaced by an eerie quiet. Which made it easy to hear Ozzie when he shouted, "The way I see it, you have two options! The first is I blow your fucking head off!"

Breath bated, Samantha stared through the front windshield at the man she thought she knew. *Thought* being the sticking point. Because this guy, the one threatening death and looking like he meant it, was someone else entirely.

"The second is you exit that van, keeping your hands where I can see them!" Ozzie continued, just as the sound of sirens blared in the distance.

"Fuck you!" Bulldog shouted, darting his head left and right, trying to think his way out of the situation. Samantha figured the biker's IQ matched his shoe size, so she wasn't holding out much hope he'd actually find a solution.

"What's that?" Ozzie yelled.

"*Fuck you!*" Bulldog bellowed again, breathing hard and fouling the air with his putrid breath.

"That's what I thought you said!" Ozzie called, his words dripping with malice. Cars began to dart around them, the passengers and drivers gaping at the scene playing out even as they fled from it. "Talk of bedroom antics gives me a boner, thanks. But that wasn't one of your choices! Now, I'm going to count to three! If you haven't exited that van by the beat of four, you're dead! Simple as that!"

Bulldog glared at Ozzie with naked hatred. "Who the fuck is this guy?" he asked under his breath. Samantha wasn't sure if he was talking to himself or to her. Didn't matter, since she was pretty sure neither of them knew the answer.

"One!"

"Fuck, fuck, *fuck!*" Bulldog hissed, his fat-fingered hands flexing on the steering wheel.

"Two!"

Samantha's heart pounded when she saw Ozzie's finger move. It was subtle. But one second, his pointer was straight against the trigger guard. The next second, it was curled menacingly around the trigger.

He's going to do it! He's going to shoot Bulldog right in front of me!

Bulldog must have come to a similar conclusion, because with a final obscenity, he yelled, "All right!" and pushed out of the van.

Cool wind rushed into the vehicle, blowing away the smell of the biker and replacing it with the scent of car exhaust and hot metal. Two police cruisers arrived on the scene, lights swirling, sirens cutting off. Traffic was now stalled in all directions as gawkers took in the drama. Despite this, Ozzie remained cool, calm, and collected as he continued to draw down on Bulldog. As if having a human head lined up in his sights was something he encountered on a daily basis.

Samantha didn't realize she was echoing Bulldog's question when she murmured, "Who *are* you, Ozzie?"

—·—

Black Knights Inc. Headquarters

"I've seen some frickin' bad shit in my time," Samantha heard Becky Knight whisper. "But this is a whole new level of suck."

"I have faith in you," Ozzie replied, settling an arm around Becky's shoulders and twanging the lollipop stick protruding from between her pursed lips.

Samantha sat on the leather sofa pushed against the stairwell in BKI's bottom-floor shop, a bag of frozen peas pressed to the knot on her head and Peanut curled beside her. The tomcat purred so loudly that she was having trouble hearing the conversation by the bike lift. Becky, Ozzie, and Michelle were all standing around the mangled body of Ozzie's beloved bike, talking in hushed tones, as if in church…or at a graveside.

She felt just awful about his motorcycle. And at the same time, so grateful. Because if he hadn't acted so quickly, there was no telling where she might be right now. Visions of a shallow grave and worms crawling out of her eye sockets drifted through her head. But even *that* didn't dampen her desire to walk over to Ozzie so she could hug him and kiss him and…*bone his brains out*! You know, to express her gratitude.

It'd been five hours since Bulldog had been shoved into the police cruiser. Four and a half hours since the paramedics who had arrived at the scene, checked her head wound, and gave her a clean bill of health. No concussion. Just a bit of swelling and some pain. And four hours since she'd been driven to the local precinct where organized chaos had ensued.

She'd had to give her statement to no fewer than five different policemen on five separate occasions.

She'd written a lengthy, four-page transcript of the entire abduction. Which, given the whole thing had lasted a little over five minutes, was a testament to her skill as a reporter who prided herself on being a stickler for details.

At some point, Washington had returned her purse and phone to her, and she'd made a quick call to Charlie, letting him know she was okay. She'd texted the same thing to Donny, who had quickly texted back: *Thank heavens! I want all the deets when you get a minute. P.S. Love your funny face.* Then she'd been fingerprinted—apparently they needed her prints on file so they could rule them out when collecting other prints from the van—her injury photographed, and the CPD had ended the day by generally poking and prodding her for any additional information she might have forgotten. Finally, she'd been pronounced drained of all pertinent details, and she'd been taken back to collect her car.

And the whole time, where was Ozzie? Well, right beside her. Still *not* touching her.

It was beginning to make her paranoid. They'd gone over this, hadn't they? She had admitted to wanting to be more than just friends, and he had admitted that the whole reason he hadn't touched her before was that he'd been afraid once he started, he'd never want to stop. When she replayed his words in her head, they thrilled her as much now as they had then. But he *had* touched her last night, touched her *so good*. And then this morning…nada.

I mean, what the hell?

Then it occurred to her…

What if he was having second thoughts? What if, between last night and this morning, he'd come to real-ize the extent of her feelings for him, come to under-stand that when she said she wanted to be more than friends, that wasn't limited to a quick game of hide the salami, and then buh-bye? And what if he was trying to ease back, create some distance between them, because he didn't feel the same way about her? After all, he may be a Casanova, but he was also a nice guy and her *friend*. If he thought his usual MO of *Love 'em and leave 'em* would hurt her, he'd do everything in his power to make sure that didn't happen.

Shit!

So, then, where did that put them? Back at square one? Him not touching her and her pretending that all she wanted was to be a pal who met him for the occasional drink?

Screw that! She couldn't go back. Not after that scene in the kitchen. Not after—

"Shove over," Christian said, coming to stand in front of her. He had a jelly-filled doughnut in one hand and a copy of *Car and Driver* magazine in the other.

She scooted to make room, and he plopped down beside her. "Ruddy hell," he said as Peanut lifted his head and meowed his displeasure at being jostled. Then the cat caught wind of the food and sat up, yellow eyes keen, crooked tail flicking side to side.

"Ruddy hell what?" Samantha mimicked Christian's accent as Peanut transferred his furry, rotund self to the back of the sofa.

"I'm surprised smoke isn't pouring from your ears, given how fast your gears are spinning." He motioned to her head with the doughnut. Peanut's eyes followed the movement with intense concentration.

"That obvious, huh?"

"Only to someone with eyes," he admitted unhelpfully. "So what are you going on about? Anything I can help you sort out?"

As a matter of fact… "Has Ozzie ever had a steady girlfriend?"

Christian blinked, the doughnut halfway to his mouth. He swallowed and lowered the pastry. "Well now, this is an eight-point-nine on the awkward scale, yeah?"

"I'm serious." Samantha frowned.

"As am I." Christian's expression was the same one he would have worn had he been sucking on a lemon. "And because I'm his friend, and because I know the two of you held a dance-off with your pants off last night, I feel obliged to remain mute on the subject of his past relationships."

"We didn't," Samantha admitted. Today, Christian was dressed in designer jeans, a cotton pullover, and black leather ankle boots that flashed the Gucci logo on the sole when he crossed one ankle over his knee.

"No?" One dark eyebrow crawled up his forehead.

"No." She shook her head. "But not because *I* put on the brakes. Hell no. I was all about the gas. *He*"—she tilted her head toward the group gathered around the bike lift—"was the one to stop things."

"Now, *that* is interesting." After a beat, Christian added, "And it explains some things."

"Like what?"

"Like the fact that he was a grumpy Gus when he crawled out of bed this morning. I thought it was because he didn't get the prize out of the cereal box again, but it's because he was forced to salute his own general last night."

Salute his own general? Where does he come up with these things?

"I'm serious." She scowled at him.

The look Christian gave her was the picture of innocence. "Again, as am I." He took a giant bite of doughnut.

"Given this recent revelation," he said around a mouthful, "I suppose it wouldn't hurt to tell you no, he hasn't had girlfriends. At least not as long as I've known him."

Samantha's shoulders couldn't have sagged any lower if someone had plopped fifty-pound newspaper bundles on them. "That's what I was afraid of."

Ozzie didn't do relationships. Ever.

Christian eyed her. "I take it you don't fancy that answer?"

"It is what it is, I guess." She sighed, feeling hard stones of disappointment and hurt tumble through her chest. "You can't ask a tiger to change his stripes, can you?"

"No, you most certainly cannot. Here." He held out what remained of his snack. "Have the rest of my doughnut. It's not quite as good as the Welsh cakes my uncle used to make. But it's close."

"I don't want it if it's a pity doughnut," she told him with a sniff.

"Why? It tastes the same."

When she narrowed her eyes, he grinned broadly.

Of course, when Peanut—moving with a speed Samantha would not have thought possible given his girth—jumped from the back of the sofa and snagged the doughnut in midair, it was her turn to grin.

"Thief!" Christian bellowed, glowering at Peanut's quickly retreating back end as the cat dashed around the corner in a blur of gray fur. "Becky, your sodding cat filched my food again!"

Becky glanced over her shoulder with a look of complete disinterest. "That's what you get for putting your food anywhere near him."

"Or," Christian said, his words heavy with irritation, "you could train that beastly feline terror to keep his grubby paws to himself."

The expression on Becky's face questioned Christian's intelligence. "You don't know much about cats, do you? Besides, you shouldn't be eating anyway. Michelle took the afternoon off work. She's making us a wonderful dinner, which you won't get to enjoy since you've ruined your appetite."

Christian sat up straighter. "Michelle cooked?"

"You cooked?" Ozzie turned to the statuesque brunette. "What did you cook? Please tell me it's lasagna. I would murder for some of your lasagna."

"Down, boy." Michelle patted Ozzie's shoulder. "No need to turn to homicide. It's lasagna."

Ozzie whooped and kissed her on the cheek. "I love you," he said, making Samantha's brown eyes threaten to turn green again. "Why'd you have to go and marry Snake? I'm a much better catch. And much better at all the bedroom stuff that—"

Michelle elbowed him in the ribs, making him wince and stumble back. Samantha should not have been relieved. The fact that she was made her want to kick her own ass.

Okay, Sammie. You've totally lost it. You're out there. Like, the lines have been clipped, and you've drifted into orbit around Planet Imajealousbitch.

Michelle glanced at her watch. "I need to pick up the kids from the babysitter." She turned and looked through the big, leaded-glass windows at a sky that was bluebird blue, not a cloud in sight. "It's a nice evening. While I'm gone, why don't you all set the picnic table? I'll be back before…" She trailed off, a blush blooming over her cheeks.

Did she just shoot me a furtive look? Samantha wondered.

"I'll be back before the bread is finished baking,"

Michelle quickly finished, leaving Samantha to assume she'd imagined the momentary weirdness.

"And dessert?" Christian asked, scooting to the edge of the sofa. If he'd been a dog, his ears would've perked up. "Did you make any of your legendary tiramisu? Please say yes."

"If you eat any more sweets," BKI's secretary said as she clomped down the metal stairs from the second floor, "all your teeth will rot out of your head."

"Speaking of sweets," Christian mumbled beneath his breath, "here comes the icing on the crappy cake that is this day."

"What's that?" Emily stepped from the last tread to stand in front of Christian, hands on hips.

"Nothing," Christian grumbled.

"Didn't sound like nothing."

"Why don't you bugger off and bother someone else?" Christian glared up at Emily. "How does that sound?"

The challenge in Emily's voice was unmistakable. "You mean on a scale of one to…uh…one?"

Samantha decided that was her cue to leave. She'd only seen Emily and Christian interact once before, and that time, she'd been surprised when neither of them walked away bloody. Setting aside the bag of peas, she pushed up from the sofa to make her way to Ozzie. Michelle headed for the door, and Becky gave her a nod before walking toward the back of the shop.

"Those two should just do it already and get it over with," Ozzie mumbled once she'd made it to his side.

She glanced over her shoulder. "Emily and Christian? Is that their problem?"

And on the subject of two people who should do it already…

Of course, she didn't dare say that aloud. Instead, she turned her attention to the bike. A tow truck had delivered the carcass while she'd still been answering questions at the precinct. She winced when she let her eyes wander over the mangled mess.

Ozzie was saying something more about the Brit and BKI's secretary, but Samantha interrupted him, needing to get something off her chest. "Ozzie..." She touched his arm, marveling at the toughness of his flesh and the sheer warmth of his skin beneath her palm. He flinched like her fingers burned. She was left to curl her hands dejectedly into fists. "I'm so sorry about...about..." She couldn't finish the sentence, just motioned with her head toward the ruined motorcycle. "She was so beautiful. I know how much she meant to you, and I just want to say—"

"Know the great thing about working in a custom bike shop?" he asked.

She blinked at the interruption. "Um, no?"

"We fix bikes." He grinned and winked.

She barely resisted shaking her fist at the sky. There he stood, looking like a bad boy but being a nice guy. He was so stinking...*perfect*.

"Stop it." She frowned up at him. *Way* up at him.

Has he always been this tall?

"Stop what?" He cocked his head, and a lock of shaggy blond hair fell over his eyebrow.

She dug her nails into her palms to keep from pushing it back. Because then, you know, *whoopsie!* Her hand might accidentally slip around the back of his neck so she could draw his head down for a kiss.

"Being so damned nice all the time," she grumbled. "You should be giving me what for. Telling me I should never have left your side to take that call. Berating me for not paying better attention to my surroundings. Yelling at me to—"

The words strangled in her throat, because he touched her. He finally touched her! His long, strong fingers wrapped around her upper arm. Since she'd shed her jacket and was wearing a sleeveless silk blouse, they were skin to skin. She could feel his rough calluses, and the nerves in her arm seemed to activate one by one until her whole right side thrummed with sensation.

Then he released her, and the momentary joy was quickly tamped down.

"You didn't do anything wrong," he told her. "Who would have thought that dipshit Basilisk would snatch you off a busy street in broad daylight? Dude obviously has way more balls than brains."

"You say that like it's a bad thing!" Emily called from her spot by the sofa, proving she could eavesdrop and argue with Christian at the same time. "But Christian's made a career of that woeful combination!"

Christian sputtered, and then the two of them were swiping at each other again.

Samantha ignored them. "And there you go again. Being all nice."

"Please," Ozzie scoffed. "A nice man wouldn't have been tempted to blow a hole in the fucker's head."

She blinked. Just for a second, it was back. That look in his eyes. But then as quickly as it appeared, it was gone.

So to recap…bad boy, nice guy, superhot warrior.

Who are you *really*? She opened her mouth to ask, but Christian and Emily's bickering picked up volume.

"I wasn't born with enough middle fingers to let you know how I feel about that!" Emily yelled. She was scowling up at Christian, who had stood from the sofa to tower over her.

"Warms the cockles, doesn't it?" Christian's tone was just this side of irate.

"*Ding, ding, ding!*" Emily acted like she was ringing a bell. "*Wrong!* Freddy, tell him what he *didn't* win. And what the hell are cockles anyway?"

Beside Samantha, Ozzie sighed and shook his head. "It's been like this since the moment they met." Then he raised his voice. "You two need to leave the drama with your mommas. Seriously, what's the matter with you?"

"She bloody started it!" Christian pointed an accusatory finger at Emily.

"And I'll finish it too," Emily declared, flush with the thrill of the fight. If Samantha didn't know better, she'd say Emily was thoroughly enjoying herself.

"You see?" Christian threw his hands in the air, then turned to stomp up the stairs.

"Running away again?" Emily called after him.

"Jolly well trying to keep from committing murder!" Christian called back.

Ozzie chuckled. Apparently he was unable to resist joining in the fun, because he yelled, "Is that a little yellow I see staining your belly, C-Man?"

Having reached the second-floor landing, Christian turned back and glowered. "You, sir, are a sack of ass." And with that parting shot, he disappeared into the conference area.

It occurred to Samantha how wrong she'd been about the men and women of Black Knights Inc. For so many years, and then again last night, she'd thought of them as dark, villainous characters. But in reality, they were simply a group of people who'd come together to build a business. And in so doing, they'd grown into a big, noisy, argumentative family.

She was struck by a keen sense of longing. It'd been a long time since she'd felt like part of a family...

Chapter 13

Basilisk Clubhouse

"Savoy says they're finished questioning Bulldog," Crutch announced, thumbing off his cell phone.

Venom watched his second-in-command light a cigarette and suck until the cherry burned orange. Seated around the big table was the Basilisks' executive committee. They had convened a secret, emergency session of Church when they got the call that Bulldog had been arrested. So besides Venom and Crutch, present were Termite, the club's treasurer, and Hawkeye, their secretary.

"Savoy also said they have him dead to rights on the kidnapping charge," Crutch went on. Edward Savoy was the best criminal defense attorney in the great city of Chicago. The Basilisks kept him on retainer. "A whole shitload of eyewitnesses saw Bulldog snatch Samantha off the street downtown. Including two cops."

"Stupid fuckin' bastard," Termite spat out, twirling his red mustache like a cartoon villain. Termite was an Irish Catholic boy, born and raised on Chicago's South Side. Which meant he used the word *fuck* with impunity.

"Bulldog was just following orders." Venom was quick to defend his sergeant at arms. Although he was pissed that Bulldog hadn't been a hell of a lot subtler in his abduction of the reporter, he didn't allow the bad-mouthing of club members. Ever. Bad-mouthing led to infighting. Infighting led to violence. And violence led to the loss of control and the loss in profits. As far as Venom was concerned, the latter was to be avoided at all costs.

"Dude's like a bull in a china shop," Hawkeye grumbled. He had lived in Chicago for ten years, but he hadn't lost his SoCal dialect. "Which is usually fine. But this job required a little finesse, yo."

"Savoy told me the pigs questioned Bulldog about Marcel Monroe," Crutch added, "but, of course, he played dumb."

"Fuck yeah." Termite chuckled. "Not much of a stretch for that fat fuck." The wrench he liked to keep in his boot was on the table. As was his habit, he spun the tool in circles.

"Enough, Termite!" Venom slammed his hand on the wooden surface. The four bottles of beer atop it jumped and rattled. "I don't wanna hear another word against Bulldog. He's gonna do time for this job. We damned well better give him our gratitude and support."

Termite swallowed and nodded. "Fuck. You're right. Sorry."

"Hey." Hawkeye turned to Crutch. "So what the heck happened to the gun Bulldog used to off the banger?"

"Same as always," Crutch assured him. "We took it apart and scattered the pieces around Lake Michigan. The cops will never find it. So as long as Bulldog keeps his trap shut—"

"Which he *will*," Venom insisted.

"Which he will," Crutch agreed. "There will be nothing to link Bulldog to Monroe's murder. Savoy says as long as we watch ourselves and don't answer any of the cops' questions, we should be good."

A thought burned in the back of Venom's brain. "What did Savoy come up with for a motive?"

Crutch laughed. "You're going to love this. Savoy says Bulldog will claim he kidnapped her to force her to write an article about a *real* MC. Apparently"—Crutch's voice was heavy with sarcasm—"Bulldog was sick of the way TV and movies portray us and wanted to set the record straight."

Hawkeye snorted. "Radical, dude."

Venom shrugged. "It's a good motive. It'll be impossible for the prosecution in his case to disprove it."

"Okay. So then, what are we supposed to do?" Termite asked. His red hair was pulled back in a ponytail, and a black bandana covered his forehead. "We have no fuckin' sergeant at arms."

"True," Venom allowed. "But more important than finding a replacement for Bulldog while he finishes his stint inside is finding out why that fat fuck of a detective brought up Iraq this morning." He drummed his fingers on the table.

"Speaking of Iraq…" Crutch said. "Bulldog said Samantha railed at him, asked him all kinds of questions when she was in the back of that van, including the who, what, and how of us getting the weapons out of the Sandbox."

"Yo! What…the…*hell*?" Hawkeye ran a hand through his scraggly blond hair. "How could she know any of that? *Shit!*"

"Cool your jets." Venom lifted a hand. "It might not be as bad as it sounds."

"Well, that's good, bro." Hawkeye's voice was laced with sarcasm. "'Cause it sounds pretty damn bad."

"Before we jump to conclusions"—Venom knew it was important to project calm even though his stomach had balled into a fist—"we needa get our hands on the reporter and find out exactly what she knows."

"Given Bulldog's botched kidnapping," Crutch said, watching a smoke ring drift toward the ceiling fan overhead, "if we snatch her, the first place the pigs will come looking for her is here." He turned and surveyed the room with its wood-paneled walls, neon beer signs, and general man-cave air. "Well, not *here* exactly." The Basilisk's clubhouse was in the basement of a flower shop owned by Termite's second cousin. Its location was only known to those loyal to the club. "But they'll come looking for *us*."

Venom waved his hand unconcernedly. "They won't find a thing. Same as always."

"So then, what's the plan?" Crutch asked. "How do we get our hands on Miss Tate?"

The thrill of the hunt filled Venom. It'd been a long time since he'd been involved in bringing down human quarry. He leaned forward, a smile stretching his lips. "I think I have an idea."

———

Emily watched Ozzie slap more lasagna onto Samantha's plate even though Samantha was laughing, shaking her head, and making a half dozen excuses for why she couldn't eat another bite.

"That last reason was so lame it needs crutches," Ozzie scoffed, forking a bite between his teeth and grinning the whole time.

"Are you still flapping your lips?" Samantha came right back at him. When Ozzie opened his mouth, she lifted a hand. "Shhh. Let me enjoy the visual image of duct tape over your mouth for just a little while longer."

"Bondage?" Ozzie waggled his eyebrows. "Now we're talking."

"Are we?" Samantha cupped her chin in her hand and

batted her eyelashes at him. "Are you *sure* you want to go there?"

"I'm a guy, sweetheart." Ozzie spread his arms wide. "I pretty much live there."

"Then what are we waiting for? Let's head to one of those outbuildings"—Samantha hooked a thumb over her shoulder to the small rectangular structures BKI used for parts storage, weapons bunkers, and a home gym—"and get it on like Donkey Kong."

"Fine by me." Ozzie acted like he was about to stand from the table.

Samantha stopped him with, "Oh, sorry. Did you think I was talking about you? I meant Becky."

Becky choked on her lasagna and reached for her glass of wine.

"If you're serious about the Becky thing"—Ozzie leered at Samantha—"I could just sit in the corner and watch."

Samantha's cheeks flushed bright red. "Okay, you big jerk. You win that round."

"I swear I'd be so quiet." Ozzie's eyes positively gleamed in the dimming light. The sun was sinking low in the sky, bathing everyone seated around the picnic table in a warm glow. "I wouldn't say a thing."

"Stop it!" Samantha laughed, raising her hands to cool her cheeks. "I already said you won!"

"Everyone heard that, right?" Ozzie pointed his fork around the table. "I won against the indomitable Samantha Tate. Record it for posterity."

The wind blew in from the river and across the huge brick wall that surrounded the back of the compound. It smelled of fish, wet vegetation, and a city that was winding down for the day.

"What did you win, Ozzie?" Franklin, Michelle and

Jake's five-year-old son, asked from his seat beside his mother. Michelle had JJ, Franklin's eighteen-month-old brother, on her lap. She was trying to feed the baby lasagna without getting most of it on his face, hands, and bib. Emily would say Michelle was only marginally successful.

"Bragging rights, squirt." Ozzie winked at the little boy. "Which is just about the best thing ever."

Franklin grinned, shoving a huge bite of garlic bread into his mouth, his little legs swinging happily. Excluding Emily, only two of the BKI women who were currently in town were gathered in the courtyard. Those who weren't on-site would find a quiet spot to conference call in when the time arrived for their men to phone from the field. The two who *were* on-site? Well, they were trying with all their might not to let their nerves show.

Luckily, Samantha and Ozzie had been doing a good job of distracting everyone with their lively banter. Intentionally, no doubt, on Ozzie's part. Quite innocently on Samantha's.

Emily took a sip of wine, pretending she wasn't *insanely* aware of Christian, who was seated across from her. That was difficult, considering he was looking all suave and handsome and so un-muss-able that all she want to do was muss him. Ruffle his hair. Wrinkle his shirt. Hide his razor.

It was becoming an obsession. *He* was becoming an obsession. To distract herself, she studied Ozzie and Samantha.

She hadn't known Ozzie before coming to work for Black Knights Inc. But from what little she'd heard, the edgy, slightly withdrawn man she'd come to know over the past few months was not the *real* Ozzie. She thought back on something Becky told her one night after they'd shared a bottle of wine. *"The man you see today isn't the same one we've all come to know and love. I mean, he still tries to joke around, still tries to smile and laugh, but everything seems contrived."*

Emily hadn't had anything to compare Ozzie's behavior to, so she'd had to take Becky's word for the difference. *Now*, however, she could see what Becky was talking about. She could see the change in Ozzie. With Samantha by his side, he seemed more like the man the others had described. Easygoing. Funny. Quick to laugh and even quicker to flash that devilishly handsome smile.

The reporter is good for him, she thought.

Of course, there was a problem. A big, honking one that started and ended with the opposite sides of the coin their respective jobs put them on.

Her mind was ripped from the problem when Franklin—who was in the middle of sneaking a ranch dressing–coated piece of lettuce from his salad and shoving it beneath the picnic table to a happily waiting Fido—asked, "What's bondage?"

Everyone choked and sputtered and tried not to laugh. Everyone except for Michelle. She did her best to glare Ozzie into the ground. "Oh, for goodness' sake. Thank you *very* much for introducing that word into my son's vocabulary, wonder boy."

Realizing he'd been given something off-limits, Franklin grinned until the adorable dimples he'd inherited from his father winked in his cheeks. "Bondage! Bondage! Bondage!" he singsonged, his feet swinging faster.

"Yessiree, Bob. You are *so* dead," Michelle swore to Ozzie just as the alarm on her iPhone chimed. She and Becky drew in so much air that Emily was surprised there was any oxygen left for the rest of the group to breathe.

It was time. Time for the ladies to find out if their men were safe and sound or…*not*.

"What?" Samantha glanced around. "What's wrong?"

"Oh, nothing," Michelle assured her, handing a lasagna-covered JJ over to Christian. "That's just the alarm letting me know the dessert is ready."

Samantha blinked. "That must be some tiramisu."

"It frickin' *is*," Becky assured her, gathering up dirty dishes. Her hands shook, but she was quick to disguise the tremor by wrapping her fingers tightly around used cutlery. "I'll help you cut it and plate it, Michelle."

"I'll help too." Samantha pushed to a stand.

"No!" a chorus of voices rang out, and Samantha instantly retook her seat, eyes wide.

"You're our guest!" Emily chirped, kicking Christian's foot beneath the table.

He scowled at her. She sent him a look that said *Little help, please?*

"Right-oh." Christian nodded, pretending to gobble the sticky, sauce-covered finger that JJ tried to poke into his mouth. For all his dandyish ways, Christian didn't seem to mind when one of the children got him dirty. In fact, he hadn't said a word last week when Penni's son's diaper failed and Christian's favorite cashmere sweater got doused with sticky, green baby poo. "Take advantage of your guest status while you can, luv. Becky tends to put newcomers to work on day three. More wine, yeah?"

"Oh…uh, sure," Samantha said, still looking bewildered as Christian refilled her glass.

"Back in a sec," Michelle said. "And you." She pointed a finger at Ozzie.

"Me?" He blinked innocently.

"Yes, you. I don't see another wonder boy around

here." It was Michelle's pet name for Ozzie. "Don't think I don't realize you were saved by the bell."

"I don't know what you're talking about." Ozzie feigned innocence.

Michelle made a mom-like *tsking* sound before turning to follow Becky inside. The call usually only lasted a couple of minutes, and it was up to Emily, Ozzie, and Christian to distract the kids and Samantha during that time.

"So what's this I hear about you turning down a little jiggery-pokery last night?" Christian asked Ozzie, bouncing JJ on his knee until the baby burbled with delight.

Okay, so not necessarily the tack I would have taken, but... Emily popped a crust of bread into her mouth and settled in to watch the show. There were two things she'd quickly learned after joining the Blacks Knights. The first was that the idea of privacy was pretty much a joke. And the second was that everything and anything was fair game.

"Excuse me?" Ozzie sputtered. Then he turned to glare at Samantha. "You *told* him?"

"Well..." The look on Samantha's face said she was praying for the patio pavers to open up so the ground could swallow her whole. "He thought we *had*, and I...I thought it was better if I set the record...uh...straight."

"So what's the issue?" Christian asked. "Your knob stop working?"

"My knob works just fine!"

When Samantha said, "It does. I can vouch," Ozzie choked. "What?" Samantha blinked. "I'm just setting the—"

"Record straight," Ozzie finished for her. "You seem to be obsessed with that, don't you?"

Samantha pointed to herself. "Hello? Reporter?"

This is better than reality TV. Emily happily sloshed another splash of pinot noir into her glass.

"What's jiggery-pokery?" Franklin asked. Now that his mother was gone, he was no longer trying to hide the fact that he was feeding all his salad to the dog. He shoved a huge handful of the dressing-covered stuff beneath the table, giggling when Fido licked his fingers clean.

"Ohhhh!" Ozzie crowed with delight, pointing a finger at Christian. "Michelle is going to *kill* you!"

It occurred to Emily then and there that with these people, and for the first time in a long time, she felt like she belonged.

———

Ozzie wasn't sure how much time had passed since Becky and Michelle disappeared inside the warehouse, but it felt like an eternity. Christian was still doing a bang-up job of distracting Samantha and Franklin by telling Samantha she should ask Franklin to recite the alphabet. *Thank heavens they've moved on from the subject of my knob.*

As Franklin singsonged the letters while Samantha and Emily kept the beat by clapping their hands, Ozzie surreptitiously glanced at his watch. Oh-nineteen-hundred-and-five. Exactly five minutes since his brothers-in-arms should have made the call back to home base.

His stomach clenched around the lasagna, and he immediately regretted his third helping. Of course, that wasn't his only regret. Not by far.

It should be me out there. I don't have a wife. I don't have kids. I should be the one risking it all. Not them.

It was the same thought he had every night at this

time. The same thought that brought with it the terrible spiral of *what-ifs*. What if he never healed enough to go back into the field? What if he became a burden to those around him, good for nothing but a joke and smile? What if they asked him to leave, to move on, to find a place that better suited his limitations?

And right behind all those *what-ifs* rolled the twin wonders of self-pity and remorse. He hated himself for…so much. For precipitating his mother's mental illness. For not pulling Julia Ledbetter out of that deadly bed in an attempt to change her mind about letting him stay. For not being with the Knights on this mission, letting them down when they needed him most. For feeling sorry for himself and turning into his father, a man who hadn't been able to move on after all his dreams were shattered.

The screen door creaked on its hinges, the ladies backlit by the interior light so that all he could see were their silhouettes.

Finally, he thought, the nerve endings in his neck and shoulders firing, making his muscles twitch. To keep from jumping up to demand a situation report, he pressed a thumb into a spot on his thigh that was particularly sensitive. The bright flare of pain kept him seated and reminded him of his place in all this.

He might love the men of Black Knights Inc. like family, but he wasn't *their* family. The women were. The women and the children. And right now, the women's worries, their fears, their daily struggle to keep it together took precedence over his.

Michelle was the first to push through the door. But her back was to him, which meant he couldn't see her expression. His heart hammered in his chest. Becky appeared next, arms laden with plates piled high with

Michelle's famous tiramisu. But she was watching her feet on the uneven flagstones. He couldn't see her eyes, and his breath burned through his lungs. Then—*bless her*—she was kind enough to lift her head and zero in on him, shooting him a quick wink.

Fuckin' A. He blew out a ragged breath and stopped applying pressure to his wounded thigh. The pain ratcheted down from sharp agony to a dull throb.

Everyone's okay. Everyone made it through another day.

"You okay?" Samantha whispered.

"Fine. Leg cramp." And that wasn't *totally* a lie. He just left out the part about having done it to himself.

Samantha reached beneath the table and placed her hand atop his thigh. Her fingers were cool, even through the denim of his jeans, but her touch sent heat racing through his blood. "Should I massage it?" she asked, completely innocently.

Dear God, yes. She should massage it. And then work her way up to massaging—

"So what's next for you, Samantha?" Becky leaned between him and Samantha so she could set the desserts in front of them. It forced Samantha to withdraw her hand, and Ozzie breathed a sigh of relief…or regret. He wasn't sure which.

"What do you mean?" Samantha eyed the layered concoction in front of her with equal parts eagerness and dismay. Ozzie understood. He was stuffed. But the tiramisu was a siren's call.

"I mean," Becky said, taking her seat, "the man who was after you is in jail. The police have no leads on who took out your informant. And they have no way to tie either the informant, the jailbird biker, or his Basilisk pals to the weapon with the Iraqi serial number. So what's next?"

Samantha shrugged and dug into her dessert. "I'm not

exactly sure. The police are going to do their thing. Oh my Lord, this is good."

Michelle beamed and nodded. "Why, thank you," she said as she plucked JJ from Christian's arms.

"They'll poke around, ask a few questions," Samantha continued, "but I think they've pinned most of their hopes on Ozzie and what his military contacts might be able to provide on the service records of the Basilisks' president and vice president."

Becky lifted a brow and turned to Ozzie. "Your... military contacts?"

"From my time in the navy." He shot her a meaning-ful look before pasting on a wide grin. "You know me. I make friends everywhere. And I've got a guy pretty high up the ladder who owes me a favor."

Which, again, wasn't *totally* a lie. General Pete Fuller, the head of the Joint Chiefs and BKI's direct boss besides the president himself, *did* owe Ozzie a favor for the time Ozzie had thwarted an attack on the general's personal computer by a group of Chinese spies.

So yeah. Not totally *a lie.* Still, Ozzie squirmed in his seat. Continuing to deceive Samantha was beginning to make him feel dirty on the inside. Like, with each couched word and misleading comment, a black stain spread across the fabric of his being.

Becky had forgone the tiramisu in favor of a cherry-flavored Dum Dum lollipop. She spoke around the stick. "And have you contacted this person already?"

"Snuck out and made a phone call while Samantha was giving her statement to the police," he said. "I'm just waiting to hear back one way or the other."

"So I guess you'll be spending the night again," Becky said to Samantha. "Or maybe a *lot* of nights. This thing sounds like it could drag on for a while."

Ozzie could easily read the strain on Becky's face. Having Samantha inside the compound kept everyone on their toes during a time when tensions were already running high. He *hated* that he was causing them more worry and stress. But what else could he do? Samantha needed his protection, and he hoped the lovely ladies of Black Knights Inc. understood that. Just as he'd protect them until his dying breath, he'd do the same for Samantha.

Whoa. Had he just lumped her into the same category as the women seated around the picnic table? Women he loved down to the marrow of his bones? Yep, it seemed he had.

So what the hell does that *mean?*

He didn't dare dwell on the answer.

"I…" Samantha swallowed and glanced around the table. "I don't want to be an imposition, so I could—"

"Forget about it." Michelle waved her off. "A friend in need is a friend indeed. You'll stay here as long as you require wonder boy's protection."

Samantha looked down at the napkin in her lap and swallowed. "Thank you." Her voice was a little hoarse. "After all these years and all the grief I've given you all, I don't think I deserve—"

Ozzie couldn't bear to hear the end of that sentence. Samantha had only done her job. And he refused to let her apologize for it. "Who's on dish duty tonight?" he interrupted. "My vote is Christian. All in favor?"

Every hand at the table, except for Christian's, went in the air. Michelle even lifted one of JJ's chubby little arms.

"It's settled then," Ozzie declared.

Christian turned to glare at him. "You, sir, are proof that evolution *can* go in reverse."

"And you, sir, are a twelve-year-old in a man suit," Ozzie was quick to come back.

"I got your twelve-year-old right here, friend." Christian feigned an American accent and reached beneath the table to grab his unit.

"Please." Ozzie rolled his eyes. "Is that supposed to be some sort of threat? I've seen earthworms bigger and scarier than anything you've got. Remember that big rain we had a couple of weeks ago, Becky? When all those worms crawled out of the ground and got stuck on the patio pavers?"

"Don't drag me into this." Becky waved her hands. "I won't be the yardstick in your—" She glanced at Franklin. "In your *johnson*-measuring contest."

"Yardstick?" Ozzie asked. He and Christian exchanged a glance. "Not ruler?"

"Just how big *is* Boss?" Christian demanded, blinking rapidly and fighting a grin. "Oh, you poor dear. I should think you need to visit your physician. And soon."

Becky blushed. "Both of you can shut up now."

"Who's Johnson?" Franklin asked.

"That's it!" Michelle threw her napkin on the table. "This meal is officially over!"

Chapter 14

"I CAN'T UNDERSTAND WHY WE'RE KNOCKING ABOUT teaching him baseball when we could be schooling him on a *real* game," Christian said as Samantha sat comfortably ensconced on a chaise longue along with the rest of the women who had hunkered down onto various pieces of patio furniture to watch Ozzie, Christian, and little Franklin toss around a baseball.

Thanks to Christian, the dishes had been cleared away and piled into the dishwasher. He had complained the whole time, but apparently, he accepted the almighty power of the group vote. The sun had long since set. A local radio station crooned R & B from a set of speakers mounted on the back wall of the warehouse beneath a rolled-up cylinder of fabric that Samantha assumed provided a canopy for the courtyard when extended. With a blanket over her knees and a third glass of wine in hand, she felt ridiculously content.

She shouldn't. She *knew* she shouldn't. There was so much left unresolved. So much left to do. But she couldn't shake a warm feeling of comfort.

It's just the wine, she assured herself, but a little voice piped up, insisting it was more than that.

"And what is a *real* game?" Ozzie asked, his hair glinting in the glow of the artificial lights bolted atop the brick wall surrounding the courtyard and outbuildings. He carefully tossed the ball into Franklin's outstretched baseball mitt so the little boy didn't have to do more than curl his glove around it to catch it.

"Why, cricket, of course," Christian declared, leaping into the air to snatch the wild throw Franklin sent whizzing above his head. The move caused his shirt to ride up, revealing his muscle-packed stomach and the trail of dark hair that started at his belly button and disappeared into his jeans.

Beside Samantha, Emily sucked in a startled breath.

Samantha couldn't fault the woman. For the last hour, she herself had been mesmerized by the flex of the muscles in Ozzie's broad back. By the shift of his round butt cheeks inside the denim of his jeans. Separate, the two men were delectable. Taken together, they were almost too much to bear. Their differences seemed to highlight the unique appeal of each. Where Christian was dark, Ozzie was golden. Where Christian was perfectly put together, Ozzie was unkempt and wild and all the sexier for it.

The dynamic duo. And their superpower is flat-out, panties-on-the-floor sex appeal.

"If we charged admission," she whispered to Emily, "we'd be millionaires by next week."

"I like the way your mind works." Emily nodded, taking a sip of wine. "But you're thinking too small. If we charged admission, sold T-shirts with their faces on them, and added a Win a Date with the Hunks contest, we'd be millionaires in forty-eight hours."

Samantha laughed. She didn't know Emily well, but the woman seemed like someone she might call a friend. Judging by the way she talked, they were both South Siders. That alone was enough to warrant instant sisterhood. "Yeah, but we'd have to share them. Not sure how I'd feel about that."

Emily turned to her, eyes narrowed. "Mind if I ask you a question?"

Samantha tensed. An inquiry preceded by *Mind if I ask you a question* was almost always of a personal nature. "If I said no, would that stop you?"

"Nope." Emily shrugged, plowing right ahead with "What are your intentions?"

A windy breath left Samantha's lungs. She had a strange sense of déjà vu. Wasn't that the exact question Donny had asked Ozzie? "What do you mean?"

"Toward Ozzie. What do you want from him?"

"Wouldn't the better question be what does *he* want from *me*? After all, he's the hot-rod bed-hopper extraordinaire." The hot-rod bed-hopper extraordinaire who seemed to be having second thoughts about taking their relationship to the next level. Ugh!

"That he may be, but he's also an amazing person. Crazy smart, fiercely loyal, and handsome as the devil himself. If you're trying to—"

Emily didn't get a chance to finish what she was saying, because Franklin piped up with "Crickets? What are you talking about, Christian?" His little lisp turned the Brit's name into *Chrishian*. "Crickets are bugs!"

Samantha wasn't sure if she should be annoyed by the interruption or relieved. *Why do all the BKI women keep acting like* I'm *the potential bad guy in this situation?* It boggled her mind.

"Yes. Crickets *are* bugs." Christian nodded, tossing the ball to Ozzie. "But cricket, singular, is a sport. The best sport on the planet besides football."

"I like football." Franklin grunted with the "effort" of catching the ball Ozzie once more tossed directly into his glove. "The Bears are my favorite team, but Daddy says they're s'posed to be shitty this year."

Every adult in the courtyard choked. Except for Michelle. "Franklin!" she sputtered, then shushed JJ, who had nodded off against her chest but stirred at her outburst. "For goodness' sake! You know that word is naughty." She narrowed her eyes until Franklin looked down at his feet and dug at the seam between two flag-stones with the toe of his sneaker.

"Sorry, Momma," he mumbled.

"Uh-huh." Michelle muttered under her breath. "And add your father to the list of men I need to murder."

Franklin's little cheeks were bright. Being scolded in front of the others, particularly men he looked up to, had embarrassed him. Ozzie quickly came to the boy's aid. "Well, Christian isn't referring to American football anyway. He's talking about soccer."

Franklin lifted his head and wrinkled his nose at Christian. "You think *soccer* is the best sport? No way! It's baseball!" To prove his point, he chucked another zinger above Christian's head.

"Americans," Christian lamented as he once again snagged the ball midair. "You're all hopeless gobshites."

"And on that note," Michelle said, "it's time to call it a night."

"No!" Franklin howled. "Ten more minutes!"

"Nope." Michelle shook her head. "You have school tomorrow, mister."

"Aw, Momma!" Franklin did the disappointed, foot-stomping dance all kids seemed preprogrammed to know. "Please?"

Michelle pushed from the bright-red Adirondack chair, patting JJ's bottom. "How many times has argu-ing ever worked with me?" she asked her older son.

Franklin slipped off his baseball mitt, shoulders slouching. With his bottom lip thrust out, he admit-ted, "Never."

"That's right." Michelle tousled his hair. "But that

doesn't mean I don't appreciate the effort. Now, tell everyone good night."

"G'night, everyone," Franklin muttered sullenly.

Michelle shook her head, her gray eyes filled with love for her pouting son. "Yes, good night, everyone."

When the trio headed toward the back door, Becky and Emily pushed up from their seats. Becky stretched her arms over her head and let loose with a noisy yawn. "I'm calling it a night too."

"Me three," Emily added, her dark hair catching the lights and shining like melted chocolate. "'Night all."

Christian was quick to add his good-byes, and before Samantha knew it, she and Ozzie were alone.

"And then there were two." He tucked his hands into his pockets and rocked back on his heels. She couldn't read the look he shot her from beneath the fan of his thick lashes. It seemed a little bashful. But that didn't make sense. Ozzie was a lot of things. Bashful wasn't one of them. "Do you…uh…do you feel like turning in? You've had a hell of a day. *Again*."

"I seem to be making a habit of that, don't I?" She downed the last of her wine and pushed up from the lounge chair, carefully folding the blanket Michelle had given her into a neat square. "But no. I'm not tired yet. Of course, if you want to—"

"No." He shook his head. "I'm still keyed up. So… what should we…uh…what should we do?"

Samantha lifted an eyebrow. Maybe it was the wine. Maybe it was the magic of the moonlight. Or, hell, maybe she was sick and tired of avoiding the subject. She blurted, "Oh, I can think of a thing or two. Both of them involve you naked."

He choked on a laugh. "Wow. You don't mince words, do you?"

"Not tonight."

"Huh." He nodded. Then, "How is your head?"

Was it just her, or was that question out of nowhere and seemingly apropos of nothing? "Fine. The wine helped."

"Good. That's good." He rocked back on his heels again.

"Why do I get the impression you're stalling?"

His eyes glittered when his gaze slammed into hers. "Stalling what, Samantha?"

"Stalling *us*," she declared with exasperation. "I mean, I get it. Last night, you played the gentleman card and put on the brakes because you thought I was too vulnerable after everything that happened. You thought I might have second thoughts in the bright light of day. Fine. Good. But here I am, standing in front of you, telling you I *didn't* have any second thoughts. So if you would kindly stop treating me like a plague carrier and pick up where we left off, I'd really, *really* appreciate it."

He shook his head and looked at the sky. It made his Adam's apple bulge in his tan neck. She wanted to lick it. Or *bite* it. "But that's just it, isn't it? All those reasons I had last night apply again tonight. You were whacked over the head and kidnapped off the street. You might pretend it's nothing, that it didn't affect you, but I know it did. And now you've had a little to drink. So maybe you're not in the right frame of mind to—"

"*Bullshit!*" she spat out, feeling heat rush into her face.

Thankfully, she wasn't alone in her affliction. A deep flush stained Ozzie's cheekbones when he blinked at her. "Excuse me?"

"That's complete and utter bullshit." And then she

decided, *What the hell. In for a penny, in for a pound.*
"You're scared shitless you'll hurt me when this thing
between us reaches its inevitable conclusion. So you're
trying to stop it from starting in the first place."

His face shuttered. "Is there…" He stopped and swallowed. "Is there an inevitable conclusion?"

"Oh, come on, Ozzie," she scoffed, ignoring the burning pain that ignited behind her breastbone. "I know your
game. You're a renowned playboy, Don Juan brought to
life. So let's make a deal, shall we? I won't do you the
disservice of pretending you're something you're not, if
you promise you won't do me the disservice of thinking
I don't know my own mind." Now that she was on a
roll, she couldn't stop. "I like you. I respect you. I have
fun with you. But more importantly, right now, I *want*
you. And whether that's for one night or two nights or
ten nights is up for discussion. But I don't, not for one
minute, think this thing can last forever."

She winced. That was the closest she'd ever come to
lying to him.

Although the rational part of her *didn't* think they
would make it to the altar, swearing *'til death do us
part*, the irrational side of her, the romantic side, the
side that had already fallen a little in love with him,
wanted exactly that. It was the same irrational, romantic,
lovesick side of her that held out hope that if she could
only get him into bed, if she could only show him that
besides friendship and laughs, they could share fiery-hot
passion, he'd change his ways and suddenly settle down.
He'd realize she was…*the one*.

*Seriously, Sammie? That shit only happens in sappy
rom-coms and cheesy romances.*

She violently quashed the voice of dissent in her
head. Okay, so yes, it was insanity. *She* was insane. But

that's what falling in love was, right? A socially acceptable form of insanity?

His face gave her zero clues to what he was thinking. So she was left with no recourse but to wait for him to tell her. One second stretched into ten. She could count the passing of time by the hard thud of her heart. Ten seconds quickly became fifteen. The breath had strangled in her lungs, and low oxygen made her brain buzz. When twenty seconds rolled by, she lost it. Patience had never been one of her virtues, but it was particularly hard to come by when her silly heart and all her far-fetched hopes were on the line.

"Ugh." She blew out a breath. "That's it. Time's up."

Stuffing the blanket under one arm, she grabbed his hand and dragged him toward an outbuilding he had shown her on the tour he had given her months ago. It housed a small gym. And since everyone in the compound was now inside the warehouse, the space promised to give her precisely what she needed.

Privacy!

Ozzie's whole life, he had given his love away.

First to the endless string of women who had come through his father's house, though none had ever stuck, because none had ever been his mother. Then to the procession of women in his own life. But *they* had never stuck, because they all thought he was the good-time guy. The man they liked for a laugh and a sweaty roll in the hay. Not the one they brought home to their parents.

He had accepted it. Expected it, even. Until now. Until Samantha…

He didn't want his time with her to be just another

wild story to add to his tally of wild stories. She was different. *They* were different. Or so he had thought.

He was a walking zombie, numbly following where she led. It wasn't until the door slammed shut on the gym and the smell of heavily bleached towels tunneled up his nose that he realized where she'd taken him.

"So how about it?" She hit the light switch.

He blinked against the glow of the fluorescent bulbs to find her standing directly in front of him, hands on hips, dark eyes glinting.

He knew exactly to which "it" she was referring. *The* it. As in doing *it*. Because he was nothing but the good-time guy, good for *it* and not much else.

A wave of hurt...of *anger* crashed over him, washing away all those lovely lunch dates and walks through the park, washing away all his good intentions and self-preservation.

Last night, he'd convinced himself that if he kept their relationship platonic, she would stick around. That he could keep his secrets *and* keep her.

So much for that.

Her words in the courtyard proved sticking around wasn't something she had ever considered. Acid churned in his stomach, and he did something he had never done before. He was cruel to someone he cared about.

"Sweetheart," he snarled like the wounded animal he was, "if you're hurting for it that badly, I'll gladly throw you a bone."

Her lashes fluttered. He saw the confusion and shock on her face. But he didn't allow either of them time to dwell on what a horrendous ass he'd just made of himself. Instead, he wrapped a hand around her arm and spun her until her back pressed flat against the door.

The blanket that had been under her arm fell to

the floor. The R & B still playing outside drifted in through the thin walls. Treadmills and weight benches were at his back. But the only thing in front of him was Samantha. Smart, sexy, stubborn Samantha. The woman who challenged him and teased him and had made him hope that perhaps there was still a little of the old Ozzie left beneath all the uncertainty and self-pity and remorse.

The same woman who had utterly crushed him with a few careless words…

Without thinking, without *allowing* himself to think, he settled his length against her, letting her feel the erection that had plagued him all damn day. She dragged in a ragged breath and searched his face.

Afraid of what she might see, what *he* might see reflected in her eyes—specifically a mirror image that looked far too much like his father—he used one hand to fist her wrists above her head and the other to lock her hips in place. Without hesitation or finesse, he slammed his mouth over hers.

He wanted to punish her. He wanted to hurt her the way she had hurt him. He wanted to…*love* her.

And that's when it hit him. He already *did* love her.

Too bad all she wants from me is a quick, dirty fuck.

Samantha wasn't sure what had happened. All she knew was that, for a moment, there had been something in Ozzie's eyes she hadn't seen before. A hardness. A bitterness. And that thing he had said about throwing her a bone? That wasn't like him. It was too coarse, too rude. Ozzie was neither of those things. But then… Oh! Then he kissed her, and she couldn't think.

His tongue was a wet, hot wonder invading her mouth

over and over. Filling her up, then leaving her empty and hungry, only to fill her up again. And his body… Holy fucking smokes, his body was a wall of hard, wonderful flesh. He rubbed himself against her, letting her feel the resistance of his muscles, the flex of his cock even as he kept her hands imprisoned in the vise of his grip.

She wanted to touch him. She wanted to stroke him and squeeze him. Not being able to was a frustration and a huge turn-on. She was at the mercy of this big, warm, wonderful man, and she reveled in the sensation of being powerless against his desires. Warmth settled low in her belly and quickly grew into scorching heat.

"Ozzie." She gasped his name when he allowed her up for a breath. The taste of him was sharp on her tongue. The sweetness of the dessert he'd eaten mixed with the flavor of the man himself until she was giddy, drunk on each unique note.

"Tell me what you want," he demanded, leaving a string of kisses across her cheek and down the side of her neck. When he reached her hammering pulse-point, he wrapped his lips around her flesh and sucked.

She felt the pull of his mouth at the tips of her breasts and lower, in her belly and in the empty, lonely place between her thighs. "You," she whispered, giving him the truth. *Her* truth. Wondering if he grasped the magnitude of it. "All I want is you. Every way, any way, just—"

She squeaked when he shoved his uninjured thigh between her legs. It wasn't a gentle move. He wasn't easy with her. But she didn't need easy. She needed hard and hot and…*him*.

With his hand on her hip, he guided her. Dragging her forward along his muscled thigh, pushing her backward. The friction as the seam of her jeans abraded the bundle of nerves at the top of her sex was delicious. She squeezed her inner muscles, intensifying the pressure, the pleasure.

"You like it quick and dirty?" When he was satisfied she'd continue the motion against his thigh on her own, he released her hip to cup her breast. Through the fabric of her shirt, she felt the heat of his palm. Unerringly, he found her nipple, squeezing it between his thumb and forefinger until it grew so hard it hurt. "Or slow and sensual?"

Both! And everything in between, she thought dizzily.

"Let's start with quick and d-dirty," she panted. "And then next time, we can do slow and s—"

He didn't allow her to finish. He pulled her shirt over her head and tossed it behind his back. Her bra was apricot satin, and he took a moment to appreciate the contrast of the color against her pale skin before he reached between her breasts and flipped open the front closure. It joined her shirt on the floor a second later. And then her hands were pinned above her head again. The position lifted her breasts, her nipples pointing up at him, begging for the heat of his mouth.

He didn't resist their silent plea.

Dipping his head, he caught one taut peak between his lips. Compared to the air inside the outbuilding, the heat of his mouth was scorching. The lick of his tongue was a flame of fire against her sensitive flesh. Her breath caught in her lungs when he flicked his tongue back and forth, her toes curling inside her shoes and her eyes rolling back in her head.

She thought his hair tickled her chin, but she couldn't be sure. She thought he reached down to thumb open the button on her jeans, but she was too overcome with the erotic joy of his mouth on her nipple and his thigh between her legs to concentrate on anything else. Of course, when she felt the rough pads of his fingers slip between her swollen folds, she knew she hadn't imagined either of those things.

"So wet," he grumbled against her breast, rubbing his fingers back and forth. Pleasure twanged through her as she bathed him in her need. "So sweet. I have to taste."

He released her wrists, and her arms fell uselessly to her sides. When he removed his thigh so he could pull her jeans and panties down over her hips, she was glad the door was at her back to support her, or else she would have slid into a puddle on the floor. The pleasure he pressed on her made her boneless. The promise of the pleasure to come made her quickly kick off her boots and step out of her jeans and panties, leaving her in nothing but her stocking feet. Ozzie impatiently pulled her socks off next, seeming to want her completely naked. And then his next words confirmed it.

"But before I taste," he said, his voice guttural with desire, "I want to look."

Samantha had stood in front of men in nothing but her birthday suit before. But none had ever been Ozzie. Ozzie...with his ability to really *look,* to really *see.* The urge to cover herself made the muscles in her arms clench. But she'd asked for this. *Demanded* it, actually. And he'd granted her request.

Fair is fair.

Flattening her hands against the door, she forced herself not to hide. Instead, she spread her feet a little wider, letting him see just how wet he'd made her, how swollen she was for him.

A strangled sound erupted from the back of his throat. He fell to his knees as if his legs could no longer support him.

Samantha had no illusions about her body. She had

strong arms and a good butt, decent boobs and a stomach that was flat enough. But there was nary a thigh gap in sight. Nor were her legs as long as she'd like them to be. And her hips? Well, let's just say there was no exercise on the planet she'd found to get rid of her saddlebags.

Still, when she dared to glance at Ozzie on his knees in front of her, she saw nothing but reverence in his eyes. He looked at her and saw something beautiful. And in that moment, she *felt* beautiful.

"I pictured you like this after I went to bed last night," he admitted, swallowing hard. "I touched myself and thought about how beautiful you are. But my imagination didn't do you justice."

Holy hellfire. He'd thought about her and *touched* himself? The erotic picture in her head made the ache between her legs almost unbearable. She squeezed her thighs together, hoping to dull the delightful misery.

He grunted as if he knew what she was doing. And maybe he did. Because he lifted his hands and forced her legs apart.

"Ozzie." His name was a plea in and of itself. But she didn't think it hurt to add, "Please, touch me. I ache, and—Oh Lord, yesssss."

He didn't hesitate to slide one thick finger inside her. Because she was so hot, so ready, her body offered little resistance. Instead, it welcomed his intrusion with a hot rush of wetness.

He made a noise. It was a breathy *unhhh* of sound. As if he couldn't stand it a moment longer, he leaned forward and put his mouth on her.

Now, Samantha had never been a huge fan of cunnilingus. The men she had dated, while wildly exuberant, had also been pitifully unskilled. They either lapped at her like a cat with spilled milk or else sucked so hard, she thought her clit might pop right off. But Ozzie…

Oh, he did neither of those things. In fact, she couldn't say for sure *what* he did, but whatever it was, it was… *wonderful*. With his lips and his teeth and his tongue— not to mention the finger inside her—he created a head-spinning, toe-curling hedonistic profusion of sensation. And before she knew it, he had built her orgasm to dizzying heights. Pleasure was a vibrant, pulsing thing inside her. Muscles she hadn't realized she possessed spasmed and quivered.

"Ozzie!" She speared her fingers into his hair. To push him away? To pull him closer? She couldn't tell. It was so good. Too good. She couldn't take it anymore and—

The sound that keened from the back of her throat was one she'd never heard before. And forevermore, she would recognize it as the noise of pure, transcendent physical rapture. Her body exploded. Pleasure pulsed. Stars burst behind her squeezed tight eyelids, coalesced, and burst again.

It was ecstasy. It was agony. And she never wanted it to end.

Chapter 15

BEAUTIFUL.

That was the only word to describe Samantha in the throes of release. The smell of her. The taste of her. The sight of her, head thrown back, hips pressed forward, body throbbing in delight.

So beautiful, in fact, that she made Ozzie hurt. Shame formed a lump in his throat. He'd meant to give her the kind of pleasure she would never forget. The kind that would make any man who came after him pale by comparison.

And he had. He was certain that he had. There was no way she could fake her quivering breasts and thighs, her flushed skin, and the fluttering squeeze of her internal muscles around his pumping finger.

But it felt wrong.

He felt wrong.

Because he hadn't done it with generosity, because there was nothing more wonderful than bringing a woman to the brink of ecstasy and then standing back and watching her fling herself over the edge. He'd done it out of malice, out of hurt and anger. Her pleasure had been her punishment.

But it had backfired.

He had tried to use sex as a weapon, but the only one wounded by the experience was him.

Well, no more, he thought. *No more wallowing. No more self-pity*.

Samantha had done him the honor of allowing him to

love her, to *make* love to her, and even if it only lasted a night or two nights or ten nights, he swore to himself he would make the most of every second. Because he *did* love her. It was clear to him now. Loved her the way Boss loved Becky, Snake loved Michelle, the way all the BKI men loved their women, with a fierce, all-encompassing devotion. And even if she didn't feel the same way about him, that didn't mean he couldn't cherish the here and now.

"Beautiful," he whispered, kissing her thigh when the last vestiges of orgasm had shuddered through her. Her taste was sweet on his tongue, making him think of the line from Warrant's song, "Cherry Pie."

Tastes so good, make a grown man cry. He got it. He totally got it.

She blew out a ragged breath and dipped her chin to look at him there on his knees in front of her. Her gaze was slumberous, gratified, and *hot*. She wanted more. More of him. More of them.

His dick was already rock hard. But the heat in her eyes made it harder still. She placed her hands on his shoulders and shoved. His position made his balance precarious. Before he knew it, he was flat on his back on the floor. And Samantha? Well, she was on top of him, straddling him.

"Where in God's name did you learn to do that?" she asked breathlessly, her voice throaty and hoarse. "Never mind. I don't want to know, just…bravo, my friend. Brav-fucking-o."

A wide smile pulled at Ozzie's lips. Only Samantha. Funny, flirty, wildly entertaining Samantha could make him want to laugh and fuck at the same time.

"And now," she said, a wicked gleam making her brown eyes black, "it's *my* turn."

He didn't need to ask what she was talking about. She made it clear when she whipped his T-shirt over his head. She paused to place a soft, warm kiss on each of the red spots left behind by her Taser and then scooted down his legs to tackle the button on his fly.

She was glorious in her nudity. Unabashedly determined to get him in the same state. He was left with a dilemma. Did he touch all those inches of smooth, pale flesh. Or did he tuck his arms behind his head and enjoy the show?

She made the decision for him when she scooted out of his reach. With a determined yank, she pulled his jeans to his knees, revealing the heft of his cock as it bounced against his lower belly and the awful, raised red flesh of his wound.

Her breath caught in her throat when she saw the extent of his injury. His jaw clenched with the effort not to reach down and cover the hideous sight. The bomb had torn away chunks of flesh and muscle, leaving horrendous divots behind. Gouges from the shrapnel that had ripped into him had formed huge, jagged scars. The surgeons had done the best they could. But they had worried more about saving the functionality of his leg and less about aesthetics.

"You got this in a motorcycle crash?" she murmured, and he almost told her the truth then and there. Then she said, "Oh, Ozzie," and surprised him when, instead of being repulsed, she leaned down and carefully, ever so gently pressed her lips to the worst of his scars. Over and over again. Beauty kissing the beast.

"It's ugly." He ground his teeth. "You don't have to—"

"Hush," she grumbled at him, still moving her soft lips over his mutilated flesh. "Scars aren't ugly. They're proof of a life lived. I just wish I could take away your hurt."

His heart Hulked out, growing so huge, he was surprised it didn't burst through his rib cage.

Sweet...

It wasn't a word he usually ascribed to Samantha, but it fit all the same. When you got right down to it, she was so damned sweet.

Her breasts hung down like ripe fruit as she continued to press soft kisses to his mangled leg. Her pert bottom stuck up in the air. It was too much. His dick flexed and bounced, and a hot drop of pre-ejaculate plopped onto his belly.

"Believe me," he told her, his voice strangled. "Right now, I don't feel anything but you. In fact, I'd say right now, I feel the best I've felt in my whole sorry life."

So true. Because for the first time in his whole sorry life, he was with a woman he loved.

"Really?" She quirked a dark eyebrow, and then the only term to describe her was *she-devil*. She ran her hands over his chest, over the erect, aching nubs of his nipples, and down the corrugated muscles of his abs. The feel of her touch was hell on his self-control. He'd never wanted a woman as much as he wanted her. "I think that's a challenge." She leaned forward to take his swollen head into her hot little mouth.

~~~

Ozzie was a big man. In every way. Samantha couldn't take all of him. Still, that didn't stop her from trying. Because *h-h-holy hell*, he tasted sweet. So hard and throbbing against the roof of her mouth.

Just like the rest of him, his cock was gorgeous. Long and thick. *Substantial* was the word she was looking for. She wrapped her hand around his base, amazed when her fingers didn't touch. And then, with deliberate slowness, she hollowed her cheeks and sucked.

A helpless gurgle sounded at the back of his throat. He had been watching her, but now his head hit the floor with a *thunk*. One hand fisted at his side, and the other fisted in her hair. Urging her onward? Telling her to stop?

Since he didn't say, she chose door number one. She bathed his length with her tongue even as she stroked with her hand. His big, muscled body bunched with tension, his hips shifting slightly as if it was killing him to hold still.

"Sweet...*Jesus*," he moaned, sinking his teeth into his lower lip.

He was so damned sexy. So damned...everything. And any satisfaction he'd given her was blown away by the renewed ache of desire. Her breasts felt heavy, the tips ultrasensitive. Between her legs, she thrummed with blood, her flesh twitching with the need to be touched.

But she couldn't stop what she was doing to him. She didn't *want* to stop what she was doing. She had been at his mercy earlier. He was at her mercy now.

"Don't hold back," she commanded, his cock momentarily slipping free of her lips. "I want you to give yourself to me."

And she did, in more ways than just this.

He lifted his head, his eyes dark with desire, slumberous with need. "Then open your mouth"—his voice was so low and gravelly, she had a hard time understanding him—"and take me."

When she did as instructed, his shaft twitched. It was all the encouragement she needed to pull him deep. Again and again. In and out in a slow, slippery glide that partnered with the stroke of her hand as she jerked him in an easy rhythm.

"Fuck," he grunted. His hips pumping. His bootheels

digging into the floor. "Just like that, Samantha. Oh God! Just like that!"

She hummed her agreement, her pleasure. Her whole body buzzed with desire, with the need for ecstasy. But it was *his* ecstasy she was most interested in, and the power she felt knowing she could give it to him.

He made gasping, pained sounds as he thrust between her lips. His movements were restrained. He was holding himself back. Drawing it out. Torturing himself with the pleasure. And the sight of him stretched beneath her, all those flexing muscles, so much…*man*, made her hotter still. She closed her eyes, pulled him deeper.

"Samantha!" He yelled her name, the hand in her hair fisting tighter, the strands pinching with tension. It was a warning. If she was going to stop, now was the time.

She had *no* intention of stopping.

She let him know by working him faster, deeper, harder. He fought it for a while longer, but it was no use. Within seconds, his big body bowed up, and she tasted the first drop of his release.

—⁓—

"What did you do the year after you left the navy?"

It was a good thing Ozzie was already flat on his back, or else her bolt-from-the-clear-blue-sky question would have knocked him on his ass. "What do you mean?"

"I mean"—she pushed up on her elbow, cupping her cheek in her hand—"you finished your contract with the navy, but for thirteen months, there's no record of you. What'd you do? Take a supersecret mission to Mars before deciding to join the BKI group and open the custom chopper shop?"

She was stretched out next to him on the floor. He'd pulled off his boots, kicked out of his jeans, and spread the blanket to create a pallet on the cold concrete. Her smooth thigh was over his leg. Her free hand absently traced the clutch of violets tattooed over his heart. And her mouth—that mouth that had just given him so much pleasure, he was still shaking with it—was twisted with curiosity.

He knew if he pulled her down and kissed her, he could make her forget this entire line of questioning. Make her moan and gasp and climb back atop him. Because, as the Borg would say, "resistance was futile." And he considered doing it. For a second. But there was already so much left unsaid between them, so much that must remain hidden.

"You realize that a secret mission to Mars would take longer than a year, right? I mean, it would be six months getting there and six months getting back, *but* you have to take into account that you'd have to stay on Mars for sixteen to twenty months until the planets realigned before you could—"

She pinched his nipple.

He usually wasn't one for mixing pain with his pleasure. But when it came to Samantha, he was up for anything. Which was probably why his spent dick thickened. "Hey! What gives?"

The teasing gleam in her eyes made him grin. He'd had plenty of women. But none had ever made him feel the way Samantha made him feel. Like they were two pieces of a puzzle clicking together. Milk and cookies. The stars and the moon. Hipsters and ironic T-shirts. Separate, they were good. Together, they were abso-fucking-lutely awesome. It was terrifying.

"Stop being so literal," she harrumphed.

"When you're talking about space travel," he assured her, "the only way I know how to *be* is literal. I would have thought my vast collection of T-shirts made that obvious."

"Ozzie…" There was a warning in her tone. It said, *Stop dicking around and answer the damned question*.

"Samantha…" He made sure *his* tone held nothing but innuendo. It said, *Why are we talking when we could be screwing each other's brains out?* And just in case she wasn't picking up what he was laying down, he trailed a finger over her satiny cheek—*man, she's soft*—and waggled his eyebrows.

She caught his finger between her teeth and gave the tip a teasing nip. And yep, right on cue, his hips flexed, and his heels dug into the floor. It was some kind of crazy, this effect she had on him.

"Why do I get the feeling you're trying to distract me?" she asked.

"Distract you?" He donned his most innocent expression. "I would never. But…did I mention that Boss keeps a box of condoms in his locker?" Hooking a thumb over his head, he indicated the row of small gray lockers lining one wall. "I mean, I'm just saying…"

"We'll get to that in a minute," she said matter-of-factly. A *zing* of anticipation shot through him. "*After*"—she stressed the word—"you answer my question."

"I was in BUD/S training." Man, it felt good to admit that. To give her an unvarnished truth.

Her eyebrows arrowed toward her nose. "Say again?"

"BUD/S training," he repeated. "Basic Underwater Demolition/SEAL. I was working to become a Navy SEAL."

She blinked once. Twice. Then a look he recognized spread over her pretty face. He'd named it her *hard-nosed journalist* expression. She smelled a story.

"*That's* why it was so hard to find out any concrete

information about you all when I went digging," she said. "You're not just a bunch of retired military men; you're a bunch of retired black ops!"

He could have said there was no *retired* about it. But there was a huge difference between telling her they used to be spec ops and admitting they were a clandestine group of private military contractors running top secret missions for none other the president and his joint chiefs.

"I knew it!" she crowed. "I knew you guys were more than you seemed! Ha! What a story this will make! Charlie's going to go nuts for it. The headline: Spec-Ops Soldiers Turned Grease-Monkey Motorcycle Mechanics."

She looked on the verge of doing a happy dance. And part of Ozzie, the *guy* part who knew he would enjoy watching all her naked bits jiggle, almost let her do it. But the *other* part of him figured it was best to burst her bubble now, before it grew too big or rose too high. "You can't write about me. About *them*." He deliberately made sure his tone was the audio equivalent of a tire iron, hard and sharp.

She immediately sobered. "Why?"

"Same reason the military and the government don't list the identities of operators even after they've left the services," he told her. "Our enemies don't care whether or not we're active duty. All they care about is getting revenge on everyone who could have been involved in a mission against them. If you print what I just told you, you'll put all of us here in danger."

She blinked and opened her mouth. Then she closed it again. He could see her struggling, the reporter in her dying to tell the story.

"*Pbwbwbwhh*." She blew out a windy breath that fluttered the wild mass of hair hanging around her face. "But grease-monkey motorcycle mechanics sounds so sweet. The alliteration alone…" She shook her head sorrowfully. "Hey, at least *knowing* is something. And it *is* something. Because it explains a couple of things."

"Such as?" he asked curiously. He hadn't doubted her, exactly. But he had worried that he would have to reiterate his point a time or two before she would give in and agree not to run with the story. That he *hadn't* had to do that delighted him and proved what an amazing woman she was. She was willing to forgo writing something that was sure to put a feather in her reporter's cap simply because…well…simply because he'd asked her to.

"Such as why you all have been dodging me for years. Reporters and men who have big, honking secrets don't generally play well together, do they?"

That was pretty much the understatement of the century. "So that's one thing. What's the other?"

"You," she said.

"Me?" He frowned. "What about me?"

"The way you *are*. The way you don't hesitate to jump onto a moving van. The way you can threaten to end a man without blinking. The way you…*look* sometimes."

Okay, now he was *really* curious. "How do I look?"

"It's not really an expression or anything, but more something in your eyes. You have the eyes of a warrior. Someone who has seen things, done things. And even though you only spent a year as a SEAL, I guess that was enough."

He wanted to tell her that the thirteen months he had spent training weren't what had put that look in his eyes. It had been all the years since. All the missions and sweat and tears, all the bloodshed and death and destruction. But he couldn't do that. *That* secret was not his to tell. So he did the next best thing. He lifted her hand to his mouth and kissed her palm. Her fingers curled around his face, holding on to the sensation of his lips.

"So mystery solved," she said. "But there's one more thing I want to know."

"What's that?"

"Why has it been so long?"

"So long since *what*?"

"Since you had sex." That delectable gap-toothed grin was back.

Uh-oh. Red alert! Red alert!

"Is it just me?" He glanced around. "Or are the walls suddenly closing in? Did they move when I was blinking?"

"Come on," she cajoled. "Surely, the reason behind your recent sexual hiatus isn't nearly as juicy as the one behind the unwillingness of the Black Knights to sit down for an interview."

The walls were *definitely* closing in. Since they were at it, he wished that they would talk to their good buddy, the floor, and convince it to open up and swallow him whole.

Given her we're-good-for-now-but-not-forever stance, he couldn't very well tell her that he'd decided to lay off the ladies until he met someone special. Until he met *her*. That was sure to send her screaming for the hills.

Had Ozzie been a clam, he would have slammed shut. As it was, his expression shuttered, and his body, stretched out beside her, became the flesh-and-blood equivalent of a two-by-four.

"I should've known you wouldn't just let that go," he grumbled, wiping a hand over his face.

His calloused palm made a rasping noise against the

short beard on his chin and cheeks. And that sound…
It was a bad-boy sound. It swirled around in her ears,
affecting her in the naughtiest possible way.

"When have you ever known me to let *anything* go?"
she demanded.

Although, in all honesty, she had let go of the whole
spec-ops thing pretty quickly, even though a bazillion
questions were buzzing through her head. *Did you
just train, or did you go on missions? What about the
others? What were they involved in? Anything I would
have heard about?* But she recognized a closed door
when she saw one. And besides, she was so happy he
had opened up to her about something so personal and
secret and potentially dangerous—*He trusts me! He
really, really trusts me!*—that it didn't take all that much
to beat back her naturally nosy tendencies.

At least not on *that* topic.

On *this* topic? Um, yeah. No way. It was too juicy.

"Right." He bobbed his eyebrows. "So you want the
long version or the short version?"

Considering she was starting to get all hot and bothered again—hard *not* to when his big body was spread
out before her like a feast of tanned flesh, crinkly man
hair, and um, the most impressive-looking penis she'd
ever had the pleasure to behold. Even semi-flaccid, he
was still long and thick and blatantly, unrepentantly
male. She figured she'd opt for the short version.

"Give me the CliffsNotes." She ran her hand down
his washboard belly, delighting when his skin quivered
beneath her fingers. It was a heady experience to make a
man like him—a former spec-ops soldier, an alpha male
raised to the nth power—shiver. "That way, we can put
those condoms to use."

"Truly?" If he'd been a bird dog, he would have been

on point. The arm he had around her tightened, and his wide-palmed hand found its way to her ass.

She pointed a finger in the air. "Hear that?" He cocked his head, straining to listen to the soft music drifting in from the speakers outside. "That's Al Green. One note of Al Green, and I become Miss MonkeySex McHornyPants."

He laughed. That low, rolling, want-to-listen-to-it-forever laugh. It did funny things to the rhythm of her heart. "Good to know. I'll keep that in mind for the future when I'm trying to get you in the mood."

The word hung in the air between them. *Future*... Was it possible? Had her plan worked? Did he realize how good they were together? How they just *fit*?

We're talking Legos, folks.

But just when she began to hope, he waved a hand through the air and quickly changed the subject. "After my injury," he said, "I was on some pretty heavy-duty pain meds. That put the chill on any nocturnal activities, if you know what I mean." She pulled a face, and he flashed her that hundred-watt smile. "Sorry. *Of course* you know what I mean. But I've been off the sauce for a couple of months now. And things seemed to be in fine working order. *Thank goodness*. Between you and me, I was starting to get concerned."

To say that Samantha was disappointed would be like calling the rain wet. But she was silly to have hoped, even for a second, that he had laid off the ladies because he'd decided to...what? Save himself for her?

For fuck's sake, Sammie.

"I mean, not to blow my own horn or anything—" He stopped abruptly, and his smile turned decidedly wicked. "No need, since you've blown it so well." Oh great. And now she was blushing. "But things *are* in remarkably fine working order." He hitched his chin to indicate his penis lying atop his belly. No longer semi-flaccid. Now, perfectly erect.

Seeing it, an answering wetness slicked Samantha's core. "Lucky for me," she said. Any disappointment she felt was replaced with longing. Longing to *be* with him. To *take* him. To make him hers for as long as he'd let her.

She bent to claim his lips, but he stopped her by pressing a finger against her mouth. "Ah-ah-ah," he said. "Turnabout is fair play. You got to ask me a personal question. Now you have to pony up the goods."

She pulled back, lifting an eyebrow. "What do you mean? I don't have any goods to pony up. I'm an open book."

"Sh'yeah right. As If I'd believe that."

"So okay," she admitted. "You got me. This one time, in eighth grade, I glued tacks to January Jolly's chair. But only because she had called me names all year long, started a rumor that I was going steady with a fifth grader, and cut off half my ponytail in art class."

Ozzie's lips twitched. "I mixed up all this fake puke at home, and then I went to this movie theater, hid the puke in my jacket, climbed up to the balcony and then, th-th-then, I made a noise like this... *hua-hua-huaaaa*..."

"*The Goonies*." She grinned delightedly, immediately recognizing his quote and giving him extra points for doing a spot-on impersonation of Chunk.

"Best movie ever made."

"Mmm..." She twisted her lips. "Second best. *The Princess Bride* is my all-time favorite."

"Hallo. My name is Inigo Montoya. You killed my father. Prepare to die!"

She laughed. She'd never felt so alive, so free, so...
herself with any other man.

"And January Jolly sounds like a real bitch," he said.
"She's lucky *all* you did was glue tacks to her chair. So
what happened?"

"Since she was wearing a short skirt that day, she suffered the full brunt of those little daggers when she sat
down. She yelped and jumped up, and the whole class
laughed. I, of course, got suspended for two days. But
it was totally worth it just to see that look of horror on
her face."

"So this killer instinct of yours isn't a new thing."
He was watching her through half-lidded eyes. "You've
always had it."

"Guilty as charged."

"Which brings me to my next question."

Samantha rolled in her lips. "Why do I suddenly feel
like the walls are closing in?"

"Apparently the problem is catching," Ozzie said,
right before asking a question that immediately tainted
the easy atmosphere between them. "So what's behind
all that doggedness? Why are you so hell-bent on uncovering secrets? I've known you long enough to figure out
it's more than just a profession. It's a calling. One might
even say it's an obsession?"

And for all they'd shared, this was the one thing
she had never been able to bring herself to tell him.
She wasn't sure why. Maybe because it felt so big, so
central to her soul and the essence of who she was.
Telling him would give him everything, everything
that was *her*. But considering all he'd shared, the
grand secret that was the pasts of the men of Black
Knights Inc.—and talk about power; he'd handed her
a boatload with that one confession—she couldn't do

him the disservice of not answering. Turnabout *was* fair play.

Still, she was dismayed to hear her voice shake when she admitted, "It all started with my father's murder."

Chapter 16

OZZIE HAD BEEN PREPARED TO HEAR A LOT OF things. He had *not* been prepared to hear *that*.

Just like the time he had jumped in front of the neighborhood girl to save her from the slavering dog, his instincts had him reaching for Samantha and pulling her down so that her head rested beneath his chin. He wanted to protect her from it all. Erase the hurt in her eyes and the hitch in her voice.

"You don't have to talk about it if you don't want to." He knew how deeply a wound like that could cut, and he cursed himself for bringing up the subject in the first place. He had done it, after months of making sure he didn't. He had thrown open her Pandora's box of deep, dark secrets.

"No," she assured him. "It's okay. I... My dad was a good man. He was a hardworking man."

And he understood her need to put that out there. Having lost a parent himself, he knew how important it was to protect their memory. "His daughter obviously takes after him."

The tension drained out of her, and she softened against him. "You know"—she sighed—"I'd like to think so. I try hard to live my life in a way that would make him proud."

"Samantha." He loved the feel of her pressed along his side, loved *her*, wished there was a way he could make her love him too. "I'm sure if your father were here right now, he'd tell you he couldn't be prouder."

"If my father were here right now, he'd probably grab my ear, haul me up, and tell me to get my clothes on." She laughed. That was the thing about Samantha. Her sense of humor was never far from the surface.

"True," Ozzie admitted. "I've never been introduced to anyone's father, but if I ever was, I'd like to think I wouldn't have my wedding tackle hanging out."

Her tone turned theatrically seductive, like she was auditioning to be the femme fatale of a really bad film noir. "But it's such nice wedding tackle."

"Right back atcha, sweetheart."

"Aw, look at us, a mutual appreciation society of two."

"Two hearts are better than one," he told her. "At least that's what the Boss says."

"Boss said that?" There was a heavy dose of skepticism in her voice. "He doesn't strike me as the sentimental sort."

"Not Boss as in Frank Knight." He laughed, trying to imagine the curmudgeonly dude who ran Black Knights Inc. spouting anything other than mission parameters or weapons specifications. "*The* Boss. Springsteen, baby."

"Oh right," she said, then fell silent for a while. Her fingers continued to toy with the tattoo over his heart. And he knew she was working herself back up to continue her tale. He waited patiently. Something this important, this *painful* couldn't be rushed. Finally, she said, "So my father had been nuts about cars his whole life. Worked most of it as a mechanic at a dealership. It was steady pay, enough to keep us decidedly lower middle class. But it had always been his dream to open his own repair shop. By the time I was a freshman in high school, he'd socked away enough to do just that. Man, I can still remember the look on his face the first morning he opened for business. It was like…" She stopped and searched for the right word. "Incandescence," she finally said.

A puzzle piece fell into place. "The Mustang… It was your father's."

She nodded. Her cheek was warm and wonderful as it brushed over the skin of his shoulder. "He rebuilt it from the frame out. After me and the shop, he always said that car was his pride and joy."

"And by keeping it, you're keeping a piece of him."

Her breath caught. "You understand."

Better than you could possibly know. "Go on."

For a moment, she gathered her thoughts. Then she said, "You've lived in Chicago long enough to realize the local government is famous for being rife with corruption, right?"

"Sure. The city of big shoulders *and* big swindlers."

"Yeah, well, our ward out on the South Side wasn't any different. We had a horrible alderman. And by horrible, I mean every bone in the man's body was crooked. He was taking kickbacks from wealthy businessmen in exchange for favorable zoning. When a slum lord who made millions putting up cheap housing took a shine to the corner my father's shop was on, the alderman was quick to get the space rezoned for residential use instead of commercial use."

"Oh, for the love of Montgomery Scott," Ozzie muttered, having seen the worst of humanity, all the violence and suffering and greed. In war, those things were normal, expected even. On the streets of the Midwest? It was a damned travesty.

"My dad was desperate to save his shop." Samantha's voice shook when she continued. "He tried for months to block the zoning change, but he was one little man going up against these pillars of the city. He finally decided the only way he could stop this alderman was to expose him as the corrupt asshole he was. Dad made a few anonymous tips to the police that ended up going nowhere, and he came to believe that a lot of the local cops were in on the racket. He didn't know who to trust, and things were coming down to the wire. The rezoning was about to go through. In a strange twist of fate, he'd just fixed the car of a fresh new reporter for the *Trib*. And he thought, aha! A tell-all in the paper. The reporter's name was Donny Danielson, by the way."

"Ah, yes." Ozzie nodded. Samantha had talked a lot about Donny over the weeks and months, but this morning was the first time Ozzie had the pleasure of meeting the man. And he got why Samantha loved him. Donny struck him as honest and true and, above all, straightforward. "Mr. Boyfriend Material."

He could feel her mouth curve into a smile. "None other. Anyway, Donny told Dad he couldn't write an exposé without irrefutable proof that the alderman was on the take. So, my dad being my dad, he bought a camera with a zoom lens and followed the alderman around for a week getting evidence of his malfeasance. Stuff like handshakes with criminals, money exchanges, that kind of thing. Then one night, Dad didn't come home." Her voice thickened. Hearing it, a lump formed in Ozzie's throat.

"His body was found in the middle of the sidewalk in front of a coffee shop the following morning. He'd been shot through the heart. His camera was broken. All his film was missing. And there were no…" Her voice broke. Ozzie was pretty sure his heart followed suit. "No witnesses," she finished.

For long moments, the only sound that intruded on the silence of the gym was the R & B drifting in from the speakers outside. Otis Redding crooned about when a man loved a woman. For the first time in Ozzie's life, he understood the line about a man trading the world for the good thing he'd found. If Samantha would only love him, he would trade it all, trade—

"I was eighteen when it happened. A senior heading off to college to major in English on a scholarship. I was going to write the next Great American Novel." She chuckled as if amazed at the naïveté of her younger self. "Like you said, I've had a killer instinct from the beginning. I was going to *massacre* those bestseller lists. But"—she blew out a breath—"Dad's death... It... changed everything. It changed *me*.

"Suddenly, I wasn't satisfied with fiction. I wanted to uncover truths, to expose corruption. But I still loved the written word, and then there was Donny. Even though he never advocated for my father to go all vigilante and try to gather the evidence against the alderman on his own, he still felt responsible for Dad's death. So he sort of took me under his wing. He became one part mentor and two parts friend." She lifted a hand, let it fall back to his chest. "So here I am, all these years later. An investigative reporter."

Tragedy had shaped both their lives, made them the people they were today. And maybe that was why he had felt a kinship with her from the beginning.

"Have you tried to use the sources you've amassed over the years to bring down the alderman?"

"Luckily, I didn't have to." She absently circled his nipple with her finger. Even given the topic of conversation, his areola contracted. The muscles in his stomach did the same. Her touch, no matter how innocent, sent an erotic blast of sensation through his body. "Donny did that for me. He was dogged in the two years following Dad's death. He turned over every rock until he finally had enough to write an exposé. A trial followed; a conviction was handed down. The alderman will spend the next fifteen years finishing out his sentence. If he lives that long. Last I heard, he was undergoing treatment for liver cancer."

Her throat clicked with dryness when she swallowed. The story didn't end there. She had more to tell him. He waited, gently trailing a finger over her delicate spine and the tattoo on her lower back. The ink was a pen lying across a sword with scrolling letters that read: How I Change The World.

Little does she know that she's already changed mine.

Eventually, she said, "He was never convicted of my dad's murder though. Donny doesn't think he was the triggerman. Figures it was one of the alderman's hired thugs who did the actual shooting. Over the years, I've tried to find the culprit, but"—she shrugged one shoulder—"so far, nothing."

There were a million things he could have said. All of them seemed trite. So he went with the tried and true. "I'm so sorry." Sorry she'd had her heart broken. Sorry she'd had no real closure. Sorry she would carry the wound of her loss for the rest of her life.

She pushed onto her elbow, gazing down at him. "I am too." There was a sheen in her eyes, the echo of tears long since shed.

He wanted to go back in time, go back to every moment she had ever cried and take her in his arms. Hug her and kiss her and protect her from the horror of the big, wide world. Then when she said, "Kiss me, Ozzie," he realized there was no place he'd rather be than right here, right now. With this woman...

There were a hundred different ways for two people to kiss…

They could kiss with passion. With hello or goodbye. With joy or sorrow. Hell, even with anger. But as Ozzie's lips moved over Samantha's, it was the first time she knew what it was to kiss with love.

At least on *her* part, there was love. Huge, crashing waves of it that washed away the ghosts of the past. There was so much tenderness in the stroke of Ozzie's tongue. So much *caring* in the brush of his big, warm hands down her back and over her hips that she dared to hope there might be a little love on his part too.

"Samantha," he whispered against her lips, his breath hot and sweet, a world of understanding, of *longing* in his tone.

"Ozzie, I—"

"Hey, you two!" Emily yelled from the other side of the door, making Samantha squeal in alarm.

When Emily followed with a loud knock, Samantha bolted upright, grabbing the edge of the blanket and wrapping it around herself. She wasn't sure if she should curse Emily to hell and back for the interruption, or kiss the woman smack on the lips. Because she was pretty sure she'd been a second away from confessing her love to Ozzie. She was so swollen with it that she'd nearly allowed it to explode out of her like an overfilled water balloon. Just…*bam!* And as with most explosions, she figured the outcome would have been painful and bloody.

Holy shit, Sammie. Get your head on straight.

Good advice. Trouble was, when it came to Ozzie, her head wasn't in charge. At first, it'd been her hormones running the show. Now, it was her heart. Her silly, hopeful, desperate heart.

"What the hell, Emily?" Ozzie called. Unlike Samantha, he made no move to cover his nakedness. In fact, he crossed his arms beneath his head and directed his question to the ceiling. Truly, he was resplendent in his nudity.

"I wouldn't have disturbed your…" Emily's voice trailed off. When she finished with, "workout," it sounded like she was suppressing a giggle. Samantha felt her cheeks heat. "But I thought you'd both like to know those military records you requested just arrived by courier. Guess they were too sensitive for email or fax. That's interesting, don't you think?" Emily's tough Chicago accent made *don't you* sound more like *doncha*.

Ozzie glanced at Samantha, one eyebrow raised. "That *is* interesting," they said at the same time.

"Pinch, poke." He gave her exposed flank one of each. "You owe me a Coke."

"Ow!" She slapped his abusive hand away. "How old are you? Seven?"

"Would a seven-year-old be sporting one of these?" He used both hands to indicate his wonderfully erect penis.

Her throat dried at the sight. For the record, that was the *only* part of her that dried at the sight. "Not sure," she admitted. "I was under the impression that erections, particularly involuntary erections, started pretty early in life."

"I'm not talking about its state." He glowered at her. "I'm talking about its sheer size and majesty."

It was hard for Samantha not to smile. But she managed, pursing her lips instead. "You have a pretty high opinion of yourself, don't you?"

He shrugged. "Maybe. But that opinion has been backed up by *many* satisfied customers." When he realized what he'd said—come on, you don't talk about past sexual partners with current sexual partners—a look of horror passed over his face. "Shit! Sorry! That was stupid. I'm an idiot."

She had to bite her cheek to keep from laughing. Ozzie was the only man she had ever known who could go from being arrogant as hell one minute to boyishly charming the next. She couldn't resist teasing him. "Save your breath." She gave him the stink eye. "You're going to need it to blow up your date later on."

Christian was sitting at the conference table on the second floor when Emily climbed the stairs. She'd already changed into what passed for sleepwear for her, silk pajama bottoms and an old pullover—or *sweatshirt* as Americans liked to call it. Although, for the life of him, he couldn't understand why.

Sounds as if one is wearing a shirt made of sweat.

"You're laughing," Emily declared, staring at him from the top step. That beauty mark was a blatant taunt. Made him have to fight the urge to kiss it.

"I laugh quite often," he informed her haughtily, delighting in the look of incredulity that spread over her scrubbed-clean face. Emily was the type of woman who needed no artificial enhancement. Her skin was clear and bright. Her lips naturally pink. In fact, he far preferred her au naturel. Perhaps because Emily sans makeup conjured up images of how she'd look the morning after a night of intense lovemaking. Mascara rubbed off. Lipstick kissed away.

"Bullshit you laugh all the time," she declared. "You laughing is like a solar eclipse. Rare and slightly terrifying to those who don't know what's going on."

She had him there. When she was around, he *didn't*

laugh. That was because he was trying to stop himself from tossing her up against the nearest wall and silencing her wicked mouth with a deep, punishing kiss.

"So what's so funny?" She cocked a hip against her hand.

He could have told her *she* was the reason for his humor. *"I wouldn't have disturbed your…workout."* He'd been ambling by the back door after fetching a cup of tea—you could take the man out of England, but you couldn't take the Englishman out of the man—when he heard her interrupt Ozzie and Samantha. She was keenly funny. Funny and bossy and sexy and…*infuriating*. Watching her cover her mouth with her hand and giggle like a schoolgirl had charmed him and tickled him in equal measure. He had been replaying the scene in his mind when she marched up the steps.

"I recognize it is your standard mode of operation to *get all up in everyone's business*, as Ozzie would say," he told her, "but some things, I prefer to keep to myself." Especially how much she affected him.

The look that entered her eyes told him to sod off. But to his surprise, there was no flurry of barbs hurled his way. Instead, she waved a hand and said, "Fine. Maintain your air of mystery."

She pulled out the chair at the head of the table, the one usually reserved for Boss. In Boss's absence, she had deemed herself BKI's stand-in head honcho.

Cheeky wench.

Tapping a finger on the recently delivered file, she regarded him consideringly. *Too* consideringly. When he couldn't take it a second longer, he blurted, "What, pray tell, are you thinking?"

"I really like your hair."

He lifted a hand to his freshly cut hair. Like everything

in his life, his hair ritual was strictly regimented. "You do?" he asked in disbelief. Emily had never complimented him before.

"Yeah." She nodded. "Tell me though, how do you get it to curl out of your nostrils like that?"

His hand jumped to his nose before he realized she was having him on.

"Gotcha." She grinned evilly, her lush lips a taunt.

Everything inside him ordered him to pull her out of that chair and crush those lips with his own. So it was a good thing Ozzie and Samantha had begun to make their way up the stairs.

———

"I don't understand," Ozzie said.

Emily watched him close the file. A deep frown pinched his brow.

"Don't understand what?" Christian asked, sipping tea.

Ozzie, Christian, Emily, and Samantha were the only ones left awake inside the warehouse. They were seated around the conference table, and Ozzie and Samantha sported the rosy, disheveled look of the recently laid. Emily felt a pang of jealousy. It had been a *really* long time since she'd gotten herself a little afternoon delight.

Or morning delight or evening delight, for that matter.

"I mean, I just did a cursory read, so maybe I'm missing something." Ozzie slid the folder to the center of the conference table. "But I don't understand why these files were redacted. Everything in there seems pretty standard for two guys who did two tours. There's some cryptic mention of an incident involving their unit and an Iraqi translator near a little town by Habbaniyah Lake, but—"

Emily must have made a noise, because Ozzie stopped abruptly, his sharp blue eyes cutting into her like the early April wind in Sox Park. "That little town wasn't called Albu Bali, was it?" she asked.

"As a matter of fact, it was." Ozzie's brow furrowed. "How the hell would you know that?"

She shook her head slightly, darting a quick look at Samantha. Obviously, it wasn't quick enough, because Samantha caught it.

"What?" The reporter blinked, glancing around the table.

No one spoke for long moments. Then Ozzie finally piped up. "I told Samantha I used to be a SEAL."

"You *told* her?" If dubiousness had a face, it would be Christian's. "You, sir, are the reason the gene pool needs a lifeguard."

"Hey," Ozzie barked. "She knows how dangerous it would be if she ever put that information in print." Ozzie dared Christian to naysay him. "So she won't. End of story."

Well, now that's *interesting*, Emily mused. Writing a story about a true-blue, top secret military operator turned custom bike builder was just the thing to launch Samantha's career to the next level, a human-interest story sure to be picked up by the Associated Press. That Samantha was willing to give up that opportunity was huge.

Very interesting.

"Emily." When Ozzie said her name, she turned her attention from Samantha to him. "I trust her. I hope you will too."

Trust was a tough one. Emily tended not to trust

anyone or anything. But Ozzie wanted to pull the curtain back, just the teeniest bit. And who was she to say he couldn't? "Okay." She nodded. "So then…cone of silence?" She pinned Samantha with a look she'd developed in her blue-collar Bridgeport neighborhood and perfected while working for the Company. It was her patented *Don't you dare fuck with me, or I'll rip your heart out* look.

Samantha lifted her chin. "Cone of silence."

Emily flicked her gaze back to Ozzie. His expression said, *Trust but also tread lightly.* She got that. Samantha being willing to forgo writing an article about former spec-ops guys turned motorcycle mechanics was one thing. Asking her to keep it to herself that those former spec-ops guys turned motorcycle mechanics were, in fact, the personal, private goon squad for the president was another thing entirely. Any reporter on the face of the planet would think the American people had the right to know *that*. Not to mention that it was Pulitzer Prize–winning material. A bigger story than the one the *Boston Globe* ran when it outed the Catholic Church for willfully keeping pedophile priests in parish churches.

So okay. Tread lightly. Not a problem. Emily had been treading lightly her entire career.

"All right," she said. "Well, since it appears we're doing a reveal, guess it's only fair I open up my trench coat. Hi." She waved at Samantha. "I'm Emily Scott. I used to be an office manager for the CIA."

Samantha blinked. Emily could see the wheels turning, grinding to a stop, and then turning again. Finally, Samantha swung her attention to Christian. "And let me guess, you're what? Retired MI6?"

"*Pfft*." Christian waved a hand through the air. "Those pansies? Please. I was SAS. That's—"

"British special forces," Samantha cut in. "Yeah, I know."

Peanut chose that moment to join them. He hopped onto one of the chairs, then foisted his rotund self onto the table. Stalking to the center, he circled once before flopping down and reclining back like a fat, furry sultan, surveying his domain through drowsy, yellow eyes.

"I guess that just leaves one question," Samantha said. Emily could have cut the tension in the room with a knife. "How the hell did all you supersecret spy types find each other?"

Like a tire with a slow leak, the pressure gradually eased. Christian shrugged. "Ever hear the saying 'It's a small world'?" Samantha nodded. "Well, the world of special operations is absolutely minuscule."

"Rrrright," Samantha said skeptically. But she didn't push it.

Emily respected the hell out of her for that. Maybe Ozzie was right. Maybe she *could* be trusted.

"So now that *that's* out of the way," Ozzie put in, "let's hear about Albu Bali."

Emily nodded. "So you guys probably don't remember the Haditha massacre of 2005."

"I do," Samantha said. "When the story finally broke, it topped the news cycle for weeks. A group of U.S. Marines killed a bunch of civilians in Haditha, including women and children. It was in retaliation for..." She stopped and screwed up her face, searching her memory. "For an attack on one of their convoys, right?"

"Right." Emily dipped her chin. "Good memory. But what you may *not* remember, because it wasn't much publicized, is that even though eight Marines were charged and tried, none of them were ever convicted. It didn't create much of a buzz here in the

United States. But as you can imagine, there was a *huge* international outcry."

"I'm sorry." Christian frowned at her. "But what's that got to do with the Basilisks or Albu Bali?"

Emily kicked him under the table. Since she wore soft, fuzzy socks, the blow wasn't very effective. "Patience, man. It's a virtue, you know."

He leaned down to rub his shin, scowling even harder. He was never so handsome as when he was scowling. Just one more reason she delighted in abusing him.

"Anyway, around the time all the shit about Haditha was hitting the fan, a squad of U.S. Army infantrymen and their trusty translator carried out a similar attack in Albu Bali. Difference there being the reason for the massacre was good ol'-fashioned bloodlust and greed. Rumors had swirled that some families in Albu Bali were sitting on a stash of Saddam's gold. But like most rumors, those turned out to be false. There was nothing in Albu Bali but thirty-four innocent civilians who died brutally at the hands of American soldiers."

Ozzie and Christian's faces registered their disgust. Neither man was a stranger to killing. But both men lived with a code. It was a simple one: ending a life was a last resort. To guys like the Black Knights, men who killed for greed or glory—or *worse*, pleasure—were the bacteria that feasted on the scum that lived at the bottom of a bog.

"Considering Haditha was in the news," Emily continued, "the powers that be inside the Intelligence community decided that Albu Bali needed to be covered up. According to them, the conflict was at a tipping point, and America couldn't withstand another punch that might shove it over the edge. My boss at the CIA· was the one overseeing the agents who went in to do the cleanup. Albu Bali was neatly swept under the rug and the infantrymen quietly discharged for *medical reasons*." She made quote marks with her fingers. "Which I guess makes sense, since they were nothing but batshit crazy thugs. And that, as they say, was that."

"Which explains why their files were redacted," Ozzie concluded. "The DOD would be super anal about these two men, blacking out anything and everything for fear something might prompt questions about Albu Bali. Unfortunately, knowing why their files were lined out doesn't get us any closer to the who or how or *where* of the Basilisks' gunrunning business—or to pinning them down for Marcel Monroe's murder."

"Follow the money!" A voice from the first floor echoed up the stairs. It was quickly followed by the sound of dog claws on the metal treads. Three seconds later, Fido appeared on the landing, tongue lolling, red bandana knocked askew and sticking up over his left ear. Delilah followed him, motorcycle helmet tucked under one arm. She took a quick glance around the room before grabbing a seat.

Fido made a loop around the table, accepting ear scratches from those willing to give them. Christian was particularly enthusiastic. Kids and dogs. They were his Achilles's heel and the only creatures Emily had ever seen crack through his tough outer shell. Finally, the dog plopped down next to Delilah's seat, curling himself around her biker boots.

"So," Emily prompted, blinking at the new arrival. "Follow the money? Care to explain?"

"If you want to find out who the Basilisks are getting their weapons from," Delilah said, fluffing out her auburn hair, "all you have to do is follow the money. They have to be paying *someone*."

"Sure." Samantha nodded. "But following the money would require not only knowing the businesses the Basilisks are running but also gaining access to their accounts. The first might not be too difficult. I think the CPD could probably provide us with a list of the Basilisks' various enterprises. But the second thing, access to their accounts, would mean getting a court order. And according to Chief Washington and Detective Carver, that isn't going to happen without more evidence of malfeasance."

"Well, the first has already been taken care of," Ozzie said, tugging on his earlobe.

Samantha's dark eyebrows formed a perfect V. "What do you mean?"

"I mean I asked Washington to email me a list of the Basilisks' holdings. He sent it earlier this evening. Thought I'd do some snooping on my own."

The V of Samantha's eyebrows deepened. "What do you mean?" she asked again. "Snooping *how*?"

Ozzie opened his mouth but seemed to hesitate.

"Bloody hell, man," Christian blurted. "She already knows SEAL, SAS, and CIA." He shot a finger gun first at Ozzie, then himself, and finally Emily. "May as well tell her you're a world-class hacker to boot, yeah?"

"Wait a minute." Delilah sat up straighter, frowning. "She knows about—"

Emily kicked her under the table. Apparently she was in a kicky mood tonight. "She knows about our pasts." She subtly emphasized the last word. "And she understands that she has to keep that information to herself."

"Well, pour me some top-shelf tequila and color me speechless." Delilah nodded her understanding. "Okay then."

"Can we circle back to the world-class hacker part of this conversation?" Samantha asked.

"My mate here has mad skills." Christian gave Ozzie a tip of his chin. "Did you never wonder how he came about his nickname?"

Ooooh, that accent. It did crazy things to Emily's pulse.

Samantha looked taken aback. "Uh, no. I guess I never thought about it. He's just…he's just *Ozzie*."

"Go on then," Christian demanded. "Tell her."

"It's not that interesting," Ozzie muttered.

"Oh, puh-lease." Delilah rolled her eyes. "Since when have you ever been one not to talk about yourself? Just tell her."

Ozzie frowned at Delilah. She frowned back just as hard. Finally, Ozzie gave in. "So I got into computers at a really young age," he said.

Because your drunk father left you alone in your room all the time, and your computer, cassettes, and VHS tapes were your only friends, Emily wanted to add. But she kept her mouth shut.

"Because of that," Ozzie continued, "I became known as the Whiz Kid. That nickname stuck all throughout school. But that year I spent in college, I wasn't a *kid* anymore, so the name morphed into the Wizard of Oz. And *then*, once I joined the navy, Wizard of Oz had too many syllables. Too much work for my CO when he wanted to scream at me. So he shortened it to Oz, which over time became Ozzie." He peeked over at Samantha. "See. Told you it wasn't very interesting."

Au contraire, Emily thought. When it came to Ozzie, Samantha found everything about him endlessly fascinating. The woman stared at him with such blatant adoration that Emily was once again hit with the interesting thought that it might be within her power to find a way to keep the couple together.

"So you asked Washington for the list hoping you could use your super-duper computer skills to hack into the Basilisks' PCs," she prompted.

"Right." Ozzie nodded.

"But then what?" Samantha frowned. "It's not like Washington can *act* on any information you might find, given it would've been obtained illegally."

"Ever heard of an anonymous tip?" Ozzie's smile was decidedly enigmatic.

"*La-la-la!*" Samantha singsonged, plugging her ears. "I'm pretending I didn't hear that."

"Well, *I* heard it," Delilah declared. "And I want in. It's been a while since I've taken on a an interesting case and—"

"Case?" Samantha interrupted. "Don't tell me. You're, like, what? Former FBI?"

"I sometimes moonlight as a forensic accountant," Delilah admitted.

"Ex-*cuse* me?" Samantha sputtered. "Who the hell moonlights as a forensic accountant?"

"She does," a chorus of voices sounded. Both Emily and Christian pointed at Delilah. In response, Samantha looked askance at them all. Like at any moment, they might rip off their faces and reveal they were, in fact, lizard aliens. Emily understood. It was a lot to take in all at once.

"Well, then." Christian shoved his chair away from the table. "Sounds as though a plan is in place. I'll toddle off to Bedfordshire"—Emily had learned that was the British equivalent of *hit the hay*—"and leave the hacking and the accounting to the experts."

"I'll come with you." Emily pushed to a stand. From the corner of her eye, she saw Christian blanch. "Oh, for crying out loud." She punched him in the arm. "Not with you to *bed*. You should be so lucky."

He didn't say anything. Just gave her a look. Then he turned and headed toward the stairs.

"You should be so lucky," she muttered again under her breath, stomping after him.

Chapter 17

VENOM WATCHED HAWKEYE AMBLE DOWN THE street toward the stolen SUV they had used to follow home the maintenance man from the Tribune Tower. The Basilisks always kept an untraceable vehicle on hand for various reasons. And their plan tonight had been to kill the asshole maintenance man and whoever else happened to get in their way, steal his security pass and uniform, and then ransack the place to make it look like a robbery gone bad.

But before they could bust into the A-hole's cookie-cutter, 1950s-era tract house, he had emerged on his front porch and moseyed down the block to the corner bar boasting a Pabst Blue Ribbon Beer sign above the door. Thinking quickly, they had sent Hawkeye in after him to suss out the situation.

That was thirty minutes ago.

Now, Hawkeye hopped into the back of the SUV. He brought with him the smell of cheap beer and bottom-shelf booze. "Dude was an open book after I got the second beer in him. So here's the dealio. He lives alone. He's looking to tie on a real pisser tonight 'cause he has tomorrow off work. Which has me thinking, brohas. We'd be better off stealing his shit now, while he's gone, than waiting for him to come home so we can wax him. He prolly won't miss his uniform or his security badge until he goes looking for 'em day after tomorrow. He'll be nursing a hangover until then, yo."

Venom had been amped to spill a little blood—*it's been too long*—but maybe Hawkeye was right. It was better to get in, get what they needed, and get the fuck out without leaving any evidence or carnage behind.

"Makes sense to me." Crutch flicked a cigarette butt out the window. The maintenance man lived in a decidedly low-class Evanston neighborhood. It wasn't like anyone would complain about litter on their lawn.

"Fine." Venom didn't try to hide the disappointment in his tone. "You two go get it done. I'll wait here in case our newfound friend decides to make an early night of it."

If he did, Venom would be waiting.

———※———

Black Knights Inc. Headquarters

"I think we're down a man," Delilah said.

Ozzie scrubbed a hand over his face, following the thumb Delilah hooked to his left. Samantha, who had pulled up a chair beside him at the bank of computers, was out cold. No surprise considering that when he glanced at his watch, he realized four hours had passed since he began hacking the Basilisks' computers, rifling through their banks statements, identifying their overseas accounts, and so on.

If you thought all that sounded really interesting, you'd be dead wrong. It was enough to put an observer into a coma. Case in point: Samantha.

"So what's the deal, Ozzie?" Delilah asked as a girlie-sounding snore fluttered Samantha's lips. Her arm was straight on the computer table, her cheek flat against the surface, her mouth slightly open. It wouldn't be long before a puddle of drool formed. "Is this just another of your legion of conquests? Or is it something more?"

He *wished* there was a way it could be something more. He wished there was a way to *make it so*, as Jean-Luc Picard would say. But there were too many obstacles between them, too many secrets. Not to mention Samantha's assertion earlier that she believed what they had was fun for now but not forever.

"Don't worry, Dee. She has no designs on me for the long haul."

"Good." Delilah blew out a breath.

"Glad one of us is happy about that."

"Ozzie—"

"No." He held up a hand. "Just…no, okay?" Then it occurred to him that maybe he was being overly sensitive. He was tired. His leg was throbbing—the damn thing *always* throbbed. And he'd been staring at his computer screen for so long, his eyes felt gritty. "I think that's enough for tonight." He punched the power button on his monitor and watched the screen go black. "We'll pick up here in the morning."

Delilah opened her mouth like she wanted to say something more, then closed it again, shaking her head. Finally, she declared, "I'm going to start rifling through the accounts you hacked, see if anything buzzes my radar."

He realized his tone was more cutting than he intended by the furrow of Delilah's brow when he said "Suit yourself," but he couldn't make himself apologize. Those twin pits of self-pity and remorse were back. They'd sprouted thick branches that threatened to strangle him as he shoved to a stand.

"Samantha…" He bent to whisper in her ear, brushing

a lock of hair behind the delicate shell. "Time to call it a night."

She came awake with a start and a curse. *Only Samantha*. Just like that, his frown turned upside down. And some of those dark emotions that had taken root were ripped out and tossed away.

"Did I fall asleep?" She blinked at him blearily.

"Sawed a few logs. Nothing major," Delilah assured her.

In the light of Delilah's computer screen, Ozzie saw Samantha grimace. "I know I snore." *Adorably*, he thought. *You snore adorably*. "Sorry." She gazed around as if disoriented. "So did you find anything?"

"Not yet," he told her. "But it's enough for one night. I need to get some sleep."

"Oh good." She nodded and pushed to a wobbly stand. "Take me to bed, Goose. Or lose me forever."

Top Gun. She quoted *Top Gun* at him.

His heart clenched. She was everything he'd ever hoped for. Everything he was doomed never to have.

———

"Your room or mine?" Samantha waggled her eyebrows at Ozzie. They were standing in the dark third-floor hallway, so she figured the effort was wasted. Still, she hoped he could *hear* the eyebrow waggle in her voice.

"You're tired," he said. "Let's agree on a rain check."

She *had* been tired. Downstairs, after hours of watching his fingers fly across not one but *two* keyboards—*he really is a Whiz Kid, a hacker extraordinaire*—she'd been exhausted. But the journey up the flight of stairs, not to mention all the thoughts of what was to come once they were in one of the bedrooms, had her awake. And horny.

"Damnit, Ozzie," she hissed. "Not again."

As soon as the words were out of her mouth, she realized how selfish they were. How selfish *she* was. She wasn't the only one to have been through the wringer these last couple of days. For heaven's sake, he'd been tasered, accosted, and cuffed by the police. He'd wrecked his motorcycle and then spent forever on his computer trying to help *her* out, trying to solve *her* mess. The poor man had gone above and beyond. And here she was, wanting something more from him. Namely, his hot bod.

"Sorry." She winced. "After everything you've done, you've got to be exhausted. And here I am—"

"Being wonderfully, delightfully *you*," he interrupted her. His warm hands found their way to her hips. His hot breath tickled her ear when he leaned down to whisper, "Sweetheart, I'll never be too tired for you. I just thought—"

"See…" She cut him off. "That's the problem with you brainy sorts. You think too much." Then she grabbed his ears and kissed the bejeezus out of him right there in the hallway.

———————

Ozzie kicked his bedroom door shut, wincing when it slammed with a loud bang.

Shit, I probably woke up the whole place.

That was the last rational thought he had, because Samantha shoved him until his back hit the wall. Then she was on him, hungrily kissing him like the breath he fed her was the only thing keeping her alive, and she wanted him, *needed* him to keep kissing her forever.

I'm game for that!

"Ozzie." When she whispered his name, her voice

thick with passion, heat washed from the top of his head to the tips of his biker boot–clad toes.

Her lips melted into him, her tongue licking flames into his mouth. She was on fire, a living conflagration threatening to burn him up. And oh! He was game for that too.

For long moments, he allowed her to run the show. Let her skim her hands all over him, her fingers testing the muscles of his shoulders, his chest, his stomach as he simply held her steady, cupping her face in his hands. Then he couldn't stand it any longer.

"I need you naked," he whispered against her lips.

He needed to feel all that was her pressed against all that was him. Needed no barriers between himself and the woman who had stolen his heart just by being her marvelous, smart, unpretentious self.

Without waiting for her permission, he pulled her shirt over her head. Her bra quickly followed. She was as eager to move things along as he was. She yanked off his T-shirt and carelessly tossed it aside. The glow of the crescent moon filtered in through the panes of the leaded-glass window, providing just enough light to show the frenzy of their fingers as they worked at each other's jeans and boots.

When Samantha stepped out of her panties, Ozzie was ready for her, waiting to take her in his arms. "Come here," he said, or *growled*. That was really the only way to describe the tires-crunching-along-a-gravel-road sound of his voice.

She lunged at him. *Lunged*. Pressing herself so tightly against him that it was as if she wanted to crawl inside. Little did she know that she was already there.

Already in his head.

In his heart.

"So soft," he whispered. "So perfect."

They were finally skin to skin, heart to heart. Nothing between them but the sweet sound of his name on her lips. And when she kissed him again, there wasn't even that.

Once again, her hands were everywhere, as if she was trying to memorize every bulge, every dip, each individual texture. And he understood. He wanted to touch every inch of her. *Kiss* every inch of her. And then when he was done, he wanted to start over from the beginning.

"Bed," she said when he moved his mouth to her ear, nipping the delicate lobe.

"As you wish," he whispered, quoting *The Princess Bride*, her favorite movie.

He realized his mistake when she stiffened, her graceful muscles locking into place.

Fuck. "As you wish" was Wesley's way of telling Princess Buttercup he loved her. So in effect, whether Ozzie had meant to or not, he had just declared his love to Samantha.

By the change in her, it wasn't something she expected to hear.

"Anything you want, you just have to ask," he quickly added, hoping she would assume his earlier words were purely coincidental. It worked. A little shudder ran through her, and she was back to kissing him like crazy.

He walked her backward toward his waiting bed. When her thighs hit the edge of the mattress, he grabbed her waist and tossed her atop the covers. He landed beside her, delighted by the giggle that sounded at the back her throat. Even *more* delighted when that giggle turned into a gasp of pleasure, because he quickly took her in his arms, framing her face between his palms so that he could reclaim her mouth.

His cock throbbed insistently against her hip, its skin on fire. She moaned at the feel of it, the heat of it. And even though he was already hard, that throaty sound turned him to granite.

But if he was granite, then she was water. Warm and liquid and moving against him. An undulating river of smooth skin and darting tongue and busy, *busy* hands.

"Please," she whispered, her fingers digging into his shoulders. "I don't want to go slow. Not this time. Please, Ozzie."

As you wish was once again poised on the tip of his tongue, but this time, he bit it back. Instead, he said, "Hell yes," and reached into his nightstand drawer, grabbing a foil-wrapped condom.

Before he could do the honors, she took the little packet from him, ripped it open with her teeth, and seconds later had him expertly sheathed. The feel of her soft, eager hands fisting the latex down his swollen length? *Holy shit!* It was nearly enough to have him going off right then and there. He had to distract himself by palming one of her perfect breasts, thumbing the hardened tip until her soft areola furled and wrinkled.

"Now. Hurry," she demanded, lying back and spreading her legs.

In the moonlight, her pale skin looked almost translucent, the rosy tips of her breasts standing out in contrast. He had never seen a sweeter or more seductive sight than her hair spread out against his pillow.

His pillow. *His* bed. *His* woman.

At least for tonight.

Moving between her legs, her frenzied breath and grasping hands urging him faster, he once again felt like his heart was too big for his chest. It pounded so hard, he marveled it didn't crack open his rib cage, exposing itself and his love for her and leaving him a wasted lump of flesh on the bed beside her.

"What are you waiting for?" Samantha whispered, making mewling, impatient noises. Her knees were on either side of his hips. She grabbed the base of his dick and angled it toward her opening. Even in the dark, he could see how swollen she was, how wet she was…for *him*.

Gritting his teeth, determined to cherish every second of their first joining, he gently flexed his hips and watched, wide-eyed and breathless, as the head of his cock disappeared into her gorgeous body.

It was terrifying the way Samantha had lost all control. Her body was not her own. It was a thing that throbbed and wanted and *needed*.

She had no sense of place and time. There was only Ozzie, rising above her like a golden god. Broad shoulders flexing, a sheen of sweat making his tan skin glow in the moonlight. "You okay?" His voice sounded like his throat had been scoured.

Her brow furrowed. *Okay? I'm in heaven! I'm with you!* But then she looked down to where their bodies were joined, just barely, just the tip of his cock buried inside her, and she understood his concern. She was stretched tight around him. And yeah, okay, so he'd felt big in her mouth earlier. Now, between her legs, he looked…*huge*.

"I take back what I said about not going slow," she said. "I think we better take this inch by inch." *How* many inches exactly, she didn't hazard to guess.

A muscle ticked in his wide jaw. His blue eyes bored

into her, cutting through the dark of the night. She could tell it took everything he had not to crash forward, not to rut as his body demanded. And most men, when being ridden hard by lust, would not have bothered to worry about her. They would slam home and apologize for it later. But Ozzie? Oh, Ozzie slowly, inexorably slowly, slid his thick length inside her.

It wasn't easy. As he speared deeper, her body clamped down, the intrusion too much. But Ozzie, patient and wonderful Ozzie, knew just what to do.

"Relax," he gritted between his teeth.

Before she could come back with a smart-alecky *Easy for you to say!* he pressed his thumb against her distended clitoris. Rubbing it side to side, up and down in a rhythm he'd learned drove her crazy, he coaxed her body into accepting his.

With a final grunt and thrust, he was seated to the hilt. His pelvic bone abraded the nerves at the top of her sex *just right*. His chest was warm and heavy as he allowed her to take some of his weight.

"You okay?" he asked again.

If she'd had a voice, she could have told him she'd never been better. But she was stretched tight, completely full. And she was so overcome with sensation that she couldn't speak. Being with Ozzie, having him buried inside, was the absolute best thing she'd ever known. He touched her in places she'd never been touched. Smoothed out every wrinkle until she wasn't sure where she stopped and he started. And the throb of him so deep inside… Her eyes nearly crossed. Her toes *did* curl. She managed a mute nod.

The words *I love you!* lodged in the back of her throat when he began to move. She wrapped her arms around him and held on tight.

Samantha was glorious.

Seeing her take her pleasure, watching how the slightest touch, the smallest change in pressure or angle made her arch and moan, was the single greatest thing ever. But *because* it was the single greatest thing ever, and because it had been so long, and because she was so...*her*, Ozzie's body teetered on the edge of release. He had to grit his teeth and fist his hand in the covers beside her head, fighting tooth and nail to keep from going off before she did.

He tried to go slow, tried to do everything just like she wanted, but she was so hot, her body rising and falling beneath his. When he hit the right spot, her hips arched off the bed. "Yes!" she cried. "Oh, Ozzie! Yes! Right there!"

Right there indeed.

He grabbed a pillow and shoved it beneath her ass. It kept her angled into the position she craved. The one they *both* craved. The one that had the sensitive tip of his cock sliding along the top wall of her channel, rubbing that swollen patch of nerve-rich flesh.

The sounds she made became low and guttural. And him? He was growling, panting, encouraging her ever higher with dirty talk that, in any other situation, would make them both blush to the roots of their hair.

He was lost in the slide of flesh. In and out. Give and take. Two bodies striving for one mutual goal.

He could have died on the spot and been happy doing it. He was inside Samantha. *Samantha, Samantha, Samantha...* Her name became a refrain that matched the rhythm of their bodies. Sliding his hands beneath her butt, he gripped her plump cheeks and lifted her higher. Increasing the pressure, the friction. Thrusting harder.

Deeper. Over and over again. When she whimpered, a desperate, kittenish sound, he knew she was close.

"Come for me, sweetheart." He buried his face in the crook of her neck, kissing the salty sweat from her skin and feeling her heart thunder against his lips. He wanted to tell her more, tell her *everything*. Who he really was, what he really did, how he really felt, but all he could say was, "I want to feel you come all around me."

She grabbed his ass as if begging him to make the pleasure stop and simultaneously pleading for more. He chose the second option, pistoning his hips faster. Harder. His balls pulled tight against his body, aching for release. And just when he thought he couldn't take any more, her thighs clamped around his hips, her back bowed, and she gave herself over to passion, crying out his name.

Feeling her body coil and release around him, feeling her bathe him in her ecstasy, forced his own release. He could no more hold back his orgasm than he could hold back the rising of tomorrow's sun. He let go…of everything. Every doubt. Every fear. All his pain. And came into her.

The whole time, she held him like she never wanted to let go.

Chapter 18

THE DREAM BEGAN AS IT ALWAYS DID. WITH JULIA nudging him awake…

"Ozzie. Ozzie! You have to go. There are rules about fraternizing on the job, and I don't want to get caught."

"I'll leave before sunup," he assured her, tossing aside the warm, damp sheets to search for a breath of air. The hotel's AC units hummed nonstop, but they held little sway over the staggering heat and humidity of the Malaysian night.

"No." She punched his shoulder. *"Get up, Ozzie. I'm serious."*

He groaned and opened one eye, seeing his clothes in a heap over by the door. He had given his all for the last two hours, and his aching muscles and heavy eyelids told the story. As did the rumpled sheets and the musky scent of sex filling the room.

Yep, he had shown Julia Ledbetter the time of her life. And now she was kicking him out. He should be used to it, but the truth was, it stung.

Every damn time.

With a grunt, he pushed to a stand and padded over to his pile of clothes. Finding his boxer briefs, he pulled them on and turned to find Julia luxuriating in bed.

"That was fun." She bit her lip and smiled coyly. *"We should do it again sometime. You think you'll ever get another assignment to assist the Secret Service?"*

By *do it again sometime, she didn't mean take his*

number and try to make a go of it. She meant if their paths happened to cross, she wouldn't mind a repeat of the night's Olympic sexual performance.

He wanted to snarl and snap. Instead, he flashed her an easy smile and said, "We can only hope, right?"

She giggled, lifting her arms over her head and stretching. "Yes, we certainly c—"

BOOM!

A terrible, earsplitting sound.

A blinding white light.

The acrid smell of smoke and burned skin.

And inexplicable pain...

Ozzie opened his eyes to see his own hot, wet blood spurting from what remained of his leg. Curling tendrils of pungent vapor filled the room. On the burning bed was Julia. Her hair was gone. So was her flesh. And her eye sockets, empty of her eyeballs, seemed to stare at him accusingly.

If he hadn't seduced her, perhaps she would be in the bath instead of the bed. If he hadn't seduced her, maybe she would still be alive.

Terrible guilt drove a dagger into Ozzie's gut. He blinked at Julia's charred remains, watching her, the whole scene, morph in front of his eyes.

Gone was the hotel room. Gone was the smoldering bed.

Now he was inside the garage of his childhood home. And Julia had become his mother. He was four years old, standing at the door leading into the house, clutching his security blanket and staring at his mother's long, blond hair pressed against the rolled-up window of her car. Her face looked blue. And puffy.

He had always thought her a beautiful angel, but she didn't look beautiful now. She looked scary with her mouth open and her eyes bulging. She seemed to be accusing him of something. Of spilling the paint on the rug. Of scaring the cat and making it scratch her. Of not being a good boy.

He held his blankie to his mouth and started to cry, unable to look away.

And then, once again, the scene changed. His mother's face was replaced by others. Others wearing looks of pity or affection or indifference or seduction. Familiar faces. Dozens of faces. Flashing in front of his eyes like a skipping movie reel.

Then the reel stopped, and there was Samantha. She stood before him, ethereal and wavering. An image reflected in water. She smiled that sweet gap-toothed smile as she waved good-bye, turning from him. Walking away. Not looking back.

He thought he knew pain. But nothing compared to the feel of his heart exploding inside his chest.

"Ozzie! Ozzie!"

He came awake with a start, blinking at the sight of Samantha hovering over him. Moonlight still streamed in through the window, showing the alarm in her chocolate eyes and glinting off the curling curtain of her dark hair.

"You were having a nightmare," she whispered, her brow knit with concern.

Yes, he was. A familiar one. And it didn't take Freud to figure out what it all meant. The two women who had died on his watch—and all the others who hadn't seen enough in him to want to stick around—they were his failures. Proof that he...

But Samantha, *she* was a new addition.

He rubbed his chest where his heart still ached and wanted to spill his guts when she said, "Was it the accident? Do you..." She scooted down until she was stretched beside him. Her head on his shoulder, her arm tight around his waist. "Do you want to talk about it?"

The cold specter of the dream slowly subsided, leaving nothing but pain, guilt, and recrimination behind.

In his heart of hearts, he knew there was nothing he could have done to save his mother or Julia. But that didn't stop the string of *what-ifs* that plagued him. *What if* he had only done this. Or *what if* he hadn't done that. *What if—*

"Ozzie?" Samantha's cool fingers smoothed the lines from his forehead and gently cupped his jaw.

"Like you said," he told her, grabbing her hand and kissing her fingertips, "it was just a bad dream."

She nuzzled his neck, tossing a leg over his waist. The feel of her silky skin, the decadent heat of her snuggled against him, chased away the last of his chills, warming his body, his soul.

She would leave him just as his nightmare foretold. And yes, it was bound to break his heart when she did, but in the meantime…

"Want to help take my mind off it?"

She pushed up on her elbow, a shadowed grin flashing down at him. "What did you have in mind, cowboy?"

He trailed his hand over the small of her back, past the tattoo he had kissed and licked earlier, until he palmed her plump, delicious ass. "Cowboy, huh? Well, cowgirl, you fancy taking a ride?"

"Thought you'd never ask." She giggled and claimed his lips in a hot kiss that scorched away any lingering memory of the dream.

There was a new sort of desperation in the way Ozzie held her, in the needy, guttural noises he made.

The nightmare had shaken him.

It had shaken *her*.

To feel him jerking beside her, to hear him moaning like his heart was breaking, had scared her to death. She wished he had told her what it had been about, wished she knew if it was the wreck or those thirteen months as a Navy SEAL or the reason he sometimes got that sad, faraway look in his eyes. But she satisfied herself that whatever the dream had been about, she was the one to make him forget it.

She straddled his hips, her slick channel cradling the evidence of his desire.

"God, that feels good," he moaned, humping upward to drag himself against her.

"Mmm," she hummed against his lips. "Keep doing that."

He grabbed her hips in his big, strong hands, pulling her down hard against him, and kept up the rocking motion. Slick skin razed against hard. Wet, sultry heat bathed hot, rigid flesh. And his kiss? It was enough to make her head spin.

The way Ozzie used his body, the way he put everything he had into lovemaking, was truly spectacular. Nothing was off-limits. He took direction and gave it with equal fervor. And before long, her orgasm built to a fever pitch.

"I'm going to come," she whimpered, pushing up so she could increase the friction, the pace of her hips sawing over his, her sex sliding over his.

"Yes, come, sweetheart. Let me watch."

Her head fell back on her shoulders. She cupped her breasts, lifting their aching weight, lightly pinching her nipples.

Ozzie made a low, growling noise of approval. When

she glanced down at him, his blue eyes blazed through the dark like laser beams. His jaw was gritted, and the tendons in his neck stood out as he watched her fondle herself.

"Help me," she whimpered, her orgasm so close. So very close. But she couldn't…quite…get…there. "Oh!" she cried out when the callused pad of his thumb worked between her swollen lips to rasp over the hard knot of nerves at the top of her sex.

That was all she needed. Her climax burst through her like Independence Day fireworks. Just detonation after detonation. *Boom, boom, BOOM!*

Samantha collapsed against him, vestiges of her orgasm making her shake.

Amazing. That was the only word he had to describe her. She was so utterly uninhibited.

He had been with a lot of women, probably more than his fair share. But he had never been with a woman who sought pleasure and gave pleasure with equal abandon.

Watching her ride his cock without ever taking him into herself had been one of the most erotic experiences of his life. And holding off against the slick, fantastic friction had taken every last ounce of his self-control.

He was so hard, quivering with the need to come.

"I need to be in you." He pulled her hair from the side of her face and whispered in her ear. "Samantha, I need to be in you so badly."

"Mmm-hmm," she hummed her approval, putty in his arms as he flipped her over until he was above her.

Her thighs clamped around his hips. Her heels dug into the back of his legs, egging him on. And her wet, welcoming sex was so tempting that he almost threw caution to the wind and plunged into her scorching heat.

But good sense and chivalry won out in the end. He shook with the effort to get a condom on. And then he shook with the effort to go slowly when he slid his burning, aching length inside her.

"You feel so good," she murmured, dragging his head down for a long, lazy kiss.

And that was the understatement of the millennium. He felt great, even though the muscles in his thigh twitched with pain, even though his heart pounded so fast, his chest ached, even though he was so hard, the skin of his dick stretched and stung.

"Fuck me, Ozzie," she instructed, her hands in his hair, her hips arching into him. "Fuck me until I come again."

And he did. In a slow, sensual dance, he rebuilt her passion while, with jaw gritted, he staved off his own. When he finally felt her clench around him, he cried out her name, letting himself go in long, endless, body-shaking spurts. And afterward, he slept a dreamless, peaceful sleep.

It was the first time he had done that in longer than he could remember.

Samantha came awake in the most delicious way.

Ozzie's big body spooned her. His lips nibbled the nape of her neck. And his fingers toyed with her nipple.

"Mmm," she hummed, stretching and smiling when she felt his erection throbbing insistently against her bottom. "What are you up to?" And was that her voice? She'd never sounded so sexy, so purr-y before. She dug it.

Apparently Ozzie did too. He flexed his hips. "I'm

working on my night moves," he whispered, nipping her earlobe and making her toes curl.

"First Bruce Springsteen and now Bob Seger? Look at you branching out beyond eighties hair bands." She snaked a hand beneath the covers to find his warm hip. Running her fingers down his muscled thigh, careful of his scars, she reveled in the crinkly man-hair that tickled her fingertips.

"I'm no one-trick pony," he assured her, rubbing his hardness against her in a slow thrust and retreat.

"Don't I know it. Carry on then." She wiggled against him, loving the moan her movement caused. "Keep working on your night moves. You'll hear no complaints from me."

He pinched her nipple, making her gasp. She tilted her head into the pillow to allow him better access to her neck. "Although," he said, "it would probably be more apt to say I'm working on my *morning* moves. You know, since it's nine a.m."

Nine a.m.?

Her eyes popped open, and the first thing she saw was sunlight streaming in through the window. She turned and looked at the glowing numbers on his alarm clock. They read 9:07.

Shit!

"Shit!" She tossed back the covers and vaulted out of bed. Her head gave a dull throb, reminding her of the injury she'd sustained, before it faded away.

Ozzie blinked at her. "Was it something I said?"

"Get dressed!" She lobbed his jeans at him even as she hopped into her own. "There's no time for a shower or breakfast. I have a noon deadline on that story Charlie wanted to bump. If I don't make it, he probably won't run it at all. And I refuse to let that sleazy jerk of a businessman get away without having his perfidy immortalized in print. People lost their jobs and retirements because of him. They *deserve* for him to have his dirty laundry publicly aired."

"Say no more." Ozzie kicked his legs over the side of the bed.

Samantha allowed herself a couple of seconds to take in all six-plus feet of his tan, golden, sex-mussed self. His hair was going every which way. There was a faint shadow of a hickey on his neck. And his dick was fully engorged and bobbing hungrily. But he didn't hesitate. He didn't complain. He just pulled on his jeans and walked over to open a drawer on his dresser, grabbing a clean blue T-shirt and pulling it over his head. When he turned around, she could see it sported a picture of Spock and read: *I find your lack of logic disturbing.*

Sweet merciful fuck, is there anyone more wonderful than Ozzie? Ozzie with his big, beautiful Navy SEAL body—she was still wrapping her mind around *that.* Ozzie with his big, beautiful computer-hacker brain. He was equal parts god and geek, and to her, that made up a perfect whole.

She wanted nothing more than to shove him back into that bed and have her way with him. But justice—and the *Chicago Tribune*—waited on no one.

Reaching for the red bra lying atop his dresser, she blinked when he snatched it out of her hands. "Nope." He shook his head. "This one's mine. A souvenir of our first kiss and the first time I made you come." He bent to pick up the apricot bra she'd been wearing the night before. "This one you can keep."

She cocked a hip against her hand. "And do you keep souvenirs from *all* your conquests. If so, that's a little creepy."

He shook his head, his eyes twinkling. "Just you, sweetheart."

A thrill of delight skimmed through her. He might be bullshitting her. But she didn't think he was. "Good answer." She winked. "In fact, it's *such* a good answer that as soon as I turn in the story, I plan to reward you by taking you into the storage closet where I'll work on my *afternoon* moves."

Tribune Tower

"Your left eyelid is twitching," Ozzie said from the spot between her and Donny's desks. The bullpen was its usual controlled chaos. And the air was heavy with the tangy scents of stress sweat and bad coffee. "What's got you pissed?"

"Is my tell really that obvious?" Samantha frowned. "Or are you just that observant?"

"Little of A, little of B." He shrugged. "But it was the litany of curses you whispered under your breath that really gave you away."

"Charlie wants to cut this quote." She pointed a finger at her computer screen where a red line drove viciously through her article's money shot. Just looking at it made her blood pressure spike. "When the douche-canoe businessman goes on the record saying his ties with the mayor are what made him a target for all these *trumped-up* charges."

"Your editor probably knows better than to drag the mayor's name into this mess. Things start to get sticky in this city when—*Ow!*" He slapped his cheeks. "Okay! Okay! I take it back. Stop trying to fry my face off with your fire eyes!"

"That's right. Don't forget whose side you're on."

"Your side." He crossed his heart. "I'm always on your side."

"Exactly." She turned back to her glowing screen. But when Ozzie's stomach grumbled for the bazillionth time, she looked over at him again. "You know, there's a Starbucks a block north. You could run down and snag us some breakfast." The clock on her computer read 11:09. "Maybe by the time you get back, I'll have this damned article done, and we can take our coffees and muffins into the storage closet." She waggled her eyebrows and leered.

He pushed out of his seat, wincing and absently rubbing his thigh. It was strange... Ozzie was so stoic about his injury, never complaining, rarely even mentioning it. In fact, were it not for his subtle limp or the occasional flash of pain across his face—or last night's nightmare?—she would never know he was hurt.

"Promise me you will not move from this spot?" he asked. "We still don't know—"

"This seat and my ass are two sides of a Velcro strip," she swore. "I won't get up even for a potty break. Oh!" She snapped her fingers. "And skip the coffee with cream and sugar. After last night, I need a double shot of espresso." While strong and bitter, the break-room coffee hadn't done the trick today.

Ozzie grinned down at her, pleased with himself that *he* was the reason she needed the caffeine equivalent of a mule kick to the backside. "As you wish." He snapped her a salute before sauntering toward the elevators.

Her breath strangled in her chest, her heartbeat a rapid *thud* in her ears. It was the second time he had uttered that phrase. The one that really meant *I love you*. But she didn't think he understood the connection he was making with the movie. When he stopped to talk to the woman who wrote for the paper's entertainment section, Samantha was *sure* he didn't realize the true meaning of the words. Because he flashed that smile and twinkled those eyes at the busty, dark-haired harlot who had a set of teeth that belonged on a toothpaste commercial.

"Flirting is second nature to you, isn't it, you big jerkface?" Samantha grumbled. Her brown eyes were *definitely* green this time.

She had to remind herself that Ozzie hadn't done anything wrong. He had promised her nothing. Agreed to nothing. *She* was the idiot who had thought that if she got him into bed, he'd see how great they were together, and then he'd automatically want to…*what*? Settle down with her and make a million babies?

Mad at herself for being a stupid, hopeful, girlie cliché, and mad at him for being so wonderful that he turned her into a stupid, hopeful, girlie cliché, she turned back to her computer screen, determined to finish the damned article. The sound of her phone ringing from the depths of her purse interrupted her.

She didn't bother to dive into the crap that was fundamental to her daily existence. Instead, she upended her purse atop her desk and snagged her phone from the pile. She smiled with relief when she saw who was calling. *Donny*. Dear, sweet Donny. He always seemed to know when she needed a sympathetic ear.

"Decided to play hooky today, funny face?" she asked, trying to sound chipper. "Or are you out following a lead? Because I have to tell you, you picked a hell of a day to be gone. I could really use—"

"Samantha," a deep voice interrupted. Whoever was on the other end of the line wasn't Donny. An icy finger slipped up her spine.

"Who is this?" She gripped the edge of her chair until her knuckles turned white. "Why do you have Donny's phone?"

"The better question is," the man hissed, his voice reminding her of a snake slithering through dry leaves, "what I'll do with Mr. Danielson if you're not out on the street in front of the building in two minutes."

Samantha glanced up, hoping to see Ozzie still flirting with the wannabe Crest White Strips model. No such luck. He was long gone.

"And before you think to call the police or tell one of your colleagues what's going on, know that the man standing by the water cooler is one of us. If he sees you do anything you shouldn't, he'll let me know, and Mr. Danielson… Well, you don't wanna know what'll happen to him."

Samantha jerked her eyes over to the man in the brown coveralls beside the cooler. To the casual observer, he didn't look out of place. The uniform, the mop bucket, the lazy way he cleaned the floor, said he was just one of the many maintenance people who kept the building spick-and-span. But upon closer inspection, she could see his baseball cap was pulled low over his eyes. And since his red, bushy beard covered the lower half of his face, his identity was completely obscured.

"How do I know you won't hurt Donny even if I *do* come down?" Her chest hurt. Why did her chest hurt? Oh yeah. Because her heart was banging against her ribs like a steel fist.

"Guess you'll just hafta take my word for it," Snake Voice said. "After all, what other choice do you have?"

He had her there. She had *no* other choice. She felt like a colony of spiders crawled over the back of her neck.

"Leave your phone," the man instructed. "Leave your

purse. Ninety seconds and counting." *Click*. The line went dead.

Samantha used three of her remaining ninety seconds racking her brain for a way to let someone know what was happening. A quick note? An SOS tapped out on her desk with a pen? Did any of her colleagues know Morse code? Of course, all of this was fantasy, since the janitor who wasn't really a janitor was watching her every move.

Swallowing the bile that climbed up the back of her throat, she pushed to a stand and shakily made her way to the elevator. Janitor/Not Janitor followed her inside, careful to keep his hat pulled low, mindful of the elevator's security camera. When she opened her mouth to say…she wasn't sure what, he gave her a terse shake of his head. She clamped her jaws so hard that the sound of her teeth clacking together echoed around the small space.

As the car descended, *dinging* the passing of the floors, Samantha prayed that Ozzie had forgotten something—his wallet or his sunglasses or *anything*—and that he'd be waiting to ride the elevator back up when the doors opened.

Once again, no such luck. The silver doors slid open to reveal no Ozzie, just the normal hustle and bustle of people rushing through the lobby as they went about their day. Janitor/Not Janitor spoke for the first time. "Thirty seconds, Miss Tate."

Goose bumps peppered her skin at the sound of his voice. It was that of an executioner. Unfeeling. Inflectionless. When she stepped from the elevator car, she realized that she'd lied to Ozzie for the first time. Not a lie by omission, like her love for him. But a flat-out, black-and-white *lie*.

She had promised she wouldn't get up from her seat under any circumstances. And here she was walking across the lobby…

Chapter 19

VENOM HAD LITTLE PATIENCE FOR WEAKNESS. AND even *less* patience for sniveling, pansy-ass men wearing ridiculously large glasses and bright-red skinny jeans.

"Shut the fuck up!" He kicked the seat in front of him where Donny Danielson was hog-tied and gagged.

The stolen SUV was perfect for a kidnapping. Its third-row seats allowed Venom to keep his pistol trained on the back of Donny's head, and the deeply tinted windows assured him no one on the outside could see what he was doing.

Even so, he felt twitchy. He didn't like idling by the curb, waiting on Samantha to come down. Michigan Avenue was busy, humming with tourists and locals out for a day of shopping. And where there were tourists and commerce, there were cops. It wouldn't be long before one of the doughnut eaters on patrol saw the SUV's blinking hazard lights and came to investigate.

Venom flexed his shoulders. Blew out a hard breath. But nothing seemed to calm his nerves. Donny's sniffling was making matters worse.

"Can you believe we went to war for assholes like this?" he asked Crutch. His VP was in the driver's seat, impatiently drumming his fingers on the steering wheel.

"Mmph," Crutch grunted. He hadn't had a cigarette since they snatched Donny from outside his apartment building. Lack of nicotine always made Crutch uncommunicative.

And speaking of snatching Donny, it had been ridiculously easy. The reporter had been fumbling with his keys, distracted by the glowing screen of his iPhone and trying to juggle a steaming cup of coffee, when Venom and Crutch pulled up beside his prissy Prius to drag the squawking little runt inside their SUV.

"I *said*," Venom snapped, shoving the barrel of his pistol so tightly against Donny's head that the reporter winced and choked behind his gag, "shut the fuck up!"

"Easy," Crutch cautioned.

"Seriously, though," Venom snarled. "I did not sweat my ass off in that damned Iraqi desert for the likes of him, tadpoles who would rather suck a dick than grow a pair of balls."

Venom was going to *love* watching the lights go out in Donny's eyes when he eventually strangled him. A bullet was too good for Donny Danielson. Real men died by lead. Snot-nosed lady-boys died by having the life strangled out of them while they looked into the eyes of a real man.

But he couldn't kill Donny yet. He might need to use the sack of shit to make Samantha talk. Nothing loosened a person's tongue quicker than watching someone they cared about suffer. He'd learned that lesson in Albu Bali.

"Look." Crutch pointed out the window. "She's coming."

Venom turned in the direction of Crutch's finger. Sure enough. Samantha and Termite hustled through the building's front door, Termite steering her toward the waiting SUV with a hand at her elbow.

Venom's heart began to pound. His breath caught at the back of his throat. Even though her eyes were wide and unblinking, her cheeks pale with fear, she was still prettier in person than in any of the pictures he'd seen online or in the paper.

Anticipation swirled low in his belly, making his

cock twitch. "This is gonna be fun," he said to no one in particular.

—∿∿—

Samantha knew the taste of fear when she slid into the second-row seat of the black SUV. It was sour, like a pickle. It thickened her spit, making it impossible to swallow.

"You okay?" she asked Donny, taking in his red eyes and disheveled hair. His ankles were duct-taped together, as were his wrists. A length of the stuff was slapped over his mouth.

He gave her a jerky nod, and relief rushed through her so quickly that she felt dizzy. Or maybe that was terror making her head spin?

"I'm so sorry I got you into this," she told him.

"How touching," came the voice from the phone.

She turned to find a mountain of a man dressed head to toe in black. He wore a ski mask. It covered everything but his mouth and eyes. When he flashed her a smile, she was surprised to see his teeth were straight and white. In contrast, his eyes were as black as night. Looking into them, she felt like she was falling into a soulless abyss.

John George Peabody III, a.k.a. Venom. She would bet her life on it.

"Good job," the guy in the driver's seat said, drawing her attention when Janitor/Not Janitor climbed into the front passenger seat. The driver was also dressed head to toe in black, with a ski mask obscuring his features.

Samantha waited for the locks to reengage as Janitor/Not Janitor closed the door and pulled on his seat belt. But they didn't.

She wasn't sure she really thought about her next

move. She just *did* it. Leaning over Donny, she grabbed the latch on the unlocked door and threw it open. Using both hands and one foot, she shoved Donny out of the vehicle. Because his hands and ankles were tied, he landed in the street in a heap.

Desperate to follow him out, she made a swipe for the handle on her door, only to hear the locks *click* into place. A split second later, the barrel of a pistol was pressed tight against her temple. "You bitch!" Venom snarled.

"Help him!" she yelled through the open door just as Janitor/Not Janitor jumped out and rounded the front of the vehicle to make a grab for Donny. Adrenaline made her brain buzz. "Help him!" she screamed again, fully expecting Venom to send a bullet crashing through her temple.

Three men in suits carrying Chipotle bags heard her second yell. They turned toward the commotion by the curb. When they saw Donny bound and kicking at Janitor/Not Janitor, one of them yelled, "Hey! What the hell are you doing?"

"You *bitch*!" Venom hissed again, grabbing a fistful of her hair and jerking her head back. Her scalp stung, especially the area Bulldog had tried to bash in, and she assured herself that was the cause of the tears that sprang to her eyes. "You stupid, fucking *cunt*!" Venom added, because apparently *bitch* wasn't enough of an insult.

The guy in the front seat yelled to Janitor/Not Janitor, "Leave him, damnit! Get in the car!"

When the side door slammed shut, Donny still out on the curb, Samantha began to smile. She'd done it. She'd saved Donny.

"You're gonna pay for that," Venom whispered as Janitor/Not Janitor hopped in and the SUV peeled away from the curb. The biker's mouth was close to her ear, his breath stinking of stale coffee.

"Doesn't matter what you do to me now, asshole," she said, and Venom pulled her hair tighter. "Donny's safe, so I win."

Samantha had always been the kind of woman to take her victories where she could get them. As for her losses? Well, she wouldn't allow herself to think about those. She wouldn't let herself think about…Ozzie.

—⁂—

Ozzie was having a great day.

First, there was waking up to Samantha in his bed. Second, there was her expression when he'd ventured to whip out that whole *as you wish* line again. He had wanted to see her face when he said it, to try to get a read on his response, and while she hadn't jumped into his arms and professed her undying love, she hadn't run for the hills either. And *then*, as if those two things weren't reason enough to celebrate and mark this day one for the history books, there had been no line at Starbucks— *unheard of*—so the whole trip had taken him under ten minutes. Which meant he was that much closer to allowing Samantha to pull him into that storage closet.

Yes, indeed. Ozzie was having a great day.

He stopped in his tracks when he got to Samantha's desk, tilting his head at the contents of her purse piled atop it. A quick scan told him the usual culprits were there, even her cell phone. The only thing missing was *Samantha*.

He glanced around the bullpen, trying to spy her dark head and black blouse. *Nothing*. A niggle of apprehension stole up his spine. He beat it down, telling himself she'd gone to the break room to grab a bottle of water, or else, despite her assurances to the contrary, she'd had to make a run to the bathroom.

Setting the bag of chocolate chip muffins—her favorite—and the tray holding their two cups of coffee on the corner of her desk—the only clean spot—he turned and headed for the break room. Smiling faintly, he lifted a hand at the sports reporter who called out a hello. Said, "Sorry, there's something I need to check on," to the dark-haired woman who kept trying to flirt with him despite him being completely convinced it was obvious to everyone that he was gaga over Samantha. And seconds later, he was standing in the break room.

The *empty* break room.

That niggle of apprehension morphed into a full-on gut punch of dread. Ignoring the pain in his thigh, he spun around and jogged back into the bullpen, checking to make sure Samantha hadn't returned to her desk—*nope*—before making a beeline for the women's bathroom.

A redhead in a blue silk shirt and baggy gray slacks exited just as he lifted his hand to knock. She jumped back and blinked at him.

"Sorry," he said in a rush. "Would you happen to know if Samantha Tate is in there?"

"Samantha…" Red stared at him, her eyes traveling over him from head to toe. Usually, he enjoyed his effect on the ladies. Right now? He wished for buckteeth, bad skin, and a beer belly.

"Tate," he gritted between his teeth. "Samantha Tate. Is she in there? This is kind of an emergency."

"Oh!" Red blinked as if coming out of trance. "No. It was just me, but I could—"

He didn't wait to hear what she could do. He turned and bolted for Samantha's editor's office. Charlie sputtered when Ozzie barged through the door, the aluminum blinds attached to the frame rattling crazily. But the man took one look at Ozzie's face and knew something was up. "What is it?" he asked, adjusting his bifocals.

"I need to see the last ten minutes of surveillance footage for the elevators, the halls, and all the exits." Ozzie cursed himself for leaving her alone. If anything happened to her, he'd never forgive himself. He'd never be able to *live* with himself.

"Why?" Charlie's sharp green eyes looked huge behind the lenses of his glasses. "What's happened?"

"I'm not sure, but I think—"

The door burst open behind Ozzie, admitting the whirlwind that was Donny Danielson. The man's shirt was ripped, his hair mussed, and there was a patch of angry red skin in the shape of a rectangle covering his lips and cheeks.

Ozzie recognized the red pants Donny was wearing. He had seen them in the middle of a crowd of people when he'd been walking back from Starbucks. He'd thought it was a street performer looking for tips. Something along the lines of the dudes who liked to bang the bottoms of five-gallon paint buckets or paint themselves silver and pose motionlessly with tourists. But no. Now that he thought back on it, there had been a furtiveness to the gathering, a nervous sort of energy.

Right then and there, Ozzie's great day turned to shit and started circling the drain.

When Donny yelled, "The Basilisks have Samantha!" Ozzie glanced around, wondering who was making that awful sound like a wounded animal caught in a trap. And then he realized...

It's me.

———

"What do you mean you lost track of the SUV?" Ozzie thundered into his phone while taking the ramp to the Dan Ryan at breakneck speed.

After Donny explained what had happened, the first thing Ozzie did was race back to Samantha's desk and rifle through her pile of crap until he located her car keys. The second thing he did after pulling her Mustang from the parking garage was call Washington. In a single breath, he gave the police chief the lowdown, told him to get out an APB on a black Ford Expedition, and demanded that Washington check the POD and CCTV cameras around the Tribune Tower for footage of the vehicle. Then Ozzie turned south, heading for the down-and-out neighborhood the Basilisks liked to call home.

He'd barely made it past North Wells Street on his way to the highway before Washington called back to say they *had* caught the SUV on city surveillance and were tracking it. Then, not ten seconds later, Washington said, "Scratch that. It's vanished."

Like it was a fucking ninja Ford or some shit.

"There aren't any cameras in that neighborhood." Washington's tone was defensive. "Every time we put one up, some criminal piece of shit tears it down again."

Ozzie had zero time for excuses. Fear and adrenaline were a toxic mix in his blood, making his stomach queasy and his head feel so light, he would not have been surprised if it popped off his neck to go sailing out the open window.

When Donny had recounted how Samantha had shoved him from the SUV, determined to save *him* instead of herself, Ozzie had wanted to simultaneously kiss her and shake her. Of course, he couldn't do either, since she was in the hands of merciless killers because he'd dropped his guard and left her alone when he should have been stuck to her side like glue.

It's all my fault.

A ball of self-reproach clogged his throat. He had no time for any of that shit either.

"Where would they take her?" he demanded, running through the list of businesses and residences the chief had given him yesterday, trying to determine the best place to hide a kidnap victim.

Victim. The word stuck in his brain like a meat cleaver. His hands curled into fists around the steering wheel, his knuckles going white as skin stretched tight over bone.

"Their clubhouse would be my guess," Washington said.

Ozzie darted around a granny in a Buick as big as a boat. She could barely see over the dashboard, which might have been why she was going twenty miles per hour under the speed limit.

"Where's that?" he demanded, working the clutch, shifting gears, and pressing his foot on the gas. The Mustang's tires ate into the asphalt. Never had he admired the horses under the hood of a classic muscle car as much as he did right then.

"Hell if I know," Washington said. "That's the thing. No one knows the location. It's a well-guarded secret. Carver and some uniformed officers are headed over to their repair shop to crack some skulls together, but—"

Ozzie didn't wait to hear what else Washington had to say before disconnecting the call. It was obvious the police didn't have the first clue where to look for Samantha. Which left him one last option. He held down the number one on his cell phone and listened as autodial connected him with the shop.

Emily answered with a cheery-sounding, "What's

up, Romeo? I thought for sure you and Juliet would be getting busy in the storage closet by now. And before you accuse me of listening at doors, know that I was minding my own business in the hall this morning when I heard—"

"Damnit, Emily!" he growled. "Shut up and listen!" He could almost *see* her pulling back from the phone. The thing to do would be to apologize for his tone. But add *apologies* to the list of things he had no time for. "The Basilisks have Samantha."

"What?" she squawked. "How?"

A muscle ticked in his jaw. *I fucked up, okay? I fucked up!* "Never mind that. Is Delilah around?"

"She's sleeping."

"Wake her up. *Now*."

He didn't have to ask twice. He could hear Emily's feet clomping up the metal treads to the third floor. A door opened with a *bang*. Emily called Delilah's name. A few muffled words were exchanged. And then Delilah's croaking voice sounded on the other end of the line. "Ozzie? Jesus, Mary, and Joseph! Do the Basilisks really have—"

"Yes!" He cut her off. "So please tell me there was some clue in their accounts that might point to where they have their clubhouse."

"Their clubhouse?" She still sounded groggy. Item number one million on the list! No time for grogginess! He needed her firing on all cylinders.

"Washington figures that's where they'll take her. But no one seems to know where—*Sonofabitch!*"

A man in a green Toyota Tundra, who obviously took driving lessons at Asshole School, blasted across three lanes of traffic to make an exit he had no business making. Ozzie slammed on the brakes so hard, the collection of handbags Samantha kept in the backseat slid onto the floorboard. He flipped the guy the bird, put a curse on the dude's cock and balls, and checked all his mirrors for more idiot drivers before he once again gave the Mustang gas.

"You okay?" Delilah asked. He could hear her feet pounding down the metal treads back at the shop. The sound of her rapid breathing told him she was no longer half asleep. He wasn't a praying man, but he sent up a word of thanks to whoever might be listening.

"Fine," he told her, glancing down at his watch. Thirty minutes… It'd been thirty minutes since Samantha had been abducted. Fuck. *Fuck!* So much could happen in thirty minutes. So much he refused to think about, because if he *did* think about it, he'd puke all over the interior of Samantha's beloved car.

"I think I might have something," Delilah said, and his heart didn't just skip one beat—it skipped a dozen. "About five years ago, a freakin' *big* chunk of change was paid from the motorcycle repair shop account to a store that specializes in game room and bar furniture. It caught my eye for a couple of reasons. For one thing, it's a store I know well. I bought my new foosball table and dartboards from them eighteen months ago. For another thing, even though the payment came from the motorcycle repair shop's account, the delivery address on the order was for a flower shop. I did some digging. Turns out this flower shop is owned by one of the Basilisks' cousins. What would a freakin' flower shop need with barstools or pool tables?"

"That's it!" Ozzie crowed, beating a hand against the wheel. "Delilah, I could kiss you."

"Mac wouldn't like that."

He ignored her. "What's the address?"

"Hold on." He could hear her typing. Then she rattled off a street and a number that was smack-dab in the middle of the Basilisks' neighborhood. "But Ozzie," she said, "you're not going there alone, right? You're going to call the police and get backup, right?"

He didn't want to lie to Delilah, so he thanked her and thumbed off his phone. Putting the pedal to the metal, he listened to the Mustang's engine roar. "Hang on, sweetheart." His whispered words were whipped away by the wind screaming through the open window. "I'm coming."

Basilisk Clubhouse

Venom disconnected his call to Crutch in the bike shop, turned to Samantha, and smiled.

Things were going off without a hitch. And Samantha, pretty Samantha, was just where he wanted her.

She had yet to shed a tear. Not when a pistol was pressed against her skull. Not when he bound her hands behind her back and slapped a length of duct tape over her mouth. Not even when he dragged her into the clubhouse, sat her atop a barstool, and taped her ankles to the legs of the chair.

He admired her for that. Admired her, and looked forward to breaking her.

Breaking the strong is always so much more satisfying than breaking the weak.

"Time for you and me to have ourselves a little talk." He ripped the duct tape from her mouth. She winced and made a small sound as a drop of crimson appeared in the middle of her plump bottom lip. The duct tape had taken some skin with it. *First blood.* That always made his dick hard.

"There's nothing to say," she growled. "Besides the fact that you're totally fucked."

"Ohh, such ugly words coming outta that pretty mouth." He delighted in the fire in her eyes.

"I thought you guys were smart," she grumbled. He could see the vein pulsing in her neck. He wanted to bite it. "Thought you *had* to be smart to run all these criminal enterprises without getting caught. But now I know you've just been lucky. Because only a dumbshit would snatch me off the street when one of his buddies is rotting in jail for attempting that very thing not twenty-four hours ago. This is the *first* place the police will look for me."

Venom grabbed a barstool and pulled it in front of her. He sat, adjusting himself until he was so close, their knees touched. He could feel the warmth of her body. Smell the fabric softener she used and something more. Something earthier. Sexier. Or maybe it was just sex? Yeah, that was it. Samantha smelled of sex.

Dirty little whore. He *liked* dirty little whores. "See, that's where you're wrong, Samantha." *Samantha*. He loved saying her name. It felt…*intimate*. "No one knows where this clubhouse is. So even if the police *do* come looking for you, they won't find you. And even if they *do* suspect the Basilisks are the ones that took you, there's no way they can prove it. Mr. Danielson can't identify us. We were wearing masks. The SUV we kidnapped you in is currently being smashed into a cube of twisted steel and plastic at a local junkyard. And the rest of the boys who were part of today's little human heist? Well, they're back at work. And we have ten people who'll swear they've been there all day long. So you see, you're not the only one with sources. But you *are* the one who's totally fucked."

Her lips quivered. *That* made him so hard, he had to reach down and rearrange himself. Samantha followed the movement of his hand. When she saw how stiff he was for her, her cheeks went white as winter snow.

"Don't worry," he told her, anticipation making him sweat. He shrugged out of his biker jacket and smiled when Samantha's eyes widened. He was a big man. *Huge*, some might say. And he loved the look that came into people's eyes when they realized they were in the presence of a predator larger and stronger and far more deadly than themselves. "We'll get to that in a bit. I promise you. But first I needa know what Marcel Monroe told you two mornings ago. Tell me what you know and how you know it, and I won't make you pay for shoving that sniveling little shit of a pansy-ass reporter out of the SUV."

He saw her teeth set, the muscles in her jaw harden.

Just as I suspected, he thought. *She's gonna be a tough nut to crack. Perfect.*

He reached out one hand, keeping the other on the butt of the pistol resting against his thigh, and started unbuttoning her shirt. *Pop* went one little button through its hole. *Pop, pop* went two more.

She shivered. Either from fear or repulsion. He didn't care which. It was all the same to him. Holding her gaze, seeing himself reflected in the wide pools of her pupils, he cupped one warm breast and squeezed. A gurgle of pain sounded at the back of her throat. It hit his ears like the sweetest music, traveling down his spine to settle in his cock.

"Samantha," he whispered, drawing out the *S* sound at the beginning of her name. "I know it's a cliché. But there are two ways we can do this. The easy way or the hard way."

"Fuck you," she snarled, her hot breath tickling his cheek.

His mouth was next to her ear, so she didn't see him smile. "Hard way it is then."

Chapter 20

OZZIE SLUNK AROUND THE BACK ROW OF SHOPS, searching for the rear door to Feeney's Flowers. It was the only place still in business in a decaying strip mall. The other shopfronts were closed and shuttered, and the parking lot in front was crumbling and full of rusting shopping carts. In fact, if not for the occasional bark of a dog or the squawk of a TV inside one of the dilapidated houses surrounding the strip mall, Ozzie would have thought perhaps he'd entered a ghost town when he parked at the curb a half block away.

Crouching low and picking his way through empty beer cans, malt liquor bottles, and cigarette butts, he counted doors. Feeney's Flowers was the fourth business down. And the motorcycle parked out back, especially when combined with the one he'd seen angled in front of the flower shop, was all the evidence he needed to know he was in the right place.

This is their den. He could feel it in the hairs that lifted over his body.

The place was perfect for the bikers. The people who lived around the strip mall were not the kind to call the law, for fear they'd be arrested on drug charges or for squatting in houses that were probably condemned. This was the kind of place where *Live and let live* was the rule. And *Die and let die* was a foregone conclusion.

The smell of poverty hung in the air, mixing with the scents of fried food and addiction. A chain-link fence separated the backyards of the houses from the alley behind the strip mall. But the fence was falling down in places, grass and trees taking over where nobody was interested in taming them. The sound of two cats fighting or fucking was obscenely loud in the relative silence.

Adrenaline poured through Ozzie's bloodstream like battery acid, making his whole body burn and the damaged muscles of his thigh twitch. It was a welcome sensation. As he descended the six steps leading down to the flower shop's basement door, he racked the slide on his Beretta. The sound of a round chambering was familiar and somehow comforting. What *wasn't* comforting was the padlock attached to the back door.

Shit, damn, dicking fuck!

They must have taken Samantha in through the front door. And since Ozzie didn't *have* that option—when running a rescue mission, the last thing you did was announce your presence with a tinkling shop bell—he was left with shooting off the padlock or waiting for the cops to arrive.

The first scenario was a no-go. The back door was made of wood. And even though it was *sturdy* wood, there was no way to ensure his round wouldn't sail through and end up lodged in someone inside. In *Samantha*, to be precise. As for scenario number two? Well, he was sure the cops were on the way. No doubt the first thing Delilah did after he hung up was put in a 911 call to Washington. But how long would it take the five-oh to arrive? Ten minutes? Twenty? Time passing while who knows what was happening to Samantha?

Yeah, no fucking way.

He racked his brain for another solution. And then it hit him...

When he parked Samantha's car, he'd noticed a bottle of compressed air lying on the floorboard. It was the kind of thing she carried around to dust off her computer keyboard or clean out her laptop. No doubt it had fallen from one of her handbags when he slammed on the brakes.

When held upright, compressed air canisters blew… you guessed it…compressed air. But the liquid inside a compressed air canister was basically Freon gas. So hold a compressed air canister upside down and spray, allowing the Freon gas to exit the can without mixing with the air, and it became a tool that froze objects solid.

Science aside, the point was that he had something that would freeze the metal padlock. As anyone who'd ever taken chemistry would know, once metal is frozen, it crystallizes and becomes brittle. Brittle metal *breaks*.

<hr />

James Gandolfini had been a large man. But Venom? Yeah, he could pull the sun out of orbit. With massive shoulders, tattoos out the wazoo, and a black Duck Dynasty beard, he was everything Samantha imagined an outlaw biker to be.

Only *bigger*.

And there was no question he was rotten to the core. A snake-mean sonofabitch who took pleasure in her pain. Which was why, despite his ruthless grip on her breast, she refused to cry out again.

"So stubborn." His hot breath fanned her ear as his thick fingers found her nipple. He rolled the tender flesh, rumbling his delight when it hardened. Samantha felt only repulsion, but her body betrayed her, muscles tightening automatically when stimulated. "So here's how it's gonna work. I'll ask you a question, and if you don't answer, I'll hurt you a lot. If you *do* answer, I'll only hurt you a little. That's how the hard way works.

And in case you've forgotten, the hard way was your choice, cupcake."

Samantha closed her eyes and waited for what came next. She was going to die here. She knew that now. Any fantasies she'd harbored about rescue, about Ozzie or Washington or Carver riding in like white knights, had been obliterated when Venom told her the location of the clubhouse was a well-guarded secret.

Ozzie's going to blame himself, she thought, a hard kernel of sadness wedging beneath her heart. It wasn't his fault. None of this was his fault. *I'm sorry*, she silently whispered to him. *I'm so sorry I got you into this mess*.

"Let's start with Marcel Monroe," Venom whispered. She hated the feel of his mouth beside her ear. It was almost worse than the hand on her breast. "I'm assuming he told you the Black Apostles are buying their guns from us?"

Her top lip curled back. She could have kept quiet. Maybe she *should* have kept quiet. The longer she refused to answer, the longer he would let her live. But she wanted to see fear in his eyes before she died. She wanted one last victory. "You have no idea the shitstorm coming your way," she hissed. "It doesn't matter what you do to me here today. The cops *know* your club is selling weapons to the Apostles. They *know* you're getting those weapons from Iraq—"

"How the fuck could they possibly know that?" The pressure on her breast increased. The pain had tears pricking the backs of her eyes.

"From a confiscated handgun used in an Apostle drive-by shooting. The serial number told the tale."

"Bullshit." A fleck of hot spit landed on her ear before he pulled back to stare into her eyes. She had to work not to retch at the feel of it. "Our weapons don't *have* serial numbers."

"You sure about that? You sure a few of those weapons haven't slipped by without first receiving stippling treatment?"

And there it was. The fear she'd hoped to see in his eyes. The uncertainty. "Fucking Raheem," he swore under his breath. "I told him not to send us any more guns until he'd replaced that fucking machine. Motherfucker is always looking for shortcuts."

"I'm assuming that's the name of your source. Which," she added with a sadistic smile, "the police will find out soon enough. See, they've got a forensic accountant scouring your accounts as we speak, and a crackerjack computer hacker uncovering all the shit you've been hiding. They even know about Albu Bali."

And *that* was the one that really did it. His dead black eyes widened. He leaned close, his mouth open in a soundless snarl.

Samantha wasn't sure what overcame her then. Maybe it was the certainty that death was imminent. Maybe it was the fighter in her who refused to go down without landing a couple of punches. Or maybe it was pure stupidity. Regardless, she saw her opportunity and took it.

Rearing back, she head-butted him as hard as she could. The bridge of his nose cracked on contact, the fragile cartilage giving way. She had only a second to feel giddy triumph before Venom shrieked his rage and backhanded her across the face. *Wham!*

Pain exploded in her cheek, making her right eye feel like it was about to explode out of its socket. The agony was so intense that she was rendered momentarily senseless. Which was why she didn't brace herself for the fall. Not that she really could have with her wrists and ankles bound, but still. She might have had the wherewithal to at least grit her teeth when his blow sent the barstool toppling.

She hit the concrete floor with a bone-jarring *crash*. The barstool disintegrated on impact. Dazed, hurting, she blinked and realized she was free. Her wrists were still tied behind her back, her ankles still taped to the barstool's legs. But the barstool's legs were no longer attached to the barstool. They'd broken apart and were now simply two sticks taped to the outsides of her calves.

Rolling onto her stomach, she inch-wormed her legs beneath her and pushed to a wobbly stand. It was awkward. The barstool legs hit the floor at an angle and dug into her thighs. Her head pounded, her face throbbed, and her heart threatened to burst out of her chest, but none of that stopped her from bolting—or, rather, awkwardly hobbling—toward the stairs leading up to the flower shop.

She probably made it halfway across the room before Venom, blood streaming from his broken nose and sticking in his beard, saw her goal and came after her. It was like being chased by a freight train. Even the noise coming from the back of his throat was inhuman, a roar as loud as a jet engine. Every hair on her body lifted.

"Help!" she screamed, even though she knew there was no one in the flower shop overhead except for the tattooed douchewad who had tipped a hat to Venom on the way in. "Help me!" she cried again as Venom caught up to her.

He grabbed a handful of her hair, stopping her forward momentum in a heartbeat as strands pulled loose and tears stung her eyes. And then he had a hand around her throat, dragging her backward. She lost her balance, suffocating in his grip as her bootheels and the too-long barstool legs scrabbled across the floor, seeking traction but finding none. Her vision tunneled. Her struggling heartbeat was a loud *whoosh-whoosh* in her ears.

Then…she was airborne. Venom launched her onto the nearest pool table. She landed hard, her hip bone taking the brunt of the impact and sending agony up her spine. She barely had time to suck in a lungful of much-needed oxygen before Venom was on her. His massive weight pinned her to the pool table's green felt top until the bones in her hands tied behind her back threatened to break.

"I'm gonna fuck you 'til you beg me to stop, you stupid cunt," he snarled, his mouth an inch from her face. "And then I'm gonna fuck you some more." Blood dripped from his ruined nose onto her upper lip and cheek. She gagged, turning her head away. But he grabbed her chin in a brutal grip and forced her to look at him, using his other hand to press the barrel of his handgun tight against her temple. His eyes were as black as the pits of hell and promised just as much punishment. "You stuck your nose into my business… *My business!*" he thundered. "And now you're gonna pay."

Still keeping the gun against her head, he released her chin so he could reach down to unbutton her jeans.

This is it, she thought. A lone tear slid from the corner of her eye. It was so hot that it burned her skin. *This is the end.* Too bad she'd never found her father's murderer. Too bad she'd never see Donny walk down the aisle with a good man. Too bad she'd never know if there could have been a future with Ozzie or if—

A metallic-sounding *bang* sounded from somewhere behind them. It was followed a half second later by the *clink* of something metal hitting the ground outside.

Samantha tilted her head in time to see the back door burst open with enough force to drive the doorknob into the drywall. Light poured into the basement in brilliant yellow rays. The man standing on the threshold was nothing but a black silhouette. Still, Samantha would recognize those broad shoulders, those lean hips, and that flyaway hair anywhere.

"Ozzie!" She choked on his name. He had found her! Against all odds, he had found her! A thunderstroke of relief blasted through her. It was quickly replaced by a flash of terror when Venom lifted his pistol.

—————

There were certain sounds Ozzie would never forget.

The drone of black flies circling a battlefield awash with bodies and blood. The shriek of dying horses high in the mountains of the Hindu Kush after a smart bomb obliterated a Taliban stronghold. And Samantha's desperate cry for help as he'd been freezing the padlock on the back door.

When Ozzie kicked into the flower shop, the first thing he saw was Venom. A mass of grizzled hair, tattoos, and bulging muscles, the biker looked like an evil cartoon ogre masquerading as a man. The second thing Ozzie saw was Samantha beneath the brute. Her face was bruised and bloody. Her shirt was torn open. And there was terror in her wide eyes when she screamed his name.

Something came alive inside him then. Something that was blackhearted and sharp-toothed. He'd killed before. Of course he had. But there had never been any pleasure in it. No satisfaction in seeing a life here one minute and gone the next. But when Venom lifted his weapon, aiming for Ozzie's head, a jolt of pure joy blasted through him when he squeezed his Beretta's well-worn trigger. With a roar of sound and fury, his weapon belched up a red-hot lead projectile that flew true and drilled that motherfucking biker straight through his evil heart.

Blood sprayed. The end of Ozzie's trusty Beretta smoked. And the biker blinked once. Twice. His mouth fell open in shock, as if he couldn't believe he had actually been bested. Venom gave a wheezy death rattle, his eyes crossed, and he fell sideways. He was so close to the edge of the pool table that his body toppled off, hitting the floor in a heap of denim, leather, and chains.

Rot in hell, you sonofabitch! If Ozzie had any saliva to spare, he would have spat on the floor. But ever since he'd heard Samantha's scream, his mouth had been bone dry.

Regulating his heartbeat as he had been taught back in BUD/S, and using the adrenaline that heightened all of his senses, he stepped over the threshold and into the Basilisks' lair. A quick three-sixty told him it was pretty much what he had expected. A long bar, two pool tables, plenty of dartboards, and a foosball table. The air was ripe with the smell of spilled beer, stale cigarette smoke, and dirty sex. But except for the dead man and the woman Ozzie loved more than life itself, the place was blessedly empty.

He counted himself a lucky bastard. When he'd kicked down that door, he hadn't known what he would be facing. Two men? Twenty? What he *had* known was there was only one guarantee in life. And that was that no one gets out of it alive. So he'd figured if he had to go out in a blaze of glory saving Samantha, it wasn't such a bad way to end it.

Still, he didn't dare let down his guard. He'd been

twenty-eight hours into a twelve-hour mission, sweating his balls off in one-hundred-and-eight degree heat, too many times to bank on this little rescue mission being over. He kept his Beretta up and aimed, quartering the room as he slowly made his way toward Samantha.

She rolled onto her side, her long hair obscuring her face as she peeked over the edge of the pool table at Venom's dead body. Blood oozed onto the floor around the biker. Ozzie wasn't sure if it was just his imagination, but he would swear Venom was already beginning to stink. Or maybe that was just the sulfuric smell of the asshole's rotten soul leaving his body on its way to hell.

A door leading to another room caught his eye. Making his way over to it, he palmed the knob and threw it open. A quick battlefield scan left, right, and center told him the place was empty except for a big table and glowing neon beer signs.

Blowing out a breath, he turned to find Samantha lying on her side, no longer looking at Venom. Her legs were splayed awkwardly, pieces of a broken barstool taped to her calves. Her shirt hung open. And a sound came from the back of her throat. It was one to add to his list of things he'd never forget.

Brass-balled, tough-as-nails, take-no-shit Samantha Tate was whimpering…

Samantha never cried.

Well, that wasn't true. She had cried for weeks after her father died, and then for a full day after Donny ran the story that brought the alderman down. But other than that? Zippo, zilch, we're talking a big, fat goose egg. And she wasn't *really* crying now. But she was on the verge, teetering on a knife's edge.

Why?

Well, because she had thought for sure she was dead. Because when Venom lifted his weapon, she had thought for sure *Ozzie* was dead. But neither of those things had happened, and now she was so overcome with relief and gratitude that it was all trying to explode out of her in—

"It's okay, sweetheart."

He was there! Alive and whole and strong and brave! He got her into a seated position, her legs straddling his lean hips, her head on his shoulder as he used the bottom of his boot to shove Venom's corpse further beneath the table.

"We have to be quick," he whispered, reaching into his jacket pocket and pulling out a folding knife. "I counted one asshole upstairs who might decide to come down and investigate if he's a dumbshit. If he's smart, he'll hop on his bike and get the hell out of Dodge." He pointed toward the back door. "Hear that?" The distant sounds of sirens drifted in from outside. "The cavalry is on its way."

It hit her then. He'd come in *alone*.

Oh, shit a brick. Now she was on the verge of crying again. "S-sorry," she sniffled, calling herself ten kinds of sniveling, soggy, want-to-kick-her-own-ass damsel-in-distress. *Yuck.*

"Nothing to be sorry about," he assured her, flicking the knife open with a *snick*. The blade gleamed menacingly under the fluorescent lights. "I'm the one who should be apologizing. I should never have left you alone."

She'd thought it wasn't possible for her to love him more. But in the moment, she did.

He didn't waste any time putting the knife to use on the restraints around her wrists. She couldn't help herself.

She turned her face into his neck and breathed him in. All those pheromones and that sweet bad-boy smell.

"No, *I* sh-should apologize. *I'm* the one who g-got you into this mess. I'm the one who l-lied." Her voice was muffled against his warm skin. When her hands came free, the first thing she did was try to wrap her arms around him and hold him close. To her surprise and consternation, she hugged nothing but air. He was down on his haunches, using his knife to cut through the duct tape around her calves.

"When did you lie?" he whispered, never looking up, concentrating on the task at hand. He was sawing one-handed because he refused to drop his weapon.

She wanted to run her fingers through his hair but didn't dare distract him. Instead, she gripped the edge of the pool table and gritted her teeth when he ripped the tape and barstool leg off her right leg.

"When I told you I wouldn't leave my desk and—"

He shushed her, cocking an ear to the sirens that were coming closer every second. "Let's both agree to be sorry that any of this happened and leave it at that." *Rrrrrip!* The second barstool leg came free, and Samantha felt like a weight had been lifted. The last vestiges of Venom and what he'd intended to do to her were gone.

Ozzie was up in a flash, grabbing her waist to hoist her from the table. Her legs wobbled when he set her down in front of Venom's lifeless body. Even though he was dead, she could feel the evil presence of the biker at her feet. And her silly heart ran a never-ending race as the electric squeal of the sirens grew to eardrum-bursting levels. The sound of car doors slamming was unmistakable.

Before they were overrun by the law and made to answer questions and give statements, she had one thing she had to make absolutely clear. It couldn't wait another second. *She* couldn't wait another second. Her fingers shook when she grabbed his leather-clad arm. "Ozzie, I—"

That's all she managed before the door separating the flower shop from the basement burst open with a *bang*. The douchecanoe from earlier stood in the threshold. And he wasn't alone. He had a mean-looking handgun with him. It was aimed straight at Samantha's head.

Her heart had just enough time to trip over itself before Ozzie yelled, "No!" and stepped in front of her, lifting his weapon and pulling the trigger.

A massive roar of sound filled the room, and something hot and sticky sprayed across Samantha's face, making her wince. When she blinked open her eyes, it was to see two things. The first was the asswipe on the top step dropping dead from the bullet that entered below his left eye and exploded out the back of his head, splattering blood and brain matter onto the door. His lifeless body crumpled like a rag doll, hitting the stairs and tumbling into the basement. The second thing was Ozzie going down on one knee like his bad leg had given out on him. He made a sound. It was a cross between a puff of air and a moan. What happened next seemed to be in slow motion.

He toppled forward, seeming to take forever to hit the concrete floor and lie motionless. Police burst in through the door to the flower shop, weapons up and aimed. Someone was screaming their head off, but it was a dull sound, muted like a shout through a goose-down pillow.

Then time righted itself. The *world* righted itself. And Samantha realized *she* was the one shrieking like a banshee.

She hit the ground at Ozzie's side, her knees crying out in agony. She paid them no heed. After all, it was her heart that was the problem. It had stopped beating the moment she saw the pool of blood growing on the floor beneath Ozzie's head.

It hadn't been one massive roar of sound that filled the room, but two *booming* shots as both men discharged their weapons simultaneously. And that hot spray she had felt? It was Ozzie's blood.

"No! No, *no!*" She screamed, struggling to breathe while simultaneously attempting to turn him over. His big body weighed a thousand pounds, but finally, she managed it.

Is he breathing? She couldn't tell. His eyes were closed. His mouth hung slightly open. And there was blood—a *lot* of blood—smeared along the left side of his face, matting his hair in a gruesome crimson tangle and running down to stain his beard.

"Ozzie!" She pulled his bloody head into her lap and shook his shoulders. "Ozzie! Ozzie!" she shrieked his name over and over until her vocal cords shredded. She angrily shook off the hands that tried to grab her and lift her away, instead rocking Ozzie's limp body.

She had survived her father's murder, two kidnappings, and Venom's assault. But she wouldn't survive this. The pain of this would kill her.

Then…he moved. Or at least she *thought* he did.

"Ozzie!" she yelled for the bazillionth time, touching his face.

One brilliant blue eye popped open. Then another. She brushed away some of the blood from his cheeks and brow.

He seemed to have trouble focusing on her. Lifting a hand to his temple, he pushed back his hair to finger the shallow groove of raw flesh where the bullet had grazed his head.

"Oh, Ozzie!" She cupped his wonderful face in her hands. His whiskers tickled her palms. The heat from his tan skin reassured her.

Then he said the most wonderful, *welcome* word she'd ever heard. "Ow."

Chapter 21

OZZIE SAT ON THE AMBULANCE'S BACK BUMPER AND let a bespectacled paramedic stitch up his scalp. She kept referring to the wound as a "head lac" which he assumed was short for head laceration. And holy shit. He was *lucky* it was just a laceration. One inch to the right, and he'd be counting worms right now. Although, there was lucky and then there was good. For most of his life, he'd been both.

He blew out a steadying breath and shifted when the paramedic hit a spot that hadn't been completely deadened by local anesthetic. She was jibber-jabbering about something. Her weekend plans maybe? But he was only giving her half an ear because he was trying to eavesdrop on the conversation Samantha was having with Carver and Washington over by Carver's unmarked cruiser.

"Called the guy Raheem," she said, and something about the name wiggled Ozzie's antenna. "The only other information I have is that they took the SUV to a local junkyard where, supposedly, it's already been smashed into a cube of mangled steel."

"That's good enough for now." Washington nodded. "That gives us enough to go on and a reason to round them all up."

"Once you *do* round them all up, you tell that maple-syrup judge of yours that they're flight risks. Bail, or lack thereof, should be set accordingly."

Fifteen minutes ago, she'd been wailing his name, rocking him in her lap, and pressing hot, desperate kisses to his face. Now, she was all business. She'd wiped most of the blood—*his* blood—off her face, and her voice was remarkably steady. A little thin and reedy from all the screaming. But steady all the same.

She is one tough cookie, he thought with admiration, knowing it must have been terrifying for her to see him go down like that. Just as terrifying as it had been for *him* to see that ass munch of a flower shop owner drawing down on *her*. The memory alone was enough to have his stomach threatening to spew its contents into the world. And since he never *did* get the opportunity to eat, chances were good those contents would be nothing but bile and acid.

"You should go to the hospital for a head CT," the paramedic said, concentrating on finishing the last stitches.

"I've had my bell rung a lot harder than that," he assured her. "Got a thick skull. Or so my boss always says. I'll be fine."

"Had your bell rung harder than a bullet?" She blinked at him, her dark eyes huge behind her glasses.

He shrugged.

"Hmm." She pursed her lips. "How long were you out again?"

"Handful of seconds."

"Probably just a minor concussion. It was a glancing blow. Still, you should practice precaution tonight. Have someone wake you up every hour."

"Done and done," he told her.

"Speaking of done," she chirped, "we're all done here."

Now that he didn't have to keep his head turned to the side, he snagged a peek at her name tag. "Thank you, Ms. Mancini."

"It's Cheryl." She grinned at him, pushing her glasses up on the bridge of her nose. "But my friends call me Cheri."

She was sweet. And *young*. "Well then, thank you, *Cheri*."

She handed him a little handheld mirror so he could check out her skill with the needle and thread. "It looks a little Frankenstein-y right now," she said in a rush, eager to reassure him. "But that's just from the swelling. Once that goes down, you'll be golden. Not to brag or anything, but I'm known around town as having surgeon's hands. My stitching is the best."

Little did she know that whatever scar this encounter left behind, it was nothing compared to the damage his body had sustained from an incendiary device. He was reminded of the way Samantha had kissed his mangled thigh, her lips so hot, her words so sweet. Despite his blood loss, the memory had his crotch tightening.

His eyes went to the woman herself. To the way she gestured while talking. To how she cocked her head, listening intently to whatever Washington told her.

He loved her. Loved everything about her. Her fierce heart and even fiercer mind. That little gap between her two front teeth and the noises she made when ecstasy overtook her. The list went on and on. And he got it now. Understood the depth of the possessiveness, the devotion, the *bonds* his brothers-in-arms felt for their women. It was all-consuming. All-encompassing. Wonderful and terrible at the same time.

Too bad it only goes one way…

Or maybe it *wasn't* too bad. Because what the fuck would he have done if it went *both* ways? He couldn't tell her who he really was. *What* he really was.

His tumultuous thoughts were enough to have him turning back to the paramedic. She was looking at him with concern. And he realized he hadn't responded.

Giving his stitched wound a cursory glance, he

handed the mirror back to her and winked. "Looks great to me."

"Oh good," she enthused, covering the stitches with a bandage before snapping off her gloves.

From the corner of his eye, Ozzie saw Carver reach into his pocket and pull out a bag of Cheetos. Just the sight of the cheesy, salty snack had his stomach grumbling.

Wish the damned thing would make up its mind. One minute, it wanted to evacuate its contents. The next minute, it reminded him that it didn't *have* any contents.

"You know," Cheri said, biting her lip. "My shift ends in thirty minutes, and I make a mean batch of linguini with clam sauce." Apparently his stomach's gastronomical songs of hunger were louder than he realized. "You could come over to my place."

When he blinked at her, lifting a brow, her cheeks flushed bright red. "Oh holy crap!" She covered her mouth with her hand. "I can't believe I just said that. That was ridiculously forward of me, wasn't it? Sheesh, I—"

He grabbed one of her hands, giving her fingers a squeeze. The poor woman had thoroughly embarrassed herself. And if he wasn't so hung up on the dark-haired reporter fifteen feet away, he would have been charmed by the pretty paramedic's proposal. As it was, the only thing he could do was ease her discomfort. "A woman who saves lives, stitches head lacs, *and* cooks?" He waggled his eyebrows. "Marry me. Marry me right now." She preened and giggled. "Alas, I'll have to ask for a rain check."

"Oh." She looked disappointed. "Sure." She regained her composure and reached into her hip pocket to pull out a business card. "This is my company card." She grabbed the ballpoint pen hooked in her breast pocket and quickly scribbled something on the little white rectangle of card stock. "And that's my cell number on the back."

He politely accepted the card, knowing he'd never use it, just as Samantha walked up to them. Faint bruises were beginning to form on her cheek and the side of her jaw, and her wrists were red and raw from the restraints. The sight of both made him want to kill Venom all over again.

"Head lac sutured and ready for action." He lifted his hair to show her Cheri's workmanship.

"So I see." Samantha's eyes were remote. Her cheeks pale. Ozzie frowned at her, trying to determine if she was in shock or… "Washington says we should go back to the shop for a while." A muscle ticked in her jaw. Her left eyelid gave one tiny twitch. "He fears a knee-jerk reaction and maybe some knee-jerk retribution from the Basilisks for the next couple of hours. He'll call us when he's got most of them off the streets and he's ready for us to head down to the station to give our official statements."

"Sounds like a plan to me." He smiled at her. Especially the part about going back to the shop. Because the shop had a bed. *His* bed.

His smile quickly turned into a frown when she didn't smile back, just nodded and looked away, blinking like something was stuck in her eye.

~~~

Black Knights Inc. Headquarters

After they got back to the shop, and after the BKI ladies had finished grilling Samantha and Ozzie and tut-tutting like old Jewish grannies over Ozzie's head wound, Samantha faked a headache and begged off on eating the Pizano's pizza they had delivered. "I think I'd rather head upstairs and try to take a nap," she said, rubbing her temple.

Truth was, she had no intention of napping. She needed some time alone. Time to finally admit the truth to herself. The truth that Ozzie was…*Ozzie*. Smart, brave, funny, sexy, and *not* the kind of guy to settle down. When she'd heard him asking that pixie of a paramedic to marry him, she'd stopped in her tracks. And then when he'd taken the pixie's card, she'd wanted to throw up.

Thankfully, she hadn't tossed her cookies. But what she *did* was find herself sitting alone in the guest room on the third floor of the BKI warehouse, the urge to cry rising in her like a tide. For a woman who never cried, she'd sure been on the verge a lot today.

Then again, bawling like a baby after realizing all your hopes and dreams are just that—hopes and dreams, *not* reality—was pretty much a given. Or so all those sappy John Green love stories and Katherine Heigl movies had led her to believe.

Another thing all those sappy John Green love stories and Katherine Heigl movies had taught was that when you were nursing a broken heart, you called your best friend. When Ozzie had taken her to the Tribune Tower to pick up her stuff before heading to BKI, she'd seen Donny just long enough to give him a huge bear hug. Now, she needed her best friend. She needed to confess that, despite all her good intentions, she'd fallen in love with a bad boy who just happened to be a wonderful man.

A wonderful man with a penchant for changing women as often as he changes socks.

Dumping her purse onto the bed, she found her phone and punched in Donny's number. He answered on the first ring. "Sammie? Everything okay, sweetie?"

She opened her mouth, but the only thing that came out was a pathetic little squeak.

"Samantha, what is it?" Donny's voice was frantic.

The whole story burst from her like a dam unable to hold back floodwaters. Everything that had happened. The way Ozzie had saved her, so bravely, so selflessly. The way they had made love, so purely, so passionately. All the things they'd said. All the laughs they'd shared. The only things she kept to herself were the Black Knights' secrets.

"I knew you were falling for him weeks ago." Donny sighed. "You talked about him all the time. And when he calls to invite you for coffee or a drink? You start to glow."

"I knew I *liked* him," Samantha said, sniffling, hugging the pillow close and burying her nose in it because it smelled of the same fabric softener Ozzie used. "I knew I *lusted* after him. But I didn't realize I *loved* him until…" She shook her head.

"Mmm," Donny hummed. "I can't blame you. I mean, what's not to love?"

"You're supposed to be *helping*," she cried.

"Sorry, funny face." Donny sighed again. "I wish I had some sage words of advice, but—"

"You've been in love before," she cut in. "Tell me this won't kill me. Tell me broken hearts can heal."

"Oh, Sammie, broken hearts *do* heal." She raked in a ragged breath, daring to hope. "But they scar like a motherfucker."

———

"Samantha…"

She came awake with a start and a curse when she felt Ozzie's big, warm hand on her shoulder. She couldn't believe she had fallen asleep.

"Samantha, sweetheart, I need you to come downstairs with me," Ozzie said, his voice so smooth, so low and seductive. Too bad she'd never allow herself to be seduced by him again. Despite Donny's assurances about broken hearts healing, she wasn't sure hers would survive more time in Ozzie's arms. In his *bed*.

"What time is it?" She rolled over, rubbing her eyes. They felt gritty.

"Twenty-hundred hours," he told her, then put it into civilian terms. "Eight o'clock."

"Did Washington or Carver call?" Her voice was scratchy. Her throat felt as dry as the white wine Donny liked to drink on their monthly "friend nights," when just the two of them spent an evening in together.

"No. Not yet. But there have been developments you're going to want to hear about."

She sat up. Her head felt like it weighed a hundred pounds. Outside, the sun was sinking low in a tie-dyed sky. It sent golden rays through the leaded-glass window that caught Ozzie's hair and turned the sandy strands into spun gold. At some point, he'd grabbed a shower and washed away the blood.

Lord, he's gorgeous. And smart. And brave. And funny. And sexy. Ugh!

"That name Venom gave you?" He offered her a hand to help her stand. She hesitated to take it. After a beat, she placed her fingers in his warm, wide palm and allowed him to pull her out of bed. Just as she'd feared, his touch, the feel of his calluses, affected her in distinctly naughty ways.

"Raheem?" She quickly extracted her hand from Ozzie's grip, hoping he couldn't feel her fingers shaking.

"That's the one." He nodded. "I've been doing some digging. A *lot* of digging, actually."

Of course he had. She'd been upstairs feeling sorry for herself and napping. And *he'd* been digging. Working. Hacking. Doing his best to find all the pieces of this crazy puzzle and put them together. For her.

Double ugh! Why does he have to be so wonderful? And why can't he be mine?

―――――᷎᷎᷎᷎᷎―――――

"Something Samantha told Washington and Carver struck a chord with me," Ozzie said, and Christian watched him type madly on the laptop sitting in front of him. The *clickety-clack* of his fingers across the keyboard echoed around the second floor and into the shop below.

Since the meeting Ozzie and Delilah had called was impromptu, only Christian, Emily, and Samantha were present around the conference table. Becky was on the phone with a client who wanted twenty custom bikes built in the next two months. And the other ladies, having once again received the call that those in the field were right as rain, were back at their respective homes taking care of their children or simply avoiding the shop while Samantha was present. Christian understood. The wives and girlfriends of the Black Knights already had enough to worry about without having to watch every word that came out of their mouths.

"That name, Raheem… I'd seen it before," Ozzie continued, grabbing a slice of cold pizza from the box on the table. "Good thing Venom was so chatty there at the end."

"He thought it was going to be *my* end," Samantha said. "So he wasn't too worried about divulging secrets."

"Don't remind me," Ozzie muttered around a mouthful of pizza.

Samantha bit her lip and glanced away.

Oh no, Christian thought, recognizing the change in the atmosphere between the two. He looked over at Ozzie, hoping for a clue to what *that* was all about. But Ozzie seemed as confused as Christian. Ozzie cocked his head at Samantha, halting mid-chew.

"What's with them?" Emily leaned close to whisper in Christian's ear, proving he wasn't the only one to detect trouble in paradise. *Also* proving Emily had sweet-smelling breath, like bubble gum and fresh coffee, and that her hair was cool and soft where it brushed against his neck.

Frowning, he leaned away from her. Odd, because what he *really* wanted to do was lean *toward* her. "Why does everyone assume I have a ruddy crystal ball capable of seeing people's motivations?"

"Why do you have to be such a ruddy curmudgeon?" she came back immediately, mimicking his accent.

"Please go on," Samantha insisted after turning back to Ozzie, interrupting any answer Christian might have given Emily. "I'm all ears."

Ozzie's eyes remained narrowed, his expression baffled. But he haltingly continued. "A man named Raheem al-Atrash was the translator with the squad of army infantrymen at Albu Bali."

"Now *that* seems like too much of a coincidence," Emily said, shooting Christian a withering glance. Cad that he was, he felt that look deep in his…*crotch*.

"I thought so too," Ozzie said. "So I did a little digging. And guess what I found?"

"He found quite a bit actually," Delilah piped up. She turned Ozzie's laptop around so everyone could see the screen where a tall, dark bloke in an Iraqi military uniform proudly posed for a picture. "Meet Colonel Raheem al-Atrash."

"*Colonel*," Samantha sputtered. "So after the greedy sonofabitch willfully took part in a massacre of his own people, he went from being an *interpreter* to a *colonel*?"

"Actually," Delilah said, "turns out that after Albu Bali, he was promoted to major. In the years since, he's risen to the rank of colonel."

"Seems one of the ways the CIA managed to keep the massacre at Albu Bali a secret was to pull some strings and get Raheem a cushy position inside the Iraqi army," Ozzie explained. "A cherry job in exchange for his silence."

"Oh, for fuck's sake." Samantha's face was the epitome of disgust.

"Welcome to the wide world of international intrigue, luv," Christian told her. Having lived there most of his adult life, he was no longer surprised by the perfidy of the players.

"Yeah?" Her brow was knitted. "Well, from what little I've seen of it, I'm not surprised you all got out as quickly as you could."

A heartbeat of strained silence followed *that* little pronouncement. Emily was quick to fill it. "So let me guess. Colonel al-Atrash is being supplied with weapons by the U.S. government."

"According to *our* military records, he is," Ozzie said.

"Meaning?" Samantha asked, and Christian noticed that she couldn't quite meet Ozzie's eyes.

"Meaning I could find no corresponding record of those weapons when I hacked into the Iraqi accounts," Ozzie said. "It would appear that Raheem is accepting the shipments himself and then diverting the guns to the Basilisks instead of sending them on to the Iraqi army."

"Can you prove this?" *Now* Samantha was directing

her gaze straight at Ozzie. The reporter in her overruled whatever else was going on.

"Not me." Ozzie shook his head. "Delilah." He pointed to the redheaded bartender who petted Fido's big, blocky head. "By digging into Raheem's accounts, she was able to follow a money trail leading back to a Panamanian bank. The *same* Panamanian bank used by one of the shell companies the Basilisks have."

"After a marathon bit of hacking," Delilah added, "Ozzie was able to get past the bank's firewalls."

"Which *themselves* had firewalls," Ozzie muttered.

"And he located some internal transfers of cash between the account of the Basilisks' shell company and the account Raheem owns," Delilah finished. "Done and done. Point A has finally been connected to Point B."

"Holy shit!" Samantha blinked rapidly. "That's… incredible."

"Yep." Ozzie ran a hand through his hair, wincing when he inadvertently hit the wound near his temple. "Seems our wild-goose chase paid off."

"So what happens now?" Samantha asked.

Ozzie blew out a breath. "It's already happening. I handed everything over to Washington, and he's handed it to the government. There are a lot of players interested in this case. The ATF, the FBI. Fuck, even the CIA."

No doubt Ozzie had also phoned General Pete Fuller and the president, alerting them to what he'd found. What was equally apparent to Christian, because he'd known both men for so long, was that the general and the president had handpicked the individuals Chief Washington gave the information to.

The wheels of the establishment… Oh, how quickly they turn.

"So…then…" Samantha shook her head, trying to

take it all in. "What happens to the Basilisks? To the guys who kidnapped me today? To..." She turned to Ozzie. "To...*you*? You shot two men."

"In self-defense." Ozzie nodded. "Washington assures me there will only be a cursory investigation and no charges will be brought."

"But...but..." she sputtered. "What happens to the bikers in the meantime, while the feds build their case?"

"Judge Maple took your advice. *And* the advice of someone fairly high up in the federal government." Ozzie shot her a smile. Samantha didn't return it. "He's holding the Basilisks without bail."

"And so the kidnapping charge? The assault charges?" Samantha demanded.

Ozzie ran a hand through his hair again. "The government will likely go after the Basilisk MC as a whole on the illegal weapons deal. That'll trump any local charges. I'd say chances are good you'll never see the inside of a courtroom. I'm sorry, Samantha. I know you probably wanted to face down the men who took you, but—"

"I don't need to *face down* anyone," she declared, her expression fierce. "I just want to make sure they all rot in an eight-by-ten for what they've done to me, to Marcel, and every innocent kid who died on the streets from a bullet fired from one of their weapons."

"At this point, given all the players involved and the fact that the U.S. government doesn't take kindly to outlaw biker gangs stealing its weapons and selling them on the black market, rotting in eight-by-tens is pretty much a foregone conclusion."

"Good." She nodded vehemently. Her eyes darted across the conference table as she worked through all the ins and outs. "And Raheem?"

"I suspect proof of his double-dealing will be handed over to the Iraqis. Believe me, whatever punishment they give him will be far worse than anything the United States might do to him. He's a traitor to his country."

Samantha shook her head. "So that's that then. It's done."

"It's done," Ozzie agreed.

"It'll be a great story when it finally blows too." Her lips twisted wryly. "Too bad my exclusive went the way of the dodo bird the minute this became an international mess instead of a local brouhaha."

Ozzie leaned back in his chair, grinning broadly. "Now, that's where you're wrong. See, I made it clear you're *still* to get the exclusive when it's time to break the story."

"How the hell did you manage that?" Then Samantha shook her head. "No, let me guess…your high-up connections?"

Ozzie winked and pantomimed zipping his lips.

"Why do you have to be so wonderful?" she demanded, her voice a little too loud.

Ozzie frowned. "Why do you make being wonderful sound like a bad thing?"

Before Samantha could answer, Ozzie's phone buzzed in his pocket. He pushed to a stand. "It's Washington." After he took the call, he pinned Samantha with a grim stare. "It's time to go make our statements."

Samantha shoved away from the table. When Ozzie grabbed her elbow to escort her to the first floor, Christian saw Samantha flinch as if Ozzie's touch had burned her. Ozzie was too distracted by stepping over Fido's wagging tail to notice.

Once the two disappeared down the stairs, Delilah piped up with, "Is it just me, or have all the freakin' hearts and flowers that have surrounded them the last couple of days begun to wilt?"

"Right?" Emily sat forward. "What do you think happened? Did Ozzie say anything while you guys were nose deep in accounts and hacked files?"

"Not a thing." Delilah shook her head. "But if you ask me—"

"Here's where I make my exit, yeah?" Christian quickly stood.

"What? Too much girl talk for you?" Emily's eyes twinkled with devilment.

Before Christian could answer, Peanut hopped onto the table in front of Emily. When Peanut stretched himself out, turning his motor over the instant Emily rubbed his belly, Christian spun on his heel.

"Come on now! Why are you always walking away from me?" Emily demanded.

Because when you pet that bloody cat with those bloody delicate fingers of yours, I want to roll over on my back and beg you to scratch my *belly!*

"I'm not walking away from you. I'm simply saving my own sodding life. If I stay to listen to you two hens go on about what's happening between Ozzie and Samantha, I'll be tempted to swallow a bag of razor blades."

The sound of the women's laughter followed him up the stairs. It wasn't until he reached the top that he realized thoughts of Emily rubbing his belly had made him hard.

Chapter 22

Chicago Police Homicide Division

"YOU READY TO BLOW THIS JOINT?" OZZIE ASKED Samantha as soon as she exited the interrogation room. Her giant purse hung from her shoulder, making her lean slightly to the left. Add that to her wildly curling hair, the mascara smeared under her eyes, and the bruises darkening on her face, and it was an understatement to say she looked a little worse for wear. Poor thing.

Washington had told his men to rake them over the coals, getting every last detail of what transpired that afternoon. And then he'd told his men to rake them again. And *again*. "With all the scrutiny this case is going to draw from all parties involved," Washington had said to Ozzie once he was released from questioning, "we have to make sure we do everything by the book. Sorry." Washington had shrugged a shoulder, handing him a steaming cup of coffee. "I know you've already had a helluva day, and I just made it worse."

"Can't fault a man for doing his job," Ozzie had assured him, accepting the coffee and grabbing one of the plastic chairs against the wall, content to wait for Samantha. He'd been sitting for thirty minutes, sipping the strong brew and wincing because the activity buzzing inside the station, even at this late hour, was enough to have his head aching. His thigh wasn't helping matters. It screamed at him. Still, the moment he saw Samantha trudge toward him, he felt nothing but joy.

She was safe. The danger to her was gone now that the Basilisks were behind bars. And even looking like she'd gone through hell in a high wind, she was still the most beautiful woman in the world.

"I am *beyond* ready to blow this joint." She plopped into the vacant chair beside him, letting her purse hit the floor with a *thud*. Despite the day she'd had, she still smelled wonderful. That powdery scent reached out to him, making his stomach muscles clench. "I feel like I've aged ten years today." She twisted her head from side to side and rubbed the back of her neck.

"Fear. Adrenaline. Shock," he told her. "They take a toll on the body."

"I need a martini and my bed." She blew out a breath that fluttered one looping strand of hair. "And then I think I'll rinse and repeat for the next two or three days. Maybe after that, I'll feel human again."

Ozzie set aside what remained of his coffee so he could brush Samantha's hair back over her shoulder. When he gave her a squeeze, her muscles were like stone. He knew of *one* surefire way to help her lose that tension. "Keeping you in bed for the next two or three days, even if I have to share you with the occasional martini, sounds good to me."

She looked away from him, her throat working over a hard swallow.

All his instincts went on red alert. "Hey. What's up?"

"I'm not going home with you tonight, Ozzie." When she turned back, her eyes looked funny. There was determination there, but also sadness.

Now his instincts weren't on red alert. They were running around, screaming like their hair was on fire. His voice was harsher than he would have liked when he cocked a brow and said, "No?"

"No." She shook her head. "I need to go home. I have

things to take care of. Plants to water. Trash to take out. That article I was working on today... Charlie texted to say he'll give me an extension."

"Was I hearing things?" Ozzie cocked his head. "Or were you talking about martinis and taking to your bed not two minutes ago."

"That's a fantasy. This is reality."

And why did he get the feeling those two sentences meant more than she was letting on? An itchy sort of desperation tightened his shoulders. "I could go with you. I've never seen the inside of your place, and I'm dying to get a gander at your sanctum." He hoped to smooth the strain in the air with a little humor. "You know, get to know the *real* Samantha, warts and all. Tell me, do you leave your wet towels on the floor and your half-empty Diet Coke cans sitting around?"

"You can't come over. I already told Donny he could."

"Right." Ozzie nodded, a muscle twitching in his jaw. "So how about I swing by tomorrow and—"

"Like I said," she quickly interrupted. "I have that article to finish. And...other stuff to catch up on."

"Right," he said again. Now it wasn't just the muscle in his jaw twitching. Those in his neck and back had joined in on the action.

If he wasn't mistaken, and given his experience, he didn't think he was, this was a brush-off. She was fucking brushing him off. Of course, he'd been expecting her to do exactly this *eventually*. But he had thought he'd have more time. Time to shore up his defenses so the blow wouldn't hurt as bad.

"Ozzie." She grabbed his forearm. Even through the leather of his biker jacket, he could feel the delicate pressure of her fingers. Fingers that'd given him so much pleasure. Fingers that belonged to the one woman on the planet who could inflict the ultimate pain. "I…" She swallowed. Her throat made a sticky sound. "I'll never be able to thank you for everything you've done for me these last couple of days." He could think of a way. It involved her not *leaving* him. "You've gone above and beyond in every way. Putting your life on the line time and again. Getting shot, for fuck's sake. Losing your bike."

"Screw the bike," he snarled.

She blinked at his outburst but seemed determined to press on. "I think you are…" She drifted off, as if searching for the right word.

When she looked at him, he saw compassion in her eyes. It reminded him of the look on Cindy Rutherford's face the day she packed up her things and left. Cindy had stuck with his father far longer than any woman before her, eighteen glorious months spanning most of Ozzie's fifth- and sixth-grade years. And he had loved her. Loved that she made chocolate chip cookies on Sunday and walked around the house in a ratty old robe and big, fluffy slippers. But his love had not been enough to make her stay. His love had never been…*was* never enough.

"I think you're *wonderful*," she finally said.

"And there you go again, making that sound like a bad thing," he gritted through his teeth. His whole body was rigid, his hands curled into fists around the seat of his chair.

"It's *not* a bad thing." Her eyes pleaded for him to understand.

Oh, I understand all right. No matter what words she used, it was the same old refrain. The one he had first heard from the women his father brought home, and then from the women *he'd* brought home. *It's not you, it's me.* The five cruelest words on the planet.

He'd ruined it when he used the line from *The Princess Bride*. He'd revealed too much of what he felt. He'd scared her. And now she was running away.

"I've had the pleasure of knowing three wonderful men in my life," she went on, each word shattering his heart a little more. The broken pieces acted as fertilizer for the hurt growing inside him, turning it into a venomous kind of anger. "My father, Donny, and now you. Your friendship these past few months"—the word *friendship* stuck in his brain like a blade—"has meant so much to me. *You* have meant so much to me."

"Why do I get the feeling this is good-bye, Samantha?" His voice sounded like he'd put it through a garbage disposal.

"No." She shook her head vehemently. "No, I don't want it to be. But—"

He didn't want to hear what followed that *but*. He shoved to a stand so quickly his plastic chair banged against the wall. She blinked up at him, her dark eyes huge.

What's wrong with me? he wanted to shout down at her. *Why doesn't anyone ever want* me? Instead, all his hurt and anger spewed forth in a deluge of vitriol. "No, I get it," he snarled. "It was fun for a while, when you *needed* something from me, but not forever. Good. Great. Since when have you ever known me to do forever?"

"That's not..." She glanced around at the police officers who had turned in their direction.

Ozzie didn't give a flying fuck if they had an audience. When she reached for him, he stepped away. He felt like that lock on the back door to the Basilisks' clubhouse after he'd hit it with a full can of Freon gas. Cold, hard, and brittle. If she touched him, he might break.

"I didn't mean to hurt you," she swore, her eyes beseeching. "I just—"

"*Hurt* me?" He frowned down at her. The ugliness that had grown inside him infected his heart and honed his tongue. "Ha! You think I'm *hurt*? Hell, woman, I'm *pissed*. After everything I've done for you, I thought for sure I'd get another five or ten good fucks before one of us kicked the other to the curb."

She drew back like he'd punched her. He hated himself for that, but he couldn't stop. "But don't you worry. My bed won't be empty for long." He remembered the card the paramedic had given him. Pulling it out of his jacket pocket, he glanced down consideringly at the number scrawled across the back. "In fact, it won't even be empty tonight. This concussion requires someone to wake me up every hour. I know just the woman to do it."

With that, he spun on his heel and left her sitting there. The noxious mix of hurt and anger inside him refused to let him turn back. Shoving through the front doors of the police station, he was startled and sickened to see the reflection of his face in the glass. He looked... exactly like his father.

Samantha Tate's Apartment, East Illinois Street

"The man sure knows how to make an apology. You have to give him that," Donny said, plucking the card from the gift basket after Samantha closed the door on the deliveryman.

This was the fourth gift basket in four days. The first had been full of Snickers bars in every size from bite-size to as big as her arm. The second had been chock-full of all the things a woman would need to give herself a luxurious at-home pedicure: pumice stone, soaking salts, and twelve different colors of glittery polish. The third basket had contained a bright-pink carryall with matching wallet and key chain. But this basket…

This is my favorite.

It was filled with all the things she'd need to make herself a killer dirty martini. Jigger, shaker, deli olives, expensive gin, and a little bottle of dry vermouth.

He knows me so well.

Better than any man before him. Which made her decision to wean herself away from him that much harder. A clean break would have been better. After he'd stormed out of the police station on his way to pork that pixie of a paramedic, she had thought she'd done just that. Ripped off the bandage in one fell swoop.

But the next day, the first basket had arrived along with a lengthy note of apology. He had begged her to forgive him for what he'd said. Explained that he'd been tired and in pain and shocked that she seemed ready to end the physical part of their relationship. Then he had assured her that he was fine going back to just being friends. That he *treasured* her friendship.

Of course, she'd forgiven him in an instant—hard not to when she, you know, *loved* the man. But still, the gifts kept coming.

Carrying the basket to her kitchen, she set it on the bar before pulling out the contents. Donny handed her the card. "*And* he's succinct," he said.

Setting the bottle of gin aside, she turned over the card. Written in Ozzie's slanting, decisive scrawl were three words: *Cheers to you.*

"I told him to stop it after the second basket arrived. I told him I forgave him. This is too much." She frowned at Donny, adjusting her sweatshirt when it slipped off one shoulder. It was her favorite. But after hundreds of washes, it was stretched beyond all recognition. It *also* happened to be the same sweatshirt she had worn the night Ozzie kissed her for the first time. Kissed her and—

She stopped the memory before it could start. Heat had already stolen into her cheeks, and if she wasn't mistaken, there was a tightening in her core. A profound sadness engulfed her. She'd never get to experience any of those things with him again. She'd never *be* with him again.

Donny hopped aboard a barstool, cupped his chin in his hand, and eyed her. "Number one," he said, "I don't want to know what you were thinking just now to make your cheeks light up like Michigan Avenue during the Magnificent Mile Lights Festival. Number two, let the man grovel if he wants. He was a total rat bastard."

"No." She shook her head. "I waylaid him. He thought we were friends having a good time hooking up. He goes to all this trouble for me, risks his *life* for me, then *bam!*" She clapped her hands together. "The moment I don't need him to save my ass, I hit him over the head with what amounted to a verbal Dear John letter. Can you blame him for lashing out?"

"*Yes.*" Donny sniffed. "I blame him for making you a mess that night. I haven't seen you that out of your head since your father died."

"The man I love told me he was headed out to bang the Betty wearing butt-fuck-me Buddy Holly glasses." She glowered at him. "What do you expect?"

"Nice alliteration." He grinned at her, opening the olive jar and stealing an olive. Chewing, he sobered. "But whether or not *I* can forgive him for what he said is neither here nor there. That *you've* forgiven him is all that matters."

"How could I not?" she asked. "You've met him. You know how amazing he is. A few harsh words spoken in the heat of the moment don't trump all the months of friendship. And they certainly don't trump what he's done for me these last few days. Besides, he assured me he *didn't* bang the Betty in the glasses."

"Well, that's something, I guess."

"I wish it weren't. Being insanely jealous is just going to make the weeks ahead that much harder."

"Are you *sure* you're not wrong about him, sweetie?" Donny asked. "I mean, there's all this." He motioned toward the basket and the others that were lined up on the counter behind her. "And he kept his word about that exclusive." Yes, he had. The ATF had partnered with the FBI to keep her apprised of the developing story with the Basilisks. In a few weeks, when the feds were ready, they would tell her to write the story and blow the lid off the whole damn thing. "Maybe he feels more for you than you realize and—"

"No." She cut Donny off. "I'm not wrong about him. He *likes* me, sure. I'd go so far as to say he likes me *a lot*. But he's *liked* a lot of woman. That's just him. The consummate gentleman playboy who, when he's focused on you, makes you feel like you're the only person in the whole world. But his focus eventually wanders. And I'm not stupid enough to think I'm any different than those who've come before me."

She blew out a breath. It hurt, but she'd grown used to the sensation over the last few days. It was just her lungs rubbing up against her broken heart. "I really wish I could hate him for it. But I can't. There's nothing malicious about what Ozzie does or who he is. There's no score keeping or locker-room talk or anything like that. He's just...*him*."

"And your lunch date with him tomorrow?" Donny asked, grabbing another olive.

Samantha decided she'd better make martinis before Donny devoured the entire jar. She crossed to her stainless-steel refrigerator and snagged the bucket from the ice dispenser. The sun was setting low in the sky, lighting up the city. Her apartment was the size of a shoebox. But, oh! What a view. She could see the entire Chicago skyline from the John Hancock Building to the Sears Tower—which had officially been renamed the Willis Tower, although no self-respecting Chicagoan would *ever* refer to it as such.

"What about my lunch date with him tomorrow?" She dumped the ice in the shaker and used the jigger to measure the liquor.

"You going to be okay?"

After pouring a little olive brine in with the gin and vermouth, she capped the shaker and gave it a good jiggle.

"Why do I get the feeling you're avoiding the answer to that question?" Donny yelled over the sound of alcohol and ice clanging against metal.

She grabbed two martini glasses from her cupboard, upended the shaker, and filled both. Only after she slid one to Donny and had taken a good tug on the other did she wipe her mouth and admit, "Because by avoiding the question, I won't have to lie to you."

"That bad, is it?" Donny took a sip of his drink and closed his eyes. "Mmm, good."

She'd developed her mad love for dirty martinis from Donny himself. He had taken her out on her twenty-first birthday. She could still remember what he'd said to her when he ordered their first drink. "Now, usually your twenty-first birthday is for bad beer, cheap vodka shots, and puking out the window of the cab on the way home. But you deserve better, funny face. We're going to start you off with the good stuff." Four dirty martinis later, she'd *still* puked out the window of the cab on the way home.

"The truth is, I don't know if I'll be okay," she admitted, the gin warming her belly but not her soul. The thought of seeing Ozzie again, of being *near* him but not being able to touch him, left her cold. "But I *have* to go. If I don't, he'll keep thinking he needs to apologize, to make up for..." She didn't finish that sentence. "And that'll just drag this thing out. I can't handle that. I have to keep up pretenses and let things deteriorate the natural way."

"The ol' friendly fade," Donny said, shaking his head before taking another sip. "Harsh."

"Don't act like you haven't done it yourself. I remember Mark Bennett. You met him for drinks and dinner less and less. Emailed and texted less and less until one day...*poof*. He was gone from your life. Never to be seen or heard from again."

"Not true. We exchange Christmas cards."

"Come on." She made a face.

"Fine." Donny sighed, running a finger around the rim of his martini glass. "So I friendly faded Mark. But in my defense, that was so much more merciful than out-and-out rejecting him. He was too nice for that."

"Exactly."

"Difference there being I didn't *love* or *lust* after Mark. How the hell are you going to keep from ending up in Ozzie's bed again? Or better yet, what possible reason will you give him for wanting to put a halt on your nocturnal activities? Activities that, by your own admission, were better than good... They were *grrrrreat*!"

Better than good or great, she thought. *Making love to Ozzie was transcendent. The man is a master.*

And *that* thought reminded her why she had decided to turn down this road in the first place. He'd acquired that mastery by being with women. A *lot* of women.

"I'll think of something," she told Donny.

But when she woke up the next morning, she still hadn't thought of anything.

Chapter 23

"WHY THE LONG FACE?"

Ozzie jumped at the question. He hadn't heard Becky come up behind him. He'd been too caught up in staring at Samantha's text message, willing it to change.

Clearing his throat and pasting on a smile—he hoped it wasn't too sick-looking—he turned away from his bank of computers. The late-morning sun always gave the shop a rosy glow. But even that wasn't enough to soften Becky's edges. She was covered head to toe in metal shavings and grease, and her expression was decidedly flinty. She always got that look when she was knee-deep in a bike build. Just so happened that right then, she was knee-deep in a bike *re*build. After five days, Violet, his beloved motorcycle, was beginning to look like her old self. Becky was a true genius.

"Long face?" He quirked a brow. "Wait. I know this one." He forced a teasing note into his voice. "It starts out… A horse walks into a bar, right?"

Becky plunked down beside him, a bottle of water in one hand and a grape-flavored Dum Dum lollipop still in its wrapper in the other. "Don't frickin' distract me with that winning smile and those quick quips. Ten minutes ago, you were grinning and whistling that *Come on, feel the noise* song by…" She screwed up her face.

"Quiet Riot, although it's actually a remake of an old 1973 Slade song," he submitted helpfully. It would also forever remind him of Samantha, the song she'd had him play on the jukebox at Delilah's bar all those years ago.

"Right." Becky nodded. "And then you get a text message, and suddenly, you look like you're sucking on a lemon. So what gives? Who was that?" She flicked a greasy finger at his cell phone.

He considered prevaricating or telling her it was none of her damned business, but what would be the point? She would find out eventually. He hadn't exactly kept it a secret that he was supposed to meet Samantha for lunch.

"It was Samantha." And just saying her name opened up another fissure in his heart. "She canceled on me."

Becky lifted a brow. "Why? Did something happen to burst all those heart-shaped balloons flying above her head?" She pointed her lollipop at him. "What did you do?"

"M-me?" he sputtered. "Why do you assume *I* did something?"

"Um, because you're a man, that's why."

"Is this one of those sisterhood situations or rules or something?" He frowned at her.

"Huh?"

"Never mind." He ran his fingers through his hair, inadvertently hitting the bandage over his stitches. The wound itched like a bitch. Soon, it would be completely healed, and he'd have nothing to show for those two crazy, amazing days with Samantha but a thin scar and the memory of her beneath him, above him, teasing him and tormenting him and giving him more pleasure than he'd ever known. Even though she claimed to have forgiven him, he got the feeling this missed date was just the first of many missed dates to come. She was in the business of disappearing from his life. He recognized the signs. "The truth is I was an ass to her, okay?"

Becky's chin jerked back. "You? I don't believe it. You're never an ass to anyone." She shook her head. "No. Wait. I take that back. You're a *smart*-ass to just about *everyone*. But I've never known you to be intentionally cruel."

"I was to her." When he replayed his words to Samantha, he felt sick to his stomach. His father used to lash out. Sometimes he had stumbled into Ozzie's bedroom in a drunken rage and slurred, "She was fine before you came! This is all your fault!" Later, when his father was sober, he would apologize. But the sting of his words never went away.

And I'm becoming more like him every day. Eaten up by self-pity and remorse. Unable to do anything about it.

"So did you…" Becky hesitated. "Did you apologize for being an ass?" She eyed him quizzically.

"Yep. In every way I know how."

"But she's still pulling away from you?"

He shook his head. "She was pulling away from me before that. Her pulling away was what precipitated my assholery."

"Hmm," Becky said.

"Hmm?" He made a face. "That's all you got for me?"

"I just don't understand it. I thought she was frickin' ass over tits for you."

"Please." He snorted.

"Hmm," Becky said again, and he was beginning to hate that word.

"Such is my lot in life."

"So what are you gonna do about it?"

"What *can* I do?" His thigh chose that moment to send a shooting pain into the base of his spine. "I'll give her up. I should be good at that by now. I've had to resign myself to giving up a lot of things, especially recently."

"What do you mean?" Becky's brow furrowed.

He hadn't realized where this conversation was going, but it was a destination he had known he would need to reach eventually. *Why not now? Everything else is falling to shit. Might as well get this over and done with.*

"I mean this." He waved a hand to indicate the shop. "I mean *us*. All of us."

"Not tracking." When Becky shook her head, her long blond ponytail shed metal shavings like sparkling silver confetti.

"Come on, Becky." His voice was hoarse. He didn't think his broken heart could hurt worse, but... *Oh joy! I sure love surprises!* "You can't bullshit a bullshitter. We both know my leg is about as good as it's going to get."

She glanced down at his thigh. It was covered by his jeans, but he felt like she could see the mangled flesh beneath. "So?"

"So that means my job at Black Knights Inc. is over." And saying it out loud for the first time was like having his stomach cut open and listening to his guts spill on the floor. "I'll never be able to go back in the field. I can't run half a mile on the treadmill without collapsing from the pain, much less hump my ass over mountains or through jungles."

"So?" Apparently she was doing her best impression of a scratched record. She kept skipping and repeating the same lines over and over. "You're still an integral part of this team. What you do with these computers..." She waved at the monitors. "It's invaluable. And your design suggestions for the last couple of custom bike jobs? Brilliant."

"It's not enough," he said around the lump in his throat. "Boss brought me on to do more than computer work. But I'm no good for more than computer work, and I—" His eyes burned. He had to stop and look away so she wouldn't see what a pussy he'd become. When he turned back, Becky whacked him on the back of the head hard enough to have him seeing stars. "Hey! I had a minor concussion not five days ago, and now you're—"

"Shut up," she hissed. She was holding her Dum Dum lollipop an inch from his nose. He went cross-eyed when he tried to look at it. "For a genius, you sure are an idiot."

Ozzie frowned. "I've been hearing that a lot lately."

"Probably because it's true. Do you really believe you're only worth something to Black Knights Inc. if you can do the job you were hired to do?"

"Well—"

"Nope." Becky plunked her water bottle down on the table. Peanut, who had been doing figure eights around the legs of her chair, hissed at the sudden noise and scampered away. "You don't get to talk. *I'm* talking."

"But you asked a question." He blinked at the rage brightening her cheeks.

"So?" She looked at him like his IQ might have fallen into the double digits. "That doesn't mean I expect you to answer!"

"Of course not," he said, completely flabbergasted.

"Do you think the only thing Frank and I have been building here, the only thing *all* of us have been building here, is bikes?"

He opened his mouth to tell her they'd been building some pretty hefty spec-ops résumés as well, but snapped his jaws shut when he realized this was another rhetorical question.

"We have been building a *family*, you big, beautiful meathead. Black Knights Inc. is more than just a business. It's a *home*. It's *your* home."

Family… Home… There was a lump in his throat he was having trouble breathing around. His whole life, he had wanted family. His whole life, he had wanted to belong, wanted to be *wanted*.

"What we have is stronger than blood," Becky went on, her voice growing hoarse. "We have bonds of the heart. Bonds of the *soul*. And all of us here at BKI would sooner chop off all *our* legs than let you leave because you have it in your fool frickin' head that you're not good enough, or that we wouldn't want you if you couldn't do exactly what you were originally hired to do." If he wasn't mistaken, her eyes were overly bright.

Oh, good. I'm not alone. Because that lump in his throat had grown to the size of Australia. "What does Boss say?" Was that his voice? It sounded like he was talking underwater. "Does he feel—"

"Frank will tell you the *exact* same thing *I'm* telling you," she cut in. When a tear trickled down her cheek, smearing a line in a patch of grease, he thought he just might die. "We've talked about it a hundred times. What this place means to us. To all of us. What the people mean. It's like being married—good or bad, sickness and health, for richer or for poorer, we are all on this wild ride *together*. Oh, Ozzie…" She sat forward, grabbing his face with her grubby hands. Someone had started a fire in his chest. A smaller conflagration burned behind his eyes. "How could you not *know* that? How could you not know how much we all love you?"

She threw her arms around his neck and hugged him tight. Damn if he wasn't on the verge of bawling his motherfucking eyes out.

—∼∼—

"Whoa." Christian stumbled to a stop in the doorway to Emily's office. "What...uh...what the bloody hell has happened? Are you—"

"Shh," she scolded him. "Come in. Sit down. I'm eavesdropping on Ozzie and Becky, and you're blocking my view." With her office door open, she had a straight shot at the bank of computers where Ozzie and Becky sat.

Christian glanced over his shoulder. "Eavesdropping on Ozzie and Becky made you cry?"

"Yes," she hissed, waving for him to come in already and take one of the two chairs in front of her desk. *For crying out loud! The man follows instructions for shit.* "It was a poignant moment." So poignant because talk of family, talk of BKI *being* a family, touched a particularly tender spot inside her. "No time to explain. Now sit down and shut up."

He eyed her for a full three seconds. Finally, he shrugged and shuffled inside. He was wearing a purple dress shirt, unbuttoned at the collar and with the sleeves rolled up. The color emphasized the bright green of his eyes, and the tailored cut made his shoulders look as wide as an Olympic-sized swimming pool. She ignored all of this—*yeah, right*—as he took a seat.

"...are you working on?" Becky asked, wiping the tracks of tears from her cheeks as she pointed to Ozzie's computer screen.

Emily had been curious about that herself. For the last few days, Ozzie had been nose deep in something. And since she was the office manager, kept apprised of every mission or project, the fact that she didn't know what was keeping Ozzie up nights meant it was something personal.

"I'm trying to track down the person hired to kill Samantha's father all those years ago."

Christian muttered something under his breath. Emily shushed him.

"Why?" Becky asked Ozzie.

"Because…" Ozzie trailed off, shaking his head. Then he glanced through the door to Emily's office.

Oh shit.

"Act like you're talking to me," she instructed Christian, careful to keep her voice low enough not to be heard.

"I would," he answered with a glower, that ridiculously sexy glower. "But you insist on shushing me. So"—Emily saw Ozzie turn back to Becky—"how am I to know when—"

"Shh!" She waved at Christian.

He gaped at her.

"Because it's something Samantha has wanted to know for years. She needs closure," Ozzie told Becky. "I can't give her everything I want to give her, but I just might be able to give her this."

"We shouldn't be doing this," Christian whispered. "That's a private conversation and—"

"Either hush or leave." Emily tried to murder him with her eyes. "I'm not doing this just to be nosy."

"No?" He lifted a brow.

"No," she assured him. "I have… *Shh!*"

He lifted his hand as if to say, *You were the one talking, not me*, just as Becky said to Ozzie, "Tell me something. Are you in love with Samantha Tate?"

The woman wasn't one for beating around the bush. Just one of the many reasons Emily adored her. Holding her breath, Emily waited for Ozzie's answer.

He tried to play it off with, "I love all women. You know me."

Becky punched him in the shoulder. "Cut the crap. I'm serious."

For a while, Ozzie remained quiet. Then he blew out a ragged breath. "I love her."

Emily nodded. She had suspected as much all along. She thought she heard Christian mutter "Stupid, bloody wanker" under his breath.

"But it doesn't matter," Ozzie said. "It's not like I could make it work with her. Not in the long run. I mean, I can't even tell her who or what I really am." He hesitated a beat before adding, "But that's a moot point anyway."

"Why is that?" Becky asked.

"Because she doesn't love *me*."

Before Becky could answer, Emily pushed up from her desk. The move was so sudden that Christian looked startled. "Becky!" she called. "I need to talk to you!"

Becky turned in her seat, metal shavings falling from her ponytail. "Can it wait? I'm kinda in the middle of something here."

"It's a time-sensitive matter!" Emily called.

With a sigh and a word to Ozzie, Becky shoved out of her chair.

"What are you up to?" Christian demanded.

"Stick around and find out."

Becky stomped to the doorway. "What's up?"

"Shut the door," Emily instructed. "I have an idea I want to run by you."

Chapter 24

Black Knights Inc. Headquarters

ONE WEEK AFTER SAMANTHA HAD CANCELED HER lunch date with Ozzie, she stood in front of the huge steel doors to the old menthol cigarette factory and warehouse the Knights had converted into their custom bike shop. Lifting her finger to ring the buzzer, she noticed its tremor.

What the hell am I doing here?

Oh right. She was here because Becky had called, asking her to stop by. The blond-haired motorcycle mechanic had said she had something for Samantha. But Samantha couldn't help but wonder if Ozzie was behind this.

She'd canceled on him twice. She hadn't been able to bear the thought of being with him without *being* with him. But now it was time to come clean. Her plan to friendly fade him wasn't working, and she couldn't continue to blow him off.

Pride be damned, she needed to tell him the truth. Tell him she loved him to the moon and back. At which point, she'd sit back and nurse her broken heart while *he* pulled away.

She glanced over her shoulder through the big wrought-iron gates at Toran. He was one of the Connelly brothers, the four burly Chicago-born Irishmen who worked guard duty for BKI. She'd come to know all four brothers over the years while trying to get the dirt on the Knights, but Toran was her favorite. He had always withstood her nosy questions with a bit of humor. Currently, he was standing in the door to the gatehouse giving her a thumbs-up.

"Go on!" he yelled in his thick Chicago accent. "Give 'em a ring! They'll let ya right in!"

She waved her thanks before turning back to the buzzer. For so long, she'd been *trying* to get into the BKI compound. Now she was being let in at will, and she couldn't even make herself press the damned buzzer.

You've never been a coward, Sammie. Now's not the time to start.

Right? *Right.* Squaring her shoulders, she pressed the button. An angry *whir* sounded inside. After a series of clicks and beeps and one mighty *clang*, the huge metal door swung open with a whispered groan.

They take their security seriously here, she thought. Then again, they *were* all former special operators or spies or whatever. Security was probably second nature to them. Plus, they had hundreds of thousands, maybe even millions of dollars' worth of equipment and custom bikes inside, and this wasn't exactly the greatest neighborhood.

As the door swung wide, Samantha girded herself to see Ozzie. Maybe she was even *hoping* to see him. That was the only explanation for why her heart plummeted when she realized it was Becky waiting to meet her. "Oh, it's you," Samantha said.

"Try not to bowl me over with your enthusiastic greeting." Becky frowned around a lollipop stick.

"Sorry." Samantha shook her head. "I just thought that maybe Ozzie—"

"He's not here," Becky interrupted. "He's taken Violet out for a test ride. She's finally road worthy again." The look Becky gave her could not be mistaken. It was the facial equivalent of *No thanks to you*.

"I really am so sorry about—"

"Never mind that." Becky waved her off. "Come in."

Samantha hoisted her purse higher on her shoulder and followed Becky into the warehouse and down a hall decorated with hundreds of rusting antique motorcycle license plates. Upon entering the shop, she blinked when Becky motioned her toward the metal staircase leading to the second floor. "I thought you said you have something to give me." She glanced around nervously.

The place looked just as she remembered. Bike lifts, rolling tool chests, a row of gleaming motorcycles in fantastical colors. It smelled the same too. Like motor oil, hot metal, and strong coffee. All of it reminded Samantha of Ozzie. Of him over by that far bike lift, telling her it was no big deal that he'd obliterated his motorcycle in the name of saving her hide. Of him at his computer, hacking away to help her solve the mystery of the connection between the weapons and the Basilisks and the Black Apostles. Of him in the kitchen, kissing her with such passion that she knew no man would ever match it and—

"Hello?" Becky snapped fingers in front of Samantha's face. "Earth to Samantha."

"Sorry." She shook her head. "I sort of zoned out for a second. What did you say?"

"I *said*"—Becky frowned at her, sounding exasperated—"that what I have to give you is upstairs. Follow me."

Reluctantly, Samantha did. But something felt off. *Portentous* might be a better word. And when she topped the stairs and saw Delilah, Emily, and Christian all seated around the conference table, her alarm grew. "Gang's all here, I see."

"Not even close," Becky assured her, taking a seat near the head of the table. "We're missing more than—"

"I was making a joke," Samantha interjected.

"Yeesh. Fell kind of flat." This from Delilah. As always, trusty Fido sat by her side. She stroked the Lab's big yellow head.

Samantha's eyelid twitched like crazy. *What the hell is going on here?* Then, in a flash, she thought she knew. She'd been dodging Ozzie. No doubt they all realized that. And they probably thought—

"Look," she said. "If you guys are worried I'll go back on my word not to write a story about your past lives, then let me assure you, I'm a woman who keeps her promises."

"Good to know." Delilah motioned toward the chair at the head of the table. "Now, have a seat."

Samantha hesitated, but after a deep breath, she made her way over to the indicated chair. Setting her purse on the floor, she smiled and scratched Peanut's notched ears when he came up to investigate. Then, figuring she'd stalled as long as she could, she straightened and folded her hands on the table. She made eye contact with every person in the room. When none of them spoke, she was forced to do the honors. "Okay, guys. Here I am. Whatever it is, let me have it. The wait is killing me."

"Can I get you some coffee?" Emily offered.

"Am I going to need it?" Samantha countered. When Emily shrugged, she shook her head. "No. I'm jittery enough without it, thanks. Let's get this over with."

"By all means." Becky grabbed the file folder in front of her and tossed it to Samantha.

"What's this?"

"Open it and see for yourself," Christian said.

After a long hesitation, Samantha did just that. Inside

were a bunch of documents she couldn't make hide nor hair of, but one thing stood out. It was a mug shot of a man with a bald head, beady eyes, and a neck tattoo that made him look positively barbarous. He seemed vaguely familiar, but she couldn't place how or where she knew him. She shook her head. "Sorry. You've lost me. Who am I looking at?"

"That's Victor Fisk," Becky said. "The man who killed your father."

Samantha's heart stopped pumping. Her lungs stopped working. The whole room did a slow tilt. "Excuse me?"

"Ozzie and I have been doing some investigative work," Delilah said. "Well, it was really just Ozzie."

"He's been laboring day and night for over a week," Emily added.

"He hacked into...uh...well, freakin' everything pertaining to that alderman you told him about," Delilah continued. "But he didn't hit pay dirt until he combed through the man's accounts. Like I always say, you have to follow the money. Together, he and I were able to pinpoint a series of withdrawals from the alderman's account that coincided with deposits in Fisk's account. The one that was particularly interesting happened the day after your father was murdered. Payoff for a job done."

Now the room wasn't just tilting. It was *spinning*. White stars burst in Samantha's field of vision.

"Fisk was a gun for hire for more than just the alderman," Christian said. "He was apprehended while doing a job for another city official about a year after your father's murder."

"The public works director," Samantha whispered, putting the face and the name with the memory of the news stories she'd read in college. *That* was why Fisk looked familiar. Donny had done a couple of pieces on the scandal and the ensuing trial for the *Trib*. They had always included Fisk's mug shot.

"Right-oh." Christian nodded.

"But…" Samantha's mind was reeling. "H-how can you be sure?"

"Ozzie paid him a visit in the pen," Becky said. "For five hundred dollars deposited in his commissary account, Fisk admitted to killing your father."

"But…maybe he would have admitted anything to get that money." Samantha tried with all her might to ignore the burning itch at the back of her nose.

"No." Christian shook his head. "Ozzie never mentioned the alderman. Fisk was the one to bring him up. He's the bloke what snuffed your father, Samantha. Ozzie sorted it out for you. It's done."

Could it be true? Could it really, *finally* be over? Thanks to Ozzie?

Something massive grew inside Samantha. A tsunami of emotion, of love, of regret, of—

"So we have a question for you," Becky said.

"What's that?" *Holy shit? Is that my voice?*

"Don't you like Ozzie anymore?"

"*L-like* him?" she sputtered, glancing around the table. "I…" She stopped herself. Licking her lips, she tried again. "I…" Nope. Didn't work that time either. "I don't like him. I *love* him," she finally blurted.

Saying it out loud felt like a benediction. *The truth will set you free*. Trouble was, it could also break your heart.

"I think he's the best thing ever, the best *person* ever. I just…" She swallowed and shook her head. That thing inside her was continuing to grow. She didn't know how much longer she could hold it back. "I can't be his friend and part-time lover. I just *can't*. I hope you understand that."

"Why part-time lover?" Becky tilted her head.

"Are you serious? You know Ozzie."

"Yeah, we do," Delilah said. "Question is, do you?"

"I…" Samantha stopped and shook her head. "I know he loves women. I know he asks every woman he meets to marry him."

"Has he ever asked *you* to marry him?" This from Emily.

Samantha was taken aback. "Well…*no*, but—"

"And didn't that ever strike you as strange?" Now it was Becky's turn.

"I…" Samantha began, then stopped and shook her head. She couldn't think. Not with so many people firing questions at her. She finally knew what it was like to be on the other side of a press conference.

"Didn't it ever occur to you that Ozzie asks every woman he meets to marry him," Delilah added, "but he never asked you, because yours is the only answer that really matters?"

Now the room wasn't tilting *or* spinning. It was beginning to narrow into a tunnel. Or maybe that was just Samantha's vision. Her chest ached with pressure. "What are you trying to tell me?" she managed.

Instead of answering her, Becky posed yet another question. "Has Ozzie ever told you why he loves eighties hair bands or *Star Trek*?"

The change in topic threw Samantha for a loop. "I asked him once, but…" She trailed off, realizing he had never given her an answer.

"Well, the reason he loves that stuff is because of his mother," Becky said. "He ever talk about her to you?"

"She died when he was four, right?"

"Killed herself," Becky clarified, and Samantha gasped, aching for the little boy who had grown into such an amazing man. "Ozzie's father fell apart. He took to the bottle in his grief and self-pity. In drunken rages, he blamed Ozzie for his mother's death."

"Sweet merciful fuck." Samantha wheezed. Her throat had closed up.

"See, she suffered from postpartum depression after Ozzie's birth," Becky went on. "She documented everything in her diary. The depression. The doubts and anxiety. The feelings of failure. Of course, at the time, postpartum wasn't widely discussed, so she suffered in secret until one day, it all became too much. She left a note saying she thought Ozzie would be better off without her. Then she went out to the garage, attached a garden hose to the exhaust on her car, threaded it through the driver's side window, and went to sleep. Forever. Ozzie grew up feeling in some way responsible for her death."

As he does, Samantha thought, her broken heart ground to dust for the man she loved.

"He escaped his father's drunken rages by locking himself in his room with all his mother's old stuff," Becky added. "Her eighties hair band cassettes and *Star Trek* VHS tapes. That's how he got to know her. How he continues to keep her close and pay tribute to her memory."

"But that's not the only way," Emily chimed in. "The *other* way he pays tribute to her is with his motorcycle and the tattoo above his heart."

And suddenly, Samantha understood. With that understanding, she was no longer able to hold back the thing growing inside her. It began to erupt, starting with a quake in her chest. "Violet," she whispered. "He named his bike after his mother."

"Yes." Becky nodded. "The bike he sacrificed without a thought. For *you*."

That's when it happened. Samantha Tate, the woman who never cried, burst into great, heaving, body-shaking tears.

"This was a bad sodding idea," Christian muttered, shifting uncomfortably in his chair.

Samantha Tate was a pretty woman, but she cried ugly tears. The sort of tears that made her whole body heave.

"No." Emily shook her head. "It was a great idea." There was a smile on her face.

"What, pray tell, could you possibly have to grin about?"

"She loves him. Like *loves* him loves him." When Christian turned back, it was to find Becky and Delilah patting Samantha's shoulders while offering her a box of tissues. "Oh, the joy of being right," Emily added, still beaming.

"There's still a long way to go yet," he warned her. "This scheme of yours could still backfire on us all."

"Ozzie's happiness is worth the gamble," Emily said.

Christian hoped so. But in the same breath, he sent up a silent prayer of thanks that his brothers-in-arms in the field were ready to be evac-ed immediately, should this grand plan Emily and Becky had schemed up not go the way they hoped. Should Samantha not *react* the way they hoped.

"Everyone agreed," Emily added, glancing over at him, that damned beauty mark making him barmy. "*You* agreed. Don't tell me you're changing your mind."

"No," he assured her. "You're right. Ozzie's happiness *is* worth the gamble." Because, like everyone else, he happened to love the obnoxious wanker.

"See." Emily pointed at his face. "I knew there was a warm heart buried somewhere under that cold exterior."

He frowned. She thought he was *cold*? When she was around, he was so hot, he wanted to shed his clothes. And then ask her to shed *hers*.

He opened his mouth to say…he wasn't sure what, but he was stopped when Becky quietly told Samantha, "Ozzie has spent his whole life being rejected by the people he loves. First there was his mother. Then there was his frickin' father. Add the women his father brought into the house who would coddle Ozzie and dote on him until they eventually realized they were no replacement for Ozzie's mother, and they ended up leaving too. And even though I don't think Ozzie ever loved any of the women he took to bed, he certainly *cared* about them. But did any of *them* stick around?"

Samantha started to say something, but Becky talked right over her. "No, they did not. We're all hoping you're different."

"But wh-what if…" Samantha wiped her red, puffy eyes and blew her nose. "What if *he* doesn't love *me*? What if *he* rejects *me*?"

"Guess that's a risk you're gonna have to take. Is he worth it?"

Samantha swallowed, searching Becky's eyes. "Yes. He's worth *everything*."

"Good answer." Delilah slapped her on the back, and Christian breathed a sigh of relief.

Becky glanced around the table. "I think it's time, don't you?"

Christian's heart clenched for Ozzie. This would be the moment of truth. The moment they'd all know if Samantha was worthy of Ozzie. Or if she would kill their careers.

Delilah placed both hands on the table and pushed to a stand. "Let's do this."

"Do what?" Samantha blinked in alarm.

"Follow us." Becky stood and motioned for Samantha to do the same. Blowing out a breath, Christian trotted after the women to the bank of computers.

Grabbing one of the rolling chairs, he noticed that Emily positioned herself directly behind him. "Here goes," he muttered.

She nodded. When he tilted his head back, he discovered her smile had disappeared. Now that the time had come, she was nervous. Which was why he wasn't as surprised as he might have been when he felt her tentatively reach for his shoulder. She needed to hold on to something. He was a daft prat to feel such joy that she'd chosen *him*.

"Christian?" Becky turned back to him. "Do the honors, will you?"

He nodded and switched on the monitor in front of Samantha. After he used the keyboard to type in the needed information, the screen flashed once before crystallizing and revealing one of the world's most recognizable faces. The president of the United States. The software they used was similar to Skype, only with a bazillion firewalls backed up by having the signal bounced through just about every satellite speeding around the earth.

"Whaaaaa?" Samantha's eyes were wide and unblinking as the president turned from looking over his shoulder. The windows of the Oval Office glinted behind his back, but they were soon obscured by the imposing presence of General Pete Fuller in full dress uniform.

The general leaned down, his rough face looking huge when he held it too close to the camera. "Oh good. We're on," he said before straightening.

Samantha swayed, grabbing hold of the edge of the computer table until her knuckles turned white. "M-Mr. P-President," she stuttered.

"Samantha Tate." President Thompson waved. "It's so nice to meet you. These folks"—he tipped his chin to include those gathered behind her; they could see themselves in a little picture-within-a-picture down on the right-hand side of the screen—"have told me so much about you."

"Th-they have?" Samantha shook her head. She was white as a ghost.

Christian understood. It wasn't every day one had a chat with the commander in chief.

"Yes, they have," Thompson said. "And that's why we're having this meeting."

"Showtime," Emily whispered, her fingers tightening around Christian's shoulder.

Chapter 25

SAMANTHA WAS DREAMING...

She had to be. She couldn't really be sitting inside BKI's custom bike shop listening to the freaking president of the freaking United States of freaking America tell her that Ozzie and the others weren't just *former* SEALs and spies and SAS officers and whatever. They were all *currently* working for him and the Joint Chiefs as some sort of supersecret government defense firm.

She pinched herself and winced at the pain. *Okay, so not dreaming.*

The instant reality sank in, she wanted to shout, *I knew it! I knew this place was more than it seemed!* But she couldn't, because the freaking president of the freaking United States of freaking America was still talking.

"...not the first president to employ his own fast-reaction force," Thompson was saying. In a navy suit with a red-and-white-striped tie, he looked very presidential. There was power in his bearing. Wisdom in his salt-and-pepper hair and sharp blue eyes. Even his voice was authoritative. "And I won't be the last. You can count on that."

He reached over to snag a bag of Haribo gummy bears, ripping open the packet with his teeth and shaking a few into his mouth. As if watching the leader of the free world have a snack wasn't enough, General Fuller, the freaking chairman of the freaking Joint Chiefs of Staff, a man who looked like he should be starring in war movies, held out his big scarred hand, and the president poured a few brightly colored bears into his waiting palm.

This is the most surreal moment of my life, Samantha thought. She was tempted to pinch herself again. "I'm sorry, Mr. President. I don't understand why you're telling me this unless…" A lightbulb flamed to life inside her head. "Are you hoping I'll break the story? Maybe spin it a certain way because I know the players involved?"

"No." Thompson shook his head. "We're hoping you love Ozzie enough not to write anything about it at all."

Samantha's mind blanked. I don't understand."

"All these folks lined up behind you…" Thompson explained, and Samantha glanced over her shoulders at the faces of the people he mentioned. They held various expressions of concern and hope. "…feel that Ozzie has a right to happiness. They think *you're* the person who can give him that happiness. But only if you know the truth about him and what he does. They're risking everything on you right now. And they asked *me* to break the news to you, because they figured it's harder to say no to your commander in chief."

Samantha's voice was a bare whisper when she said, "What do you mean they're risking everything on me?"

"I mean, the missing members of Black Knights Inc. aren't at a conference. They're either in Syria, disrupting the Islamic State's supply lines, or they're in Europe hunting down the identity of an international crime lord responsible for everything from human trafficking to piracy to the selling of illegal goods."

Samantha turned around again, blinking at the people behind her. She'd thought the tension in the shop was due to her presence, to the fact that she'd dogged them for years and then suddenly was foisted upon them as a guest. But that wasn't it at all.

"I have evac plans in place to pull them out of harm's way should you decide you can't keep this secret, should you feel compelled to write it up as fodder for the American public," Thompson continued, and Samantha once again turned to face him. "And if that's what you want to do, I won't try to stop you. I won't have the Secret Service quietly disappear you." She could tell by his enigmatic smile that he could do just that.

"You can pen the piece and accept the awards it'll no doubt win you. And I'll deal with the fallout on my end. But know this. Every single member of Black Knights Inc., people who came to your rescue and took you in when you needed protection, will spend the rest of their lives looking behind them, waiting for their enemies to make a move on them or their families."

This was big. Bigger than big. It was *huge*! The stuff they gave out Pulitzer Prizes for.

And I can never write a word of it.

She struggled with that knowledge. Struggled with the part of her that felt everything was better in the light. But that struggle only lasted a second. Whether or not this was a secret that deserved the light was beside the point. Like the president said, these people, the Black Knights, deserved her silence. They deserved her loyalty. But more importantly, *Ozzie* deserved it.

"I understand." She swallowed around the giant lump in her throat, shaking with the enormity of the information that had been handed to her.

President Thompson narrowed his gaze. "Meaning what?"

"Meaning your secret…" She turned to the group. "Meaning *all* your secrets are safe with me."

The collective sigh of relief was nearly enough to ruffle the hair around her face.

"Told you I was right about her." Emily nudged Christian.

One of the two massive garage doors at the front of the shop began to open. "Ozzie's back," Becky said. "You ready?"

Samantha shook her head, her heart pounding. She was absolutely *reeling* from everything she'd heard. But all that melted away, because…*Ozzie*. "Ready?" She looked at Becky like the woman might have six heads. "Hell no. I'm scared to death."

"You'd be an idiot if you weren't," General Fuller muttered, still noshing gummy bears. "Telling someone you love them, letting yourself be that vulnerable to another human being, is one of the most terrifying things a person can do."

Samantha blinked. Did the freaking head of the freaking Joint Chiefs really just say that to her?

"Ah, Pete." The president clapped a hand on the general's forearm. "I love it when you let your inner tender heart out to play."

"Fuck off," the general said, his image leaving the camera's field of view. "I need some coffee."

So surreal, Samantha mused in amazement. Then she turned at the sound of biker boots on the metal treads. Ozzie topped the stairs, pulling off his helmet and shaking out his shaggy hair.

"What the hell?" He eyed them all. Samantha knew the moment his gaze fell on her. She felt his eyes roaming over her face like a physical touch.

"And here's where I take my leave," President Thompson said. "I suggest the rest of you do the same." He leaned forward, and the computer screen went blank.

Samantha could sense the group shuffling away, heading into various offices. She didn't turn to watch them go. She only had eyes for Ozzie.

Pushing to a wobbly stand, she walked over to him on gelatinous knees. She didn't remember him being so tall. *Has he grown?* Or so broad-shouldered. *Has he been hitting the gym extra hard?* But she did remember his eyes. Those blue-sky eyes that looked at her and really *saw* her.

"Have you been crying?" were the first words out of his mouth. A muscle ticked in his jaw as his gaze darted to the office doors through which his friends and coworkers had disappeared. "What the hell is happening here? Did they threaten you? I'll fucking—"

"No." She grabbed his arms. His motorcycle jacket concealed the warmth of his skin, but there was no concealing the way his muscles bunched at her touch. "No one threatened me."

"I don't understand." He frowned down at her. "Why are you here? Why was the president on the monitor? Why—"

"We'll get to that later," she assured him. "First, there are three things I want to tell you."

He blinked, the pulse in his tan neck pounding like crazy. "Go on."

This was it. The moment of truth. Her heart stuttered. The breath in her lungs burned. She could feel herself chickening out, so she hurriedly said, "The first thing is *thank you*."

His chin jerked back, that wonderful square chin covered with that delightful light-brown beard. "For what?"

"For finding Victor Fisk for me. For spending all that time and effort and money—"

"Goddamn Becky," he growled. "She never minds her own fucking business. I was going to mail that information to you with a letter explaining—"

Samantha went up on tiptoe and cupped his face in her hands. It made the words strangle in his throat. He searched her eyes. "The second thing is…I know."

She could feel the muscles in his jaw working beneath her palms. "Know what?"

"All about who you really are. What you really do. And don't worry, your secret is safe with me. *All* of BKI's secrets are safe with me."

There was dawning understanding in his eyes. His Adam's apple bobbed in his throat. "Why would they tell you about—"

"Because they knew you never would," she cut in. "Because they thought you had a right to have your truth known. Because they love you." His whiskers abraded her palms. And she wanted nothing more than to kiss his velvety lips. But there was one more thing she needed to tell him. *The* thing. The one that would make or break her.

"And the third thing?" Ozzie blinked rapidly, his eyes overly bright.

Here goes. "I'm in love with you," she blurted.

He sucked in a startled breath.

She could feel every one of his muscles lock into place. "I apologize for the unpolished delivery, but it's true. I'm in love with you. It's that simple and that complicated. And I know…I know you probably don't feel the same about me. Which is why I've been pulling away. But I'm not pulling away anymore. I'm jumping." Yes, she was. Breath held, eyes closed, she was jumping. "Because that's what love is, a leap into the void with the hope that someone is there to catch you."

―⁂―

Ozzie couldn't believe his ears. His friends, his colleagues, his…*family* had risked everything by telling Samantha the truth. And Samantha? She was willing to go against everything she stood for, against her very nature, to keep that truth a secret.

It was too much. *They* were all too much.

He was seconds away from bawling his motherfucking eyes out. And since the last thing he wanted to do in this moment, the best moment of his entire sorry life, was prove what a vulnerable wreck he really was, he distracted himself by tenderly framing Samantha's pretty face.

"I'm going to kiss you now," he told her, his voice a gravelly parody of itself.

"O-okay." She blinked up at him.

As he leaned close, he noticed with relief that all her bruises had faded. That was the last rational thought he had, because the minute their lips touched and her wide eyes fluttered shut, he was drunk on the taste of her. It was the sweetest thing he'd ever known. He could put a name to the flavor of her candied mouth now. It was love. *She* was what love tasted like.

She loves me! She loves me! She loves me!

He wanted to howl it at the moon. Wanted to take her upstairs and make love to her until they were both sweaty and spent. But what he did instead was pull back and give her the truth that had been in his heart for so long. She thought love was a leap into the void? "I'll catch you," he whispered.

She gasped and searched his face. And then he watched as tears filled the indomitable Samantha Tate's eyes.

What a woman, he thought. *My woman*. And never had two words sounded so sweet.

"I'm so fucking sorry I had to lie to you," he swore. "I wanted to tell you the truth a million times, but—"

She shoved a finger over his mouth. A finger he couldn't help but kiss. "Don't." She shook her head. "Don't apologize for that. There were so many people depending on you to keep quiet. It's such a burden and—"

"But you probably feel like you don't really know me," he insisted.

"Oh, I know you." She grinned up at him. "I know you're smart and loyal and funny."

A muscle twitched in his jaw. "Not so funny. Not all the time. There's darkness in me, Samantha. And for years, I've tried to hide it behind jokes and gibes and…" He trailed off, needing her to hear the truth of him, wondering how to explain it. "I learned to be charming because it made people like me. It made them want to stick around. But I'm not always the good-time guy. Sometimes I get broody and—"

She didn't allow him to finish. She went up on tiptoe and threw her arms around his neck. Her wonderful smell filled his nose, and the feel of her soft breasts against his chest provoked a familiar hunger. "I don't want happy-go-lucky all the time, Ozzie. I just want you. All of you. Funny and sad. Light and dark. *All* of you."

A shudder shook him.

"Now, say it," she whispered in his ear, her warm breath tickling his skin and making his muscles clench with need. "I need to hear the words, Ozzie. I need you to tell me—"

"I love you." And there it was. The greatest truth of all. "I love you. I *love* you," he vowed, holding her so tight. "I'll say it a million times if that's what you—"

A sudden pain shot through his thigh, taking his breath away. He stumbled back, grabbing the rail beside the stairs for support. *Great.* Of all the times for his wound to make itself known. But he guessed he'd better get used to it. The injury was a part of him now. Just like his liver and lungs. Just like…Samantha.

"What it is?" Her brow furrowed in concern.

"My thigh." He rubbed the fucker, willing the agony

to subside. When it did, he blew out a breath. "Sorry to ruin the moment."

She tenderly touched his wound. Her fingers were cool through the denim of his jeans. Not trusting his leg to continue to support him, he rested his weight against the railing and pulled Samantha between his thighs.

"So what *really* happened to your leg?" she asked quietly, running her hands through his hair.

"Remember when the president's daughter's security detail was taken out in Malaysia a year ago?" he asked. *Damn, it feels good to hold nothing back.*

"That was *you*?" Samantha's eyes were wide as saucers.

He scratched his hairy chin, shifted uncomfortably. "I was…uh…I was with one of the Secret Service agents in her hotel room. We had—"

Samantha covered his mouth with her hand, making a face. "Spare me the details."

Ozzie's broken heart reknitted itself then and there. And it was stronger, bigger, *happier* than it had ever been before. "Are you jealous?" He flashed her a seductive grin.

"You bet your fine ass." She scowled. Grabbing the lapels of his biker jacket in both hands, she jerked him forward. "You're mine."

He shouldn't take such joy in her possessiveness, but he couldn't help himself. She wanted him. *Me! She wants me!* "I'm yours," he assured her. "Always and forever."

That seemed to placate her. She smiled that gap-toothed smile he loved so much. "Damned straight."

"Anyway, she had kicked me out." He shook his head, thinking back on Julia Ledbetter. She had been a sweet woman even if she *had* wanted nothing more from him than a quick slap and tickle. And he would never get over the guilt he felt that he had lived when she had died. "It's what saved my life. I was across the room getting dressed when the incendiary device the terrorists planted under her bed detonated. But even across the room, the blast was big enough to do this." He massaged the mangled muscles of his leg.

"So many *huge* stories"—Samantha shook her head and stuck out her bottom lip—"and I can't write any of them."

A kernel of doubt lodged in his brain. "Samantha, this life…it's…" He searched for the right words. "It's a burden. Keeping these secrets, especially when your job is to uncover secrets… It will weigh on you. And there's no one you can talk to about it. You can't tell Donny or—"

Again, she placed a cool finger against his lips. And again, he couldn't help himself. He kissed it. "I can tell *you*. I can talk to *you*." Then she leaned in, pressing her forehead to his, and said the most amazing thing. "You're worth any sacrifice, any burden, any secret. Oh, Ozzie, to me, you're worth *everything*."

And damnit! He was ready to bawl his eyes out again. So, *again*, he distracted himself the only way he knew how. He covered her mouth with his and kissed her until tenderness turned to desperation, until sweetness became desire.

His fingers found their way beneath her shirt. Her skin was so soft and smooth. Her silky tongue speared into his mouth over and over again, making him throb and—

"Bloody hell!" Christian's deep booming voice thundered from one of the offices. "You two need to get a room!"

Samantha giggled, hiding her face next to Ozzie's.

"I'm game," he whispered in her ear. "Are you?" She

pulled back and searched his face. He could tell something was bothering her. "What is it, sweetheart?"

"I...uh...know this is soon, probably too soon, but I just want to make sure you know where my head is."

"Okay?" He frowned at her. "Where is your head?"

"It's in love with you."

"Thought we'd established that. My head is in love with you too. Not to mention my heart and my soul and many of my favorite body parts."

"And I want to be with you. *Forever*." She went on as if he hadn't spoken. "I want to marry you, Ozzie." His heart started pounding for all it was worth. "Do you..." She trailed off, shaking her head. "*Will* you marry me?"

It was a question he'd asked a hundred different women a hundred times. But this was the first time anyone had ever asked him. He was filled with so much joy that he was surprised it didn't explode out of his ears. Voice thick with emotion, he smiled and gave Samantha just three words. He knew she would understand exactly what they meant.

"As you wish."

*Keep reading for a sneak peek of the next
Black Knights Inc. book*

FUEL FOR FIRE

"THERE MUST BE A BETTER WAY TO GET THIS JOB DONE."

Dagan Zoelner noted his own thunderous expression in the mirror hanging on the wall near the front door before returning his attention to Chelsea, sullenly eyeing her when she leaned close to her reflection to apply lipstick in a shade that could only be described as take-me, big-boy pink.

When she blew a kiss at him in the mirror, a coiling awareness tightened his gut. Then she turned and gifted him with a look that would have made a lesser man instinctively reach to protect his balls.

"Lands sakes alive, Z! You're going to whip out your misogyny *every* morning?" That husky voice of hers... it *did* things to him, and she planted her hands on her fantastically curvy hips. The woman was built like a Kardashian, no doubt about it, but the familiar stance reminded him not of a Kim or Khloé, but of a pint-sized Wonder Woman.

All she's missing are the gold cuff bracelets and the flowing black hair.

Because while Chelsea's hair was dark and shiny, it was as short as a little boy's. A *pixie* cut, he thought it was called. And that word described Chelsea Duvall perfectly.

With her smooth café au lait skin, her copper-colored eyes that frequently glinted with mischief, and the sprinkling of freckles like cinnamon across the bridge of her button nose, she was an ethereal creature. One he wanted to put in a gilded cage so he could keep her safe from the cruel world. And, more importantly, from the likes of Roper fuckin' Morrison.

"It's not misogyny. It's a cold, hard fact. You're not qualified for this kind of work."

"Oh sweet Jesus!" She tossed her hands in the air. She was unaware that the movement caused her blazer to gape open, revealing a set of spectacular breasts that stretched tight the fabric of her lavender blouse. "It's déjà poo. As in, I've heard this crap too many times before."

"Frequency doesn't make it any less true." He ripped his eyes away from the vast landscape of her chest because…you know…he refused to be *that guy*.

Even so, it didn't escape his notice that her amazing rack was partly to blame for the position Chelsea currently found herself in…the position of pretending to be Morrison's personal assistant when, in truth, she was waiting for an opportunity to plant a virus in one of Morrison's computers. Once she did that, the Black Knights back at headquarters in Chicago would hack into Morrison's systems and get the information they needed to prove, once and for all, that he was the notorious Spider.

For months, they had tried to ferret out Spider's true identity with no luck. Then, with the release of the Panama Papers, the detailed attorney-client information for more than 250,000 offshore companies and the identities of those companies' shareholders and financial transactions, they had found the proverbial needle in the haystack. The papers had uncovered a tie between Morrison and a diamond mine in Angola. Which wasn't all that unseemly on the surface, right? A man of Morrison's means—estimated net worth fourteen billion dollars—who owned a media empire of a hundred newspapers and dozens of television stations in both the United States and the UK, had investments all over the world, Africa included. But it just so happened that the Black Knights and the CIA had reason to believe that that *particular* diamond mine was owned by the shadowy Spider.

It had been a clear case of a transitive relationship as far as everyone involved had been concerned. If A equaled B, and B equaled C, then A equaled C. Morrison was Spider. The trouble came in trying to prove it. They hadn't been able to hack into Morrison's systems from the outside because, according to BKI's hacker extraordinaire, the renowned Ethan "Ozzie" Sykes, "Morrison's firewalls have firewalls." So that had left them with only one option. Get someone on the inside.

Enter Chelsea Duvall.

She had volunteered for the job with one unforgettable sentence: *I'll get so close to Morrison that he won't be able to take a piss without me giving it a shake*.

Dagan had exploded. He'd told her and everyone else at the early-morning meeting, "There's not a snowball's chance in hell Chelsea will be the one to do this. She's an analyst, not a fuckin' field agent!"

But he'd been outvoted.

Apparently Chelsea was the perfect pawn to use in

the chess match with Morrison because the man was known to hire and surround himself with women who possessed certain…physical attributes. Read: Ladies built like brick shithouses. And Chelsea's back story about wanting to quit her job with the Bureau of Land Management—that was her CIA cover—move to England, and go to work for Morrison was exceptional for two reasons. One, it was believable. And two, it happened to be one hundred percent true.

Less than two weeks after that fateful meeting at BKI headquarters, it became known that Morrison had fired his PA. Twenty-four hours later, Chelsea's resume had been in Morrison's hands. Forty-eight hours after *that*—time no doubt used by Morrison's security team to vet Chelsea top to bottom—she had been on a plane to London to sit for an interview.

Just as had been predicted, Morrison had taken one look at Chelsea—and her…uh…*myriad* delightful features—and hired her on the spot. That was the good news.

The bad news? Well, on top of being an evil and lecherous old fart, Morrison was incredibly paranoid. In the four and a half weeks Chelsea had worked for him, not once had she been allowed to enter either his home office or the office he kept in downtown London to use the thumb drive she meticulously sewed into the lining of her jacket or slacks or whatever other item of clothing she happened to wear to work that day.

Morrison not only *locked* the doors to his inner sanctums, but gaining access to the rooms required a retinal scan and voice recognition. Getting around the voice recognition part wasn't too hard. Chelsea had already made a secret recording of Morrison saying the pass phrase. But the retinal scan? Short of offing the asshole and plucking out one of his eyeballs, they were at a loss. *Something has to give.*

Dagan was convinced that *something* should be Chelsea's job with the handsy bastard. They could prove that Morrison was Spider some other way. One that didn't involve her subjecting herself to Morrison's unsubtle leers, roving hands, and blatant sexual innuendos.

"I'm just saying"—he eyed her mulish expression—"if you were going to get the chance to plant the virus, it would've happened by now."

"Says who?" She thrust out her chin. It was small and pointy, and he had the oddest urge to bend down and kiss it.

"Says me."

She rolled her eyes and adjusted her glasses. "And you're the ultimate authority...uh...*why?*"

"Let me see. Maybe it's the hundreds of successful missions I've—"

"Lord have mercy," she interrupted, slipping into the unhurried drawl that revealed her southern roots. "You realize if I wanted to commit suicide, all I'd have to do is climb your ego and jump down to that place where you keep your humility."

Before he could think of a good comeback, she continued. "And, sure, okay, let's stand here and go through all the reasons I'm not qualified for this kind of work. *Again.* No, really. I love beating a dead dog. You go first. And then when your arm gets tired, I'll jump in. Ready? Go."

"Bloody hell!" Christian, a former SAS officer in the British Army who, for reasons known only to a few, had left Her Majesty's Army to go to work for Black Knights Inc., called from the kitchen. "Would you two stop trading verbal punches? It's too early in the morning. I haven't finished my first cup of tea, and all that blathering is giving me a sodding headache!"

"Oh, now you've done it. You've gone and angered the Brit," Colby "Ace" Ventura said, sauntering up beside them and planting a kiss on Chelsea's cheek.

Before coming to work for the Black Knights, Ace had been a crackerjack Navy pilot, hence the nickname "Ace"—although there was some speculation that his last name and the Jim Carrey movies had played a part in his *nom de guerre*. Dagan respected the shit out of the guy. But right now? Well, he was hard-pressed not to punch the fucker in the mouth. If the guy's lips were busted, maybe *then* he'd keep them to himself.

But the dude's gay, one might argue.

Didn't matter. When it came to a man's mouth on Chelsea, Dagan's green-eyed monster made an appearance. Because the fact of the matter was, despite their daily verbal boxing matches, he *liked* her. Had since the first time he met her back at Langley all those years ago when she'd given him an Intelligence report in a confident, businesslike fashion. Looking at her, he had seen nothing but soft curves. Listening to her had revealed a sharp mind.

It was a wonderfully complex juxtaposition, and Dagan had determined to get her in bed on the double. But since he had rarely been stateside back then, the opportunity had never arisen. And just as he had been poised to return to the United States for a good, long stint, an op in Afghanistan had gone horribly wrong, and five people had paid for his mistake with their lives. Afterward, he'd been fired from the CIA quicker than you can say, *Clear out your locker, dickhead*. And as if all *that* wasn't bad enough, following his expulsion from the Company, he'd briefly gotten himself involved with a corrupt senator.

Both of those screwups were black stains on his character. He was convinced that a woman like Chelsea, a woman who was upright and true, wouldn't give him the time of day. Not knowing what she knew about him.

"Do you have everything you need?" Ace asked Chelsea, handing her a travel mug of coffee. "Perhaps you could use some Mace? Or electric underwear so every time that old bastard *accidentally*"—Ace made the quote marks with his fingers—"rubs your ass, he gets a nasty shock?"

"Thank you, Ace honey." Now it was Chelsea's turn to smack a kiss on Ace's cheek. "I don't know what I'd do without you."

Dagan's inner six-year-old stomped his foot and sullenly shouted, *What about me? I'm* always *looking out for you!* But he quickly reminded the little brat of Afghanistan and Senator Aldus. *She wants nothing to do with the likes of us, and you know it.*

"My pleasure. Teamwork makes the dream work, am I right?" Ace winked at Chelsea. He really was a handsome bastard. All blond hair, sea-blue eyes, and a physique that looked like it belonged in an underwear advertisement.

Dagan's jealousy was ridiculous. But that didn't stop him from wallowing in it when Ace opened the front door and Chelsea walked into the hall that led down four flights to the hustle and bustle of London's streets.

After the door shut behind her, Ace took one look at Dagan's face and sighed. "Come with me, Werewolf of London," he said. It had been a running joke since they took up residence. The town. The beard. Dagan got it. He just didn't think it was nearly as funny as the rest of them did. "Let's get some of Christian's tea in you. Maybe it will settle your nerves."

"If only it were that easy," he muttered, allowing Ace to pull him through the living room and into the kitchen.

Sitting at the small circular table in the corner was Christian. The three of them made up the team that had volunteered to move to London to provide Chelsea with support. And after living together in such close quarters—the flat only had two bedrooms, so all three men were bunked in one room—and with no real purpose except spending their days poring over every bit of Intel and research they could find on Morrison, a.k.a. Spider, they'd taken to busting each other's balls more frequently than usual.

Case in point…

"What happened to my bagel?" Ace demanded after opening the toaster oven and peering inside.

Christian glanced at the remains on his plate and grinned.

Ace spied the half-eaten bagel. "You shit-swizzling breakfast stealer!" He had a rare talent for coming up with imaginative insults. "I had that toasted perfectly!"

Christian picked up the bagel, studied it from all sides, then took a considering bite. "Indeed it is," he said around a mouthful. "Thank you."

"I should rip off your dick, shove it down your throat, and feed you your own ball sac for dessert. But rumor has it, you sport a microwang, and I don't want to strain my eyes trying to find it."

Aw, yes. The attack on the size of a man's meat. Classic.

Dagan jumped into the fray, happy for the distraction. Anything to take his mind off Chelsea. "You going to let him dis your doodle like that, Christian?"

"This rumor is easy to refute." Christian stood and reached for the top button of his jeans.

"I'll thank you to keep your man stick to yourself." Emily Scott sauntered in from the living room.

Whoops. Dagan had forgotten to mention *her* as part of the team that had come to provide support for Chelsea. Although for the life of him, he couldn't understand how. Emily, the former secretary to an FAS, a foreign area specialist inside the Central Intelligence Agency, and current BKI office manager, was the one who had kept the refrigerator stocked these last few weeks in London and the one who twisted their ears when the laundry piled up. Without her and her Mother Goose ways, they'd likely be living on pork and beans and wearing three-day-old underwear.

"Hand to God, I'd rather have my right eye gouged out with a toothpick than see Christian's dick," she continued, projecting a toughness that he knew covered a soft, gooey center. Emily *cared* about all of them. She just didn't like to show it. "There's enough testosterone floating around this place without the addition of naked wagging wangs."

"Once again," Christian said, "let me point out that you didn't *have* to come with us. No one twisted your arm." His hoity-toity English accent made it sound like *yoor ahm*.

"And leave poor Chelsea to fend for herself among you three animals?" Emily snorted. "Not likely."

And great. Dagan had enjoyed a brief reprieve, but one mention of Chelsea and his brain was firmly fixed on her. He *hated* that she was alone in that big penthouse with Roper fuckin' Morrison. He hated worse that he couldn't come up with a better plan to prove Morrison was Spider so that she wouldn't *have* to be alone in that big penthouse with Roper fuckin' Morrison.

"And speaking of Chelsea..." Emily continued. When she turned to Dagan, she rocked the eye daggers of doom. "I really wish you would refrain from giving her grief every morning. The poor, innocent woman has enough on her plate without you piling on."

Innocent? There was a word. When it came to Chelsea, Dagan's thoughts didn't live in the same zip code as innocent.

"All that shit on her plate is precisely the point," he insisted. "She's not—"

"Qualified or trained to do this kind of work. Blah-blah-blah. But news flash: she's doing a bitching job regardless. And instead of sending her off every morning feeling like a can full of squashed assholes, maybe you could try sending her off feeling like she can conquer the damned world. Step up your game or keep showing up as lame, man. Jeez."

"And how would you suggest I make her feel like she can conquer the damned world?" He took a sip of the tea Ace passed him. The Earl Grey wouldn't do a thing to soothe his nerves, but it *would* soothe the roiling in his stomach at the thought that his words to Chelsea, meant to be cautionary and to express his concern, were instead making her feel bad about herself. *Shit.*

"A dozen body-shaking orgasms should do it," Emily said.

Dagan choked on his tea. "*Excuse* me?"

"It's as obvious as the nose on your face."

"What is?"

"That you're hot to trot for our resident undercover CIA liaison."

Author's Note

For those of you familiar with the vibrant city of Chicago, Illinois, you'll notice I changed a few places and names and embellished the details of others. I did this to suit the story and to highlight the diversity and challenges of this dynamic city I call home.

Acknowledgments

As always, kudos to my hubby. Sweetheart, when I said I couldn't spend one more winter in Chicago, you whisked me away to New Orleans for two whole months. The majority of this book was written on a belly full of gumbo and étouffée, after Mardi Gras parades and second-line shenanigans, and while sitting on the banks of the mighty Mississippi. Thank you for always being up for an adventure.

Big thanks to my editor, Deb Werksman, and my agent, Nicole Resciniti. Ladies, you always make my books shine. Thank you so much for your dedication and unwavering support. You're both amazeballs, and I couldn't do any of this without you.

Mega props to my readers. Thank you all so much for following me and the bunch at BKI on these crazy journeys of love, laughter, and life lived on the edge. Here's to many more! Cheers, and happy reading!

About the Author

Julie Ann Walker is the *New York Times* and *USA Today* bestselling author of award-winning romantic suspense. A winner of the Book Buyers Best Award, Julie has been nominated for the National Readers' Choice Award, the Australian Romance Reader Awards, and the Romance Writers of America's prestigious RITA award. Her books have been described as "alpha, edgy, and downright hot." Most days, you can find Julie on her bicycle along the lakeshore in Chicago or blasting away at her keyboard, trying to wrangle her capricious imagination into submission.

Be sure to sign up for Julie's occasional newsletter at: www.julieannwalker.com. And to learn more about Julie, follow her on Facebook: www.facebook.com/julieann walkerauthor and/or Twitter: @JAWalkerAuthor and/or Instagram: @julieannwalker_author.